STALKED

THE BOY WHO SAID NO

Also by Patti Sheehy

The Boy Who Said No: An Escape to Freedom

STALKED
THE BOY WHO SAID NO

A True-Life Novel

PATTI SHEEHY

OCEANVIEW PUBLISHING

SARASOTA, FLORIDA

This book is a work of fiction. Names, characters, businesses, organizations, places, and incidents either are the products of the author's imagination or are used fictitiously. Any resemblance to actual events, businesses, locales, or persons, living or dead, is entirely coincidental.

ISBN: 978-1-60809-248-2

Illustration copyright © 2013 by Emily Baar

Published in the United States of America by Oceanview Publishing, Longboat Key, Florida
www.oceanviewpub.com

10 9 8 7 6 5 4 3 2

PRINTED IN THE UNITED STATES OF AMERICA

This book is dedicated to my amazing husband and friend, Robert J. Hunter. And to my whole crazy—and wonderful—Sheehy family, especially my daughter, Patricia.

ACKNOWLEDGMENTS

I would like to acknowledge Frank Mederos for providing the basis for this story, for his keen memory, his patience, and attention to detail. He has been central to the writing and promotion of both *The Boy Who Said No: An Escape to Freedom* and *Stalked: The Boy Who Said No*, and I owe him a great debt of gratitude. He is not only my partner, but also a dear friend. My sincere thanks go to his wife and family for their understanding of the time demands in introducing these books to the world.

My husband, Robert Hunter, made writing my books possible through his unwavering support in holding the fort, running errands, and cooking endless meals, while I slaved away at the computer. Hats off to Bob!

The success of *Stalked* depends partly on the success of *The Boy Who Said No*. Hence, I owe a debt of gratitude to Christopher Walter and the Board of Trustees of the Haddon Heights Public Library for naming *The Boy Who Said No* One Book Haddon Heights and for their work in the book's successful launch.

Thanks to my family for their support, especially my father, William V. Sheehy Jr., and my brother, William V. Sheehy III, for their exceptional efforts in promoting *The Boy Who Said No* to their colleagues, neighbors, and friends. Their efforts exceeded all expectations, and I am truly grateful.

Civic organizations, book clubs, and individuals too numerous to mention contributed to the success of my first book by inviting Frank and me to speak to their clubs. You know who you are. Thank you, thank you, thank you.

The International Thriller Writers (ITW) organization played a key role in getting *The Boy Who Said No* off to a memorable start at an honorary event that remained fresh in my mind for months.

I want to thank my amazing friends, Patty and Rich Israel; Patrick and Michelle Delaney; Barbara and Tom Gardner; Laura and Ted Todd; Rose Fitzgerald, Joyce Herrman, Carol Larro, Nancy Gulick, Lin Sweeten, Dorie Gilchrist, Carol Beahm, Maureen D'Andrea, Ellen Youseffian, Sue Comfort, Peg Carney, Ruth Griesback, Anne McAdams, the folks at the Kennedy Health System, and so many others who went out of their way for Frank and me by opening their homes to host book events.

Thanks to the crew at Oceanview Publishing: Pat and Bob Gussin, Frank Troncale, David Ivester, and Emily Baar for their continued professionalism. Kudos to Susan Hayes for superb editing and to George Foster for another dynamite cover design.

PREFACE

In *The Boy Who Said No: An Escape to Freedom* we follow the harrowing adventures of Frank Mederos, a member of Fidel Castro's Special Forces, as he defects from the army, spends five months on the run from his fellow soldiers, and makes a desperate escape by boat to Key West, Florida.

When Frank arrives in America his trials are far from over. While he works to make a life for himself, sinister forces in Cuba plot his destruction. This is his story—a tale of love, loss, courage, and friendship.

Stalked: The Boy Who Said No is based upon countless hours of interviews with Mr. Mederos. He was able to attest to the parts of the story that directly involve him. In many areas of this narrative, however, Frank knows what set events in motion and how they played out, but the details of what happened in between remain in shadow.

As a result, many scenes, descriptions, and dialogue have been written based on how Frank imagined them to have occurred knowing the characters, time frame, and history. Liberties were taken in creating material that Frank could only surmise, given the outcome of events. The experiences of Frank's former commanding officer, Pino, in the cane fields and in the Soviet Union as well as the interactions among the Cuban operatives are fictionalized.

Nonetheless, the skeleton of this story—Frank's attempted recruitment by the CIA, his relationship with Magda and Chris, his life as an immigrant, and his encounter with his friend Lazo and the Cuban operatives in the hills of north Jersey—are true. Thus, *Stalked: The Boy Who Said No* is called a true-life novel.

The names of some characters have been changed to protect the privacy of family members and those still residing in Cuba.

No friendship is an accident.
—O'Henry, *Heart of the West*

STALKED
THE BOY WHO SAID NO

CHAPTER ONE

Lieutenant Pino picked up the phone. The forty-year-old Cuban military officer had one message for Commander Martinez, one sentence that would change the course of his life. He didn't bother to identify himself when the commander answered.

"It's over," he said. "The son of a bitch has escaped."

"Jesus Christ. When?"

"Just now!"

"How?"

"The American Coast Guard picked him up. We intercepted the radio transmission."

"Christ almighty, this is all I need!"

The lieutenant took an audible breath, but did not respond.

"I want you back at base, pronto, Lieutenant."

"Yes, sir."

"And you'd better have one hell of an explanation for this." The phone went dead. Pino lifted his chin as if he were preparing for a fight and signaled to his driver to start the engine.

CHAPTER TWO

Lieutenant Pino arrived at base at four p.m. Sensing his mood, his driver remained silent during the trip, regarding the lieutenant cautiously in the rearview mirror. The lieutenant seemed agitated, his hands fisted, his mouth twitching uncharacteristically. Thick blue veins throbbed at his temples, looking as if they were about to explode. He appeared shell-shocked and bone-tired.

The driver pulled into base and opened the door of the Russian-made jeep. Pino stepped out of the vehicle and straightened his back. He glanced at his watch, then at his driver. His eyes were hard as cement.

The base was unusually busy with men scurrying in different directions in frenzied activity. They saluted smartly when they saw the lieutenant, but Pino detected a trace of fear in their eyes. He found this unsettling. He knew it was going to be a long, trying day.

Before the lieutenant walked three feet, he was told to report to Commander Martinez's office. He tightened his shoulders and hastened down the hallway.

The commander stood against the open window, red-faced, nostrils flaring. Pino sucked in his breath. He had seen that expression on the commander's face before, and it never preceded anything good. Martinez stabbed Pino with his eyes, turned, and lowered his chin. A thin layer of fat settled above his collar.

"Shut the door, Lieutenant," he barked. The older man's eyes were flinty, his lips starched.

Pino turned slowly to close the door, hoping to buy a little time to think. He pivoted to face his commanding officer.

"So, we have a situation," Martinez said curtly.

Pino blinked, dreading this conversation. "A situation?" he countered. It was an instinctive reaction. He knew full well what the commander meant. He also knew this meeting would involve no fiery tango, no point-counterpoint. He could offer no real defense. He had gambled and lost. Now, there would be hell to pay.

"What situation?" mocked the commander. "You told me an hour ago that Mederos has escaped—picked up by the American Coast Guard. I'd call that a situation. Wouldn't you, Lieutenant?"

Pino bit his bottom lip, not wanting to respond. He hesitated a moment and looked at the ceiling. He needed a drink—a double scotch. Finally, he nodded and said in a strangled voice, "Yes, sir."

"Can't hear you, Lieutenant. Speak up!"

"Yes, sir."

Martinez shook his head in exasperation. "What do you have to say for yourself?"

Pino straightened his spine as his stomach dropped away. "Couldn't be helped, sir. We did everything possible to bring the worm in."

Pino's commanding officer looked incredulous, as if he were still trying to process what had happened. The air in the room grew as still as that preceding a tornado. Pino looked at the commander, and an image of a Cuban boa flashed before his eyes, its body coiled, its jaws unhinged to consume its prey. Like the rodents it attacked, Pino felt he was about to be asphyxiated, eaten alive.

"Everything possible, Lieutenant? Everything possible?" The commander paused, trying to quell the roar in his ears. "I'll tell you what was possible," he spat. "It was possible that we followed procedure in this situation. It was possible that we notified the police, the Committees for the Defense of the Revolution (CDR), the goddamn militia. It was possible that they would've posted Mederos's picture on every window and on every telephone pole in this goddamn city, in the goddamn country if necessary." He shook his head.

"It was possible that Mederos would've been arrested the day he defected." The commander's voice climbed an octave as he concluded his monologue. "It was possible that this whole damn fiasco could've been avoided, and Mederos would rot away in some rat-ridden jail." He hesitated a moment, giving his words gravitas. "For your information, Lieutenant, that's what was possible."

The commander exhaled loudly, eyes blazing. Pino stiffened. He felt like all the oxygen had been siphoned from the room, and he was gasping for breath. Only he wasn't. "But *you!* You, with your stubbornness, your willfulness, your know-it-all attitude, you made all of that *impossible.*"

Pino squeezed his lips together and lifted his chin, but said nothing. The room seemed suddenly hollow, devoid of power on both of their parts. The clip of boots hitting pavement drifted through the open window. The sun cast a puddle of yellow on the linoleum floor.

When the commander spoke again, his voice was hoarse, almost a whisper. "You and your damn arrogance will cost us plenty, Lieutenant. Both of us. Do you understand?"

Pino bit the inside of his cheek and returned the commander's glare. He felt a tickle at the back of his throat but resisted the urge to cough. *Bile*, he thought. The two men stood in silence.

"Make no mistake about it," said Martinez. "We're through with this little game of yours. Your so-called state of emergency at this base is officially over." He scoured the lieutenant's eyes. "I am in charge now. And, as your commanding officer, I'm placing you under house arrest."

Pino blanched. His body grew rigid, fear cramping his stomach. Small beads of perspiration dewed his hairline.

"I've notified the administrator at headquarters in Managua, and a delegation is on its way to deal with the issue," said Martinez. "They will arrive first thing tomorrow morning. Meanwhile, you are confined to base. You will not leave, you will not go home, you will not go anywhere until further notice. You know the drill. Am I making myself clear?"

Pino nodded. He opened his mouth to speak and then thought

better of it. The commander looked like he would brook no argument. Still, he felt he had to defend himself. Finally, he said, "How could you do this to me? You know how loyal I've been to the Party."

The commander's eyes widened. "Christ almighty, Lieutenant. You just don't get it, do you? This isn't about being a loyal communist. It isn't about being an educated Marxist. It isn't about being a good soldier. This is about being a total asshole!" He turned and pointed outside. "Do you see what's going on out there, Lieutenant?"

Pino looked out the window. He had been so self-absorbed that he had barely noticed what was happening around him. Now things were becoming clear.

"Mederos knew everything about our operation—Christ, nobody knows that better than you." Martinez shook his head in frustration. "He's probably spilling the beans to some eager little CIA officer right now. This is a matter of vital importance, Lieutenant. Even an imbecile like you knows that."

Pino took a step backward, watching the commander carefully as he crossed to the other side of the room. A couple of minutes elapsed before Martinez spoke again.

"I've ordered the men to take measures to protect us—Cuba—from the consequences of Mederos's treason. God knows what the imperialists will do with the information he provides them. They could attack at any time—take out our missiles before we have time to move them. That's why this base is in such an uproar."

Pino remained mute as a mime, knowing full well that Martinez spoke the truth. He exhaled loudly as the commander opened the door and signaled to the soldiers standing guard outside. They advanced quickly and surrounded the lieutenant, while he stood like a bronzed statue, his icy eyes staring straight ahead. To Pino's chagrin, Martinez ordered the soldiers to escort him to his office.

Pino walked stiffly down the hall while the soldiers held his arms. He could feel their condemnation. He could feel their hatred. Humiliation burned his cheeks.

He checked to make sure his shoulders were back and down. He didn't want to appear stressed in front of the men. Not now. He puffed his chest, trying to look less vulnerable. He worked to keep his breathing regular. He worked to control his rage. But he startled like a frightened alley cat when his thick office door slammed shut behind him.

Pino looked at his large mahogany desk, at his black telephone, at his gray filing cabinet. But in his mind's eye he saw a narrow cot, iron bars, and a pitted porcelain basin. *Is this my future? My life?*

He knew a similar crime in Russia would prompt a sentence of hard labor in the ice-laden camps of Siberia where your fingers, toes, and ears would blacken and wither from frostbite. Or you could be sent to work the uranium mines in the Urals where your teeth would rot from the roots from radiation and your hair would drop in clumps, leaving your scalp red, scaly, and exposed. At least there weren't any uranium mines in Cuba. And the country was warm. But Cuban jails were no picnic either.

Pino stomped around his office. "Damn Mederos!" he muttered. "Damn him! Damn him! Damn him!" He lifted his arm and threw his fist into the cinder block wall, leaving scraps of skin behind. He shook his hand to release the pain, and then drew it to his mouth to suck out the sting.

Years of work, years of study, years of kowtowing to the likes of Commander Martinez and to Lieutenant Brown and it's come to this? For what? For one little worm?

A shudder surged through the lieutenant's body. His stomach clenched as a headache bloomed behind his eyes. He sat down at his desk and shuffled a few papers. He signed some forms, wondering whether this would be the last time he ever conducted official business. It was too much for him. He dropped his pen and stared at the wall. *How could I, a person who drinks scotch from Waterford tumblers, ever survive some concrete cesspit? Besides, it wasn't my fault. I tried everything. I did my best.*

Pino rested his forehead on his fingertips while a fury as dark and black as lava churned his belly. He worked to control it, to harness it. As bad as things appeared right now, he knew he would be the victor. He would prevail. When he put his mind to something, he always did.

CHAPTER THREE

Accompanied by two soldiers, Pino headed back to his room in the officers' barracks, located in the imposing mansion once occupied by a wealthy Cuban landowner. It was just past eight p.m. He climbed the five marble steps and entered the commodious lobby filled with gilt-framed oil paintings and fine European antiques.

A Tabriz carpet covered the floor beneath a leather couch. The first movement of Mozart's Symphony no. 40 in G minor played softly in the background. Cuban military officers were treated well. Pino nodded to the sergeant on duty before ascending the wide interior staircase.

A soft breeze wafted through his bedroom window as Pino unbuttoned his shirt and removed his hat. His body was lean and muscular, and he worked to keep it that way. He fell to the floor and did a hundred push-ups before he removed his shoes and squared them at a right angle to the wall. Tomorrow morning he would set them outside his door to be polished.

The lieutenant performed his usual evening ritual of showering and brushing his teeth before he climbed into bed. The mattress was firm, effortlessly supporting his back and weight. He set a glass of water on a cherry-veneer bed stand, anticipating a long night ahead.

Tomorrow the brass from headquarters would arrive, throwing their weight around, asking a million questions. He could picture their faces, stern and ruthless, their mouths tight wads of condemnation, their eyes stony and accusing.

He could hardly believe it had come to this. *If only that imbecile at the Coast Guard station had followed my orders, this never would've happened.*

That's always the way, isn't it? You give some miserable peasant a little power and it goes to his head. Hell, if the Cuban Coast Guard had done what I ordered, we would've gotten Mederos before the Americans did. All that babble about triggering an international incident was just stupid talk.

Suddenly, Pino felt hot and sticky. The paddle fan twirled overhead, but the room was closing in on him. He sipped some water, kicked off his upper sheet, and banged his feet against the mattress. *How could Mederos elude me for so long? He must've had help. He wasn't smart enough to pull this off alone. But who?*

Pino ran through the possibilities in his mind. *Manny? Lazo? Lieutenant Brown?*

Nah, Brown was too smart for that. He was far too fond of Mederos, but he wouldn't actually help him escape. That would be treason. He would be executed for such behavior. And he knew it. He'd never risk it. But the other two? They were always palling around with Mederos. Thick as thieves. They'd do anything for each other. That's the way it is with the Special Forces.

Pino rubbed his forehead with the palm of his hand, trying to soothe his pounding headache. *What difference does it make now? Any way you look at it, my goose is cooked. Still, it would help to point a finger at someone else when the hard questions are asked.*

Suddenly, he remembered the smirk on Jabao's face the night Mederos vanished into thin air. *What did he say?* He tried to recall the exact words. *"Do you think you are going to find Mederos here? On his own turf? Impossible."* He sighed. *Maybe it was inevitable. Fate. Destiny. Whatever you want to call it. Christ. What am I thinking? Something like this wasn't meant to be. Mederos was a menace, a wart on the face of communism. A cancer that needed to be excised, removed forever.*

Pino sat up in his bed. His vision blurred for a moment before the face of Frankie Mederos pirouetted before his eyes. It was as if he were right there in the room with him. "You stinking bastard. You've screwed up everything. My whole damn life is ruined because of you." It barely registered to Pino that he was talking to himself.

The lieutenant slammed his right fist into his left palm, feeling the force of his self-inflicted pain. He stifled a scream, imagining his fist connecting with Mederos's jaw. He wanted to mangle his face, to bash in his brains.

"I'll get you, Mederos. I'll get you, Mederos. I'll get you, Mederos," he said in a voice loud enough to be heard through the walls. He repeated the oath like an ancient Buddhist chant sung in a monastery high in the Himalayas. The words looped round and round in his head and on and off his tongue until the morning light wedged itself through the shutters. Then he slowly lifted his body from the bed to face whatever the day might bring.

CHAPTER FOUR

Glancing out his office window, Pino watched as the delegation from Managua drove onto base. Looking starched and official, two captains and three first lieutenants disembarked from their vehicles. They saluted the guards and asked to be taken to Commander Martinez's office.

Martinez greeted the delegation and gestured for them to be seated. Pitchers of iced tea and coffee sat on a sideboard along with a tray of sliced mangoes and fresh pastries. The commander took his position behind his desk while the other officers settled themselves in wingback chairs.

Captain Carrilles, a man of fifty with a deep, sonorous voice, spoke first. "We are here regarding your call to headquarters about a member of the Special Forces who escaped. We need a full accounting of what happened—step-by-step, starting with you."

Martinez leaned back in his chair. "I'll tell you what transpired to the best of my ability."

"Start at the beginning, Commander." Martinez nodded to First Lieutenant Rodriquez who extracted a pad from his jacket and began scribbling notes.

"Tell me what you know about Mederos."

The commander wove his fingers together and placed his hands on his desk. "Mederos was recruited into the force because of his good grades and his previous service to the country."

"What service? Be specific."

"He served in the National Literacy Brigade and spent time in the Sierra Maestra helping farmers harvest their crops."

"Go on," urged Carrilles.

"He was our best operator—could shoot the missiles like nobody's business. He hit a ship out at sea during military exercises. Everyone was impressed, including Raúl."

The captain inhaled, making a wheezing sound through his nose. "Anything else?"

"He trained new recruits."

"So, he was an asset to the force?"

"Yes. Smart. Good at math. Likeable enough. That's about it."

"What about his knowledge of operations?"

"He knew everything someone in his position would know."

"Besides what he knew as a member of the force, did he possess any special knowledge that might make this situation more dangerous?"

Martinez looked at the ceiling, thinking for a moment before blotches reddened his cheeks.

"What is it, Commander?"

"Now that I think about it, he took inventory of the missiles."

"Goddamnit! When?"

"Several times."

"When was the last time?"

"Right before he left."

"So he knows where our missiles are kept, their number, and kind?"

"He does."

The captain's eyes bulged. "This is even more serious than I thought."

Martinez's stomach growled, and he cleared his throat. "I know."

"Did Mederos ever give any indication that he was a counterrevolutionary?"

Martinez thought for a moment. "No. At times he was too out-spoken for his own good—a bit of a hothead—but nothing you wouldn't expect from a man his age. He had some run-ins with Lieutenant Pino over political issues, but he never indicated that he didn't support the revolution."

Carrilles nodded. "When did he first disappear?"

"He was supposed to demonstrate the rockets at the Multi-province Military Exercises in Las Villas at the end of November, but he never showed up. He was nowhere to be found."

"What did you do?"

"We searched the base, of course, and questioned the men, but no one knew anything about the situation."

"Why didn't you call headquarters and tell us what was happening?"

"He hadn't taken his gun, which led us to believe that he wasn't trying to escape. He had a girlfriend, and we thought he might have family issues. Frankly, it occurred to us that he might've gotten her pregnant and needed time to sort it out."

"This is highly irregular, Commander."

Martinez took a deep breath. "I know, sir, looking back—"

"Did anyone search for him?"

"Lieutenants Pino and Brown visited his family members, ransacked his home—that sort of thing. But to no avail."

"Then what?"

"After a couple of weeks, I told Pino that we needed to report the situation to headquarters. But he refused. Said it was a political matter, and he was taking charge of the base."

"Because?"

"Because Mederos had such deep knowledge of our operation."

"And you let him?"

"I had no choice."

"You still could've informed headquarters."

"I could have, if he hadn't forbidden me to."

"He forbade you from making a report?"

"Yes, sir. He said he could handle the situation himself, said there was no need to get anyone else involved, including the militia. I think he was afraid of being embarrassed."

"And you went along with that?"

"There was nothing I could do. He became obsessed with finding Mederos—carried on about it day and night. He wasn't thinking clearly. He finally got so worked up he sent the entire force after him."

"What the hell are you talking about?"

"He sent the Special Forces out to find him. He said they knew how he thought, and they would be in the best position to bring him in."

"And you didn't stand up to him? You were in command, why the hell not?"

"I have to admit I felt powerless in this situation, sir."

Carrilles shook his head in disbelief. "So powerless you couldn't pick up a goddamn phone and call headquarters?"

Martinez lowered his chin and remained silent.

The captain shook his head and stared at the commander.

"This is beyond belief! This isn't bad judgment, Commander. This is lunacy. We are going to get to the bottom of this."

"Do you want me to ask Lieutenant Pino to join us?"

"Hell, no, Commander. We have plenty of people to talk to before I speak with that idiot. Besides, if I got my hands on him right now, I'd kill him. Get Lieutenant Brown in here. *Now.*"

Brown appeared in Martinez's office looking solemn and shaken. He had joined the military before Fidel came to power. Much of the land his Haitian family had worked so hard to acquire had been expropriated by the State under the Agrarian Reform Law of 1959. Brown had no time for the communists, but he was smart enough to keep his opinions to himself.

Brown was in charge of operations for the Special Forces unit, while Lieutenant Pino oversaw political affairs at the base. Pino relinquished authority to Brown in military matters, and Brown conceded to Pino in political matters. The two lieutenants disliked each other and vied for power. Pino had declared Frank's escape a matter of national security, making it a political matter that fell under his authority.

Brown regarded Captain Carrilles warily. He saluted, took a seat near the window, and folded his hands.

The captain shifted in his seat. "Commander Martinez informs me that Pino sent the entire Elite Counterattack Force after Mederos. Is this true?"

"Yes, sir."

"Why didn't you say something? Speak up? Call headquarters?"

"I am a soldier, Captain. My first duty is to obey orders. When my two commanding officers agree on a course of action, and that course of action is *not* to inform headquarters, that's what I do."

"So you felt powerless in this situation, Lieutenant?"

"It wasn't a matter of feeling powerless, Captain."

"Then what was it, Lieutenant?"

"It was not my duty to go over their heads, sir. I am a soldier, a graduate of the military academy. I obey orders."

Carrilles gritted his teeth and glared at Brown. He waited a moment to regain control of his emotions. He turned to the officer at his right to make sure notes were being taken.

"Were you \at the Coast Guard station when Mederos escaped?"

"Yes, sir."

"Describe what occurred there."

"We got word that Mederos was in one of two boats filled with worms headed for the Florida Straits. A Guatemalan freighter had spotted them and had radioed the American Coast Guard to pick them up. The communication was intercepted, and Pino ordered our Coast Guard to go after them."

"What about the director of the Coast Guard station? Didn't he have anything to say?"

"He was furious that Pino was trying to take over. He went along with him for a while, but he eventually recalled our boats. Said he didn't want an international incident on his hands. Evidently, members of his family were aboard one of the boats. I'm sure it influenced his decision. He and Pino argued, and the lieutenant lost. That's about it."

Carrilles thought for a minute and then stood up abruptly. The rest of the officers followed suit.

"I've heard enough for now," he said. He turned to Martinez. "I am shocked and appalled at your spinelessness and recklessness in the midst of a critical situation. What kind of weak sister are you to allow this to happen under your command?" He practically spit out the words. "You are the most pitiful excuse for a commander I've ever seen."

"I—"

"Shut the hell up, Commander. I've heard enough nonsense. As of now, you and your officers are under house arrest. Members of our delegation will take over the base until your replacements are appointed. Meanwhile, we will escort Pino to Managua where he will be held under guard until arrangements are made for his trial.

"Your actions could prove devastating to our great nation. Our delegation will investigate further to make sure no conspiracy was involved in this worm's escape. If we find evidence to that effect, you—and anyone else involved—will be tried for treason. As you know, the penalty for treason is death. Meanwhile, you are relieved of your command."

Carrilles turned to Brown. "I respect that you were following orders, Lieutenant. But for the time being, you are also relieved of your command. Perhaps, with further instruction, you can be salvaged to better serve the revolution. Time will tell. You are to report to the military academy for additional leadership training."

The captain turned to his first lieutenant and said, "I will need to speak to all members of the Special Forces regarding this matter. Get me a list of men, and schedule interviews as soon as possible."

The delegation saluted and walked out of the office, leaving Brown and Martinez ashen and spent.

CHAPTER FIVE

After bidding farewell to the US Coast Guard, Frank Mederos and his party climbed aboard a bus headed to Freedom House, an agency that provided immigration, health, and settlement services. The agency, which served as a sort of refugee hotel, was located near the airport in Miami.

The group was a motley crew, their hunger for life, liberty, and safety now supplanted by their urgent need for a hot shower, dry clothes, and a decent meal.

The party numbered twenty-nine: two women awaiting child-birth, several traumatized children, adults of all ages, including Frank and his Uncle Luis. It took them a while to regain their land legs, the undulant motion of the sea clinging to their limbs like burrs to cotton.

They had been fed and issued blankets aboard the Guatemalan freighter *Gran Lempira*. Now Dixie cups filled with water were distributed and quickly consumed. Suffering from dehydration, many of the refugees urgently requested refills. They gulped down water as if they'd never had a drink.

Although exhausted and bedraggled, the group was electric with the talk of their adventure. To Frank's chagrin, his Uncle Luis was carrying on as if he were the hero of the voyage when, at the height of their crossing, he had begged Frank to take the boat back to Cuba to avoid what he thought would be certain death at sea.

Frank had ignored his urgings, rendering Luis striated with fear and momentarily speechless. But Frank understood his feelings. He was familiar with the kind of cold terror that could sluice through your body so rapidly it obliterated rational thought. He had tasted it, faced it, overcome it.

When Frank was younger, he regarded his uncle as a brave, loyal man. It was why he had asked Luis to hide him from the authorities—no small matter. If caught, Luis could've been sent "to the wall"—shot for harboring a fugitive. Yet he and his wife, Rosa, welcomed Frank into their home without reservation or complaint.

Their hospitality had meant more to Frank than a roof over his head—it had meant his life. Rosa had washed his clothes, slaked his thirst, and fed his body. What's more, she had put her life and the lives of her two daughters at risk. For a mother, this was remarkable. No wonder she'd been a bundle of nerves.

Although his uncle was unemployed and strapped for cash, Frank was surprised when he asked to go to America with him. Luis had been a truck driver for Coca-Cola and had lost his job when Fidel nationalized the company. Coke absconded with its secret formula, and the company that replaced it produced a product that few people wanted to drink.

Now, Frank watched Luis effusively recount their experience as if he were a major player in their success. Frank looked at him askance. This was a real eye-opener for him. For the first time in his life he got the impression that his uncle was not the man he thought him to be.

Amid the commotion and babble, Frank's thoughts turned to Magda. In the six months since he'd seen her, he missed her like an amputee misses a leg. His longing had reached a fever pitch. He wanted the comfort of her familiarity, the sureness of her unbidden support, the normalcy of being with her and doing something as simple as taking a walk. He planned to call her at the first possible moment to reassure her that he had escaped Cuba alive and to hear the excitement in her voice when she heard the news.

He needed her touch like he needed water. He needed her laughter like he needed air. He had survived a dangerous and circuitous path to reach her, and he was on the cusp of realizing his dream. What more could a man want?

When the group arrived at Freedom House, they were welcomed

as heroes, congratulated on their success, and praised for their courage.

Once the excitement subsided, they were issued clean clothes, soap, shampoo, a toothbrush, a razor, and a fine-toothed comb. Frank grabbed his toiletries and hastened to the men's room.

He glanced in the mirror and studied his face, surprised at his reflection. His skin was blistered from the sun and caked with brine. His hair was askew, matted and curled with oceanic debris. Bits of seaweed clung to his beard, and fine red lines netted the whites of his eyes like ivy crossing a wall. He ran his tongue over his lips and tasted salt, the essence of the sea that was so much a part of him.

His hands gripped the sink, as tremulous as wind chimes. He lowered his head, hoping the tide of adrenaline would stop flooding his bloodstream. He wondered what toll it had taken on his body during five months of running from the authorities, five months of crushing fear, five months of knowing he'd put his own life and the lives of his loved ones in mortal danger.

But he was young and strong. At nineteen he considered himself almost invincible. He nudged the thought from his mind. This was not a time for morbid musings, but rather a time for celebration.

A cruciform of sunlight bounced off the mirror, prompting Frank to shield his eyes with his fingers. It splintered in a brilliant flash—here for a moment and gone forever. Frank smiled, thinking it was a good omen.

Frank slathered his skin with shaving cream and dipped his razor into warm water. He drew the blade across his cheeks, enjoying the familiar rasp as the razor cleared a path through his beard. It was a simple thing. He was beginning to feel better already.

He brushed his teeth and ran the bristles of his toothbrush over his tongue, hoping to refresh his mouth and to obliterate the taste of the sea. He removed his clothes, knowing he could never bring himself to wear them again, and stepped into the shower. He twisted the valve and closed his eyes as a warm stream of liquid washed over him like baptismal waters. A shower had never felt so good.

He reached for the bar of hard-milled soap that sat in its dish like a jewel in a Tiffany box. It felt like polished granite. He admired its blue-green marbling and brought it to his nostrils. He inhaled the aroma of Zest, thinking it was the most refreshing scent he had ever encountered. He scrubbed his body vigorously and shampooed his hair, once, twice, thrice. He rinsed. When he ran his fingers through his hair, it squeaked like hinges hungry for oil. He smiled, listening to the sighs of other men as they performed similar rituals.

Once everyone freshened up, they gathered in the dining hall for cheeseburgers, French fries, and a salad moistened with Wishbone dressing. The rolls were soft, the beef well done. The refugees spanked bottles of Heinz ketchup with their fists to release the stubborn condiment. They passed a plate of crisp pickles and a basket filled with potato chips. Frank ate ravenously, consuming three burgers, which he chased down with two glasses of iced tea.

The group sat for a while after the meal was finished, talking about where their respective journeys might take them, while listening to the rattle of dishes and silverware. Women in white uniforms stripped paper tablecloths from wooden tables. They scrubbed counters and tabletops with squirt bottles and sponges. Disinfectant fumes scented the air. Ceiling fans twirled, and a vacuum cleaner hummed in the corner.

The refugees lined up to complete various forms and to go over the sundry details regarding their admittance into the country. Due to their number, the authorities requested that they limit their phone conversations to ten minutes a day.

Not knowing Magda's number, Frank called Magda's uncle who lived in Miami to see if he could obtain it. Her uncle had been involved in the Bay of Pigs invasion and was thrilled to learn of Frank's escape. They laughed and exchanged family news. He assured Frank that he would do well in the States and promised to call him the following day with Magda's number. Comforted, Frank smiled at the thought of soon seeing his sweetheart.

By nine p.m., exhaustion blanketed Frank like snow. He was

escorted to his sleeping quarters and assigned a bed. Despite his fatigue, he lowered his body to the floor and did a hundred push-ups—a habit he was reluctant to break.

He folded his clothes into a neat pile and placed them at the foot of the bed. He climbed into bed in relief, grateful to have a safe place to sleep. The sheets smelled of detergent, sunshine, and bleach. They felt fresh and clean beneath his skin. He rubbed the bottoms of his feet against the smooth fabric for the sheer pleasure of it.

The smell of the sheets reminded Frank of his mother. His mind wandered to the last time he saw her. It had been a brief encounter, a scant fifteen minutes, a surreptitious meeting to exchange final farewells. Her eyes were red and swollen from crying, and her face was stricken with the thought of losing her son to jail—or worse.

Neither of them knew whether Frank would survive his escape. He could have been shot. He could have drowned, or been eaten by sharks, a fate that had befallen thousands of Cubans who had braved such a journey. His odds of survival were slim.

His mother looked at Frank with such tenderness he feared his heart would shatter. The stress of knowing her firstborn child faced such an uncertain destiny had etched deep lines in her face. Frank tried to reassure her that all would be well, but they both knew he was spouting platitudes. He could offer little balm for her suffering. She wished him farewell with a voice hoarse with sorrow. Her eyes were dry, but her words were wet with tears.

Yet she did not cling to him for solace, she did not try to stop him, she did not warn him of danger. Instead, she pulled Frank to her bosom and told him she would hold him in her heart forever. Hers was quiet, intense grief, a nod to the inevitable, a mother's greatest gift: a willingness to let go.

Frank recoiled at the thought of having put his mother, his father, his grandfather—his entire family—through such pain. They deserved better. They deserved a son who would look after them, who would provide them with comfort and support, both emotionally and financially, in their old age. But he'd faced a terrible choice:

his country and his family, or his darling Magda and freedom. He had looked to the future, calculated the risks, assessed his skills, and made his decision. He had to go.

With luck, determination, and the help of friends, he had survived. He was alive, safe. But the possibility of never seeing his mother again, the woman who had changed his diapers, warmed his bottles, and nurtured him his entire life, skewered his heart.

It was almost too much to bear. So Frank leaned his head against the pillow and turned his thoughts to Magda. She embodied all the qualities he wanted in a woman: an incisive wit, an elfin sense of humor, and a keen intelligence. Of course, it didn't hurt that her breasts lent a soft curve to the drape of her blouses, that her waist turned into her hips like the stem of a champagne flute, that her arms were as soft and smooth as chocolate pudding.

Wise beyond her years, Magda saw things in a thousand hues of gray, careful not to judge people whose backgrounds and experiences differed from hers. Her voice was sweet and lilting, and she had a softness to her that reminded Frank of a lullaby.

But beneath that velvet exterior resided a will of steel. Magda was a risk taker and encouraged others to follow her lead, especially when it came to matters of right and wrong. Had it not been for her insistence, Frank might not have escaped Cuba, might not have conceived of it, might not have chanced it.

But the couple faced a pivotal point in their personal lives and in their nation's history. Frank was uncertain how much of Magda's understanding of the future was her own thinking, and how much was influenced by her family. It was probably a combination of the two. But Magda was prescient, exhibiting wisdom as rare in a young woman as a fly in amber.

While many Cubans hoped for, wished for, longed for, Fidel's ouster, Magda's family, the Hernándezes, knew it was not going to happen, at least not in an acceptable time frame. They believed Fidel was going to ruin Cuba. They knew he was strong and determined. He and his cronies had guns, prisons, and vile methods of torture.

And they were using them on anyone who took the slightest issue with the regime.

Worse yet, Fidel had instituted mandatory military service for young men, starting at age fifteen. Men had to complete three years of military training and then had to serve in the army reserves until the age of twenty-eight. While serving in the army, a man was forbidden to leave the country for any reason.

The previous year, while sitting in Magda's aunt and uncle's living room, her family made their case to Frank. Magda's father, Sergio, began the conversation. "The family has decided to immigrate to the States so young Sergio and Rigo won't be drafted." While Frank was surprised, he knew the last thing the family would want was for these cousins to advance Fidel's treachery. They had to get out, to make a life for the family in a place where Fidel had no power.

Silence enveloped the room. Magda shot Frank a pleading look while her father continued. A vein throbbed at his temples. "Magda says she loves you, and she won't go anywhere without you. We can't leave her here to fend for herself."

Frank was speechless. The air thickened. Family members stared into space for a moment before Magda's mother asked Frank the burning question: "Would you be willing to take a chance to escape Cuba to be with Magda?"

Sergio turned to Frank with the full fabric of his dilemma etched in his eyes. Frank had never seen him look so serious. "You making it out of the country is vital not only to you, but to me, to Magda, to all of us."

The family's arguments were persuasive. But defecting was no simple matter. Not for someone in the force. And it had been every bit as daunting as Frank had anticipated. But he had made it. He was free. No matter what the future might bring, he was on a far different path than he would have been in Cuba. And it was all due to Magda. She had challenged Frank to rebirth or death, and Fate had favored him with the former.

Luckily, he had come to the States with assets. While he had no money, he had his sweetheart and her family, and he knew their love and support would help get him though the challenges to come. They had applied for visas, eventually got them, and left the country legally. What's more, Magda was smart and had an excellent facility for math and language, far better than Frank's. She ran circles around him in many things, and he admired and respected her abilities. At the same time, she let him be the hero of their story. A smile grazed Frank's lips thinking about her.

After a while he began to doze. He traded the memory of Magda for a dream that was as clear and vivid as if it were in Technicolor. His mind filled with images of flowers and rain, of sinister things growing and multiplying. He envisioned guns, branches, wires, tubes, dying things, things he had not yet encountered and was at a loss to understand.

He woke with a start, knowing he was standing on the brink of a brand-new life. He was exiting the familiar, the known, and entering a land that would be a place of solace and refuge or a place as treacherous and uncertain as the one he had left.

He closed his eyes for a moment, trying to recall the images' shape and nature. But they shifted and dissolved like smoke in the wind before he could retrieve them. He only knew they had elicited feelings of foreboding. A word came to him: *Nevermore!*

Frank gazed out the window, thinking. Did the images pertain to some hidden danger, some nameless threat, some calamity that would strike him unawares in the months or years ahead? Or did they point to events he had avoided by fleeing Cuba? Had he dreamed of pain averted or pain to come? Or, perhaps, he had dreamed merely of poetry. "Quoth the raven, 'Nevermore.'" Edgar Allan Poe.

Dread rattled Frank's nerves. He tried to ignore his trepidation, but his feelings were not to be vanquished. He shivered and climbed out of bed. Sweat sheathed his body.

A gentle breeze carried fresh air through the window. A squirrel scampered across the windowsill, stared, and departed. A wren trilled a greeting in the distance.

Frank yawned and stretched. A ray of sunshine performed a petit jeté on the wall above the bed frame, warming the room and filling him with hope.

He had some issues to address before his reunion with Magda. Despite his dream, he was in high spirits. He was reenergized. He had made it to America, and he was ready for whatever life would bring.

CHAPTER SIX

Lieutenant Pino stood before the five-man military tribunal at La Cabaña Fortress in Havana. Located next to the sixteenth-century El Morro Castle, the fortress had served as a military base and prison for more than two hundred years.

During the Cuban Revolution, it was here that Che Guevara oversaw Revolutionary tribunals and executed suspected war criminals, traitors, informants, and former members of Batista's secret police. None of this was lost on Pino.

The delegation investigating his case had spent four days determining whether a conspiracy was involved in the escape of Frank Mederos. Members of the Special Forces were interviewed individually and in groups. They were grilled about Mederos's behavior and comportment while he was part of the force, as well as the officers' motives and actions.

Since he arrived at the fortress, Pino had rehearsed what he would say during his trial. He spent hours before a mirror, practicing his gestures and responding to possible questions. He wasn't about to be caught off guard. Still, he was riddled with anxiety.

Standing erect before the tribunal, he pulled a monogrammed handkerchief from his pocket and dabbed the corners of his eyes. He glanced at it, carefully refolded it, and returned it to his pocket. A gray-haired man named Captain Vasquez saluted Pino and ordered him to be seated. The captain's face was stitched with resolve. He adjusted the 9-millimeter pistol at his side and glanced through his papers before looking at Pino. A perfunctory smile skimmed his lips.

"Good morning, Lieutenant."

"Good morning, Captain."

"I assume you have reviewed and understand the charges against you."

"Yes, sir."

"For the record, Lieutenant, you serve as political commissioner for the Santa Maria base?"

"Correct, sir."

"And on the thirteenth of April, 1967, Frank Mederos, a member of the Elite Counterattack Force and an Anti-tank Guided Missile (ATGM) operator, escaped Cuba, was picked up by a Guatemalan freighter, and was subsequently rescued by the US Coast Guard."

"Yes, sir."

"Could you describe the circumstances surrounding his escape?"

Pino narrowed his eyes. "Mederos was a traitor. He had no respect for authority. On more than one occasion he challenged communist doctrine." He paused.

"Continue," said Vasquez.

"His girlfriend came from a wealthy family. She and her parents were headed for the States. Evidently, Mederos was madly in love with her and was bound and determined to join her."

"Did you know of his relationship with this girl?"

"He kept quiet about her. I didn't know of his relationship before his escape, but later I learned that a couple members of the force had met her."

Vasquez scribbled a note.

"How did Mederos escape?"

Pino tilted his head upward and studied the ceiling. "I'm sorry, sir. Do you mean the last time he tried?"

A hush fell over the room. Pino knew immediately that he had blundered. It was a slip of the tongue that would cost him dearly. His skin warmed as his neck reddened.

Vasquez's eyes grew wide. "The last time?" He leaned forward, confusion marking his face. He cleared his throat. "Are you telling me Mederos tried to escape more than once?"

Pino swallowed his fear and lifted his chin. Vasquez glanced at his fellow interrogators, perplexed. He had not heard about this additional escape attempt during his fact-finding mission. When he hesitated, Captain Enchemendia, another officer on the tribunal, interrupted the questioning.

"Let me get this straight," he said. "You're telling us that a member of the force, a man under your jurisdiction, a man who had full knowledge of Cuba's top military secrets, tried to escape not once, but more than once?"

Pino lowered his chin. Sweat gathered at his armpits. A rivulet of perspiration dripped down his sides.

"Yes, sir," said Pino, the hoarseness in his voice revealing his distress.

Enchemendia was a detail man, someone who never played loose with the facts. He pursed his lips and scribbled a note. When he finished, he peered at Pino over the top of his glasses.

"How many times did Mederos try to escape, Lieutenant? Be precise."

"Twice that I know of, sir."

"Could it have been more than twice?"

"Yes, sir."

The captain's lips trembled, and his eyes grew flinty. "Why wasn't the worm stopped? Detained? Properly interrogated?"

"I tried after the first time—"

"You tried? Why didn't you succeed?"

Pino stiffened. He wasn't about to take the fall for what had transpired.

"Lieutenant Brown countermanded my orders, sir. He said we didn't have solid proof of the worm's intentions."

"Go on."

"Mederos failed to return to base after his weekend leave. Instead of coming back Sunday night, he showed up Monday morning. He claimed he had gotten drunk with his buddies and had slept it off in the park. I didn't believe a word of it."

"Why's that?"

"I smelled gasoline on his clothes and figured he had tried to escape by boat, and it hadn't worked out."

"What did Mederos say?"

"He claimed the smell was alcohol, and Lieutenant Brown bought his story." Pino paused, licked his lips, and added, "Brown favored Mederos."

The captain drew his fist to his mouth with one hand and tapped his pencil eraser on the table with the other. He looked pensive.

"Did you inform anyone regarding this, Lieutenant?"

"Commander Martinez was well aware of the situation, sir."

"You didn't answer my question, goddamnit! Did you inform anyone else—anyone at headquarters—on either occasion when Mederos tried to escape?" Enchemendia's voice was gravelly, his stare incendiary.

Pino blanched. "No, sir."

"Why the hell not?"

The questioning was not going the way Pino had anticipated. While preparing his testimony he had ignored the fact that the tribunal might ask him about prior escape attempts. In the back of his mind he hoped the issue would not arise. Now that he had surfaced it himself, the fallacy of his thinking was painfully evident.

Pino sat stiffly silent. He went cold somewhere deep inside. His breathing became labored, irregular. Every muscle in his body burned with fear. He looked down and began picking his well-manicured nails. He stretched his fingers and studied them. Then he folded his hands so as not to appear fidgety.

Enchemendia cleared his throat. "I asked you a question, damn it." His voice was thick with frustration. He glowered at Pino and slammed his fist on the table. A pitcher of water rattled in protest, prompting several birds to abandon their perch on a branch outside the window.

Pino glared at his inquisitor, eyes defiant. A feeling of heaviness pervaded the room. Enchemendia stared back, unblinking. For a moment the two men remained locked in visual combat. Then the captain wrinkled his nose as if smelling something repugnant. He glanced at his papers.

"I understand from Commander Martinez that you declared a state of emergency at the base. Is that correct, Lieutenant?"

"Yes, sir."

"Under what authority?"

Pino jutted his chin. "Under my own authority."

"How so, Lieutenant?"

"Mederos was not a communist. He had no loyalty to the Party. When it became clear to me that he had escaped, it became a political situation. I had no idea what Mederos would do, what information he would disclose, and to whom. There was too much at stake. As you know, in cases of political emergencies, the political commissioner takes charge." He hesitated for emphasis. "Under such circumstances, I take command."

Enchemendia shook his head sternly. "For the record, Lieutenant, the fact that Mederos escaped did *not* give you the authority to take over *anything*. If you had the God-given sense to call headquarters and discuss this situation with us, we may have offered a very different solution—one that might've worked."

Pino surveyed his shoes before answering, "Yes, sir."

"Commander Martinez also states that he repeatedly asked you to inform the Committees for the Defense of the Revolution, the army, and the militia regarding Mederos's escape and you refused. True, Lieutenant?"

Pino's chest heaved with panic. He sat as rigid as an ice sculpture, trying to ignore the fact that his heart had fallen into an irregular rhythm. He opened his mouth to speak, then hesitated, afraid his voice would betray his emotions. "I—"

"It's a simple question, Lieutenant. Yes or no?"

Pino marshaled his breath, bit his lower lip, and mumbled, "Yes, sir."

"I assume you knew you were disobeying standard military procedure."

Pino calculated his response. He considered defending himself, but the tone of the questioning made him think better of it. Finally, he said, "Yes, sir."

Enchemendia looked down for a moment and rubbed his forehead. When he looked up, his eyes blazed with fury. He fixed Pino in his line of sight.

"How the hell did you plan to find Mederos then?"

Pino lifted his chin, convinced of the appropriateness of his actions.

When he spoke his voice was filled with righteous indignation. "I sent the force after him, sir."

"So we understand," bellowed the captain. "Commander Martinez informed us of this. So did other officers. And, I might add, none of them came to your defense."

"I—"

"Shut up, Lieutenant. You are beyond arrogant. If you'll pardon the expression, I'm beginning to think you are fucking crazy. Why the hell did you do this? I want to hear it from your own lips."

Pino exhaled, his eyes radiating disdain. "Without a doubt, it was the right course of action. I knew members of the force would understand how the worm thinks. They'd be in the best position to bring him in. I figured together we could outsmart him, that it would be a sure thing."

"Was it, Lieutenant?"

Pino lowered his head and answered sheepishly, "No, sir."

Vasquez studied Pino. He had been listening closely. It was time for him to speak his mind. A moment passed before he let loose with a storm of words. "Christ almighty, Lieutenant! Don't you know the mission of the force?"

Pino knew this was a rhetorical question. He was prepared for a rant. He sat like a sphinx while Vasquez continued. "The force is here to protect our homeland, to protect our citizens from imperialist aggression. To be an example of the best, the very best that the Cuban military has to offer. It's not your goddamn plaything. Soldiers are not here to roam the streets searching for one stinking worm who takes it into his warped little brain to chase after his girlfriend in America. That's someone else's job. It's not the job of the force."

"But—"

"But what, Lieutenant?"

Pino knuckled the beveled edge of the table. Beneath his hard exterior, he felt exposed, vulnerable. His lips crumpled into a thin wavy line.

"I thought—"

"You thought, Lieutenant? I don't think you thought at all. Rules and regulations are written for a reason. They are the very foundation of our military might. Who the hell do you think you are to ignore them?"

Suddenly, the air became still, stagnant as pond scum. A motor hummed in the distance and the fluorescent lights flickered overhead. Pino bit his lip as a rictus of pain tugged at the left corner of his mouth.

"I know how men like you think, Lieutenant, and if you thought about anything, it was about saving your own goddamn ass."

Vasquez sat back in his chair, making no effort to disguise his disgust. He gestured to First Lieutenant Torres, who served as a political investigator, to continue the questioning.

Torres gave Pino a long, penetrating look before beginning his interrogation.

"How long was Mederos on the run, Lieutenant?"

Pino stared at the ceiling fan, thinking. "About five months."

The members of the tribunal exchanged meaningful glances.

"Five fucking months?"

"Yes, sir."

"And how many men did you have chasing him, Lieutenant?"

"It depended. Some days more than others."

"Don't beat around the bush, goddamnit! How many of our fine soldiers spent their precious time chasing Mederos around Havana?"

"Upward of three hundred." Pino's voice was barely a whisper.

"You're telling me you sent three hundred members of the Special Forces—three hundred of our top men—on a mission to apprehend a single soldier, and you couldn't manage to catch him? What kind of fool are you, Lieutenant?"

Torres enunciated the word fool so it unwound like a rubber hose. The epithet brought a vivid image of his father to Pino's mind. *How many times did he call me a fool while I was growing up? How dare Torres call me that!* Pino shifted his body in his chair, but remained silent.

Torres continued, "Even if you thought that engaging the force was the right course of action, Lieutenant, why did you continue for so long without informing the authorities?"

"For the sake of the revolution, I believed it was my duty to bring the worm in. I figured he was still in the country, hiding with his relatives. At one point we were right on his tracks. I even—"

Pino stopped short, realizing what he was about to say would make him appear even more incompetent.

"You even what, Lieutenant?"

Pino tightened his lips. Sensing his defiance, Torres raised a fist.

"You are going to tell me, goddamnit!"

Pino exhaled and attempted a feeble smile as he computed the situation. There was no point in covering up his actions. It would all come out eventually.

"I even had him at gunpoint. He was standing right in front of me. I took several shots at him, but Mederos was so slippery he bolted and ran through the sisal. My men searched every tree, every bush to flush him out. But he was nowhere to be found." Pino hesitated. "I lie awake at night trying to figure out where he went. He disappeared into thin air."

"You make him sound like Houdini."

Pino sighed. "What can I say, sir?"

Vasquez closed his eyes as if he couldn't believe what he was hearing. He held up his hand to interrupt Torres. Torres nodded for him to proceed.

Vasquez sipped some water before beginning. "So you had this man in your line of sight, he outmaneuvers you and then, with hundreds of well-trained soldiers at your disposal, you fail to bring him in. Is that what I'm hearing, Lieutenant?"

Tension bloated the air like water filling a balloon. Pino wrinkled his nose before replying, "Yes, sir."

Vasquez sat for a moment, mesmerized. He shook his head in dismay. When he spoke, his voice resounded with authority. "What you have done not only violates fundamental military procedures of the Revolutionary Armed Forces, it makes a mockery of the basic tenets of Marxism. You of all people should know that. As a communist you do not act as an individual. You do not put the needs of yourself above those of the Party. As political commissioner you have been drilled and re-drilled on these concepts. My conclusion is you either failed to learn your lessons, or you chose to ignore them."

Pino started to speak.

"Shut up, Lieutenant. You are not to utter another word." Vasquez glanced down and shuffled some papers. "According to your own admission, you mobilized the unit in total disregard for its safety and the safety of the Cuban people."

"Yes, sir."

"As a result of your pride and belligerence, the Americans probably know every aspect of our defenses: how many missiles we have, where we store them, what their range is, how we deploy them, and God knows what else."

The statement hung in the air like a rotting corpse. "You are a disgrace and a menace, Lieutenant. That is a given. The question before us is whether any part of your sorry ass is still salvageable."

Vasquez leaned back in his chair for a moment before placing his elbows on the table. He looked at the defendant. Fear stalked Pino's eyes. It was vile and venomous, scaling his skin like a snake climbing a tree.

"Have you anything to say in your defense, Lieutenant?"

"I am a member in good standing with the Party. I have been well trained—"

Vasquez cut him short. "You may have been well trained, Lieutenant, but you failed to learn your lessons. Anything else?"

Pino's limbs felt like mush, and he wondered whether he'd be able to exit the courtroom by himself. He didn't want to stumble. He blanched to think he might need help. He refocused his attention on the captain and mumbled, "I believe in our great revolution—"

"Enough, Lieutenant."

Pino's face paled white as flour.

Vasquez closed his folder. "Your loyalty is noted, Lieutenant. But make no mistake; there will be hell to pay for your actions. Court is recessed for three hours while we consider your sentence."

Vasquez pounded the gavel, and Pino was escorted out of the courtroom.

CHAPTER SEVEN

Immediately following breakfast at Freedom House, the men who had served in the Cuban military were separated from the rest of the refugees for an official debriefing. They were taken to a room located on the ground floor of the Opa-locka Airport in Miami. The letters CIA were etched in gold on a plate-glass door.

Frank was introduced to Agent Santo, a Cuban-American with piercing brown eyes. The agent had a thick mane of curly brown hair. He carried himself with confidence, and he spoke fluent Spanish.

As a CIA agent, Frank expected Santo to be dressed in a dark suit, but he was wearing casual clothes, an expensive watch, and a gold ring boasting a clear ruby. The stone glowed a vibrant red in the sunlight. Frank stared at the ring for a moment, wondering whether he'd ever be affluent enough to own one.

Frank had heard a lot about the agency while he was part of the force, and none of what he was told was good. But he never believed half of it, and he was willing to keep an open mind.

After shaking Frank's hand and welcoming him to America, Santo ushered him into a sunlit room with a large wooden table surrounded by six sturdy chairs. The agent gestured for Frank to sit while he took the seat at the head of the table.

Santo studied Frank for a moment before saying, "So you were in the Revolutionary Armed Forces."

"Yes."

He opened his briefcase to retrieve a form while he continued talking. "What did you do?"

Frank smiled briefly, knowing what he was about to disclose would likely surprise Santo.

"I was a member of the Elite Counterattack Force."

Santo looked up and sucked in his breath. His brow furrowed as he grabbed a notepad off the table. He clicked the button on his ballpoint pen and stared at Frank. His face assumed an expectant look. He began to speak in a low, modulated voice.

"You know as well as I do that the Cold War is a war of intelligence. As you can imagine, the CIA would be very interested in learning what we can about Cuba's munitions, strategies, and capabilities. It is a matter of national security."

"Yes, sir. I understand."

Santo hesitated. "I'm sorry, but I must ask you this before we proceed: are you a member of the Communist Party?"

"No, sir. I was a member of the Special Forces, but I have no respect for communists."

"May I ask why?"

"I think they're a bunch of thugs."

Santo regarded Frank closely. "But you were a member of the force, one of Fidel's elite."

"I was, but that didn't mean I agreed with him, his philosophy, or his policies."

"What did it mean then?" asked Santo, sharpness edging his voice.

Frank examined his interrogator's face, thinking Santo knew more than he let on. "You are Cuban, I presume."

"Yes."

"Were you born in the States?"

"No. But this isn't about me."

Frank smiled knowingly. "Then I don't think I need to explain."

Santo shrugged. "Okay, have it your way."

The two men sat in silence for a moment, lost in their own thoughts. Frank remembered the day he was chosen to be a member of the force, the first day he laid eyes on Lieutenant Pino. He had looked at that clean-shaven man with his close-cropped hair and wondered how their lives would intersect. Little did he know the impact they'd have on each other one day.

Santo gave Frank a moment to reflect before he asked, "Would you be willing to cooperate with us, Mr. Mederos?"

Frank smiled slightly. He was feeling at once excited about talking about his experiences in the force and exhausted after his long ordeal at sea.

"Please, call me Frank."

"Okay, Frank. And call me Carlos."

The men smiled at each other, knowing full well that they each had a long story, the details of which neither would likely ever know.

Carlos sat back in his chair and tapped a Camel out of its pack. He tilted the pack in Frank's direction and offered him one.

Frank waved his hand. "Thanks, but not now."

Carlos placed the cigarette between his lips and lifted a gold-plated lighter to its tip. The flame flared briefly. He snapped the lighter shut and placed it next to the glass ashtray on the table. He drew a deep breath, held the smoke in his lungs, and tilted his head upward. He exhaled a long line of smoke.

"I'm going to assume you'll be honest with us," he said.

Frank looked at him, thinking about how often he had dreamed about this moment, had thought about how good it would feel to offer information that might help destroy Fidel's regime. An image of Abuelo flashed through his mind. Frank knew his grandfather would be proud to see him sitting here about to help the Americans. Frank sighed, visualizing his grandfather. His sigh was louder than he expected, and he felt slightly embarrassed.

He locked his gaze on his interrogator, hoping he hadn't noticed. "Your assumption is correct," Frank said in a voice that was barely a whisper.

Carlos raised his pen. "Let's start from the beginning."

Frank closed his eyes for a moment as Santo touched pen to paper. "How old were you when you joined the force?"

"Seventeen."

"And you were in the army before that?"

"Yes."

"Why were you selected?"

Frank smiled to himself. "I'm not quite sure. I think because I can read and write. I'm literate."

"Any other reasons?"

"I attended a government-run school after I served in the Literacy Brigade."

"Where did you serve?"

"In the Sierra Maestra. Tried to teach farmers to read."

"Did you succeed?"

"As well as anyone, given the circumstances."

Carlos nodded his understanding.

"How well do you know the Sierra Maestra?"

"Fairly well," Frank said, having no idea why he was being asked this question. "I lived there on and off three times. I'm familiar with the geography." He watched Carlos make a note.

"Where was the government school?"

"On the outskirts of Havana. Nice facility. But I hated the propaganda."

"So?"

"So I escaped."

Carlos arched his eyebrow. "Escaped?"

"Yes," Frank said smiling. "It was kid stuff really. A bunch of my friends came and rescued me. On bicycles no less. We must've been quite a sight."

Carlos tossed his head to the side, indicating he had no interest in this topic.

"Getting back to the force."

"Yes?"

"How many men are in the force at any one time?"

"Between three hundred and three hundred and fifty. Men come and go."

"What was your position?"

"I was an Anti-tank Guided Missile operator—ATGM."

Carlos's eyes shone briefly. From his reaction Frank could tell Santo knew precisely what he did. But Santo was a shrewd interrogator. Since there was no way to corroborate Frank's story, he needed to make sure Frank knew what he was talking about.

"Who supplied the equipment?"

"It was Russian made."

The light in Carlos's eyes told Frank he was familiar with ATGMs and their capability. He seemed satisfied with Frank's answer.

"What did you do specifically?"

"I launched missiles."

"Were you good at it?"

"I could hold my own."

Frank studied Carlos as his lips flattened and curled inward. He knew the agent was hoping he could tell him a great deal more about the missiles. Frank possessed the kind of information the agency wanted.

"Where are the missiles stored?"

Frank smiled slightly while Carlos watched him. "Is that all you need to know?"

Carlos leaned forward in his chair, expectantly.

"I want to know a lot of things, Frank, but that certainly ranks high on the list."

Frank nodded, but remained silent. He looked out the window. A hummingbird sipped nectar from the coral blossoms of a hibiscus bush. It reminded him of a helicopter. He wondered how the bird could possibly suspend itself in the air the way it did. That was the kind of thing military engineers all over the world would study.

Frank looked at Carlos. "Do you have children?"

"Two," he said. "A boy and a girl."

"Helluva world to raise kids in."

Carlos cleared his throat as a film of perspiration slicked his forehead. He took a deep breath. "The location, Frank," he said softly. "Where's the location?"

Frank looked at him and exhaled. "You aren't going to believe this."

"Try me."

Frank sat back in his chair, momentarily lost in thought. Carlos watched him closely. Frank rolled his head in a circle to release the tension in his neck as Carlos eagerly awaited his response. Frank's mind flashed back to when he was first taken to the place the missiles were kept.

He remembered being blindfolded and driven from base to an undisclosed location. At the time, he had no idea where he was going, but he knew enough not to ask questions. Not a word was spoken on the trip. As they drove, Frank became increasingly nervous that Pino had discovered his plans to escape. If so, he was being escorted to his execution. No trace of his remains would be found. That's how things happened.

Frank's gaze drifted to the palm trees rustling in the breeze, and a shudder coursed through his body. Suddenly, the hairs on his arms stood on end. He ran his hands briefly over his arms to warm them.

Carlos fixed his eyes on Frank. There was a long silence before he said softly, "Frank, you've got to help me out here. It's important."

Frank turned his head back to Carlos and nodded. "I know," he said. He hesitated a moment and took a deep breath. He was about to provide the CIA with the very information Pino feared he would disclose if he ever got to the States. That's one of the reasons why the lieutenant had pursued Frank so relentlessly. In a very strange way, this was Frank's moment of triumph. But he didn't feel triumphant. Instead, he felt a profound weariness.

Frank looked at Carlos and said softly, "The missiles are located in chicken coops."

Carlos's eyes widened as if he hadn't heard right. "Chicken coops?"

"Yes, chicken coops."

Carlos sat back while he processed this information. "How do you know?"

Frank smiled briefly. "I was there. I was blindfolded, but I learned the exact location later."

"Then we have a lot to talk about."

"We do. But right now I'm hungry."

Carlos hesitated a moment, thinking. "Then let's get some lunch."

The men pushed back their chairs, walked down the hall, and stepped outside. They blinked against the Florida sun. Jasmine scented the April air. They got into Carlos's black Buick and drove to a mom-and-pop restaurant in Little Havana. The owner greeted Carlos warmly and escorted them to a small table at the back of the restaurant near the kitchen. They heard pots and pans clang against a stainless steel sink.

Since Frank had arrived in America, he felt as if he couldn't get enough to eat. He devoured two roast pork sandwiches piled high with meat and roasted peppers and finished off the meal with a tall glass of iced tea. Carlos watched Frank eat with satisfaction. He waved to the waitress to bring him another drink. Frank smiled his appreciation and wiped his mouth with his napkin.

"Tell me about your family, Frank."

Frank nodded, thinking about them. "My parents live in a small house in Guanabacoa. My father works in a fertilizer factory. Backbreaking work. Long hours. He takes the night shift for extra pay. Money is tight. My mother's a housewife."

"Siblings?"

"Yeah, a whole bunch." He laughed thinking about them. "Little rascals. I'm the oldest."

"Aunts, uncles?"

"Another whole bunch."

"Anyone else you were close to?"

"My grandfather—" Frank started. His voice cracked a little, and he stopped speaking.

Carlos regarded Frank with curiosity but remained silent. Finally, he nodded as if to signal Frank to continue. Frank cleared his throat.

"Other than my parents, I was closest to my grandfather. Smart man. If it weren't for what he taught me, I would've never made it."

"What did he do?"

"For a living?"

"Yes."

"He was a fisherman."

"What did he teach you?"

"Survival skills—how to read the stars, the currents, and the wind. How to outsmart the communists."

"So, he wasn't a communist?"

"Hardly! He was a religious man. He hated communism. We used to have long talks about it."

Carlos smiled as if remembering something. Then he dropped his napkin on the table and signaled the waitress for the bill.

When they got back to the office, Carlos gestured for Frank to again take a chair. He flipped through his notes before turning his gaze toward Frank.

"We were talking about the location of the missiles," he said.

"Yes."

"Where is the facility located?"

"Not far from the airport in Rancho Boyeros."

Carlos raised his eyebrows. "The airport? That's a highly populated area."

"I know. They did it on purpose."

Carlos nodded slightly.

"Why?"

"For protection against enemy attack. They figure the Americans won't bomb a site where too many civilians could get killed. Propaganda and all that."

"I understand. Can you describe the facility?"

Frank pulled his chair closer to the table. "Several buildings are lined up next to each other. Chickens are kept on either end of the buildings to make it look like a real chicken farm. You'd never suspect it was a missile storage facility."

"Where are the missiles kept?"

"Underground."

"How do you access them?"

"Through a trap door in the floor. It's well disguised."

"Do you know how many missiles are kept there?"

"Precisely."

Carlos regarded Frank curiously. "How do you know that?"

"I took inventory. I counted all the missiles and recorded their serial numbers."

"How many are there?"

"Upward of a thousand."

Carlos leaned back in his chair and whistled. He sat up straight again and made another note.

"Is there any way to identify the missile sites from the air?"

"I doubt it. They've gone to great lengths to disguise the operation. It would look just like a chicken farm from the ground or from the air."

"Could you locate it on a map for me?"

"Of course."

Carlos reached behind him and unrolled a map of Cuba. He handed him a felt marker, and Frank circled the area in question. Carlos stared at it for a moment and then excused himself. Frank heard him speaking in hushed tones to someone in the hallway. When Santo returned, he looked more relaxed.

"This is important information," said Carlos. A hint of a smile danced on his lips. "I appreciate you being so forthcoming."

Frank nodded.

Carlos glanced at his watch. "That's about all for now. I have other men I must interview. I'll pick you up in the morning. We'll talk more then."

As they shook hands, Frank thought about what Lieutenant Pino might do if he ever got wind of what he had just disclosed to the CIA.

CHAPTER EIGHT

The next morning Carlos arrived at Freedom House around ten o'clock to pick up Frank. He was dressed in crisp chino pants and a madras shirt. They stopped for a light breakfast of coffee and bagels and chatted about baseball on the way to the office. Carlos was a Yankees fan and had an impressive knowledge of the sport, regaling Frank with stories about Yogi Berra.

Once they arrived, Carlos escorted Frank to the conference room and then stepped away to discuss a matter with someone in the hallway. It only took a few minutes. Frank could hear snippets of a hushed conversation, but he couldn't understand more than a few words.

Frank settled back in his chair, beginning to feel more rested. He stretched his legs and gazed outside. The sun poured into the room through the open windows and created golden squares that waltzed across the floor.

His mind drifted to his days with Magda. He pictured her dancing in her poodle skirt to the steady beat of "Secret Agent Man," and he smiled at the irony that he was about to talk to the same.

He recalled Magda standing in her blue bathing suit looking out to a sea that stretched to the unfathomable shores of America as curls of foam nibbled her toes. He imagined her standing next to a hibiscus bush, its ruby flowers opening to greet her. He knew he was romanticizing, but he didn't care.

It had been a long six months since he'd seen her, and more than a lifetime of events had transpired. He wondered whether she wore her hair the same way, whether she liked her new school, whether she dressed in American-style clothes. It was inevitable that she had changed. But how?

Carlos entered the room, interrupting Frank's thoughts. He took a seat at the end of the table, perpendicular to him. He seemed relaxed but distracted.

"I forgot to ask," he said amiably. "Did you sleep well?"

"Like the dead."

"Are they taking good care of you? Do you need anything?"

Frank smiled, rearranging his body in his chair. "Everything's great."

"Good."

Carlos righted the folder before him, opened it, and glanced at it briefly. He scrutinized Frank as if assessing him for some unknown reason. Feeling uncomfortable under his gaze, Frank shifted in his chair.

"There are a couple of things I'd like to talk about today," said Carlos.

"Fine. Whatever you want."

Carlos placed his elbows on the table and leaned forward. "First, I'd like to hear your take on Fidel."

"Personally or politically?"

"Both."

Frank thought for a moment, considering how to express his feelings. He had strong views on the subject. But thinking about what Fidel had done to Cuba invariably made his head pound and his insides clench. He didn't want to get into a full-blown discussion on the matter. It would be emotionally draining. It was time to look toward the future, and he was determined to make short shrift of the topic.

Frank closed his eyes for a moment before he spoke. "Castro's an enigma."

Carlos rested his chin on his fisted hand and waved his fingers in a gesture for Frank to continue. "Go on."

Frank hesitated. "For one thing, he studied under the Jesuits, yet he's determined to do everything possible to dismantle the Church."

"Are you Catholic, Frank?"

"Born and raised."

"Religion is important to you?"

"Of course."

Carlos folded his hands in front of him. "Any other thoughts?"

"Fidel was trained as a lawyer, yet he's totally disregarded the rule of law." Frank waited a moment, editing his thoughts. Anger fortified his voice. "He claims to be a man of the people, but he runs Cuba like a police state. Anyone who disagrees with his policies is labeled a worm. People have no rights—you can land in jail for the slightest transgression. Not to mention being shot on sight."

"Do you know people who've gone to jail, Frank?"

"I do."

"Friends of yours?"

"Friends of mine."

"And people who have died?"

Frank's mind formed an image of Joey López, his sparkling brown eyes, his mischievous grin. The boy had been shot and killed during an aborted escape attempt. Frank had saved him from drowning a few weeks earlier when they tried to leave Cuba together. He was only thirteen. Tears filmed Frank's eyes, and it took him a minute to regain his composure. "Yes," he said. He did not want to elaborate.

Carlos allowed Frank a moment to recover. "What do you think of Fidel politically?"

"Politically, he's a disaster. The country is in a state of chaos. People are hungry. Unemployment is through the roof. Store shelves are empty. Nothing works anymore."

Frank was working up a head of steam. He stopped talking and looked out the window. Carlos regarded him with concern. Frank thought about his mother trying to find basic ingredients for cooking: sugar, flour, meat, and beans. He remembered his father waiting in long lines to get her what she needed, only to return home angry, humiliated, and empty-handed.

He thought about the Committees for the Defense of the

Revolution, friends and neighbors spying on each other, reporting every move to the authorities. He remembered how the bureaucratic restrictions imposed on fishing had robbed his grandfather of his greatest pleasure.

Frank shook his head and said, "Fidel is the worst leader Cuba has ever had—even worse than Batista. He has single-handedly destroyed the country."

"Your country," clarified Carlos.

"No, *the* country," countered Frank.

"Isn't Cuba your country?" asked Carlos, driving home his point.

"No, Cuba *was* my country. Now, America is my country."

Carlos nodded, studying Frank. A vague smile played at the corner of his lips. "But don't you care about what happens to Cuba, what happens to your family, the circumstances under which they live?"

Frank bristled at the question, wondering about Carlos's implication. He crossed his arms. "Of course I care. I worry about them all the time."

"Of course," Carlos repeated.

Carlos studied the ceiling for a minute, pondering something. His eyes darted back and forth in a minuet while he thought. Frank straightened his spine.

Carlos returned his gaze to Frank, and said, "Would you like to see Fidel overthrown? See someone else in power?"

"Yes, as long as that person isn't Raúl. He's as bad as Fidel. They'd both have to go for Cuba to recover."

Carlos's smile waned. "You are in a good position to help make that happen, Frank."

Frank looked at Carlos, curious. "How so?"

Carlos's eyes became laser focused. A minute elapsed before he spoke in a tone as somber as a funeral dirge. "I don't want you to answer right now, Frank. Give yourself a couple of days to think about it."

"Think about what?" Frank's heart began to race.

Carlos knitted his brows, creating two vertical creases that sliced his forehead. "Think about working for us to help overthrow Fidel." The agent's lips turned upward, but his eyes did not smile. They were grave, serious. Frank wasn't sure what he meant, but he had his suspicions.

"Help you? In what way?" Frank's larynx betrayed him, his voice was hoarse and ragged.

"We need people on the inside to feed us information."

"I don't understand," Frank replied with false calmness. A seed of panic sprouted in his gut.

"Having been a member of the Special Forces, it would be easy for you to infiltrate the Cuban army—"

For a moment Frank failed to follow Carlos's train of thought. Then he did. He gulped a breath as his heart dropped like a block of cement. "You're suggesting I return to Cuba?" He could hardly believe what he was hearing.

"Yes, men like yourself often do."

Frank felt a seismic pressure change, like a hurricane was forming in his brain. He tilted his head to the side and rolled his shoulders to relieve a muscle spasm. When he completed the circle, he looked at Carlos and said, "I'm sorry. Let me be clear. You want me to spy for the CIA?"

"Yes. I'm inviting you to work for us—for the agency." Carlos hesitated a moment, searching Frank's face for a sign of acceptance. But there was none to be found.

"I know what you're thinking, Frank. You're concerned about your safety."

Frank scrutinized him, trying to get his mind around his proposition. He felt a sense of vertigo and a little nauseated. Being offered a job with the CIA was the last thing he had expected to happen that morning.

"You would be well protected. The agency has already infiltrated many areas of the Cuban military. Our people are excellent at what they do—they would be there for you."

A raft of emotions competed for purchase in Frank's throat: fear, confusion, and anxiety. He thought about his dealings with Lieutenant Pino, and crystals of perspiration erupted at his hairline. For a moment he re-experienced the fear he felt when Pino was shooting at him during his escape. He remembered hiding in a spider-infested cave. He remembered escaping his pursuers by swimming underwater and breathing through a reed.

He looked down, attempting to relieve his anxiety by examining his cuticles. Feeling chilly, he rubbed his arms with the palms of his hands. Frank's first reaction was to reject the offer, but his thoughts were jumbled. He was fraught with emotion, so he hesitated to speak.

Carlos looked at Frank for direction. He awaited his response. Frank opened his mouth, not knowing what words would emerge. "I—"

Carlos raised his hand. "Hear me out." His voice was graveled, like it was running small rapids.

Frank felt depleted, exhausted. "All right," he said, exhaling.

Carlos stood, unrolled the map of Cuba and grabbed a pointer sitting on the ledge of the blackboard. A draft rattled the map against the wall. Carlos glanced at Frank before turning his attention to the image of Cuba.

"You were stationed in the center of Cuba—here," he said. "To avoid detection we would send you to the far end of the island." He pointed to the Sierra Maestra. "It's hundreds of miles from your former base."

"I'm well aware of the location," Frank said a little too sharply.

"Several people in the Cuban command structure work for us. They'll have your back at all times should anything go wrong."

Frank shook his head in dismay. "What would you need me to do?" His voice sounded high and slightly shrill.

"We'd need you to feed us information regarding strategy, weapons, troop movements, matters of high importance to our national security." Carlos waited for Frank to absorb this information, and then added, "You may be involved in disinformation activities, suggesting certain things are true that aren't."

Frank curled his lips inward and looked at Carlos skeptically. "I understand."

Carlos studied him for a moment and returned to his seat as Frank worked to corral his feelings.

"I'm not saying this isn't dangerous work. It is. But you would be well compensated."

Frank did not respond. Carlos fingered the folder before him and shuffled some papers. The overhead lights flickered. A fly buzzed a screen in entreaty, searching for an opening, desperate for a way out. The silence lengthened before Carlos said, "Let me outline what we have to offer." He glanced at Frank. "If you agree to join us, you will receive further details from our personnel office."

"Fine," said Frank, hoping his lack of enthusiasm wasn't too obvious.

"First, we'd waive the waiting period for American citizenship. You would be granted it immediately."

Frank nodded, eyes wide.

"You would undergo a rigorous education and training program, with special emphasis on English."

"I could use English lessons."

"As a government employee, you'd be entitled to our generous benefit package, including full health benefits for you and your family. If you remain with the agency, you will be enrolled in our pension program. Are you familiar with pensions, Frank?"

Frank blushed slightly. "I'm sorry, no."

"Depending on your length of stay, the government would provide you with a very comfortable retirement income."

Frank's mind drifted to his father. He had no such benefit, and Frank thought about what a difference it would have made in his parents' lives. Even though retirement was far off for Frank, the idea was appealing. He wondered whether pensions were common in America, or whether this was a unique opportunity.

Carlos turned a page in the folder. "We will provide you with a generous financial package. I won't go into the figures right now, but it's enough for you to buy a car and put a down payment on a home for you and that girlfriend of yours."

"Magda," Frank said, surprised that Carlos hadn't used her name.

"For you and Magda," he corrected.

"I see," said Frank vaguely. He was trying to sound coherent, while ignoring the heaviness gripping his chest.

"Of course, there's room for negotiation. But joining the agency would give you a great start in this country—a real leg up."

Frank considered for a moment. Carlos was intent on his mission. He reminded Frank a little of himself.

"I share your goals regarding the overthrow of Fidel—that goes without saying," said Frank. "And I appreciate the offer. But this is a lot to take in."

"I understand. But I urge you to think seriously about this, even if you decide to do it for only a year."

"Why a year?"

"Joining the agency would help ease your transition to this country. Finding a job can be difficult for new immigrants. If they do find work, it is usually menial and low paying."

"I imagine it is."

"Of course, we would like to get you into the field as soon as possible, while your knowledge of Cuban military operations is still fresh. But after a year, we would reevaluate your assignment, perhaps bring you back to the States." Carlos hesitated, smiled, and added, "Besides, a year isn't that long, is it, Frank?"

Frank looked at Carlos, wondering how he could possibly say such a thing. He thought about months spent on the run from the army, endless nights longing for Magda, terror-filled hours on the dark, open sea.

"No," he said slowly. "A year can be an eternity."

Carlos looked at Frank, comprehension dawning on his face. "Of course," he said. "A year *can* be an eternity. But the agency would use its considerable resources to make sure things go as smoothly as possible for you."

Frank looked pensive. "What are you thinking?" asked Carlos.

"Knowing the military the way I do, I'm not sure you could protect me. Could you give me more details on how that would be done?"

"That's classified information you would be privy to once you agree to come on board."

"Would I be able to return home periodically?"

"We would make every effort to make that happen, but I can't promise anything right now."

Frank nodded. "Thank you for the offer. It's very generous. But I'd like to think about it, if I may."

Carlos stood. "You have a couple of days. Mull it over before we meet again. Tomorrow the army will debrief you. I'm sure you can provide them with important details regarding the force's operation in Cuba."

"I'm happy to oblige."

"Good," said Carlos, standing. "We'll talk again on Thursday regarding you joining our team."

"Yes, sir," Frank said, gulping his breath.

Carlos hesitated and looked Frank in the eye. "You know this conversation is strictly confidential. Do not mention it to anyone—anyone."

"I understand, sir."

The two men shook hands. Frank had a lot of thinking to do.

CHAPTER NINE

It was time to take a walk. Whenever Frank had a problem as a child, he would stroll with his grandfather through the park and they would talk. Abuelo taught Frank to look at issues from different angles, examining them like shards of glass in a kaleidoscope. He had played a great role in the development of Frank's critical thinking.

Facing this important decision, Frank wished his grandfather were there to counsel him. For a moment, the possibility of never seeing that dear man again stung his heart.

Frank's biggest concern was being able to provide for Magda and himself. He had no idea where or how to find a job. His only experience was in the Cuban military, and that would be of no use to him in finding employment. He wasn't even a high school graduate.

When Fidel instituted mandatory military service for boys age fifteen and over, it robbed Frank of an opportunity for high school and college degrees, at least in Cuba. What's more, English had never been his strong suit, and he worried about how quickly he could learn it. The agency would provide him with a job and English lessons, neatly solving both problems.

Frank tried to imagine being back in Cuba after working so long and hard to leave his country behind. He tried to imagine providing intelligence to the Americans. He tried to imagine providing disinformation to the Cuban military.

But as soon as he did, his thoughts turned to Magda. The idea of being separated from her a moment longer than necessary sapped his soul. The memory of her lips, the sound of her voice, and the softness of her skin reverberated in his brain like an echo off a fjord.

Their relationship was solid as silver. But he wondered about the timing. Was he sacrificing their future financial stability for his immediate needs and desires? Was he being selfish in wanting to be with her right away? In the long run, would a year in the agency make a difference to their lives together?

With the agency, Frank would have a direction, a position, a career. Without it, he'd start at the bottom, just another Spanish-speaking immigrant in search of a job.

That night Frank went to bed feeling anxious and restless. He tossed and turned for hours, examining the alternatives in his mind. *This is an opportunity of a lifetime. Would I be foolish to turn it down? If I joined the agency, Magda would be disappointed, but she'd support my decision. She'd wait for me. That's not the question. The question is whether I can wait to be with her.*

And then there's the risk. Carlos says the agency would have my back, that they would protect me. But could they? Really? I have my doubts. And what would happen to Magda if I weren't there to care for her? She has her family. But still—

Frank turned on his side and tried to empty his mind. After a while, he fell into a deep sleep. His eyes shifted beneath his lids like they were dancing under the stars. As daybreak approached, Frank heard a strange sound, a yelp that jerked him awake. It emanated from deep within his throat. He bolted upright and then fell back upon the pillow, haunted by an image that sat on the cusp of his consciousness.

Abuelo once told him it was easier to remember a dream if you returned to the same position you were in when you awoke. Frank turned on his side and slipped his hands beneath his head, trying to recapture fragments of a dream that was quickly dissolving.

He closed his eyes and Magda appeared in a dotted Swiss dress, her hair arranged in beribboned braids. She was holding the hand of a blue-eyed boy, a familiar boy, one Frank had seen before. They were smiling and saying something he couldn't hear.

The dream was slipping away. Frank clung to it like a man holding onto a lifeboat. He felt the roll of the ocean and heard the shriek of seagulls. The air was cool and redolent of salt and fish. The boy was calling Frank's name, faintly at first, then louder. He was beating a drum. A word rang out across the open sea, sounding as sharp and as clear as a foghorn.

Frank sat straight up. He glanced at a fellow refugee snoring in the next bed. He knew this word, this call, this command. It was the same word this boy had used when Frank was trying to decide whether to board the Guatemalan freighter.

He relaxed as the tightness in his chest dissolved like Jell-O in hot water. He smiled, knowing exactly what to do.

CHAPTER TEN

The next couple of days Frank spent with various army personnel who peppered him with questions regarding military operations in Cuba. They asked him about the distance and velocity of rockets, their depth of penetration into steel, the kinds of vehicles used to transport them, and the location of fuel.

Frank identified items of interest in films they had of Cuban military parades and thought he recognized himself in one of them. The army personnel were respectful and grateful for Frank's time and input. They concluded their discussions with mutual respect.

That night Frank had trouble sleeping, thinking about his upcoming meeting with Carlos. He was not looking forward to informing him about his decision. During their short time together, Frank had developed a genuine respect and fondness for the man. Carlos was smart and compassionate, a combination Frank valued.

Frank was in full agreement with the agency's goals, and he knew he could help. But the idea of reentering the vortex that was Cuba cramped his throat. The next morning, as they drove to Carlos's office, Frank approached the subject. "I know you want an answer regarding our discussion the other day."

Carlos raised a hand to stop him.

"Let's wait until we get to the office to talk about it," he said. Frank could tell from the disappointment in his eyes that he knew what he was going to say.

"All right."

When they arrived at the office, Frank settled himself in a chair and turned toward Carlos. "I'm sorry. The thought of telling you my decision has been weighing on my mind. I hate to disappoint you, but I cannot accept your offer. I—"

Carlos gestured his acceptance. "No need to explain. Your priorities are your priorities. You have every right to your decision. You must do what's best for you. This is America, you know."

Frank smiled. "Thank you for that. I appreciate your consideration. But there are more important things I want to do right now—like getting married."

"I understand," said Carlos. He looked out the window and said in a tone that surprised Frank, "It's hard to argue with love."

Frank nodded, not wanting to pursue the subject.

Carlos closed the manila folder on his desk and turned to retrieve another one sitting on his credenza. He smiled at Frank. "If you aren't going to join the agency, can you help us in another way?"

"I'll do whatever I can."

"I'm sure you are aware of Alpha Sixty-six, the organization of Cubans in America who are dedicated to overthrowing Fidel."

"I've heard of them."

"They are a very disciplined group, and they number in the thousands. They are involved in clandestine operations. They keep a low profile. Most Americans have never heard of them. They are better known in the Cuban community, but they keep a tight lid on disclosing their activities. They are well armed and well trained, and they will stop at nothing to undermine Fidel's regime."

"Most of them are refugees, I understand," said Frank.

"Yes. Some of their members participated in the Bay of Pigs operation. The CIA works with them on a variety of security issues, including getting people in and out of Cuba."

"I see."

Carlos cleared his throat. "It would be a great help if you could supply us with information on anyone in Cuba who might be willing to cooperate with us."

"Cooperate with the CIA?"

"With the CIA and with Alpha Sixty-six, if necessary."

"I'd have to think about it."

Carlos exhaled. "Why don't you start by telling me about who helped in your escape."

Frank took a deep breath. "I made three escape attempts, and a lot of people helped. But in terms of army personnel, it was my friends Manny and Lazo. They covered for me at the base so my absences weren't noticed."

"They took a big risk."

"They did," said Frank, feeling guilty that he had made it to the States and they had not. "They were fellow ATGM operators. If it weren't for them, I'd be rotting in jail. Or worse. In any event, I wouldn't be sitting here talking with you."

Carlos touched the end of his pencil to his lips. "Describe Lazo for me."

"He's a light-skinned mulatto. Five foot ten. Well-built. Neat dresser."

"Smart?"

"Very. He's also well spoken, charming, and sophisticated."

"Do you trust him?"

"I've already trusted him—with my life."

"That says it all."

"I guess it does."

"Where does he live?"

"In Guanabacoa with his family. I've been to his house many times."

"Describe his house for me."

Frank wrote down the address and color of the house and handed it to Carlos, who added it to his file.

"Can you tell me a story Lazo would recognize?"

Frank thought for a moment and smiled.

"What?"

"At one point Lazo was in charge of a basketball team for the force. One night we left the game early and went to a nightclub in Havana. I forget the name. If it comes to me, I'll let you know.

Anyway, Manny, Lazo and I spent a couple of hours drinking and dancing with the girls.

"Lazo met a girl named Regina—a real looker. He flirted with her shamelessly. She had a few too many drinks and ended up dancing on the bar. Lazo decided to join her, but he was so tipsy he fell off and landed flat on his face. We all laughed ourselves silly. Except Lazo. He was mortified. None of us will ever forget that night."

"Perfect! That's just what I needed." Carlos penned some notes in a slanted script before looking up again.

"And Manny. Could you describe him?"

"Sure. Manny's about five-foot-eight, slight build. Not very strong. Again, very smart. Well read. His math and analytical abilities made up for his physical shortcomings."

"How so?"

"He could figure out equations needed to determine a rocket's trajectory in a blink of an eye, which made him one of the force's best operators. Lieutenant Brown was willing to overlook his physical limitations because of it."

"Sounds like a smart cookie."

"He is."

Carlos made another note. "Where does he live?"

"In Regla, not far from the oil refinery." Again Frank wrote down the address for Carlos.

"Can you give me a list of other men in the Special Forces who hated the communists?"

Frank took pen to paper, wrote down several names, and handed his notes to Carlos.

"Is there anything else you'd like to say before we conclude our discussions?"

Frank thought for a moment. "Keep in mind that new recruits are inducted into the army twice a year, in June and December."

"Meaning?"

"Lazo and Manny will get out of the army in December. The

timing may be an important consideration, should you decide to contact them."

"I appreciate that," said Carlos. He stood up and smiled. "Well, I think that's about it for you."

"I'm free to go?"

Carlos extended his hand. "It was a pleasure getting to know you, Frank. I hope our paths cross again someday."

"Likewise."

"Perhaps we will have a drink together when Fidel is overthrown."

Frank nodded. "Perhaps."

Carlos hesitated. "One more thing: I was wondering why you decided not to join the agency."

The truth halted in Frank's throat like a heel of stale bread. He looked at Carlos, wondering whether the agent would understand. The last thing he wanted was to appear foolish. He faltered for a moment and then reclaimed his courage.

"There's a boy," he said. "I have no idea who or what he is. But he guides me when I need him."

Carlos knitted his brows. "A guardian angel?" His tone of voice did not betray his views.

"Call him what you will. But I trust him. I dreamed of him standing beside Magda. I was trying to decide whether to go to her or to join the agency. The boy looked at me and said: 'Come.'"

Carlos did not respond. He shot Frank a look so penetrating it felt like it scraped the back of his skull. "Interesting," he said. The men walked down the hallway without further comment.

When they reached the door, Carlos took Frank's hand in both of his. "I wish you the very best in America."

"It seems daunting."

"You'll do fine."

"Thanks."

"Good luck with Magda and good luck finding a job."

"Thanks again."

Frank smiled and walked into the bright glare of freedom.

CHAPTER ELEVEN

Wedged between two farmers, Pino sat on the backseat of an old, dilapidated bus, fumes belching out of its tailpipe, its rusted fenders covered with a thick coat of grime. Someone had etched the ubiquitous "*¡Cuba, sí, Yanqui, no! ¡Venceremos!*" "Cuba, Yes, Yankees, No! We will win!" with their finger on the filthy back window. As the bus lurched along the rutted dirt road running through Matanzas province, Pino closed his eyes, his muscles moving in rhythm with the sway of the vehicle.

It had been a long couple of weeks, full of loss and humiliation. Mederos's escape and his own trial and conviction had left Pino shaken to the core. The tribunal had not only robbed him of his rank, it had stripped him of his dignity. The thought pained him like a blow to the head.

If he were lucky, Pino might be able to rebuild his career from the bottom up. Who knew what the future might bring? Even so, that would take years, maybe decades to accomplish. The very idea drained blood from his face.

Pino shook his head, trying to come to terms with the fact that he was packed into this wretched bus loaded with lowlifes. He worked to distract himself by silently repeating slogans of the revolution: "*Viva el socialismo! Viva Fidel! Socialismo o Muerte!*" He scowled as a mosquito buzzed his ear. He waved it away, attempting to recall better days.

Pino was settling into his seat, lost in his thoughts, when the man sitting to his right sneezed, a sloppy, wet eruption that spread a nasty mist that landed squarely on Pino's cheeks. He was a beefy man with bushy eyebrows, known as Emmanuel. He grunted and lifted a filthy hand to wipe his nose. The former lieutenant eyed him with disgust, retrieved his handkerchief from his pocket, and dabbed his face. He exhaled loudly, and leaned away. *These people behave like pigs. And to think I'm going to have to live with them.*

Emmanuel didn't take kindly to Pino's condescension. "What the hell is wrong with you?" he said, revealing a mouth devoid of adjoining teeth. "Ain't you ever seen a man sneeze before?" Pino grunted, lowered his chin, and cast Emmanuel a venomous glare.

There was something about Emmanuel that reminded Pino of his father. A memory flashed through his mind, an image of his father sitting at the kitchen table, his calloused hands caressing a bottle of rum, his teeth fuzzy with lack of brushing.

Hygiene was never his father's long suit.

At the time, Pino had just finished reading a book on the history of Spain. He was smart and he knew it. But his father put no value on intellect or education. Being a tough guy was all he cared about. He pointed an accusing finger in his son's direction.

"Knowing that shit ain't worth a bag of beans," he said. "Ya just wastin' your fuckin' time. Ya ain't no better than me. Cut from the same cloth, we are. I ain't made nothin' of myself and ya ain't gonna either."

At that moment, Pino vowed to get out, to prove his father wrong. He began to spend his free time studying instead of playing, repeating his multiplication tables in his head while doing chores, sitting in the front seat at school, rising to the top of his class. He was well on his way to success when the revolution came. He sensed opportunities and took advantage of them. By his mid-thirties, he was well respected, a member of the Communist Party. And now this.

Pino rearranged his body and looked out the window. Fields of sugarcane drifted past his eyes like clouds in a storm. The former lieutenant was of Spanish descent. He had light skin and gray-green eyes—a color with no real name—and the sun had never been easy on him.

This will be tough. Hard labor is supposed to be. But at least the tribunal took my loyalty and service to the Party into consideration when it came to sentencing. At least I wasn't executed or sent to jail. It could be worse. A lot worse.

When the bus groaned to a halt, Pino grabbed his small suitcase and descended two stairs to greet the torrid heat. A foreman, a burly, no-nonsense man named Castillo, shouted, "This way, men." The contingent followed a narrow dirt path to a rough wooden bunker with a corrugated tin roof. Pino scrutinized it. It was beaten and bent, and Pino figured it probably leaked. He was right.

As the door opened, a pack of rats scurried into a nest of shadows. The air was a fog of mildew, rodent droppings, and eye-watering cigarette smoke. Two heavy beams ran the length of the building, providing a place for hammocks to be strung. Upward of one hundred men slept there, barely two feet apart.

Pino looked at the other men, hoping to find someone who seemed to have had military experience, someone to whom he could relate. For a fleeting moment, he wished he had someone to talk to, a woman perhaps, someone sympathetic to his plight. One man was busy picking his nose. Another was scratching his ass. His prospects didn't look promising.

Pino stood in line with the other men, selected a hammock from a pile on the ground, and strung it neatly between two poles. He plucked a handful of cane leaves from between the web of the hammock and threw them on the dirt floor.

The men lined up to be issued a tin cup and a plate. The handle on the plate was dented and Pino shuddered, imagining the quality of food it would hold.

The next morning Castillo roused the men at dawn. Each was issued a pair of knee-high leather boots. Most of the *macheteros* already had the straw *campesino* hats needed to protect them from the sun's scorching rays, but Pino did not. The foreman cast him a scornful glare and then begrudgingly handed him one. Pino returned his stare.

The former lieutenant glanced at the hat, knowing it was too small for his head, but Castillo seemed to be in no mood to sort it out. The hat sat a couple of inches above Pino's ears, causing his hair to jut out on both sides. Pino railed inwardly, appalled that the hat made his head look like a winged moon.

Working the sugarcane harvest required backbreaking labor under a relentless sun. As the country's leading cash crop, Fidel was deeply invested in the harvest's success. But rumor had it that this year's quota would fall far short of its target. Although everyone from professors to prisoners had been conscripted to work the fields, there were never enough hands at harvest time.

Pino's gaze swept the scene. Sugarcane waved in a haze of dust that misted the air a yellowish brown. Nineteen-foot stalks stood proudly beneath a topaz sky, dwarfing even the tallest men. The sky boasted puffs of white cottony clouds that grazed the horizon.

Pino's eyes were drawn to the black tendrils of smoke rising against the gently rolling hills. The fire spread rapidly across the field, eating the cane like a full-throated dragon. Fires were set to rid the cane of its dense leaves and facilitated the cutting of the unharmed stalks. Also, it was easier to burn the refuse than to cut and transport it to the sugar mills.

The men waited with machetes in hand while flames jumped into the air, sparks flying, leaves crackling like popped corn. A breeze fanned the blaze and carried the smoke downwind, stinging the men's eyes and lungs. Pino bent in a spasm, lost in a fit of coughing. The man next to him nudged him forward, and the men began marching toward the freshly burnt cane, careful to avoid areas that were still ablaze.

The cane needed to be cut at its base to maximize the harvest. The men worked until the sun dropped below the horizon, stopping occasionally for a long drink of water from a common jug. Ragged guayaberas clung to backs soaked with perspiration. The gleam of men's teeth and the whites of their eyes provided the only contrast to faces blackened with soot.

At the end of the day, the men repaired to the mess hall for what passed for dinner, assailing their food with grime-encrusted hands.

Pino was horrified. The menu usually consisted of overcooked rice, limp beans, and stale yams. The men grumbled through their meals. They were rarely served meat.

Some nights the men bathed. The nights they were too exhausted, they didn't. The smell in the barracks was horrific, a mixture of sweat and rodent droppings. Pino covered his nose with his arm while he slept.

It didn't take long for Pino to notice that the method used to harvest the cane was inefficient. Often lazy and unmethodical, many of the men stood idly by or cut the cane stalks haphazardly. Random piles of cane sat rotting in the fields, requiring too much time to be picked up and placed in carts. Pino watched this procedure with growing frustration. *What jerks. Harvesting cane isn't rocket science, yet they're managing to screw it up.* One day, his frustrations became too much for him. He had to speak up.

He gestured to the field of cane and hollered to the men. "Can't you see what you're doing? Cut a whole row of cane at one time, god-damnit! Jumping around the way you are is a frigging waste of time."

The men looked up, startled. For a moment no one spoke. Then a muscular man named Pablo stepped forward. He had a grizzled beard and obsidian eyes that glinted with rage. "Who the hell do you think you are you to tell us what to do?" he barked.

"That's right, give him hell, Pablo," shouted his fellow cane cutters.

Pino turned toward Pablo as a small group of men formed behind him, itching for a fight. His stomach lurched, and he felt a stab of fear. But he wasn't going to back down.

"I thought there might be one decent *machetero* among you," spat Pino. "But obviously not. This place is a goddamn mess."

Pablo stepped forward, raising his fists menacingly. "Shut the hell up, you bastard!"

Pino faced Pablo head on, hatred rising in his chest like steam. He was sick and tired of having to deal with the likes of these people. *Why should I, a former lieutenant in the Revolutionary Armed Forces, have to put up with this nonsense?*

Pino's eyes grew flinty. Adrenaline coursed through his bloodstream like flour through a sieve. It had been a long time since he'd been in a fistfight. But he was ready. In fact, he welcomed it. It would provide a much-needed release of the tension that had riddled his body for the past several months.

Ever since Mederos had escaped, Pino had felt tightness in his chest, his shoulders, his cheeks, tension that even exercise did not relieve. He sized up his opponent. He looked strong but none too bright. Pino wasn't worried. He would prove to be faster, smarter. After all, he was a man who got things done. *This bastard has no idea who he is dealing with. I'll flatten him with one punch.*

Pino planted his feet firmly in the soil and raised his fists. He was confident, resolute. As he did, the sun crept over the hills, striking Pino on the chin. It wouldn't be a minute before the rays cleared the tree-tops and burned into his retinas. Pino raised his head, preparing for the sun's intrusion into the altercation.

Suddenly, the man who had sneezed on the bus appeared out of nowhere, waving his arms in the air. "What the hell is going on here?" he shouted. The crowd parted like the Red Sea to let him through.

Stepping forward, Pablo replied, "This bastard thinks he's a hot shit. Thinks he knows it all. He's trying to tell us what to do."

Emmanuel turned to Pino. A look of satisfaction netted his face. "Oh yeah? Well, this little prince has had a chip on his shoulder since day one—too fancy to even watch a man sneeze."

Emmanuel grabbed Pino by the front of his shirt. "So you think you're better than everyone else? You think you're an expert at cutting cane? Well, maybe it's time we all teach you a goddamn lesson. One you won't forget."

The men mumbled in agreement. Emmanuel moved toward Pino and shoved him backward, throwing him off balance. As he did, Pino's heel hit a depression in the dirt. His ankle twisted and he turned his body to his right, falling into the cane's flaming residue. Licks of fire jumped at the disturbance. Pino issued a brief croak of surprise and extended his hands to break his fall. He was struggling to protect his face. But he failed.

The first thing Pino noticed was searing pain around his jaw. Then he felt the stinging in his hands. He felt like a thousand bees had attacked them. He let out a yelp and waved his hands at the wrists. The flames whispered up his calves. Then his knees met the burning leaves, then his arms and thighs.

Frantic, Pino levered himself to his feet and limped off the field. The ground pitched beneath him, and he concentrated on retaining his balance. He could feel the heat on his legs. The fire was devouring his pants. The smell of his burning flesh made him want to retch.

Pino fell to the ground and rolled his body in an effort to extinguish the flames. The pain spread from his ankles to his waist like oil on the open seas. He slapped his thighs with his hands to put out the fire, only to find that he was causing himself even more agony. The men watched in amazement, unsympathetic to his predicament. Smiles bloomed on their faces and snuffles of laugher drifted over their heads. One by one they turned and walked away, muttering "Good!" and "Serves the bum right!"

Pino curled his body into a fetal position. He wanted to pound his fists into the sunbaked ground, but he knew he shouldn't. It would just exacerbate the pain. He wanted to teach the bastards a lesson. He wanted a shower and a decent bed. He wanted a scotch. But most of all he wanted his ribbons, his medals, his rank. He wanted his life back. Pino raised his fists to the sky as if to curse the gods. But he knew there were no gods. Instead, he let out a bloodcurdling scream. He cursed the smoke, the sweat, and the smoldering cane. He cursed the stupid cane cutters. He cursed the searing sun.

But most of all, he cursed the day he ever laid eyes on Frankie Mederos.

CHAPTER TWELVE

A scattering of crystal stars winked overhead as Frank boarded the red-eye flight for Newark. It was three a.m. The people at Freedom House had been more than accommodating: they'd been terrific, handling paperwork and escorting the refugees through the airport.

Besides supplying Frank with a Social Security card and working papers, they had paid for his and his uncle's plane tickets and had given them each five dollars to get started in America. The red-eye was a cost-saving measure.

Telling Frank it might be cold in New Jersey, they issued him a gray wool coat with a black satin lining. He laughed out loud when he tried it on. It was so long it nearly brushed the ground, making it difficult to walk. Frank had never worn such a heavy coat. The weight of it felt strange on his shoulders. But he accepted it in good humor.

He was about to take his first flight. He had no idea what to expect, and he was unabashedly excited. He made his way down the narrow aisle, glancing at the stewardess. She wore a neat blue uniform boasting gold buttons as shiny and bright as her smile. Frank nodded to her, tucked his scant belongings in the overhead compartment, and exhaled as he settled himself in his seat.

Uncle Luis sat down next to him, and they looked at each other in amazement.

"Can you believe this?" said Luis. "A week ago we were fighting the waves in the goddamn ocean, and now we're sitting here like a couple of kings."

Frank smiled in agreement and glanced at his watch. "Just a few more hours," he said.

"What's the first thing you're going to do when you get there?" asked Luis.

"Kiss Magda. And you?"

"Have a beer."

"At the crack of dawn?"

Luis shrugged. "Why not? Celebrate!"

Frank laughed. "Yeah, why not?"

Frank looked out the window for a moment to see a man remove a ladder from the side of the plane. He turned to Luis and asked, "Did you talk with Rosa after dinner last night?"

"Yeah, she and my girls were going to your parents' house for breakfast."

"Good. It'll help keep their minds off you being gone."

Luis nodded. "Do you miss her?" Frank asked.

"Not yet," said Luis. "Been too busy with everything else." Frank stretched his legs and pushed the button on the side of his seat, realizing it made the back of the chair recline. He shook his head in wonder.

He had watched enough American TV to form a clear impression of the States as a place full of modern buildings, flashy cars, and fashionable shops. He was aware that the Vietnam War was taking its toll on American lives and threatening the presidency of Lyndon Baines Johnson. Besides that, he knew little of American history and politics. He had much to learn.

The sudden roar of the airplane engine startled him. He fastened his seatbelt and listened as the stewardess provided safety information. Although Frank couldn't understand her, he followed what she said by looking at the images on a cardboard card located in the pocket in front of his seat. There were pictures of floatation devices to be used in case of emergency. Frank considered the possibility and then banished the thought.

The plane shuddered and began to taxi down the runway. The

power of its forward thrust was startling, like nothing Frank had ever felt before. His heart beat a staccato rhythm as he watched the wings tilt and the plane lift off the tarmac. His spine hugged the back of the seat as the plane gained altitude.

Once the aircraft leveled off, he rearranged his body, thrilled to have a window seat, even if they were flying in the middle of the night. He watched as the line of lights grew smaller on the runway. As the plane ascended, he could make out the outline of the Florida coast, ragged in the bright moonlight.

Frank felt it strange to be so far above everything. He thought about his family in Cuba and wondered whether his mother was sleeping. He figured she was more likely up saying her rosary and worrying about him.

He looked around. Some passengers were reading and some were dozing. Light snoring and occasional murmurs filled the plane, but Frank was far too excited about seeing Magda to even consider napping. Besides, flying was so mind boggling, he couldn't imagine missing a minute of it.

He was amazed at the size of America. The plane had been in the air for almost two hours, and it was still flying. Frank had no idea New Jersey was so far from Miami.

Frank's life had offered him little opportunity to learn about American geography—and even less about New Jersey's. He knew it was in the north of the country, and it had cold winters, but that was about it. He tried to visualize the landscape. Magda had mentioned the Jersey shore, and he hoped it was as beautiful as Cuba's.

Two stewardesses wheeled a refreshment cart down the aisle, offering the passengers something to drink. The aroma of coffee filled the air. Some of the passengers sat up to accept food, while others slept, oblivious to what was happening.

Luis and Frank watched as other people lowered their food trays, fascinated that they were built into the back of seats. They both ordered coffee. Luis stirred some sugar into his cup and extracted the spoon. He laid it carefully on a napkin with the name Eastern

Airlines imprinted in a blue serif font. It created a dark-brown oval that expanded and seeped through the paper. Shortly thereafter, they were served a breakfast of bacon and eggs.

"I wonder what Union City is like," Frank said, taking a bite of buttered toast.

"Who knows?" said Luis. He considered for a moment. "Maybe it's full of bars and beautiful girls. Wouldn't that be nice?"

"I've got my own beautiful girl," Frank said, smiling.

"You and that girl," laughed Luis, shaking his head. "You'd think she was a goddess or something."

Frank flashed him a mischievous smile.

Luis looked at Frank as if he knew what he was thinking and grunted. He considered Frank an incurable romantic.

The stewardesses collected the breakfast trays, and Frank took a halting walk down the aisle to use the smallest bathroom he'd ever seen. When he returned, he climbed across Luis, reinstalled himself in his seat, and looked out the window as the plane began a slow, sonorous descent. The captain's voice filled the cabin, asking everyone to take their seats and fasten their seatbelts for landing. His words were like music to Frank's ears.

Frank looked out the window as a patchwork of silver-and-white cylinders came into view. They were entwined by a tangle of tubes and pipes that curled and crossed like snakes sprouting from Medusa's head. Small waste fires leapt toward the sky.

Frank had never conquered his fear of snakes. He shivered a little, thinking it might be a bad omen. A brace of doubts ran through his mind, and he chased them away like a housewife sweeping cats from her stoop. His breath caught in his throat as he watched white lights blink through fat puffs of black-and-gray smoke that smudged and grimed the reddening sky.

He could tell that this was a gigantic industrial complex, perhaps an oil refinery, larger and more robust than anything he had ever seen. He feared noxious fumes would soon assault him, and he covered his nose with the palm of his hand. He turned and looked at a man sitting in the seat behind him. He had red hair and a long, white beard. He smiled and shrugged. "Newark," he said as if saying the word explained everything. Frank nodded, confused.

His mind returned to Cuba, to prisms of light bouncing off crystal waters, to swaying trees crowded with bananas and coconuts. He thought about plucking sun-warmed strawberries off the vine, about butterflies kissing the velvety faces of sunflowers. None of that was evident here. If this was New Jersey, it looked like a harsh and unwelcoming place. A chill crawled up Frank's spine.

The sun burned off a post-dawn fog as the plane descended. A few trees stood outlined against the morning light. Their branches were stark and bare, winding and twisting like Japanese brush strokes against the pink-marbled horizon. None boasted fringed leaves. *They must have different trees here*, Frank mused.

The plane thumped down, briefly lurched, shivered, and then stopped with an earsplitting squeal. The lights flickered on. Those who'd been dozing awakened with long yawns. The cabin clicked with the removal of seatbelts as people began standing, stretching, and pulling their luggage from overhead bins. Frank slipped on his coat and ran a comb through his hair.

He pushed Newark's industrial images from his mind and focused his thoughts on Magda. He could hardly believe he was this close to seeing his sweetheart again. He glanced at his watch. The plane had landed fifteen minutes early. Frank's excitement was so palpable he was afraid it would lift the lapels of his coat. He was smiling from ear to ear.

Frank's neck and face flushed with anticipation. He turned to his uncle, beaming his pleasure. He felt like sharing his happiness with the passengers on the plane. But he couldn't articulate his feelings in English, and he knew few people would understand his Spanish.

Luis and Frank deplaned to the tarmac with haste and enthusiasm and strode with purpose to the terminal. As Frank entered the waiting room, his eyes searched for Magda. This was the moment he had dreamt about, the moment for which he had risked his life, the beginning of their life together in America.

The airport was much larger than he had anticipated with hundreds of people milling about: waiting for tickets, checking luggage, and looking for gates. A man announced something in English over a loudspeaker, but Frank couldn't understand what he said.

Frank stretched his neck and scanned the area. He looked back and forth, but saw no sign of Magda. She was always so punctual. He was sure she wouldn't be late. Panic collected in his pores as a thousand dark thoughts raced through his mind. For a moment, his gaze winked out of focus.

What if something happened to Magda and her family on the way to the airport? What if they were in a car accident? What if there was trouble with the authorities?

Frank turned to Luis. "Do you see them?"

Luis squinted. He was nearsighted and had lost his glasses at sea. He said that squinting improved his vision, a concept Frank didn't understand. Luis shook his head. "Not yet," he said.

Frank's mouth went dry, and he began to perspire. He ran his forefinger around the inside of his collar to relieve a sense of pressure. When he withdrew it, his finger was wet.

She has to be here. She has to be! I don't think I could stand it if something happened to her. Frank stopped for a moment, removed his overcoat, and rolled up his shirtsleeves. He gulped a mouthful of air and tried to calm his racing pulse. He remembered the pledge he and Magda had made to each other a couple of years ago never to doubt each other's love. He relived the scene in his mind, and it calmed him. He relaxed his shoulders and took a deep breath.

Then, out of the corner of his eye, he spotted someone who resembled Magda. She had the same straight line to her spine, the same tilt to her head, the same fall of ebony hair cascading down her shoulders. She was wearing a navy-blue coat with leather buttons and penny loafers. Frank saw her speaking to a man he didn't recognize, nodding in response to something he was telling her.

Frank's heart began to gallop in his chest. He strained his eyes to see her. Just then a heavyset man walked in front of her, obscuring the view. When he passed, the young woman turned. She looked in his direction, lifted her hand to her mouth, and screamed a one-note cry: "Frank!"

Magda ran toward Frank, graceful as a gazelle, the susurrus of her leather shoes on the linoleum sounding like the sweet wash of waves.

"Magda, Magda, Magda," Frank said, trying to convince himself that this person running toward him was real. They held their arms out to each other, awaiting the moment of union as if they were playing out the scene in slow motion, every second magnified, every inch of air between them an obstacle to overcome. When they touched, it was like they had returned to the womb. For a moment, Frank felt deliciously whole. Safe.

He embraced Magda and showered her face with kisses. Her family hurried to join them, exuberant, beaming. Magda kissed him back, and they held onto each other for dear life. Frank saw Magda, smelled her, felt her. His senses, which had hungered for her for many long months, were finally satiated.

Frank grabbed Magda by the waist and lifted her high into the air, delirious with joy. When he lowered her to her feet, she looked him up and down and squealed, "I can't believe it's you! It's really *you.*" She looked like a toddler at Christmastime, smile wide, eyes bright, just as Frank remembered her.

Laughing, Frank pointed at himself. "I can't believe it's me either," he joked. He wrapped his arms around Magda, not wanting to let her go. He lifted her face with his forefinger and cupped her cheek tenderly with the palm of his hand. He searched her eyes, noted the flush pinking her cheeks, and traced her lips with his thumb. They were dressed in a rose-colored gloss that made them look fuller. It was the first time Frank had seen Magda in lipstick. *She looks like a woman now. Just like her mother.* When his lips found hers, they were as soft as suede. He nibbled them hungrily, wanting the kiss to last forever.

When their lips finally parted, Magda nestled her head against

Frank's chest as he locked his arms around her back and gently stroked her long, thick hair. Her heart thumped against Frank's chest, and his heartbeat soon fell in rhythm with hers. They stood like that for a few minutes before Magda's father, Sergio, reached out to shake Frank's hand.

"We were afraid you might not make it," Sergio said amiably. He patted Frank on the back.

"There were times when I thought I might not make it either," said Frank.

"That's an understatement," added Luis.

"Well, we'll have to hear all about it," said Sergio. He grabbed Frank's bag from the floor and swung it over his shoulder. Frank greeted Magda's mother, Estel, and her brother with enthusiastic hugs and kisses before he embraced Magda's Aunt Sophia and Uncle Rigo.

Sophia and Rigo held a special place in Frank's heart. They had been among the many people who had risked their lives to ensure his escape. If it weren't for them, Frank might not even be alive. Their son, Rigo Jr., stood behind them, smiling broadly. He had just turned fifteen, and his parents' emigration to America had enabled him to avoid being drafted into the Cuban army.

"Happy birthday, Rigo," said Frank.

Rigo laughed. "After all you've been through, I can't believe you remembered."

The group walked toward the doors wreathed in smiles while Frank held Magda's hand. They were so excited to see each other that everyone was laughing and talking at once. Their enthusiasm had reached the point that people in the airport were looking and nodding to them. A young man with sideburns and a mustache gestured to Frank, and said in Spanish, "Just married?"

"Not yet," Frank replied.

"Well, don't let her get away."

"Not on your life! You have no idea what I went through to be with her."

Magda looked up at Frank, radiant. The man nodded and waved. Magda's father had borrowed a second car for Rigo to help transport everyone home, and the group split up. The cars followed each other. Feeling on top of the world, they made their way to Sophia and Rigo's small apartment.

Frank was so intent on looking at Magda and holding her that he didn't bother to look out the windows. There would be plenty of time to take in the sights later.

When the group arrived at their destination, they scrambled up the two flights of stairs, trying to modulate their voices so they wouldn't wake the neighbors. They were a battalion of giggles and good cheer. Sophia drew the key from her purse and matched it to the lock. It yielded with a click and the door opened wide.

The living room, while small, was warm and welcoming. Luis and Frank collapsed on the sofa while Sophia went to the kitchen to make some coffee. Magda and Estel helped, and the rattle of dishes and silverware filled the air. The familiar aroma of freshly brewed coffee was enough to make Frank weep.

The women served a breakfast of fruit, eggs, cereal, and bread. A pitcher of orange juice sat atop a white tablecloth. Food never tasted so good.

Magda laughed and hugged Frank, the love and adoration in her eyes making Frank feel like everything he'd been through had been worth it. The group spent the rest of the morning talking. Frank touched on his dealings with Lieutenants Pino and Brown. He explained how different they were and what roles they had played in his escape.

He told them about the need to commandeer a boat because the one they were in was too overloaded to make the journey. Luis described the terror as they slipped into international waters, and Frank told them a little about their long night on the open sea.

Frank and his uncle took turns recounting their experience with the Guatemalan freighter that picked them up, relating how they feared it might be a Russian ship that would return them to Cuba for execution. They described their relief when the American Coast Guard arrived to bring them to Key West. Their audience listened somberly and attentively, amazed that the two men had managed to escape.

Frank draped his arm around Magda as she snuggled against him on the couch. Feeling her body next to his and smelling her lightly perfumed skin stimulated urgent feelings in Frank. He tried to suppress them by listening to stories about Magda's school and hearing about life in Union City, the place she now called home. Talk turned to housing, jobs, and the cost of living in New Jersey.

After a while, Frank's adrenaline rush subsided, and his body informed him that he needed sleep. His eyes began to droop, but he didn't want to let go of Magda.

Magda looked at him. A mix of love and sympathy filled her eyes. "Here," she said pointing to the sofa. Frank stretched perpendicular to Magda on the couch, and she took his head in her lap. She stroked Frank's forehead as he nestled his body close to hers. The sun rose and spilled across his face, warming his cheeks.

Estel adjusted the window blinds to shade Frank's eyes. Frank held Magda's hand, rubbing his thumb over her polished nails. She ran her forefinger along Frank's eyebrows, coaxing stray hairs into place. He smiled, content.

Frank thought about Magda and their future together. Years of Friday nights spent playing pinochle and dominoes after a long week of work. Years of Saturday nights spent laughing and joking with friends. Years of Sunday mornings spent trading newspaper sections and drinking coffee as black as Texas oil.

He pictured Magda looking beautiful on their wedding day and even more beautiful on their twenty-fifth wedding anniversary. He imagined waking up to her when he was old enough to have deep wrinkles around his eyes, and she was wise enough not to notice.

He thought about the children they would have, two boys and

two girls. He imagined pushing them high on a swing on summer nights before telling them bedtime stories about Cuba.

He believed that someday their children would meet his parents, their grandparents. He hoped Abuelo would live long enough for their children to get to know him, their great-grandfather, Frank's fishing partner, the man who had made his journey to America possible by teaching him what he knew.

Frank thought Fidel would be overthrown, and he and Magda might return with their family to Cuba. They would walk along the *Malecón* as the sea spray needled their calves. They would show their children their childhood homes and the school where they met. They would drive to the rugged hills of the Sierra Maestra, narrating stories about Fidel and his rebels and showing them the place where all the trouble began.

Or. Or, perhaps, Cuba would never recover from its economic devastation. Instead, Frank's family could come to America to enjoy its bounty. Perhaps they would also live in Union City. For a moment, he pictured his jubilant relatives waving as they stepped off the airplane.

It had only been a matter of months since Frank had seen his family, but he missed them terribly. It was awful to leave them behind—not to hear their voices, not to enjoy their company, not to know whether he'd ever see them again. It created an ache in him that nothing but the love of a wonderful woman could begin to ease.

But he had that. His sweet Magda was sitting next to him, her hands smoothing the tension from his forehead, her body warming his. He nodded silently, soothing himself with the idea that their life together would go on forever. It was a comforting thought.

But it was not to be.

CHAPTER THIRTEEN

Political investigator First Lieutenant Torres completed his interview with Foreman Castillo at the sugar plantation where Pino was doing hard labor. Not liking what he had heard, he decided to talk with the former lieutenant.

Torres asked Castillo to relinquish his office so he could speak with Pino in private. The foreman agreed, walked out to the hallway, and began hollering orders to the cane cutters out the window.

Pino soon arrived at Castillo's office looking tired and disheveled. Gone was his starched, polished look. Gone was his fine haircut. Gone was his neat manicure.

He strode into the room clad in muddy shoes and dirty clothes. His face sprouted a wiry beard. His limbs were covered in blisters as red and angry as boiling lava, even after several weeks of burn treatment at the clinic.

Pino saluted Torres and stood at attention until Torres asked him to be seated. The foreman's desk consisted of an old door thrown atop two construction horses. A coat of brown dust covered his papers. The room was airless and stifling hot. A small electric fan circled lazily in the corner, humming, but providing little relief from the heat.

Torres completed writing a few notes before looking up at Pino. He dropped his pen and sat back in his chair, shaking his head in consternation.

"What are we going to do with you, Pino?"

The former lieutenant jerked his head at the remark. It sounded like something his father would say as a prelude to a beating. He took a step backward. He was unsure whether this statement required a response, so he remained silent. He had long since concluded that in instances like this, the less said the better.

Torres shook his head in dismay. "I'm told you started a fight."

Pino began to speak, but Torres raised a hand to stop him. "I've heard what Foreman Castillo has had to say. Now I'd like to hear your side."

Pino looked at him, eyes defiant. He waved his arm in a circle to indicate the scope of the plantation. "This place is a pigsty. There's no order around here, no control. What's worse, nobody cares about the work. The men are a bunch of bums."

"Bums?"

"Yes, bums."

"So you got into a fight because the men are bums?"

"No, sir. I got into a fight because I was trying to bring some discipline to this operation."

"And—?"

"And the men resented it and started a fight."

"That's not what I hear," said Torres. Pino stared at him, knowing enough to allow him to finish his thought. "I hear *you* started the fight by ordering people around."

Pino shook his head from side to side. "They needed to be told what to do. They were wandering around like dazed cattle. The cane wasn't being harvested properly."

"So you took it upon yourself to tell the 'bums' how to do it?"

"It had to be done. Time was being wasted—"

Infuriated, Torres slammed his fist on the table. "When are you ever going to learn your lesson, Pino?"

Pino's face drained of blood and his skin prickled with fear. He grimaced and issued a small sound. "What lesson?" he said, a little too sharply.

"The lesson that you are part of a team—that you are not in control of everything—that there exists a chain of command—that you can't take matters into your own hands."

Pino lowered his head. *It's the same old shit. They don't give a damn about my years of training, about my intellect, about my leadership skills. They just want me to follow some half-assed rules like a brainless nitwit. Well, if that's what they want, that's what they'll get. I'll play whatever game they want to get out of this stinking hellhole.*

Torres continued, "How long will it take before you comprehend that it was this same kind of arrogance that got you into this fix in the first place?"

Pino straightened up and stared at Torres. *I'm smarter than this guy. I'll outwit him. He thinks he's in charge, but I control my own destiny. I'll say whatever he wants to hear.* A moment of silence elapsed before Pino said, "I understand, sir. It won't happen again."

"I hope you *do* understand, Pino. This is not the only place where you can do hard labor. If you don't straighten up—and straighten up fast—you'll look back at this time as a fond memory."

Pino blanched and nodded while Torres gathered his papers. "I'll be checking with Castillo and with your comrades every two weeks regarding your behavior. I don't want to get a report like this ever again. Am I making myself clear?"

"Yes, sir."

Torres started to walk out the door and then stopped, turned, and looked at Pino. "One more thing," he said.

Pino glanced up, startled. "Yes, sir?"

Torres looked Pino up and down before his gaze settled on his jaw. As he did, Pino fingered his wound. He knew it detracted from his looks, and he was not happy about it. He had always prided himself on his appearance.

Torres hesitated a moment and said, "Take care of those damn blisters, for chrissake. You look like hell."

"Yes, sir."

Torres smiled slightly, saluted, and left Pino staring at the wall.

CHAPTER FOURTEEN

Frank woke up eager to explore Union City. After seeing Magda off to school, he donned his coat and strolled down Bergenline Avenue. The air was raw and chilly, and a watery sunlight glinted off aluminum grates that webbed storefronts. Factories belched black smoke, casting a mantle of smog over the city.

Frank thought he might look out of place in his new hometown, but that wasn't the case. Throngs of people crowded the sidewalk. They walked in unison as if attached to each other and attended their business lost in thought. He passed sari-clad women with red bindis and pink lipstick, blue-eyed mothers with towheaded children, and black men with dazzling teeth and dreadlocks capped with rough plastic beads.

The crowd pushed him along, speaking a cacophony of languages—English, Spanish, Chinese, Vietnamese. As he buttoned his coat against the cold, he accidentally elbowed a long-haired man about his age. The man's eyes were glazed and dark as ink. His beard fell like rain over his tie-dyed shirt. Grumbling, he fanned his fingers into a peace sign. Enough dirt resided under the man's fingernails to grow turnips. Not knowing how to respond, Frank lowered his eyes and kept walking.

Frank's feelings vacillated between joy and sadness. Although he was thrilled to be in America, a longing welled up inside of him, a homesickness that he feared might haunt him forever. As his feet traveled the cement sidewalks, he longed for the smell of Cuba's rich earth, the call of seagulls, and the throb of bongos that livened the streets of Havana. The only music to be heard here blasted from radios of Pontiac GTOs and Mustang convertibles.

Union City offered nothing as nature intended. Signs were every-where—metal signs, wooden signs, neon signs—jockeying for posi-tion, plastered on buildings, and hanging like slaughtered cattle from poles and pipes. They proclaimed the merits of Chinese restaurants, coin-operated Laundromats, and check cashing stores. Most were writ-ten in English, their messages a mystery to Frank. He was frustrated to not be able to read them. The architecture was intriguing—not what he had expected. He thought Union City would resemble Cuba the way Miami did. He believed American cities would look pretty much alike, but they didn't. There were no pastel-colored houses, no orange-tiled roofs, no wide verandas to corral the breeze.

The city was crowded and confusing. Frank was disoriented by the lack of elbow room. Not that his home in Guanabacoa was big. It wasn't. But at least he had space to breathe. Here everything was bunched together, like plants competing for sunlight on the forest floor.

Buildings leaked into each other, one row house indistinguish-able from the next. Images from television screens bounced off window panes, allowing him a furtive glimpse into private lives, private spaces. But doors were locked, hospitality in retreat.

Frank saw eyes that bespoke fear as they watched passersby behind lace curtains or through slatted venetian blinds. It was so different from his uncle's house where he had to hide under the bed from his pursuers because the door remained open all day so friends and neighbors could come and go at will.

Although it was April, an apron of broken snow, remnants of a long-forgotten blizzard, lay in cindery mounds on the sidewalks. Ice piles shed water from their bottoms into gutters clotted with trash. The ice lay a half an inch off the sidewalk as if suspended by an unknown force. He had seen pictures of snow sitting light as bubbles on trees, filigreeing branches in sparkling white. He never imagined snow as hard as shells, languishing like a rotting corpse, oozing its essence into the ether.

Overhead, a tangle of wires cross-hatched a dull gray sky, and he realized how much he had taken for granted in Cuba—the scent of wild lime and vanilla, arcades of coral stone archways, lizards changing color with the light, macaws grooming neon-green feathers. A crow screamed its rage, devoid of color. *Even the birds are black here*, he thought.

Frank walked up the street until he found a bookstore. To his surprise, it served Spanish-speaking people. He strolled down the aisles, admiring lavishly illustrated dust jackets. He was amazed at the number and variety of goods freely available to anyone willing to pay the price.

The store carried books, records, and greeting cards with ornate typefaces. They were designed to celebrate various occasions—birthdays, weddings, anniversaries, and graduations. No one hassled him or monitored his ration. No one forced him to wait in line. No one humiliated him for the sake of "the cause." Frank's heart quickened like the click of castanets. He felt free. He felt liberated. He felt good.

An attractive woman in a twin sweater set approached Frank, asking if he needed help. She spoke Spanish. For the first time that day he felt at home.

"Do you have any American history books written in Spanish?" Frank asked. The woman looked at him as if this were a common question.

"Where are you from?"

"Cuba."

"Have you been in the States long?"

"I just arrived."

"A lot of Cubans settle in Union City. I don't know why, but they do. It's probably because they know people here."

"That's why I'm here," said Frank. "Where are you from?"

"El Salvador. I'm Maria. Maria Reed," she said, extending her hand.

Frank shook it. "Reed?"

"It's my married name."

He nodded, looked at his chapped hands, and plunged them into his pockets.

"Follow me and I'll show you the books," she offered.

They walked past several cardboard boxes, half open and brimming with merchandise, before they stopped at a table stacked with history books. One had a picture of George Washington on the cover. Another was about the US Constitution.

"What are you looking for?"

"I'm not quite sure."

She handed him a book about Thomas Jefferson. A picture of a brick-domed building adorned its cover. She glanced at it. "That's Monticello, Jefferson's house."

"Nice."

"He designed it along with a whole lot of other things. He was a genius—like Benjamin Franklin."

"It looks interesting. But I need something more general."

"Of course," she said, smiling. She pulled a hefty book from the shelf. "This is a good one. It covers American history from the time of the Pilgrims to the end of the Korean War."

"Who were the Pilgrims?"

She grinned. "You'll hear more about them at Thanksgiving."

Maria's answer failed to enlighten Frank, but he was hesitant to ask her about Thanksgiving. He leafed through the book. It contained several images of American presidents along with pictures of the two World Wars.

"This is perfect. How much?"

"Twelve ninety-nine, plus tax."

Frank paused, having no idea whether that was a good price. "Is that a lot?"

"It's about right for a hardback. Shall I wrap it for you?"

Frank's face grew hot with embarrassment. "I'm sorry. I don't have any money right now. I have to find a job. I'll come back later."

The woman's eyes sparkled, and Frank's spirits lifted.

"Okay," she said. "Good luck!"

Frank walked out into the afternoon air, and the crowds seemed less intimidating. At least he knew where he could buy books. A smile danced on his lips. He had the feeling that life in America would be different, but doable. If there were Cubans in Union City, he knew he could make his way.

CHAPTER FIFTEEN

The next day Magda's father told Frank about an apartment house that had rooms available.

"It's not very big, but it's a start," he said.

"How much?"

"Sixteen dollars a month."

"How far is it from here?"

"Only a couple of blocks. Close enough for you to see Magda without having to walk too far."

That was all Frank cared about. He turned to his uncle. "We've got ten dollars between us. With the housing voucher they gave us at Freedom House, it's enough for the first month's rent."

Luis grunted. "Let's take a look. But we'll have to get jobs—and fast—or we won't be able to pay the bill for next month."

They walked down Bergenline Avenue to inspect the room, wending their way up a narrow staircase to the third floor of an old building. The walls hadn't seen a coat of paint in years. Two creaky beds were shoved against the wall with a narrow space separating them.

An old dresser stood beneath dusty fiberglass curtains that hung askew and appeared to house a family of spiders. Green linoleum squares curled upward to reveal dried black adhesive. Frank sat on the bed. The room was musty and airless, and the one small window was painted shut. Frank looked at it and figured he could loosen the paint with a screwdriver. Still, he felt claustrophobic. He couldn't imagine living in this room for any length of time. But the price and location were right. So he and Luis signed a month-to-month lease.

It was time to look for work. Luis quickly found a job as a dishwasher in a small Cuban restaurant. As luck would have it, Magda's father, Sergio, had a brother who worked in a factory in Clifton, New Jersey—not far from Union City—and he put in a good word for Frank. The factory laminated fabric, and Frank was hired to work the second shift—seven p.m. to seven a.m. He carried eighty-pound rolls of cloth on his back before placing them on a compressor to be stretched, steamed, and laminated. The plant was old, airless, and dusty. But it was a job.

Dazzled by American consumer goods and hungry to obtain them, Luis focused on making money. He made friends quickly, and in little over a month he obtained a more lucrative job. Frank asked him about what he did on several occasions, but Luis failed to enlighten him. Frank had too much going on in his own life to give much thought to Luis's evasive answers. One day Luis asked Frank how much money he made.

"A dollar sixty-seven an hour," Frank told him.

"What's that come to a week?"

"Around sixty bucks, depending on overtime."

"That's bullshit. Why would you work for chump change like that? I sure as hell wouldn't."

Frank dismissed his uncle's statement as bravado. He figured Luis was working at a job that paid little more than his own—he couldn't imagine otherwise. But he was wrong. Luis was buying things that Frank could only dream of affording.

Luis filled the room's small closet with expensive clothes, expensive shoes. A gold watch encircled his wrist. He smoked pack upon pack of cigarettes, puffed on cigars, and purchased beer and liquor by the case. He didn't speak fluent English, and he didn't have any particular skills. Where was he getting his money?

While Luis's job obviously paid well, it appeared to involve people of questionable character. Luis began partying late into the night. He'd return to the room singing in Spanish and staggering from drink. Sometimes his friends accompanied him. Frank feared he and Luis would be evicted.

Meanwhile, Frank's life developed into a predictable routine. He hitched a ride to work with a Cuban who lived in the city, paying him five dollars a week for transportation. He volunteered for the least desirable jobs in the factory, and he worked all the overtime he could get.

Luckily, he befriended a factory supervisor who spoke Spanish, Italian, and English. He was young—about twenty-eight. Bruno took Frank aside for a talk one day.

"You seem ambitious, Frank. And I like you. So I'm going to give you a piece of advice. It's good to speak Italian, and it's good to speak Spanish. But if you don't speak English in this country, you're screwed."

Frank knew Bruno made sense. "What's the best way for me to learn English?"

Bruno looked at Frank and said, "Find yourself a tutor."

CHAPTER SIXTEEN

Frank spent almost a week thinking about how to find a tutor before it hit him—the woman who worked at the bookstore might be able to help. She was friendly enough, and he figured she probably knew a lot of people in the area. It was worth a try.

Around ten o'clock the next Saturday morning, Frank returned to the bookstore, hoping Maria was working. He spotted her at the back of the store. She was leaning down, unloading boxes, her long black hair hanging toward her feet.

Frank walked up behind her. "Hi," he said. She looked up expectantly.

"Oh, it's you!" She smiled and straightened up. "I thought it was someone else."

"No, just me."

"What brings you here?"

"I have a favor to ask. I hope you don't mind."

"Shoot," she said.

"I'm looking for someone who teaches English."

"For yourself?"

"Yeah."

"That's easy. There's a guy right around the corner—a friend of my brother's. They served in Vietnam together." She thought for a moment. "In fact, I think he's Cuban."

"Cuban?"

"Yeah, he got wounded in the war and then had a terrible accident on top of that. He's in a wheelchair."

"What kind of accident?"

"He backed his wheelchair into an elevator that was being repaired. Unfortunately, nobody put a sign up to that effect. The elevator doors opened, and he fell down the shaft."

"Jesus!" said Frank. "What's his name?"

"Marcos Rodriquez."

"Is he any good?"

"That's what I hear."

"How can I find him?"

Maria pointed out the window. "Make a right at the light. Red door, first-floor apartment. Number one ten—it's on the mailbox. Just knock on the door. He's always there. Tell him you're a friend of mine."

"Thanks, I will."

Frank walked out of the store, beaming. *What a stroke of luck. A Cuban English teacher!*

Frank walked around the corner, easily finding the apartment building. He knocked on the door and heard the muffled sounds of children playing. "Just a minute!" came a woman's voice. For a moment he thought he might have the wrong apartment. Then the deadbolt slid and the door opened. Frank looked at a freckle-faced girl with tightly coiled ringlets the color of sunrise. Her eyes were warm and green behind horn-rimmed glasses.

"Can I help you?" she asked.

Frank sighed, knowing he'd have to make himself understood in English. "My name is Mederos. Frank Mederos. English lessons?"

The young woman smiled broadly. "Yes, yes. I'm Lauren. Come right in." She removed a coloring book and a can of Play-Doh from the couch and gestured for Frank to take a seat. "He'll be with you in a minute," she said, nodding in the direction of her husband.

Marcos sat with his back toward Frank, talking on the telephone. When he wheeled himself around, Frank realized he was missing both legs. Marcos finished his conversation and hung up.

"What can I do for you?" he said in Spanish. His hair curled over his collar. A red bandana hung at an odd angle around his neck. Frank tensed.

"I'm a friend of Maria's—from the bookstore. She said you give English lessons."

Marcos gave Frank the once-over. "It depends."

"On what?"

The tutor lifted his chin, almost defiantly. "On whether I like you or not."

"Okay," said Frank tentatively. He shifted his body on the couch.

"Tell me about yourself," said Marcos.

"I'm Cuban."

"Obviously." Marcos responded without a trace of a smile.

"What do you want to know?" asked Frank.

"Why did you leave Cuba?"

"To be with my girlfriend, Magda."

"Any other reason?"

Frank hesitated, wondering what to say.

"Were you in the army?" asked Marcos.

"Yes," said Frank. Marcos seemed to sense Frank's apprehension. "What did you do?"

"Special Forces."

The muscles in Marcos's face tightened. "You were a communist?"

"Quite the contrary."

"Then why the force?"

"It happened. I was selected. I had to serve."

For a moment a shadow passed over Marcos's eyes. "No, you didn't have to serve." His voice was low and leathery. "You had a choice. We all have choices. You could've escaped."

Frank felt like the wind had been knocked out of him. He looked at Marcos, trying to fathom his thinking. From what Maria had said, Marcos had served in Vietnam. He had been in war. He knew what it meant to follow orders.

Frank looked past him to the maple tree whose branches were shyly greening outside the window. A robin landed on the windowsill and pecked the peeling paint, looking for sustenance. A few moments passed before he responded.

Frank looked at Marcos's eyes. They were as brown and big as olives. "I did escape," he said in a voice that was almost a whisper. Unspoken negotiations were contained in these three words. Marcos exhaled.

"Plane?" he said.

"Boat."

Marcos gave Frank a long, hard look and then briefly closed his eyes. Something profound passed between the two men and remained suspended like dust motes. They sat in silence, their thoughts taking them both to a different place, a different time.

Finally, Marcos turned to Frank, and murmured, "I believe you."

The men remained silent for a few more minutes, listening to the children's voices rise and fall in play. The sizzle of grilled cheese sandwiches emanated from the kitchen.

Then Marcos cleared his throat. "Did you graduate from high school?"

"No, I—"

"No matter," he said, waving his hand. "You'll need to get your GED."

Frank nodded, not knowing what he was talking about, but hesitant to ask. "All right."

"Do you work?"

Frank nodded.

"My only available time is from nine to ten in the morning."

"I work nights. I'm finished by seven and home by seven thirty. Nine is fine."

"How often do you want to meet?"

"Often. I want to learn as quickly possible."

"Five days a week?"

Frank hesitated, wondering whether he could afford to come that often.

"How much do you charge?"

"Five dollars an hour."

Frank did a quick calculation. Tutoring would make things tight financially. On the surface, it appeared he couldn't afford it. On the other hand, he figured Marcos was making what he was making because he could speak English, and he was making what he was making because he couldn't. He'd have to work it out.

"Five days a week," said Frank.

"Two other students will work with us," said Marcos. "It's not a private lesson. We only speak English—no Spanish. Just so you know."

"Okay."

Marcos nodded and extended his hand for Frank to shake. Lauren emerged from the kitchen, pushed her glasses up her nose, and wished Frank a warm good-bye.

When he reached the door, Frank turned to Marcos and said, "One question: what's a GED?"

"Sorry. It's your high school equivalency degree. You'll need it to do just about anything."

"Is it hard to get?"

Marcos looked Frank up and down. "It will take work. But we'll get the job done. I've done harder things."

Frank nodded and replied, "So have I."

CHAPTER SEVENTEEN

At nine o'clock sharp Frank arrived at Marcos's apartment, ready for his first English lesson. He knew a few English words and phrases, things Magda and his Cuban teachers had taught him, jingles he had heard on television, curse words he had learned at work. But he had no grasp of grammar or syntax, and his vocabulary was weak. He had much to learn.

Marcos wheeled himself to his kitchen table and introduced Frank to two other men who were taking lessons. The students nodded to each other. Marcos began speaking to them in English as Lauren busied herself folding laundry.

The lesson reminded Frank of his time in Cuba's Literacy Brigade, the nights he spent teaching a peasant family to read and write in the hills of the Sierra Maestra. Little did he know at the time that he would be a language student himself one day.

Marcos taught "conversational English," and Frank had no idea what was going on. He sat bewildered, understanding little of what Marcos said. Marcos would point to objects and name them: lamp, table, rug. Frank repeated the words, but they vacated his mind the minute they left his tongue. Bone-tired from work, he tried to focus.

Having studied with Marcos for some time, the other men had a firmer grasp on the language, easily answering questions Marcos posed in English. Their progress gave Frank hope that he would eventually succeed.

When the lesson was over, Frank thanked Marcos and walked back to his room. The sun was shining, and he was looking forward to some sleep. He trudged up the stairs and reached into his pocket for his key. When he opened the door, he found Luis drinking with his friends. Empty whiskey bottles littered the floor and ashtrays overflowed with cigarette butts. Frank kicked a beer can out of his way.

Luis stood to greet Frank, swayed, and plopped on the bed. His buddies lounged about as if they owned the place. It appeared as if they'd been there all night. Frank tried to corral his anger. He scowled and announced that he needed some sleep. He hoped the men would up and leave, but no one made a move.

Out on the street a car door opened, closed. Frank looked out the window and saw four men dressed in dark clothes. They appeared dirty, rough. They were all stocky, with thick necks and determined gaits. Looking both ways, they approached the building with caution. Frank heard footfalls on the stairs before a set of knuckles pounded on the door. The rapping came with the insistence of a staff sergeant.

Luis jumped off the bed like a squirrel avoiding an oncoming car, spilling his can of beer in the process. He licked his fingers and wiped his hand on his pants. Everyone in the room grew silent.

Luis stepped into the hallway, leaving the door half open. He spoke to his visitors in a hushed tone. As he did, his drinking buddies got up, looked at each other in alarm, and made their way past the thugs. Eager to leave, they wasted no time going down the steps. Frank strained to hear what was being said, but he could only make out snippets of conversation.

After a few minutes, the thugs departed. Frank watched them climb into their car. Their tires squealed as they sped away.

Luis reentered the room and sat on the bed. He looked at once sheepish and belligerent. The room became so quiet you could hear a handkerchief land on sand. Luis lay down on the bed and turned his body to face the wall, without removing his clothes.

"What was that about?" Frank asked. Luis rearranged his pillow, but didn't turn around. "Who were those people and what did they want?" Silence.

Frank sighed and sat down on his bed. He rested his forehead on the palm of his hand before looking up. "Look, Luis, I have no idea what you've gotten yourself into, but it doesn't look good to me. You need to lose these friends of yours, and you need to figure out how to bring Rosa and your girls to the States. I don't like where your life is going without them."

"Lay off me, will you?"

"I'm not laying off. I live here too, and I deserve some answers."

A moment passed before Luis turned to face Frank. He grunted. "Rosa's not coming."

Frank looked at his uncle, astonished. "What are you talking about? She's your wife. That was your plan."

Luis held Frank's gaze for a moment. He looked chagrined. "I said she's not coming. That's that."

"Is she sick?"

"No."

"Are the kids sick?"

"No."

"Then figure out how to get her here, damnit. There's gotta be a way. You can't give up."

"I'm not giving up. I don't want her."

Frank sat back, alarmed. "Because you feel like you can't support her?"

"It's not that—"

"Then why?"

"I don't want her here, that's all. I don't need to explain myself to you—case closed."

Frank waited a moment, digesting this news. A vision of Aunt Rosa, her hair bundled atop her head, danced before his eyes. She was high-strung and nervous, but she'd do anything for anyone—she had a heart of gold. Luis was lucky to have her, and Frank couldn't imagine him living without her. If she didn't come to the States, Frank might never see her or his cousins again. He wondered how they would manage without Luis. It saddened him to think about it.

"Don't you love her?"

"She's always riding my ass. Besides, she wouldn't understand my life here."

"You mean she wouldn't approve of your friends," Frank said with a touch of sarcasm.

"That, and other things."

"What other things?"

"None of your business, Frankie. Back off, will you?"

"All right. But you're making a big mistake. You can't treat your family like table scraps."

"It's my life. Besides, who are you to tell me what to do? I'm older than you. I'm a grown man. I know what I'm doing."

"Forget I mentioned it."

Frank undressed and climbed into bed, wondering what in the world had gotten into his uncle.

CHAPTER EIGHTEEN

When Pino entered Foreman Castillo's office for his semimonthly meeting with Torres, he found the first lieutenant sitting in the foreman's chair with a folded copy of *Granma* in his lap.

The trees rustled against the window. A thunderstorm had just passed. In a few minutes the cool air would be vanquished by humidity.

Pino's skin was still scabbed, but his blisters were healing. He watched Torres sip coffee from an old, tin mug, wondering how their meeting would unwind.

The former lieutenant had been exceptionally well behaved during the past two weeks, and he figured the report on him would reflect improvement in his attitude and behavior. Pino watched Torres stand and smile. He accepted an offer of coffee and sat when the lieutenant gestured to a chair. Pino occupied the edge of his seat, feet flat, back straight. He waited for Torres to begin the conversation.

"How's it going?"

"Fine," replied Pino.

"You seem to be healing well."

"I am."

"Good. Have you been getting along with the other men?" Pino gritted his teeth and raised his chin to expose a column of throat. A gallery of sores dotted his neck. He crossed his arms in front of his chest like a brick wall. But he kept his expression neutral.

Why should I have to worry about getting along with anyone? If things were the way they should be, people would be worried about getting along with me.

Pino looked out the window. A breeze dislodged water drop-
lets from the trees, creating a crystal shower that puddled on the
walkway. A heat haze shimmered over the cane fields, but dark
clouds still loomed in the distance. The rain could resume at any
time. Watching the sweat drip off the faces of the *macheteros*, Pino
renewed his vow to play the role required of him.

"Yes. I'm getting along well with the men."

Torres nodded his approval. "What do you attribute that to?"

Pino took a hard swallow, weighing his words. "I'm minding my
business, following orders, and not taking charge." He lifted his chin
in a gesture of defiance. "I believe that's what's required of me."

Torres nodded. "Good. So you're learning to follow the rules?"

Pino looked at Torres, determined not to be his own worst enemy.
He knew it was necessary for him to modify his behavior to save
his skin. But it wasn't easy.

"Yes, I'm following the rules."

"Have you given more thought to the Mederos business?"

Pino pushed his teeth together and clenched his jaw. "Yes, and
I admit to being hardheaded."

"Explain."

Pino hesitated, formulating an answer that would please the
lieutenant. "My zeal in getting Mederos clouded my thinking. I
should have pursued him using other methods."

"So you admit your mistake?"

Pino closed his eyes. This was more difficult than he had anticipated. He knew he had made the right decision to go after Mederos
the way he did. Even if he had informed the CDRs, the militia, and
the police of Mederos's escape, they wouldn't have been able to
catch him. He had done the right thing, despite its outcome. Now,
he was forced to play this juvenile game that mocked his efforts.

An image of his mother crossed Pino's mind. She was standing
in the kitchen wearing a striped yellow apron. She tapped him on
the shoulder and handed him a colander and a pot of black beans
that had been soaking in water.

"What do you want to me to do with them?" he had asked.

"Strain and contain them," she replied.

That's what I need to do now, thought Pino. *Strain and contain my emotions. Get control.*

"I made a mistake, a big mistake," said Pino convincingly. "I put my own ego ahead of the Party, ahead of the cause. I was arrogant, and I am truly sorry."

"That's good to hear," said Torres. "Admitting your mistakes is the first step toward rehabilitation."

"I understand, sir. I have every intention of making amends for my mistakes."

A hint of a smile lifted the corners of Torres's mouth.

"I'm pleased to know you feel that way. I will see you again in two weeks. Keep up the good work."

"I will, sir."

Pino saluted Torres and left the office.

CHAPTER NINETEEN

On a Friday night at the end of April, Magda and her mother visited Frank in his room for the first time. He had made his bed and tidied things up for their arrival, aligning his shoes and banishing his clothes to a drawer. He had no concept of housework. In his eyes, the room looked fine. But he was still nervous, hoping to make a good impression on his future wife and mother-in-law. When the two women arrived, their smiles disappeared. They looked horrified.

"This is awful, Frank," said Magda. "How can you live this way? This bedding is all tattered and torn. It looks like a bunch of rags."

"It's what was here," Frank offered by way of defense.

Magda rolled her eyes. "You need new linens. Let me pick some up for you."

Frank smiled. If this was a preview of what it would be like to be married to Magda, he liked it.

Frank glanced at his watch. "I'd go with you, but I have to work."

Magda shrugged. "Mother will come with me. By the time you get home, we'll have you all fixed up."

By the following morning Frank had forgotten their conversation. When he walked into his room, he marveled at the transformation. The floor was mopped. The lampshade had shed a layer of dust. A plaid curtain hung at the window, and a new spread covered the bed. Magda had even nailed a crucifix above the headboard. A jingle Magda sung sprung to Frank's mind: "It's so easy when you use Lestoil."

Frank switched on the fan. He lay back on the bed, propping his head on his folded arms. He closed his eyes and had just begun to drop off to sleep when Magda and her brother, Sergio Junior, knocked on the door. Magda walked in, smiling. She looked proud.

"Do you like it?" she asked.

"It's great! Thanks."

"I got you sheets. Here, help me make the bed." Magda ripped the sheets from the plastic bag and nodded for Frank to take the other side. She removed the spread, fluffed the sheets, and tucked them in using hospital corners. Frank wondered where she had learned that trick.

Once they made Frank's bed, the three of them decided to take a walk. It was a beautiful spring day, perfect for a stroll. They set out in good spirits. A couple of blocks from Frank's rooming house, a Cuban man approached them. He began speaking to them in Spanish. His name was Pedro.

He was tall for a Cuban and rail thin. Gray threaded his hair and his straggly beard. Rimless glasses sat on his nose, and a faded flannel shirt with missing buttons hung open over a ribbed undershirt. A large cross announced his Catholicism from a black cord around his neck.

Pedro wanted to know where they were from, how long they'd been in Union City, and how they liked America so far. He seemed friendly enough, not a bad sort, although Frank suspected he was high on something. Once they told him a little about themselves, he turned to Frank and said, "Man, did you hear about the refrigerator?"

Frank wrinkled his brow. "What refrigerator?"

"The one on Palisades Avenue."

"Sorry, I have no idea what you're talking about."

Pedro ignored Frank's statement. "Do you need a refrigerator?"

Frank thought for a moment. "Yeah," he said. "I could use one. I live in a room with my uncle. There's no place to store food."

"Then let's go get it."

"What do you mean?"

Pedro looked at Frank like he was a simpleton.

"There's a good refrigerator just sittin' on the street. If you need it, go pick it up."

"You mean steal it?"

"Nah, I mean take it."

"What's the difference?"

"The difference is that the people don't want it no more. So it ain't stealin'."

What Pedro was saying was so far removed from Frank's experience that he couldn't get his mind around it. "They threw it away? Just like that?"

"Yeah, people here do that kinda shit all the time!"

Frank shook his head. "You gotta be kidding me. Why would someone throw away a perfectly good refrigerator?"

"I don't know about it bein' perfect, man. But I'm telling ya, the real deal is just sitting out on the sidewalk waitin' for the takin', if you know what I mean."

"No, I don't know what you mean."

"Jesus, man! What the hell is wrong with you? You think I would lie to you about sumptin' like that?"

"No," said Frank. "But it doesn't make sense. You saw it yourself? Or you just heard about it?"

The man pointed to his eyes with the first two fingers of his right hand. "These eyes," he said. "No stinkin' rumor. Hell, if I needed a refrigerator, I'd take it myself."

"So you're telling me there's a refrigerator—a real refrigerator— just sitting on the pavement where anybody can claim it?"

"That's exactly what I'm telling you. Are you hard of hearing or sumptin'?"

Frank closed his eyes for a moment. *I've literally just gotten off the boat. I can't risk going to jail over a refrigerator. What would my parents think? What would Magda's parents think? On the other hand, this guy may be telling the truth. And we could use a refrigerator.*

Frank glanced at Magda. "What do you think?"

She shrugged. "What do I know?"

Frank looked again at Pedro. "Is it legal to haul away something like that?"

"Hell, yes. People do it all the time."

"And the police don't care?"

"Nah! I've lived here for almost a year. I know how things work in this country."

Frank threw his head back and laughed. "Well, what are we waiting for? Let's go get it."

"That's the spirit!" said Pedro.

"We're going to need a rope and a hand truck," said Frank. "Do you know where I can get them?"

Pedro thought for a moment. "My brother works at a bodega on Twenty-Sixth Street. Wait here. It's not far. I'll see what I can do."

About fifteen minutes later, Pedro returned with the hand truck. "One of the wheels is kinda funky. The rubber is missin', and it don't move quite right."

"It'll have to do," said Frank. He grabbed the hand truck from Pedro and started rolling it down the sidewalk. "Let's go! We can't waste any time."

Young Sergio ran beside Frank, hoping for an adventure.

"How far away is it?" Frank asked.

"Not far. You'll see," said Pedro.

They walked five blocks, the hand truck rattling and squeaking along the pavement. Two dogs, a Brittany spaniel and a black Labrador, were sniffing a garbage can as they passed. Their ears sprung up, and they wagged their tails furiously.

They decided to tag along.

It was the morning rush hour, and traffic was heavy. Cars and trucks honked and darted past each other, jockeying for position. The contingent walked at a brisk pace, wanting to claim their prize before someone else did.

They walked four more blocks, and Frank began to get suspicious.

He turned to Pedro. "You aren't kidding me, are you? This thing really exists?"

"No shit! It'll be there, unless someone's already picked it up."

They had just finished walking another block when Sergio started screaming and jumping around. He pointed to a large white object sitting on the curb. "There it is! Do you see it?"

Frank shielded his eyes from the sun and looked where Pedro was pointing. Sure enough, a full-size refrigerator sat on the curb.

"Bingo!" he said. Sergio was so excited he hugged Pedro. The dogs sniffed the refrigerator and pawed beneath it. A line of cockroaches emerged from the motor, stopped, and then quickly retreated. Pedro stood proudly beside the appliance, while Magda jumped around like a child.

"Wow!" said Frank. "It looks brand-new."

"See, I told you," said Pedro.

Frank and Pedro wedged the hand truck beneath the refrigerator and positioned it on the platform. It tipped backward. They steadied it before inching it down the street. The right wheel wobbled and scraped the pavement. When it refused to budge, Frank stopped to adjust it.

Pedro chased people off the sidewalk, hollering, "Make way—valuable merchandise coming through!" His beard flapped in the breeze, and his hair hung over his face like wet spaghetti. He was oblivious to the impression he created.

When they reached the corner, Pedro walked into the middle of the street, stopping traffic by holding his arms in a T-position, palms out. He was talking in a crazy quilt of Spanish and beatnik English, punctuated with heavy doses of profanity.

Annoyed drivers hollered out their car windows, honked their horns, and made obscene gestures. When cars tried to pass, Pedro stood in front of them like an animal escaped from the zoo. Looking disoriented, he gestured frantically, eyes wild. He screamed, "Can't ya see what's happening? Damn important work is going on." To lend credence to his statement, he pointed to Frank holding onto the refrigerator for dear life.

When traffic permitted, Frank eased the refrigerator down the curb, over the potholes, and across the street. Heaving for breath, Pedro and Frank maneuvered the refrigerator up the opposite curb.

After repeating this routine for five blocks, Pedro ran out of steam. Panting, he said, "Maybe we should just leave the damn thing here. It probably don't work anyway. Why else would somebody throw it out?"

"What are you talking about?" said Frank. "We've come this far. We're going to get this thing home. If it doesn't work, it doesn't work. But we're gonna try, damn it!"

Pedro grumbled. "Well, I gotta have a smoke."

"All right."

They sat down on the curb, knees to their chests, feet tucked close to the gutter. The refrigerator stood beside them like a pillar of salt. Frank was hoping Pedro wouldn't leave them in case something went wrong.

The Brittany ran in circles, a bundle of nerves. The Lab drooled. Drivers beeped and waved like they were watching a carnival. Periodically, Pedro grunted something unintelligible and flipped them the peace sign.

Frank turned to Pedro and asked, "You do this often?"

"Nah, not too often," he said, as if this were a serious question.

Suddenly, the whole thing struck Magda as funny.

"What?" said Pedro, fearing she was laughing at him.

"Look at us," she said. "Four Cubans, two dogs and a refrigerator! We should be in the circus."

They all started to laugh.

Magda's brother stood up. "We could form a club—the FC and R—Four Cubans and a Refrigerator."

"Yeah, man," said Pedro. "Get tie-dyed t-shirts and all—FC and R!"

Magda's nose began to crinkle the way it did before she erupted with deep belly laughs. Soon the four of them were lying on the sidewalk, holding their stomachs. When their laughter subsided, someone would say FC and R, and it began all over again. The group had no idea how loud they were. Frank looked up to see a policeman coming.

"What's going on here?"

Frank suddenly felt guilty. He sobered up, stood, and addressed the officer. Dread gripped his stomach. *What was I thinking? I chanced going to jail for a stupid refrigerator? One that might not even work?*

"We found this refrigerator in the trash," explained Frank. "And we're trying to get it home. It's not against the law, is it?"

Frank closed his eyes for a second, hoping the officer would agree. The officer hesitated while perspiration gathered under Frank's arms. He wondered what kind of jail time you'd get for hauling away a discarded appliance. He looked at Magda and pursed his lips, sorry he had gotten them into this mess. This was the last thing they needed. Fortunately, the officer spoke Spanish.

"It's not against the law," he said. "But I don't want you holding up traffic. How far are you going?"

Frank heaved a sigh of relief.

"Not far," said Pedro.

Yeah, thought Frank. *Just another hundred blocks or so.*

"Move it along," said the police officer. "I'll stop traffic for you while you cross the street."

Frank and Pedro steadied the refrigerator while Sergio pushed. When they got to the rooming house, Luis was sitting on the steps, smoking. They rested on the stoop before trying to get the refrigerator up three flights of stairs. The stairwell was narrow, and Frank was afraid they'd gouge holes in the walls. Halfway up the staircase, the tenants on the upper floor started walking down. Pedro hollered to them like he was directing traffic.

"Stop! Go back! You can't make it! I'll let you know when it's okay."

Frank pulled the refrigerator up the stairs while Pedro and Luis pushed it from below. When they pivoted the refrigerator over the last step, they sighed in relief. Having caught their breath, they tilted the refrigerator into Frank's room.

Magda moved a table back from the wall to make space. The group stood back and looked at the refrigerator as if it were a piece of fine sculpture. Michelangelo could not have been more proud.

Magda grabbed the electrical cord and searched for an outlet. She glanced at the prongs and plugged in the refrigerator. For a moment there was complete silence. Then the motor jumped to a hum. Frank opened the refrigerator door, and the light came on. He waved his hand and felt cool air. When he opened the freezer, the air remained warm.

"The refrigerator works, but the freezer doesn't."

"That's why they threw it away," said Pedro, as if this weren't obvious to all.

"Doesn't matter," said Magda. "At least we have a refrigerator."

Frank pulled Magda close to him and kissed her. Her lips were warm and sweet. When he released her, she smiled.

"Our first refrigerator," she said happily. "Let's make a toast."

"I've got some beer," offered Luis.

"Of course," said Frank, rolling his eyes.

Luis leaned down and pulled a six-pack of Budweiser from beneath his bed.

Magda grabbed some plastic cups off a shelf. Luis uncapped two beer bottles with his teeth and poured them each a cup of beer.

Frank raised his glass and said, "To the FC and R."

"To the best refrigerator money didn't buy!" added Magda. They all repeated, "To the FC and R." Then they drank some very warm beer.

CHAPTER TWENTY

After all Frank had been through to get to Magda, he was eager to start their life as husband and wife. Although the couple spent several hours together a week, they were seldom able to see each other without the presence of a chaperone.

Magda complained to her parents that her American girlfriends could go bowling and to parties alone with a boy, but she could not. But Magda's lobbying fell on deaf ears. Her parents, especially her mother, would not hear of it.

"I don't care what your American friends do," scolded Estel. "You are my daughter, and you will do things *my* way, the respectable way, the Cuban way. Our traditions will not be trampled by the American lifestyle."

Given her parents' mind-set, Frank worried about their response when he asked for Magda's hand in marriage. Although they could rightly argue that Magda was too young for marriage, they knew Frank had risked his life to be with her. What's more, they had pleaded with him to do so.

One rainy Friday night Frank mustered the courage to approach them about the matter. He was nervous and excited, feeling he was on the verge of fulfilling his dream. He knew he'd be unable to provide Magda with many creature comforts at first, but he was young, strong, and hard working. Given time and opportunity, he would make a good life for them. Besides, Magda had never shown much interest in material goods.

He practiced what he would say several times and smiled at the thought of Magda's parents officially accepting him into the family.

Frank's talk with Magda's parents was short, and it did not go as Frank anticipated. Magda was not present during the conversation. He left the Hernándezes' apartment, stunned. Frank walked a few blocks before going back to his room, grateful for the fresh air. He needed time to digest the evening's events and to deal with a raft of conflicting emotions.

He climbed the staircase to his room, his heart heavy and his head down. A headache took shape behind his eyes. When he opened the door, Luis was lying on the bed reading the sports page of *The Star-Ledger*. Knowing what Frank had planned for the evening, he looked up expectantly.

"How'd it go?" asked Luis.

Frank bit his bottom lip. He didn't want to have this conversation. He knew Luis would give him a hard time, and he wasn't in the mood. He shook his head, sat on his bed, and removed his shoes. He stripped off his socks and threw them on the chair. A police car drove by, lights blinking, siren whining. Frank felt exhausted.

"Well?" prompted Luis.

Frank sighed and looked at his uncle, bracing himself for a barrage of criticism. "I'm getting married."

Luis lifted his eyebrows and dropped his paper to his lap. It rattled slightly. He straightened himself up and rearranged the pillow behind his back. "For someone who went through hell and high water to marry that girl, you sure don't look happy."

He was right. Frank closed his eyes and heaved a bone-weary sigh. "I am and I'm not."

"What kind of talk is that?" said Luis. "Either you are or you aren't. You're talking in circles. What the hell's the matter?"

"Magda and I are getting married in May."

"Good. Where?"

"City Hall."

"City Hall?"

Frank nodded. "The justice of the peace is performing the ceremony."

"So, what's the problem?"

"The problem is that Magda is only seventeen, so she needs her parents' permission to get married. Her father put up some resistance about her age, but the real issue is that her parents want her to get married in the Church."

"And?"

"And that doesn't happen overnight. You have to talk to the priest, go through counseling, schedule the church, and announce the banns of marriage. It takes time. You know the drill."

"I'm confused," said Luis. "I thought you were getting married at City Hall."

"We are. But that's just their way of placating us. It's a placeholder. Magda's parents are calling it 'an act of good faith,' but they don't consider it a real marriage."

"So?"

"So although we'll be legally married, we can't sleep together until we're married in the Church. And that can't happen until August."

Luis's eyes widened, and he let out a whistle. "So you'll be married, but you can't sleep with your wife?"

"That's the deal."

"That's just messed up," said Luis a little too loudly. He thought for a moment. "You're going along with this?"

Frank sighed. "Yes."

"Then you're messed up too. Besides, I don't see why you'd get married once, let alone twice. As far as I'm concerned, marriage is just a trap."

Frank closed his eyes. He didn't want to hear Luis's philosophy on marriage. "Don't start," he said.

"I don't know what to say then."

"Then don't say anything."

Frank expelled his breath, feeling despondent. All he wanted, all he ever wanted, was to be with Magda. The idea of waiting any longer made his organs weep.

Luis rewarded Frank's statement with a nasty laugh before saying, "You're messed up."

"Maybe I *am* messed up," Frank admitted.

"Why would you put up with this?"

Frank waited, formulating his thoughts. "Because I'm going to be married to Magda for a long time. There's no point in getting off on the wrong foot with her parents—it's not worth it. It would kill her. Besides, I don't have a choice."

Luis rolled over and grabbed a pack of cigarettes off the nightstand. "I guess not," he said, lighting up.

Frank shrugged, trying to make the best of the situation. "Three months isn't very long in the grand scheme of things."

Luis shook his head. "Then why get married by the justice of the peace at all?"

"Because Magda and I want to make a commitment to each other. We've been through too much not to be husband and wife."

"But you'll be married in name only—it makes no sense." He thought for a moment, tapping his cigarette against the glass ashtray. "By the way, if you want a woman, I know where to get you one."

Frank shook his head, exasperated. "You don't get it, do you, Luis?"

"No, I don't," said Luis. An annoying smirk swept his face.

"What are you thinking?"

Luis's smirk broadened. "I can't wait for the guys at the factory to hear you can't sleep with your own wife. You'll take a ribbing of a lifetime over this."

"I will if they find out."

"They'll find out all right," said Luis confidently. "Marriages are listed in the newspaper. Besides, when my friends come by, they'll see that you're still living with me. There's no way to keep it a secret."

"I don't give a damn what anyone thinks," said Frank. "It's nobody's business. Magda and I are getting married. It'll be legal. She'll be happy. That's all I care about."

"Can you take her to the movies by yourself?"

Frank sucked his breath through his teeth. "Enough with the questions, Luis. I don't want to talk about it anymore."

Luis snuffed out his cigarette and dropped his head back onto the pillow. "It sounds crazy to me, but you do what you have to. Just remember, I have connections—I can get you a woman whenever you want."

"Connections," Frank muttered to no one in particular. He turned off the light and went to sleep.

CHAPTER TWENTY-ONE

It was a hot, humid, July morning, and Frank had just gotten home from his English lesson. He put his books on his nightstand, raised his arms over his head, leaned down, and touched his toes. The stretch felt good. He did a few push-ups and sat on the chair.

The room was a mess. Cigarette butts littered the floor. Ashtrays overflowed, and the odor of stale beer filled the air. Frank thought it was bad enough that Luis partied there, but he should at least clean up afterward. He had complained to Luis about it several times, but to no avail.

Frank shook his head in frustration and removed his shoes. His feet were red and soaked with perspiration. He wiggled his toes as his uncle turned the doorknob to let himself in. Luis offered Frank a small smile as he closed the door.

Exhausted, Frank was in no mood for idle chitchat. There was talk of a layoff at the plant, and his English lessons were not going well. He needed some sleep, but he knew something was bothering Luis. His customary half smile was nowhere in sight, his cheeks were flushed, and his forehead was webbed with angst.

"What's going on?" asked Frank.

Luis shook his head, agitated. "They're rioting in Newark," he announced.

Frank didn't know what his uncle meant by the remark, and he didn't want to know. He closed his eyes, annoyed. Frank stood, unbuckled his belt, and placed his watch atop his books.

"Did you hear what I said?" snapped Luis.

"I heard you."

"Well, what do you think?"

"I don't know what you're talking about. Who's rioting?"

"Some taxi driver named Smith was arrested. The police beat him up. The whole city's going nuts."

"Can we discuss this later? I just got home. I need some sleep."

Luis leaned against the wall like a wooden puppet, absorbed in his thoughts. Frank was afraid he'd pursue the subject.

"What do you think will happen?" asked Luis. Anxiety graveled his voice.

"How would I know? Other than landing at the airport, I've never been to Newark. Besides, I'm too tired to think about it."

Luis shot Frank a nasty look and mumbled. It sounded like he said he had something important to do, but he swallowed his words.

"Pardon?"

"I'm going out for cigarettes," said Luis. Puzzled, Frank watched his uncle close the door behind him.

Frank walked down the hall and curled his hand around the bathroom doorknob. The bathroom was small and the floor needed a scrubbing. After stripping off his clothes, he stepped into the shower and turned the spigot to the thunder of rushing water. He adjusted the showerhead and let warm water drench his body. He lathered his skin with a sliver of Ivory soap left in the dish. The bar slipped out of his hand and floated in a couple inches of water at the bottom of the tub.

Floating objects always triggered bad memories in Frank. His throat constricted, as he thought about the thousands of Cubans—mothers, fathers, and children—who had died trying to escape Cuba. *And for what? For one man's insanity?* He tried to push the images from his mind.

The building's plumbing was showing its age. The pipes groaned and lurched, making the Formica walls bulge and vibrate. Frank rinsed his body and turned the faucet as tight as he could to minimize the drip, drip, drip that had yellowed the tub. He toweled his hair and stepped onto a ragged bath mat. It felt gritty beneath his feet.

With a bath towel around his waist, Frank walked to his room and plopped on the bed. The mattress was lumpy, and the box spring squeaked beneath him. He doubled his pillow under his head to boost its heft and stared at the ceiling. A motorcycle outside his window roared to life and screeched down the street.

A large horsefly banged against the window screen, desperate for freedom. Feeling the urgency of its struggle, Frank got up, pulled the screen, and released the insect from its torment. He reached for the small fan perched on a chair and switched on the toggle. Waves of cool air wafted over his body as he drifted off to sleep. He dreamt of marrying Magda.

Upon waking, Frank put on light pants and a blue summer shirt. He walked to the local deli, climbed a chrome counter stool, and ordered coffee. Men were leaning over each other's shoulders, intent on reading an article in *The Star-Ledger*. Beneath the headline about twenty thousand more troops going to Vietnam was a story about Newark. Intrigued, Frank wished his English were better.

Frank turned to a burly Spanish-speaking man dressed in an undershirt and jeans. His face was weathered, and his eyes were watery blue. Frank had seen him at the deli before.

"What's it say?" asked Frank.

"A bunch of niggers are out to kill people. If they want to act like animals, they should send them back to Africa. What's it to you?"

The man skewered Frank with an incendiary stare. Frank stared back until the man looked away. It was hot. People were on edge. It was the kind of atmosphere where the smallest thing could spark a fight.

Frank glanced at the clock above the door and wondered what Luis had planned for the day. Despite the oppressive heat, he felt a chill. The hairs on the back of his neck rose to attention.

The burly man tossed the waitress a nickel for the paper and turned, leaving the stool spinning behind him. A bell tinkled as he left the store. The other men returned to their seats and gazed into their coffee cups.

■　■　●

The entire day an air of apprehension hung over Union City like boiled smog. Rumors circulated that looting had escalated in Newark and an angry mob had attacked the police station with bricks and Molotov cocktails.

When Frank got back to his room, Luis was there, agitated, and pacing the floor like a panther. "What if all of Newark burns down?" he asked. His tone bordered on desperation. "What if no one can get in or out?"

Frank shook his head in consternation. "What's got you so worried? It's not like it's happening here. At least not yet."

Luis said something Frank couldn't decipher. Then he grabbed his cigarettes and walked out the door.

First thing Friday morning, Frank visited the local newsstand. The line to buy newspapers was longer than usual, and he felt lucky to get one of the last *Star-Ledgers*. On the front page was a picture of a police officer examining a patrol car with a trashcan embedded in its rear window. Another picture showed a policeman barricaded behind a grate once used to protect a pawnshop.

After handing the vendor some change, Frank folded the newspaper beneath his arm. He hurried to Marcos's house, more aware than usual of his surroundings.

He knocked on the door and waited for Marcos to roll his wheelchair into a position where he could open it.

Marcos smiled when he saw Frank. "Hey, man, what's up?"

"I was hoping you could help me." Spreading the newspaper on his kitchen table, Frank pointed to the article about Newark.

"What's it say?"

Marcos scanned the article and glanced up at Frank. He addressed him in Spanish.

"It's bad."

"Go on."

"The coloreds are burning and looting stores in Newark. They're wrecking people's houses, beating up white folk, and smashing windows with bricks."

"Christ almighty."

"A bunch of stores are on fire."

"They're torching stores?" Marcos nodded.

"Has this ever happened before?"

"Not that I know of, but there's a first for everything."

"Thanks for your time," said Frank.

Luis was slumped in a chair, his face white as rice, when Frank got back to the room. As soon as he closed the door, Luis said, "We've got to talk."

With his elbows perched on his knees, Luis raked his fingers through his hair. He didn't even look at Frank.

"I have to go to Newark tonight," he said.

Frank shook his head and took a deep breath. "What? Why?"

"I've got to see somebody—it's business."

"Business, my ass!" Frank knew where this conversation was headed, and he wanted no part of it.

"I need you, Frank. I can't go there alone. Not with the riots and all."

"You shouldn't go there at all. Nobody should. Besides, the police must've cordoned off the city by now."

Luis looked distraught. "I thought of that," he said, folding his arms across his chest. "It's just that—"

"Jesus effing Christ! People are burning down buildings, smashing storefronts with bats. What's so damn important that you need to go there? We could get killed!"

Luis shot Frank an imploring look. "I could get killed if I don't go there tonight."

Frank shook his head, working to control his disgust and rage. "So what is it, Luis? What's so important that you have to risk your life to go to Newark? What are you into—drugs, numbers?"

Luis opened his mouth, but Frank raised his hand to stop him. "Don't tell me. The less I know about your 'business,' the better off we'll both be."

Luis drew a finger to his mouth and liberated a hangnail with his teeth. A drop of blood formed at the corner of his nail.

"I'm sorry. I wouldn't ask you this if I didn't need—"

"This is insanity!"

"I know. But I need backup. You're the only one I can count on."

Looking at Luis, Frank expelled a breath. His uncle moved his hands over each other like he was rinsing soap. Frank had seen him exhibit that nervous habit before.

"What about all of those buddies of yours, the ones who hang out here whenever they feel like, drinking whiskey and beer and doing God knows what else?"

"They're not like you. You were in the army. You know how to fight. Besides, you owe me one."

Frank shifted his body and clenched his fists as blood rushed to the surface of his skin. In fact, he did owe Luis one—probably more than one. There was no denying it.

Luis's statement hung in the air like a hooked fish. Frank hesitated, considering the situation. He didn't like the sound of it. God only knew what they'd be getting themselves into. This was very dicey business. On the other hand, Luis was family, and he'd been there when Frank needed him.

Luis stared out the window, his shoulders hunched, his hands roving the air in front of him. When he turned around, he said in a ragged voice, "Are you going to help me or not?"

Suddenly the air seemed listless. Frank frowned, wishing the whole situation would go away. He rubbed his forehead with his fingertips.

"All right," he said. "You're right. I do owe you one. But I'm only doing this once. It makes us even. Don't ever ask me to do anything like this again. Do you understand?"

Luis nodded.

"What time do you need to go?" asked Frank.

"I need to meet someone at ten tonight." Luis looked at his nephew and said, "You are saving my ass here, Frank."

"All right. We'll leave around nine. When we get there, conduct your business, but don't hurt anybody, you hear?" Frank walked toward the door. "I've got to call my boss about not coming to work."

Luis offered Frank a wan smile. Frank left, hoping they'd survive the night.

CHAPTER TWENTY-TWO

Just after nine p.m., Frank left his room to wait on the front stoop for his uncle. His stomach felt queasy and a headache was in full bloom. He had just sat down when Luis pulled up to the curb in a red Ford Mustang. He turned off the car and got out, his right arm outstretched, a key ring dangling from his forefinger. A gold chain circled his neck and a broad smile lit his face. His mood had changed considerably since that morning, and Frank could see why.

"Hop in," said Luis, handing Frank the keys. "I want you to drive. Enjoy yourself! Get a feel for what a new car is like."

"Are you crazy? You're taking this thing to Newark? You might as well just paint a target on our backs."

Luis laughed. "Where's your sense of adventure? You've done more dangerous things than this. Loosen up. Have some fun!"

"I've done more dangerous things. But I didn't do them for fun. Whose car is this anyway?"

"Whose car do you think it is? Don't be such a worrywart. Just get in—relax."

Frank opened the door and settled himself into the driver's seat. It *was* a beautiful car. He let out a whistle while patting the dashboard. "Impressive!" he said, looking around. He beeped the horn and turned the lights on and off.

"Yeah," said Luis. "Power steering, power brakes, dual exhausts—the works."

"Amazing! How much was it?"

Luis jabbed Frank playfully on his shoulder. "It doesn't matter,

Frank. If you're in the right business, things practically pay for themselves."

"Uh-huh," said Frank.

"You could have one, too, if you stopped wasting your time working in that stupid factory."

"Don't start, Luis."

"Yeah, well, it don't pay the bills. Not like this, eh, Frankie?" Frank released the emergency brake, annoyed.

"Where are we going?" he asked.

"To a candy store next to Universal Shoes, just up from Springfield Avenue and Bergen Street."

"I've never been to Newark. I have no idea where that is. Is it anywhere near the riots?"

Luis looked chagrined. "Pretty close," he said. "I'll direct you as we go along."

"Why in God's name are we going there?"

"An old lady does business outta there."

"Out of a candy store?"

"Yeah."

"How old is she?"

"Must be pushin' eighty."

Frank shook his head.

"Is there anywhere else you have to go?"

"I have to meet someone at—" Luis looked up, thinking.

"Where?"

"I forget the name of the street. I'll know it when I see it."

"That's just great! We're driving into a goddamn riot, and you don't even know where we're going?"

Luis grumbled, "I told you, I'll know it when I see it." He settled back in his seat, looked out the open window, and unwrapped a stick of Doublemint gum. He stretched the wrapper, licked the inside clean of sugar dust, wadded it into a ball, and threw it out the window.

Frank turned the key and the motor jumped to a roar. He put

the car in gear and pulled away from the curb. They sped along the highway with the windows down, the breeze caressing their faces.

"What do you think of the car?" asked Luis.

"Nice—real nice. Where did you get it?"

"None of your damn business where I got it."

"Is it yours? Do you own it?"

"Damn straight."

"All right, I can see I'm not going to get any answers out of you. At least nothing truthful."

Frank drove as far as he thought was safe and then parked the car on the side of the road. Luis spit out his gum and lit a cigarette. They started out on foot. The night was one of egg-frying heat, the kind that causes nerves to fray and tempers to rise. A sallow haze hugged the horizon, evidence of the number of stores ablaze. Frank wiped a line of sweat from his forehead, trying to ignore the fear clawing his stomach.

"It doesn't look good. Are you sure you have to conduct this 'business' of yours?"

"It'll be okay," said Luis, a crack in his voice betraying his words. "We'll get in and out fast."

Frank found his pronouncement less than comforting. They walked along a broken pavement blighted with refuse. A chain-link fence topped with a whorl of razor wire lay crushed on the sidewalk.

As they got closer, the city looked like a war zone. It was theater of the extreme, a freewheeling carnival of hate and greed. Nothing was normal. No vestige of civilization remained in sight.

Black-and-white police cars were parked at jaunty angles to protect firemen wielding hoses. Streams of water rose high into the air, creating a mist so thick it was like strolling through a sponge. Flames licked the sides of buildings like dragon's breath. People were hollering and elbowing each other, jockeying for position to loot. Frank and Luis had never seen anything like it.

Police flashers broke the cloak of darkness, reddening puddles that reflected the grimness of the scene. Thick ash stung their lungs.

They buried their noses in their forearms, trying to avoid the soot that was ringing their nostrils.

People staggered about looking dazed and confused. Old men with canes shuffled along the sidewalk, shaking their heads in disbelief. A young woman walked by clutching her child in one hand and her meager belongings in the other. Frank knew instantly that the fires had left her homeless. He looked into her panicked eyes and reached out to steady her. But she stepped away, ducking her head in fear.

Looters were everywhere, some as serious as sledgehammers, others giddy with glee. It was as if the entire city had been granted a license to steal. A bare-chested teenager hurled a trashcan through a store window. The sound was deafening. A shower of plate glass fell like hail on the sidewalk, splintering into a thousand pieces. Frank could almost visualize molecular bonds being shattered. He stepped back, shielding his eyes as shards of glass crunched beneath his feet.

The interiors of multistoried buildings gaped empty, riot-shredded shells mocking hope. Some merchants had painted "Soul Bro" on the faces of their buildings in a futile attempt to thwart looting.

Frank looked to his right to see a young man—no more than thirteen—stumble under the weight of a console television set. He was biting his lip, his forehead oozing sweat. He weaved across a sidewalk tangled with dented appliances and clothes still clinging to hangers. Someone pushed him, and he dropped the TV on his foot. A police siren swallowed his screams.

Frank directed Luis's gaze to a burnt-out shell of an overturned car that littered the street like a discarded snakeskin. With its underbelly exposed, its wheels spun aimlessly at a smoke-filled sky.

A sharp crack rang out as if something were being ripped from its hinges. Startled, Frank looked up to see a flaming beam fall from a burning building. It was headed right for him. He covered his head with his arms and leapt out of the way. The beam crashed to the street only feet from where Frank stood. Sparks jumped into the air, singeing his legs like splattered grease. He brushed them off with the palms of his hands.

Frank walked a few feet and tripped over something solid, unyielding. He looked down in grim amazement to see a leg sitting in a pile of rubble at a right angle to the sidewalk. It was a woman's limb with a nicely shaped calf and a high heel shoe hanging off a pretty foot. It was charred and half buried in debris. The violence had eaten its color. A chill tingled his spine just looking at it. His stomach clenched and his pulse thundered at his temples. He sucked in his breath and jumped back.

The scene felt surreal, like a painting he'd seen in a book his grandfather owned. Time stretched, elongated. His face felt hot, flushed. A wave of nausea washed over him, and he leaned against a building to get his bearings.

Frank raised his hand to his mouth, afraid he was going to vomit. His forehead felt clammy. He bent over and tried to quell the roiling acid in his stomach. It took him a minute to catch his breath. When he looked again, he realized the leg was part of a dismembered mannequin. He heaved a sigh of relief.

When Luis saw Frank's reaction, he began to laugh. It was a cruel, pitiless sound, a caterwauling commensurate with the night's events. "What? Did you think it was real?" he asked.

Frank looked away, embarrassed at his own reaction, and disgusted with his uncle's. He felt a sense of dislocation. He wanted out.

Frank turned to Luis and said, "I've had enough! Do what you want, but I'm going home."

Luis stopped laughing. The alarm that rose in his eyes was too obvious to miss. "You can't leave. Not now!"

"The hell I can't," Frank shouted. He turned on his heel and started jogging toward the car.

Luis hesitated a moment and then began running beside him. "Wait! We have to talk. Don't go. I need you!"

"You don't need me," said Frank. "You need your head examined. And so do I for being here."

"I need *my* head examined? What about you? Working all night in that filthy factory for minimum wage when you can make real money working for me. When are you gonna wise up?"

"That's a discussion for another day," said Frank. He quickened his pace.

"But you owe me!"

"I owe you. But I didn't go through hell to get out of Cuba to die in a place like this. I have no dog in this fight."

"So you're backing down on your word? You promised to help me."

Frank stopped and glared at Luis. "Let me make myself clear. What you do is your business. I have no say in it. But this is madness, and I'm going home."

Frank turned and started running.

"Stop!" screamed Luis. His voice sounded shrill and desperate. "We're so close. Just give me a little time. You can stay here if you want. Wait in the car. I won't take long."

Frank slowed his pace as his uncle caught up to him. "I don't think you heard me. I'm leaving. *Now!*"

"You're abandoning me? Just like that?"

"No, I'm going back to our room. Call it what you will. You can come—or not. It's up to you."

Luis looked around frantically, his dark features signaling disbelief. He jumped around like a boxer before an opening match. His eyes darted back and forth. He resembled a wild dog trying to get its bearings.

He made a small sound, raised his fingers to his mouth, and chewed his thumbnail. A moment of silence elapsed as Frank and Luis glared at each other. Then Frank turned and walked toward the car. "Hey!" hollered Luis.

Frank shook his head and continued walking. His uncle followed. Reaching the car, he opened the door, and settled himself into the driver's seat. He was grateful to still have the keys and relieved to be in the safety of the vehicle.

Luis stood next to the Mustang, looking like he was going to kick the tires. Frank wasn't sure whether he'd get in or not. He didn't care. He turned on the ignition and put the car into gear just as Luis opened the passenger door. He hopped into the car, stretched his legs, and slumped into the seat. He untied his sneakers, loosened his shoe tongues, and propped his feet on the dashboard. The smell of sweat filled the air.

A moment elapsed as Luis stared into space. Then he turned to Frank, and said hoarsely, "This is probably for the best. I bet the old lady wasn't there anyway."

"Yeah," grunted Frank. "Probably not."

Frank started driving down the road as Luis plucked a cigarette out of a pack and lit it. He threw the match out the window, inhaled deeply, and switched on the radio to the sound of The Supremes. Then he turned to Frank and said, "You still owe me."

Frank glued his eyes to the road. He didn't respond.

CHAPTER TWENTY-THREE

At eight-thirty in the morning on August 12, 1967, Magda stood before the full-length mirror in her mother's bedroom, adjusting her lace wedding veil. Her hair lay in thick curls around her shoulders. A white organza dress embroidered with seed pearls grazed her high heel pumps.

Frank couldn't sleep the night before, thinking about how Magda would look in her gown, and how he would feel walking back down the aisle arm in arm with his bride. His eyes misted just thinking about it. It truly was a dream come true.

He had arranged for Bruno, his supervisor from work, to wait outside Magda's parents' apartment in his blue Buick Riviera. His job was to chauffeur her to St. Augustine Roman Catholic Church in Union City.

Located on New York Avenue, the church was a modern, triangular-shaped building with rectangles of stained glass that rose to a peak in the front. A large cross adorned the building's brick façade.

Twenty people filled the pews to witness the ceremony, including all of Magda's relatives living in the States and some friends Magda and Frank had made since they had arrived in America.

Frank stood at the altar with Magda's brother, who served as best man. The gold wedding bands, which Frank had purchased the week before, rested securely in his pocket.

The organist began playing the soft strands of music, and Frank's heart skipped a beat. A few more guests wandered in and sat in the pews.

Frank adjusted his tie and stood a little straighter. Magda's mother,

Aunt Sophia, and Uncle Rigo walked down the aisle and occupied the front pew. Tears dewed their cheeks.

A moment of silence, almost sacred, transpired before the organist began playing Mendelssohn's "Wedding March." All eyes turned toward the back of the church. Carrying a bouquet of white roses and carnations and holding her father's arm, Magda slowly proceeded down the aisle, beaming all the way. She nodded to her guests, and then turned to Frank and smiled. She never looked more radiant.

Sergio stood for a moment at the altar and kissed his daughter on the cheek before giving her hand to Frank. He then joined Magda's mother in the front pew. The opposite pew—the one that would have held Frank's parents, siblings, and grandparents—sat as empty as a mask after Mardi Gras.

Frank had written to his family to tell them about his upcoming marriage. He hoped they had received his letter and were thinking of them. For a brief moment, he felt the presence of Abuelo. Wherever he was, Frank knew he was happy for them.

Magda and Frank turned toward the priest, who made the sign of the cross, kissing the gold crucifix that circled his neck before letting it drop to his waist. He nodded to the altar boys and ascended the stairs to begin the service, while Magda and Frank knelt before him on red-carpeted stairs. Two floor fans cooled the air as the priest began to speak in Latin. Frank could hardly focus on the Mass.

Young Sergio gave a reading from scripture in Spanish, and the priest urged Frank and Magda to remain faithful to the Church and to each other. He spoke of love and children. Frank was so eager to get married, he thought they'd never get to recite their wedding vows.

Just when he could stand it no longer, the priest came down the steps and stood before the couple. His eyes twinkled. He delivered a blessing and a short sermon about the sanctity of marriage.

Then he turned to Frank, and said, "Repeat after me: I, Frank Mederos, take thee, Magda Hernández, for my lawful wedded wife, to have and to hold from this day forward, for better or for worse, for richer or for poorer, in sickness and in health, until death do us part." Frank's heart skipped a beat. He said the words with tears streaming down his cheeks. A hush fell over the congregation.

The priest turned to Magda. She reached over and wiped a tear from Frank's face with her thumb. Frank took her hand in his and kissed it. She enunciated her marriage vows to Frank in a strong, clear voice. He nodded, savoring every word.

"The rings, please," said the priest. The best man extracted the rings from his pocket and handed them to the priest. Frank took Magda's hand and slipped the wedding ring on the third finger of her left hand next to the trinket ring he had given her in Cuba. The night before the couple had discussed whether Magda would continue to wear that ring, and she insisted, saying it was an emblem of their love that she would wear until the day she died. Frank was secretly pleased.

The priest waited as they placed the rings on each other's fingers. Then, raising his hand in the sign of the cross, the priest said the sweetest words Frank had ever heard: "Frank and Magda, I join you together in holy matrimony, in the name of the Father, the Son, and the Holy Ghost." The priest turned toward Frank and said, "You may now kiss the bride." Frank pushed Magda's veil aside and kissed her on the lips. When he finished, she kissed him again. And again. Everybody laughed.

The recessional music began, and they exited the church in a flurry of excitement and confetti. They stood for a few minutes outside the church to take photographs before going to Sophia and Rigo's apartment for a small reception. Sophia had decorated the table with white flowers, candles, and tulle. She served a generous buffet accompanied by Cuban coffee and several homemade desserts.

Around four o'clock, Bruno drove Frank and Magda to the Port Authority in New York City so they could catch a bus for a long weekend in the Pocono Mountains in Pennsylvania. At a friend's suggestion, they stayed at a place called Cove Haven Resort on Lake Wallenpaupack. The honeymoon suite had a heart-shaped bed and bathtub. Mirrors reflected the light. The bedspread was fluffy and red. Candles and a jar of pink bubble bath sat on the bathtub's ledge, waiting to be opened. Seeing them, Magda blushed, and then laughed merrily.

"Well, we paid for it, we might as well enjoy it."

Frank took Magda in his arms, more excited than he'd ever been in his life. He had recently turned twenty. Magda was almost eighteen, smart and beautiful. It didn't get better than this. They tumbled into bed together, and Frank kissed her passionately, removing her clothes as he went. He couldn't believe he was actually touching her, holding her, kissing her in places he had only dreamed about. They couldn't get enough of each other.

At one point, Magda pulled away from Frank and laughed. "What about the bubble bath?"

"The hell with the bubble bath," said Frank. "We'll use it in the morning."

They made love over and over, gently, passionately, until Magda finally drifted off to sleep, exhausted. Frank couldn't imagine life could be this good. He turned on his back and smiled. His bride was everything he had hoped for and more. She boosted his confidence. She gave him hope. She made him laugh. She was his partner, his lover, someone with whom he could navigate this strange new world. He thanked God for the gift of her.

The events of the past year flashed before his eyes. He was proud of himself. He had achieved his goal to get to America and to marry Magda. He had struggled against the devil and won—at least for now.

His thoughts turned to his family and how much they would have enjoyed seeing him get married. Their wedding would have been much different in Cuba, attended by scores of people—siblings, aunts, uncles, cousins, neighbors, and friends. His mother would have worn a lace dress and a hat decorated with feathers. Abuelo and his father would have roasted a pig—if they could get one on the black market. Music would have brightened the air, and dancing would have greeted the dawn. But they would not have been free.

Suddenly, Frank heard a noise outside and froze, listening. His adrenaline spiked. He recognized the hoot of an owl and the rustle of what was probably a raccoon. Moonlight spilled through the curtains and a breeze warmed the room. Still, a chill enveloped his body.

He shook his head, thinking that once you've been a fugitive, fear stalks you like a lion. Long after your escape, long after your acquaintance with freedom, it appears out of nowhere. For Frank, it manifested itself in startled responses to quick gestures, to sudden noises, to unexpected events. The smallest thing could trigger fear in him.

Evil forces inhabited dark, sullen dreams, leaving his skin crawling and his sheets wet with perspiration. Terror could ambush him at the sound of a voice or in simple gestures—the nod of the head, the set of a jaw—anything that bore the slightest resemblance to his hunters.

His brain thirsted for the familiar, hungered for patterns, and sought links to what had already transpired. His response to the unknown was a survival mechanism, a shortcut to knowledge, and a recipe for torture.

He silently chided himself on how often he imagined things these days, how often he second-guessed what was happening. He reassured himself that he was in a safe place, a place of romance and love, a mountain refuge where no one could hurt him or his wife. There was no need for apprehension or alarm.

Exhaling, Frank turned on his side. Magda shifted her position and reached for him. He felt her slender arm encircle his waist and her firm breasts brush the hair on his back.

He listened as her breathing became softer, more rhythmic, grateful for her presence as she entered the world of dreams, and he remained still, his eyes open, his heart pounding, his imagination conjuring phantom shapes in the dark.

After a hearty breakfast, Frank and Magda went swimming and then tried their luck at horseback riding. Magda's horse was old and stubborn and spent most of the time eating grass by the side of the road. Frank tried to move him along, but the horse just neighed and shook his head, which made Magda laugh.

At lunch they met a group of four couples, friendly young people who told them things about the States they couldn't even begin to imagine. Frank's English was not good enough to understand most of what was said, but Magda got the gist of it. Her years of study at a private school in Cuba were paying off.

They heard stories about vacationing in the Grand Canyon, a hole so large and deep it took hours to ride to the bottom on a mule. They heard about a horseshoe-shaped waterfall in New York that dropped a hundred and fifty thousand gallons of water a second. They learned about a national park in the West with geysers, salt flats, and bubbling mud.

The men discussed investments and real estate and told them that you could get a mortgage or a car loan with a small down payment. They talked about careers in banking, insurance, and medicine. Magda's ears perked up when she learned you could make a good living by using math.

These stories opened a whole new world to the newlyweds, and they realized there was more to America than living in Union City or working in a laminate factory in Clifton.

When Frank and Magda got home, they rented an apartment on Kennedy Boulevard, and Luis helped Frank move the legendary refrigerator into the kitchen. The couple bought a bed, a table and chairs, and a damask tablecloth for entertaining.

They painted the walls eggshell white and the woodwork Williamsburg blue. Magda hung ball-fringed curtains at the windows, which helped cozy up the place. They found some Peter Max posters at a yard sale and nailed them to the living room wall. Sophia gave them dishes, flatware, and kitchen utensils. Their oven mitts were thick and plaid.

Frank was thinking about blueberry pie.

CHAPTER TWENTY-FOUR

Lazo and his fellow ATGM operator, Manny, had helped Frank in many ways during his efforts to escape. They had covered for him on guard duty and lied to the authorities regarding Frank's whereabouts. They had full knowledge of their friend's intentions and his plans to defect, which could be construed as treason.

Lazo and Manny were interrogated after Frank's escape. They claimed no knowledge of the event and were delighted when the focus shifted to those in charge, especially to Lieutenant Pino. Frank's escape was considered so serious that the top brass at the Santa Maria base were relieved of their duties and replaced by new officers.

Many soldiers knew that Pino's case had gone to trial, and there was much speculation among the privates as to what happened to him thereafter. But an official account was never provided. The officers seldom mentioned his name. It was as if Pino had dropped into a black hole in space. Which was just fine with Lazo.

Every night for months, Lazo awoke in a cold sweat over what he had done. It wasn't as if he wouldn't do it all over again. He would. Recently, Lazo's fear had retreated to the suburbs of his mind. It had morphed from a cause of panic to a nagging concern.

A couple of days before the ceremony for the graduates of the Special Forces, Commander Lucas summoned Lazo to his office. He was sitting at his desk when Lazo entered. He stood and extended a hand for the soldier to take a seat. For some reason, the commander insisted on calling Lazo by his first name, a highly unusual practice.

The commander's desk overflowed with binders and papers scattered at various angles. A map of Cuba and a photo of Fidel hung on the wall behind his desk, and a framed photograph of his wife graced a bookshelf. Lucas glanced at a paper and then turned his attention to Lazo.

"I have news, Lazo. The Russians have decided to relinquish the majority of the training of the new recruits to us."

"Is that so, sir."

Lucas opened his desk drawer and scrambled through some clutter until he found what he wanted. He withdrew a book of matches and a pack of Populares, lit a cigarette, and blew a ring of smoke upward. He rotated the cigarette in his hand, studying it as if it could provide an answer to a troubling question.

Lazo coughed to refocus Lucas's attention. "Is there something I can do for you, sir?"

The commander looked up, as if shaken from a reverie. "The fact is, Lazo, I would very much like you to be part of our team."

"Team, sir?"

"The permanent reserves."

"Thank you, sir. But why me?"

Lucas chuckled. "I thought that would be obvious to you." He dropped his match into the ashtray. "You are one of our best ATGM operators. But more than that, you're a helluva good instructor. You've assisted in the training of new recruits for almost six months now, so you've got some experience under your belt." He hesitated and smiled. "Besides, you've been a big help to me during this difficult transition. I've had my hands full taking over from Commander Martinez, and you've stepped up to the plate, especially with the weaponry. That's not an area in which I'm well versed."

"I'm glad to have been of service, sir."

Lazo's thoughts turned to Lieutenant Pino. If it weren't for him, Martinez would still be in charge, and Lazo wouldn't be afforded this opportunity. *I wonder whether Pino is dead? No, he's probably in jail. That's what usually happens to those who don't follow military procedure. In any event, things have been much more pleasant without him.*

The commander interrupted Lazo's thoughts. "As a member of the reserves, you would interview new recruits and determine who should serve as drivers and who would be more suited to be ATGM operators. You would train them on the current equipment as well as on the new Russian weapons. I don't need to tell you, this is a very responsible position."

"I understand, sir."

"Once you graduate from Special Forces, you'll have a month to decide whether you want to join the permanent reserves. Meanwhile, I will draw up plans regarding who you would report to—that sort of thing—so you could begin your work as soon as possible."

"I will give it serious thought, sir."

"I hope you do, Lazo. You've been a real asset to me, and I would welcome your continued support and advice."

"Yes, sir. I've learned a lot working with you too."

Lucas nodded his appreciation. "A word of caution: jobs are not easy to find these days. As part of the permanent reserves you would receive a guaranteed income as well as further training in military weapons, strategy, and tactics. Take that into account when making your decision."

"It is very generous of you to make me this offer."

"Do you have any questions?"

"May I ask about the salary, sir?"

"You would serve one week a month for a salary of ten dollars. But more importantly, you would continue to be an integral part of the Revolutionary Armed Forces and the vital work that goes on here." Lucas paused. "Of course, you could make a career out of the military. But I get the impression you'd rather do something else. Is that true?"

"I'm keeping my options open, sir. I haven't made my mind up. I have a lot of thinking to do."

"You do."

The men saluted each other.

"I look forward to learning of your decision, Lazo."

"You will be the first to know. Thank you, sir."

"One more thing," said Lucas. "It has been decided that from now on, all new recruits to the Special Forces must be members of the Communist Party. As you know, the bond and loyalty between members of the Special Forces has traditionally been very strong, perhaps too strong. You protect and die for each other if necessary.

"But that bond cannot supersede loyalty to the Party and to the State. Special Forces members often confuse this issue. This cannot stand. We must bring in new recruits whose loyalty to Cuba and to the cause remains above reproach. We got burned once with Mederos and the traitors who helped him escape. And the chain of command is not going to allow that to happen again."

Lazo inhaled and managed to utter, "I understand, sir."

He would not sleep well that night.

CHAPTER TWENTY-FIVE

Lazo had a decision to make. For three years he had served as an ATGM operator, a highly skilled position that left him unqualified for just about any job outside the military. He was ambitious, but he also knew securing even modest employment would be a challenge.

The day after finishing his three years of mandatory military service, his family and friends threw him a party. Due to the embargo, his parents served a modest buffet of rice, beans, and fresh fruit. The occasion was short on food but long on laughter and good wishes.

The weather was lovely, sunny and breezy, a good day for a walk. Once Lazo said good-bye to the last of his guests, he decided to visit Frank's grandfather. He had always liked the man and remembered how often Frank had turned to him for advice.

Not finding him home, he went to see Frank's parents who lived nearby. They often received telegrams and letters from Frank and had filled Lazo in on their son's life in Union City. Lazo knew nothing about New Jersey but vowed to learn more.

He spent the next two weeks looking for work. He asked everyone about possible jobs, applying at hotels, restaurants, factories, and bodegas. He stopped at an auto-repair shop, informing the owner of his mechanical skills. But he took one look at Lazo's clean hands and groomed nails and waved him away in bemusement.

Needing some time to think, Lazo grabbed a blanket and hat and headed to the beach. He spread his blanket on the sand as seagulls roamed the sky. The sun was beginning to drop, and the water shimmered beneath it. Lips of waves licked the shore.

Lazo was enjoying the moment. For someone who had had

precious little leisure time during the past three years, this day seemed nothing short of miraculous.

Resting his head on his knees, Lazo traced a labyrinth in the sand with his finger, drawing each maze a little different. It helped him to focus and to forget his troubles. When he looked up, he saw a familiar figure strolling toward him. The man threw one leg to the left, making a half circle as he walked. Lazo recognized the gait. He raised his hand to shield his eyes.

"Is that you, old buddy?" came a friendly voice.

"Matia! God, it's good to see you. How are you?" said Lazo.

"Fine, just fine! I haven't seen you forever. What've you been up to?"

Lazo dug his feet into the sand and curled his toes. The sand felt damp and refreshing. He wriggled his toes and stood on the balls of his feet. A little girl ran by, her kite fluttering in the breeze. Rows of pink ruffles decorated the bottom of her bathing suit.

"I just finished my stint in the army."

"Special Forces, right?"

"You old fox! You never forget a thing."

"It must feel good to have it over."

"Yeah, it's nice to be able to relax a bit."

"So what are your plans?"

"I don't know. Find a job—like everyone else. Or at least try. I'm not having much luck."

"It's tough out there—a lot of people are out of work." Matia thought for a moment and then slapped his forehead.

"What?"

"Just the other day my boss asked me whether I knew of anybody who was getting out of the army and might need a job."

"You're kidding me."

"No."

"Where do you work?"

"At the oil refinery—Nico Lopez." He gestured in the direction of Belot, across the bay from the Havana harbor.

Lazo's heart sank. "I don't think I'd qualify. Aren't the jobs there very technical?"

"Some are, but Tomás is looking for someone with an ability to learn. He's looking for a man to train."

"That sounds almost too good to be true. Tell me about Tomás."

"He's an engineer, a family man—a good father. I met him on the beach one day, and we started talking."

"And—?"

"We went for a drink and hit it off. He's a great guy, a lot of fun—good sense of humor. I told him I was out of work, and the next thing I knew I was working at the plant. I couldn't have been more surprised myself."

"What do you do?"

"I'm a technician."

"How long have you worked there?"

Matia looked up, calculating. "Almost three years."

"That's as long as I've been in the military. How'd you avoid the army?"

"I got a deferment. They let me off because I worked in a facility vital to national interest."

"Lucky bastard! Do you like it?"

"What's not to like? The pay is great. I've learned a lot. And it's air-conditioned!"

Lazo whistled. "Air-conditioned? Man, that could be the best part of the job." They laughed and looked out to sea. A seagull mimicked their laughter.

"Want me to put in a good word for you? Maybe I could get you an interview."

Shoulders sagging, Lazo said, "I doubt it. Don't you need a security clearance?"

"We have to be careful. There's lot of resentment against the oil company, especially since Fidel took it over from Esso. We even had a bombing a few years back."

"I remember."

"But you shouldn't have a problem, not with having been part of the force. I'll set you up for an interview, if you'd like."

"Could you?"

"I think I can pull it off."

Lazo beamed. "Damn, that would be great."

Three days later, Lazo sat in the refinery's personnel office, filling out an application. When he finished, he walked to the lobby and handed the paperwork to the receptionist. She took it with a smile, telling him that her boss would be with him shortly.

A few minutes later Tomás arrived. Lazo rose to greet him, and they shook hands. "I'm Tomás Valdes, but you can call me Tomás."

"Call me Lazo."

"Okay, Lazo."

Tomás, a trim man with thick hair and bright eyes, extended a hand toward a chair. "Please, be seated."

Tomás sat down and scanned Lazo's application. "I see you just finished up with the army. What are your plans?"

"I'm not sure. I've been home for a couple of weeks, and I just have two more weeks to figure it out."

"What did you do in the army?"

"Special Forces."

Tomás dropped the file and looked at Lazo. "What did you do for the force?"

Lazo felt apprehensive about answering the question. "I'd rather not say."

Tomás waved his hand in dismissal. "That's your prerogative. I was just trying to determine your level of skills."

"I understand."

Tomás grew more serious. "So do I." They sat in silence for a minute.

Tomás glanced again at Lazo's application. "You have two years of college—very commendable. We need educated people—people who can follow directions, people who can think."

"I would've finished college, if I hadn't been drafted."

"I see it all the time." Tomás thought for a moment. "Would you be willing to take a test for us? In order to make an offer, we would need to assess your skills."

"Do I need to study?"

Tomás chuckled. "No, it's not that kind of test."

"What kind of skills are required?"

"Basic intelligence—analytical skills, math abilities, that kind of thing."

"Sure, that'd be fine."

"Good. There's a lot of competition for these jobs, and we have to be certain we select the right person."

"I'm honored just to be considered," said Lazo. "It sure beats picking coffee or working the cane fields. And those are my only civilian prospects at the moment."

"We like to hire through word of mouth," said Tomás, ignoring Lazo's comment. "Matia speaks highly of you. He's known you since kindergarten?"

"We go way back."

"Matia's a good man. Trustworthy."

"He is."

"Trust is an important thing to me. I've worked here for seven years, and I sit on the board of directors. I'm interviewing you on Matia's recommendation. I trust him. Trust his judgment. Trust his opinions."

Lazo nodded, wondering what Tomás meant, but he was unsure how to frame the question. *There's something a little off about all this emphasis on trust. But, again, this is an oil refinery.*

Tomás looked at Lazo with an intensity that was almost frightening. "Can I trust you?"

"I'm trustworthy," said Lazo.

Tomás nodded. "You mentioned your civilian options. What are your military options?"

The question surprised Lazo. He didn't think Tomás had been

listening that closely. *There's more to this guy than meets the eye. He's sharp—doesn't miss a thing.*

"I could make a career out of the military."

"Does that appeal to you?"

Lazo shook his head. "Not really."

"What else?"

"I could just do my regular stint in the army reserves until I'm twenty-eight and try to find a job on the outside. Or—"

"Or what?"

"Or I could become part of the permanent reserves and continue to train the new recruits."

"Train them on what?"

"Various aspects of weaponry."

"So you'd remain current with all the new weapons coming out of the Soviet Union?"

"Yes, what they are and how to operate them."

Tomás leaned back in his seat and touched his fingers to his chin. "But if you did that, you'd still be able to work for us."

Lazo's heart quickened. "Yes. Time would allow me to do both."

"Would you like my opinion?"

"Of course."

"Well, it's none of my business. But if it were up to me, I'd take advantage of the opportunity to be part of the permanent reserves."

"Why do you say that?"

Tomás smiled. "I like that."

"Like what?"

"Like that you asked a follow-up question. It shows you have a curious mind—that you don't take things at face value. That kind of thinking could be a real asset to us."

"Thank you, sir. But why *did* you recommend the permanent reserves?"

"It'll keep you in the know. Help you maintain your connections. There's nothing wrong with that."

"No. Nothing wrong with that."

Tomás stood, signaling the end of the interview. "The receptionist will administer the aptitude test. If you perform the way I expect, we will both have something to think about."

"I hope so."

Tomás glanced at his watch. "I must run. I have an important appointment. Stay in touch."

"Will do," said Lazo.

His jaw unclenched and his shoulders relaxed as he watched Tomás walk out the door.

CHAPTER TWENTY-SIX

A week elapsed before Tomás called Lazo for a second interview. During that time, Lazo had given a lot of thought to his future. He didn't want to make a career of the military, but the idea of serving in the permanent reserves held some appeal. It would give him extra income. Tomás thought it was a good idea, and Lazo respected his judgment. After all, Tomás had made a success of himself.

Lazo entered the conference room to a waiting Tomás. The older man stood and pumped his hand.

"Glad to see you again."

"Good to see you too," said Lazo.

"Sit, sit," said Tomás, gesturing toward a wooden chair on the opposite side of the conference table. "I have great news for you." Lazo smiled and took a seat. "What?"

"The scores on your aptitude test place you in the top tenth percentile."

Lazo lifted his eyebrows. "Really?"

"Yes, we rarely see scores this high."

"What does that mean?"

Tomás sat back, lightly holding the arms of his chair. "It means you have a job if you want it."

Lazo leaned forward, elated. "Wow! I don't know what to say."

"You probably shouldn't say anything until you hear the particulars."

Lazo beamed while Tomás opened a folder. "First things first. If you don't mind, you will report directly to me."

Lazo shifted his body in his chair. "Great."

"I need help with new Russian equipment, and I believe you are the right man for the job."

"I'm flattered you think so."

"Once you learn to operate the equipment, you'll train six men at a time for a period of weeks. When you finish, you'll oversee one of our key operations."

"This would be a permanent position?"

"Permanent as long as your performance remains satisfactory—and I have no doubt it will. A man with your abilities should be able to enjoy an exemplary career at the refinery."

"It sounds promising." Lazo thought for a moment. "I hope you don't mind me asking, but can we discuss my salary?"

"Your salary would be forty dollars a week."

Lazo looked at Tomás, wondering whether he had heard him correctly. He made a mental calculation. The figure sounded far too high. "A week? You're talking a hundred and sixty dollars a month?"

"I hope that meets your expectations."

Blinking, Lazo let out a whistle. This was four times what most Cubans made no matter how hard they worked. He couldn't believe his good fortune. He'd be working in a nice facility, close to home, with a great boss and an enviable income. He couldn't ask for anything more.

"One other thing," said Tomás. "I've been thinking about that position you talked about in the permanent reserves."

"I've been thinking about it too," said Lazo. "I got the impression from the last time we spoke that you thought it was a good idea."

Tomás scrutinized Lazo as if he were seeing him for the first time. "I do."

"So, if you were me, you would take it?"

"If I were as young and as smart as you, I wouldn't hesitate."

"Really?"

"Think about it, Lazo. The army is willing to teach you something for free, to invest in your future. These are precarious times. The more knowledge and money you have, the better."

Lazo had considered how he would use the money. He could help his parents. Save to get married. Establish an emergency fund. Ten extra dollars a month was nothing to sneeze at.

"You're right," replied Lazo. "I'm in no position to turn down money."

Tomás nodded. "It would be a good move for you—it would help guarantee your future."

"I put a lot of stock in your opinion, sir." Lazo hesitated while making his final decision. He was not about to let these opportunities slip through his fingers. "If you'll have me, sir, I'd be honored to accept the position at the refinery."

A smile brightened Tomás's face.

"And on your recommendation, I'll also join the permanent reserves."

"Good man," said Tomás. "You've made two sound decisions today."

Lazo beamed at the compliment as Tomás took him by the elbow and walked him to the door.

"I'd like you to start in a couple of weeks, if that's good for you."

"That's fine. I'm looking forward to working with you, sir."

Tomás shook Lazo's hand and said, "Welcome aboard. I think we're going to have a very interesting future together."

Lazo nodded, smiled, and began to hum a few bars of "We Can Work It Out," his favorite Beatles song, as he exited the building.

CHAPTER TWENTY-SEVEN

Day after day, week after week, Pino made it his business to re-press his need to take charge of situations that screamed to be fixed. He watched as food spoiled in the kitchen, as garbage clung to dinner plates, as machetes rusted in the rain. He bit his tongue. He didn't say a word. Others might be left to rot in a place like this, but Pino knew what it would take to get out.

Like a chronic disease, the cane fields caused Pino blinding headaches, lower back pain, and nasal congestion. He suffered from muscular fatigue, sun poisoning, and bouts of intestinal distress from poorly prepared or rotten food. His hands became calloused, his eyes bloodshot, and his arms blistered from the sun.

Yet the former lieutenant endured it all without comment or complaint. He tried to tame his nightmares of Mederos slipping out of his hands like a greased pig, while sleeping next to men who snored and snorted all night. He even complimented his fellow laborers on their work.

True to his word, Torres appeared every two weeks to speak to Castillo and to the other cane cutters regarding Pino's attitude and behavior. He asked probing questions and took copious notes. Pino did everything possible to ensure a good report.

Little by little, Torres and Pino began to bond. They spent hours engaged in long discussions, mostly because Torres wanted to explore Pino's attitude toward the Party, but also because he found it a pleasant way to pass the time. Although Pino was humorless and pedantic, his mind was as sharp and quick as a switchblade.

Lengthy discussions about socialism, communism, and Marxism

ensued, convincing Torres that Pino, while pigheaded, arrogant, and impulsive, had a deep and impressive understanding of political philosophy and military history.

After discussing the harvest, Torres would pepper Pino with questions, hoping to gain some insight into his thinking. One day, after they had been discussing Cuban-American relations, Torres sat back in his chair, drew a cigar from his pocket, and lit it. He took a long pull as he balanced his feet on the edge of the desk.

Torres rotated his cigar in his mouth. He looked out the window and said casually, "Do you think the Yanks will invade again?"

In a tone of smug self-assurance, Pino said, "It depends on how foolish they are."

"And if they do?"

Pino looked at the ceiling, and said, "If they do, there'll be hell to pay. Our men are well trained, and our weapons are state-of-the-art."

"But the Americans are well equipped."

"The Americans would be at a great disadvantage. They can fly in their troops, but their weapons and fuel must come by ship. Unless they commandeer our refineries, there's no way to win."

Torres shook his head. "That could happen. You can't underestimate the Americans."

"I'm not underestimating them. But the Cuban navy is strong, and the Soviet navy is even stronger. The Special Forces are adept at sinking ships—we've got top-notch ATGM operators who are more than up to the job."

"That may be so, but the Yanks could surprise us."

"Surprise is a powerful weapon in the hands of the aggressor. Look at Pearl Harbor. But our troops are in a constant state of readiness, and contrary to what the Americans think, Cuba's intelligence operations are extensive and reliable. We beat the imperialists during the Bay of Pigs, and we'll beat them again. We'll be more than ready for them if they come."

"You sound eager to engage them."

"Damn right I am." Pino grimaced and spat on the floor in an uncharacteristic gesture of disgust. Although Pino's voice was dry and raspy from sugarcane dust, it was full of conviction. "Since their Congress passed the Platt Amendment, the Americans have come to regard Cuba as nothing more than their plaything, their little gold mine. They've ravaged Latin America for decades, stolen our resources, exploited our people, and lined their pockets on the backs of our peasants. Their greed knows no limit."

"So you think we'd win?"

"Without a doubt. Cuba is leading the Southern Hemisphere in the fight against aggression. We're the only Latin American country with the guts and the resources to stand up to the Americans."

"Do you think the Special Forces would bond together to fight the Marines?"

"Yes!"

"Do you think they would die to fight the Marines?"

"Of course."

"You think their loyalty to the State is that strong? Stronger than their loyalty to each other?"

"I do!"

"If that's true, why did Mederos defect? And why did fellow members of the force help him escape?"

When Pino did not respond, Torres continued, "Since Mederos's escape, changes have been made regarding the recruitment of Special Forces."

Pino's eyebrows lifted. "What kind of changes?"

"The brass at Managua has decided that from now on all new recruits must be members of the Communist Party. Cuba spends a lot of time and money training these men. We must ensure that we are not creating super soldiers that can later turn on their country."

"Like Mederos."

"Just like Mederos."

"And if it doesn't work?"

"If it doesn't work, the Special Forces will be abolished."

Pino thought for a moment. "I think Mederos was an aberration. He was a worm. He doesn't represent the force."

"You feel strongly about this."

"I do."

"And you're sure we can beat the Americans?"

"Cuba is a peaceful nation. But if the Americans push us, they will find us to be far more powerful than they think." The former lieutenant raised a fist in a gesture of defiance and his voice climbed half an octave. "We will not only win. We will crush the imperialists!"

Torres's lips creased into a satisfied smile as he fingered the ash from the end of his cigarette into an aluminum ashtray. It tipped slightly and rattled against the desk.

"Would you like to play a role in defending Cuba should that time come?"

Pino looked at Torres incredulously. *Have I not demonstrated the depth of my love of my homeland during these long months of discussions? Have I not made it clear to this man the depth of my patriotism?*

"Of course," said Pino in an annoyed voice. "Given the opportunity, I would die for my homeland. I thought you might know me well enough by now not to doubt my devotion to my country."

Pino studied Torres for a moment, wondering about the purpose of his questions.

Torres stood, smiled, and left the room without a rejoinder.

CHAPTER TWENTY-EIGHT

To Lazo's delight, his friend Matia had invited him to his house for his daughter's birthday party. Matia had told him that their boss at the refinery, Tomás, would be there, and it might be a good opportunity for the two of them to bond outside of work. Lazo arrived at Matia's house around four o'clock, bearing a gift.

After talking with the family for a while, he wedged himself next to Tomás on the couch, balanced his plate of food on his knees, and set his beer on the floor. He gobbled a plate of rice and beans, and forked some ripe mangoes into his mouth. Wiping his face with a paper napkin, he turned to Tomás and said, "Great food."

Tomás nodded, rubbed his stomach, and stood. "It's a little stuffy in here. I need to get some air. Want to join me?"

"Sure."

Lazo motioned to Matia that they were leaving, closed the door, and began walking. Heads down, hands buried in their pockets, they strolled three blocks before Lazo broke the silence. "How well do you know Matia?"

Tomás looked up at the sky, thinking. "We met several years ago. He's one of my best employees—smart, dedicated, and loyal. I'm very fond of him."

"He's a great guy."

They passed a barbershop and a stray dog joined them, wagging his tail and sniffing Lazo's leg, his breath hot on his ankles. Lazo bent down, massaged the dog's ears, and scratched him lightly under his chin. The dog rewarded him with an affectionate nuzzle and a high-pitched murmur.

"Do you like dogs?" asked Tomás.

"Yes. Our family would love to have one, but it's not a good time. Rationing hardly provides the family with enough food to feed the kids, let alone a dog."

It was a quick response and the wrong thing to say. Lazo covered his mouth with his hand, afraid the comment could be construed as counterrevolutionary. He looked for his boss's reaction, but he seemed unconcerned.

"I know what you mean," said Tomás. "It's the same everywhere."

Lazo exhaled.

"What about hobbies? Is there anything in particular you like to do?" asked Tomás.

"I like to read and hang out with my family. I play baseball and basketball when I get a chance. What about you?"

"The same. But Matia and I do some things outside of work—it's pretty interesting stuff." He tilted his head sideways. "In fact, I thought it might be something for you to consider."

Maybe they play basketball together and will invite me to shoot some balls. But that hardly qualifies as "interesting."

"Interesting? Like what?"

"Things—" Tomás lowered his voice and scoured the area with his eyes. "Things that are good for Cuba, things that will help you earn some extra money and will make a difference."

"Sorry, I'm not following you."

A woman walked by carrying a large package wrapped in brown paper. Her oily hair was streaked with gray, her shoes were worn, and the hem of her dress was uneven. Tomás waited for her to pass before he continued. "To tell you the truth, Lazo, we're both very concerned about what's going on in this country."

"I see."

Tomás cleared his throat and looked around again as if surveying the area. They walked a half block before Tomás turned to Lazo, and said, "You know, we're very fortunate to be working at the refinery. Times are tough."

"Of course. Most of my friends are out of work. They'd die to have my job."

"My point exactly—unemployment is high."

"Even my father is looking for a job," Lazo added. "He used to bartend at one of the casinos, but since so many hotels have been nationalized—"

Tomás cut him off in mid-sentence. "It has me worried."

"Me too."

"The situation is more serious than it appears."

"How so?"

"Between the bad economy and the American embargo, the Russians are subsidizing Cuba to the tune of billions of dollars a year. They've been buying our sugar at inflated prices and selling us oil at deflated prices. But sooner or later, they'll want their money back. When they do, Cuba will belong to the Soviets."

Tomás waited a minute for Lazo to absorb what he said and then asked, "What do you think?"

Lazo was startled at this turn in the conversation. This was not the kind of thing people discussed, not if you valued your life. "I haven't given it much thought."

Tomás shot him a sympathetic look. "Believe me, it's an issue," he continued. "Unfortunately, it's not the only issue."

Lazo worried a piece of mango from between his teeth with his tongue. The conversation was getting dangerous. He wondered whether to make some excuse to go back to the party. He didn't want to end up in jail for a slip of the tongue.

Reaching the corner, the men turned and started walking back in the direction of the house. Lazo pulled out a pack of Populares, extracted a cigarette, and tapped it lightly against the package.

"Do you have a light?"

Tomás drew a book of matches from his breast pocket, opened it, and passed a red match head against the strike pad. It made a rasping sound before the cardboard stem crumpled. He mumbled something and threw the match to the sidewalk in disgust. He steadied his hand and tried again, successfully.

Lazo pulled the smoke deep into his lungs and allowed a minute to elapse before gesturing toward the house. He wanted to anchor the conversation in safer waters.

"Nice party."

"Yeah," said Tomás. "It's good some people can still afford to throw a shindig like this."

"Agreed."

"But parties don't make up for being unable to travel like we used to."

Lazo wondered why Tomás kept making provocative statements. It was as if he were trying to bait him. He felt confused. He searched his mind for a safe response.

"Where did you travel?"

"I used to take my wife to Spain once a year to visit her family. They are great people. She misses them. So do I."

"It must be difficult."

Tomás kicked an empty can. It rattled like it was full of pebbles. He looked around and whispered, "It's not right that you can't leave the country. Hell, you can't even go out of town without informing the CDRs."

"True. But there's not much we can do about it."

A strange look crossed Tomás's eyes. "Well, we're doing something—"

Just then Matia yelled, "Come everyone, it's time for dessert."

Tomás patted Lazo on the back. "We'll continue this conversation later."

"All right."

Lazo walked back to the party, thinking. *Why is Tomás talking to me like this? Is this some kind of trick, a trap to get me to say things against the regime?*

When they got back to the house, Lazo cornered Matia. "What's up with Tomás?"

"Whaddaya mean?"

"We went for a walk, and he was talking politics."

"And?"

"He was saying things he shouldn't. I've never seen him like this before. Do I need to watch my ass around this guy?"

Matia waved away Lazo's concern. "It's not a problem."

"Not a problem for you. But Tomás is my boss. I don't want to alienate him. On the other hand—"

Matia raised his palm for Lazo to stop. "We can't talk about it now—I've got to help my wife with the party." He winked. "Otherwise she might kill me."

Lazo looked at Alina who was busy pouring coffee and plating slices of birthday cake. It was pound cake, no frosting. Still, it was a special treat.

"I understand. But you've got to help me. I was walking on eggshells out there."

Matia nodded, took his place beside his wife, and handed a plate to a guest. Someone put "Born Free" on the record player, and people started to sway in rhythm to the music. A few people began singing the lyrics under their breath: *Born free, as free as the wind blows—*

Lazo wandered around making small talk, while trying to banish the conversation with Tomás from his mind. When the party got too noisy, he walked outside and sat on a bench beneath a coconut tree. He brushed away some tree droppings and placed his coffee cup next to him.

The sun was bright, the air crisp. He closed his eyes for a minute, enjoying the music. Someone put on "Barbara Ann." *Ah, ba ba ba ba Barbara Ann, Ba, ba, ba, ba Barbara Ann.* It was his favorite song. The beat was so compelling he felt like dancing. While tapping his foot to the rhythm of the music, he looked up to see his boss heading his way. He inched himself over so Tomás could join him on the bench.

"Sorry our little talk got interrupted," said Tomás.

"It's okay," Lazo said with a hitch at the end of the word. Tomás looked around to make sure they couldn't be overheard. "Look,

Lazo, do you mind if I continue our conversation where I left off, or should I stop? I don't want to make you feel uncomfortable. It's your call."

"I don't know what you mean."

"I think you do."

Lazo and Tomás stared at each other in silence before Tomás looked down at the grass. He rested his elbows on his knees, lost in thought. After a minute, he straightened his body and turned toward Lazo.

"Do you remember your job interview?"

"Of course."

"Do you recall that I told you I value trust—that it's very important to me?"

"I remember it clearly."

Tomás's face grew stern, and he looked Lazo in the eye. "Well, I need to know whether I can trust you."

"I told you then that I'm trustworthy, and I meant it," said Lazo. He stood and looked over his shoulder. "But, if you'll excuse me, right now I need to use the john."

"Sure. Take your time."

Lazo went into the house, grabbed Matia by the arm, and pulled him aside. "I've got to talk to you—now!"

"Why?"

"I'm in the middle of a conversation with the boss. And I don't know how to handle it. He's going on about trust in a way that's making me nervous. He's been egging me on to say things against the communists."

Matia smiled. "Calm down, will ya? Tomás is a good man. He won't betray you. Stop worrying."

"You're sure? I need to be sure."

"I wouldn't mess with you on something as important as this."

Alina came up behind Matia and handed him a jar to open, nodding to a couple of guests who had arrived late to the party. She smiled at Lazo.

Lazo fixed his gaze on Matia. "All right, I believe you."

He went back outside, his curiosity trumping his fears. He was dying to know what Matia and Tomás were doing. It occurred to him that he wouldn't mind being involved in something exciting, something important, something that, as Tomás said, would "make a difference."

Lazo reclaimed his seat next to Tomás and sipped his coffee. "You started to say that you and Matia are doing some things to make extra cash. Is it something you can talk about?"

"It's a private matter. But there may be opportunities for us to explore. Not today, of course. But if you're interested, we could get together and talk about it sometime—just the three of us." Tomás stood. "No obligation, of course."

"It sounds interesting."

"It is." Tomás put his hands on his hips and executed a back-stretch. His ribcage pressed against his shirt, its architecture laddering itself against the green cotton fabric. He covered his mouth and issued a long yawn. "I'll see you at work on Monday. Maybe we'll get a chance to talk next week."

Tomás nodded his respects, and walked into the house to say good-bye to his hosts, leaving Lazo to wonder what the hell their conversation had been all about.

CHAPTER TWENTY-NINE

Lazo spent all day Sunday thinking about his discussion with Tomás. The man was smart and savvy enough to survive the politics inherent in his job. So why would he engage in such reckless behavior? Had the conversation gone a little further, it could be construed as treason. There was a lot for Tomás to lose. But what was there to gain?

Matia's reaction was equally puzzling. He wasn't rattled at all. In fact, he acted blasé. It appeared that they were involved in something clandestine. But what?

Although Matia had reassured Lazo that he could trust Tomás, he felt more comfortable questioning Matia about the issue. Spotting his old friend in the cafeteria, he sidled up to him in the food line.

"I'd like to talk to you when you get a chance. It's about Saturday."

"Sure." Matia looked around. The cafeteria was crowded. The clank of dishes and the rattle of silverware filled the air. Someone had just spilled soda on the floor, and a woman was wiping it up with a rag. She glanced up at Lazo and smiled.

"Let me eat my sandwich, and then we'll go outside for a smoke," said Matia.

"Sounds good."

The men ate their lunch in silence and then walked outside. Matia leaned against the building, drew a cigarette from a cardboard pack, and offered Lazo one. When he declined, Matia lit his cigarette, puckered his lips, and blew a quick series of smoke rings.

Lazo watched as they grew larger, wobbled, and then disappeared into the air.

"What's up?" asked Matia.

Lazo shaded his eyes against the sun with his hand. "That was an interesting conversation I had with Tomás on Saturday."

"So I gather."

"Tomás said you two are involved in something where you earn extra cash."

Matia nodded. "We are."

"But he didn't say what."

"I doubt he would."

"Pardon me for asking, but are you stealing from the refinery?"

To Lazo's surprise, Matia threw back his head and laughed.

"No, my friend, that's the last thing in the world we'd do. Tomás and I do everything possible to remain above reproach. We try very hard not to draw attention to ourselves."

"I'm sorry, but from what Tomás said it made me wonder—"

Matia stopped Lazo. "No need to apologize. We're making money but not in the way you think."

"I don't understand."

"Look, Lazo. You see how the communists live. You see their beautiful homes, their fancy cars. They aren't scrimping and scraping. They aren't living the same lifestyle as the rest of us."

"I know," Lazo said, a little testily.

"And you know better than anyone the kind of weaponry Cuba has at its disposal—the guns, the tanks, the missiles."

"I do."

"Then you must also know that Cuba can't afford all this stuff. Who do you think pays for it?"

"The Soviets, of course. And China to a lesser extent."

"Right."

"So?"

"So little by little Cuba is being swallowed up. Not only our economy, but also our ideals, our mores, and our way of life. We've turned into a little Russia. They used to call Batista a puppet of the Americans. But Fidel is a puppet of the Soviets. And, believe me, I'd rather be a puppet of the Americans any day."

Matia extended his fingers and studied them for a moment. "The way I figure, if you really care about what's happening to Cuba, if you care about what's happening to us, to our families, then you have to *do* something about it. You can't stand by and let it happen. Do you know what I'm saying?"

"Yes and no. I understand what you're saying about Cuba, but I don't understand what you and Tomás are doing."

"It's nothing special, nothing more than lots of other people are doing. Tomás introduced me to this line of work, and I'm glad he did. We provide some very important services."

Lazo thought for a moment, refining an idea that had been floating at the edge of his consciousness since Matia's party.

"The way you're dancing around this subject makes me wonder whether you're involved in counterrevolutionary activity."

Matia didn't respond. "Tell me, Matia, are you planning to blow up the refinery? Are you a saboteur?"

"Not exactly."

"Then, what?"

"We work more with information gathering and dissemination."

"Christ almighty, can we stop beating around the bush and speak plainly? I'm not going to rat you out if that's what's worrying you."

"I'm not worried about that."

Lazo studied his friend's face. A web of lines edged the corners of Matia's eyes, wrinkles he hadn't noticed before. He looked around before asking, "Are you working for the CIA?"

Matia did not respond. He dragged on his cigarette and blew the smoke out his nostrils. A minute marched by, then two. The rattle of dishes rose from the cafeteria kitchen. The question hung in the air, raw and ripe.

Lazo was not about to let the question go unanswered. He lowered his voice to a whisper. "Are you telling me you're a CIA operative? That you spy for the Americans?"

"I'm more than that, Lazo. I'm a patriot of Cuba, a true patriot. The CIA provides me with the tools and information I need to help free our country from this cancer Fidel calls the 'revolution.'

"Contrary to what the government says, there are a lot of good people in the CIA—people who are as concerned about what happens to Cuba as you and I. They understand what it means to fight for freedom. What's more, they are the only people on the planet who have the power and the guts to save us."

"I understand. And I'm sympathetic to your convictions. But aren't you afraid?"

"Sometimes. But we have the US government behind us. They've promised Tomás and me safe passage and safe haven in America should either of us need it."

Lazo shook his head. "It's hard to believe."

"I know. It took me a while to get used to the idea too."

"How long have you been doing this?"

"Three years."

"Have you run into any problems?"

"We've had a couple of close calls. But it's gone smoothly for the most part."

"And you get paid for this?"

"Yes, but that's not what motivates us."

"I'm sure it's not. But out of curiosity, how do they pay you?"

"Every other week."

"In US dollars?"

"Most of the money is deposited into a US bank account for my kids' education and in case something happens to me. I'm also paid in pesos."

"Aren't you afraid the authorities will find out that you have a bank account in the States?"

"C'mon, Lazo, we're in the intelligence business. The bank account is listed under a fictitious name. Nothing can be traced to me."

"Do you have any idea how many Cubans are involved?"

"With the CIA?" Matia waved his hand in a grand gesture. "Thousands."

"That many?"

"Yes, thousands of Cubans are providing information to the Americans. And thousands of Cubans are in the States providing information on America to Fidel. It's the Cold War, for chrissakes. It's all about information."

Lazo thought for a moment. "Why would Tomás get involved in something like this? He's got a good job, great pay, and security. He has a lot to lose."

"He does. But like the rest of us, Tomás was born and raised here. He cares what happens to Cuba, and he's in a good position to help. He was approached by the agency and decided it was the right thing to do." Matia paused. "Never underestimate Tomás. He is well respected within the oil industry as well as within the intelligence community."

"So, is Tomás your boss in the CIA as well as at the refinery?"

Matia nodded. "He heads up the entire Havana operation."

"Jesus!" Lazo thought for a moment. "But what made him think it was safe to approach me without knowing my political leanings? All he knew was that I was a member of the Special Forces, hardly a recommendation for the CIA."

Matia smiled smugly. "We are far more careful than that, Lazo. We had targeted you long before you came to work at the refinery."

Lazo felt stunned, bewildered. He was trying to control his burgeoning anxiety. "What are you talking about?"

"The CIA informed Tomás that you might be amenable to our cause, and we made sure you came here to work at the refinery so we could groom you."

"How could the CIA possibly know what I think?"

"The agency learned from a friend of yours that you might be someone we could recruit."

"What are you talking about? What friend?"

"Frank Mederos."

Lazo paled. Fear rose in his chest, heavy and primal. He had carried the burden that he could be executed for his part in Frank's escape for months, lying awake at night imagining what would happen if anyone found out. He wondered how much Matia and Tomás knew about what he had done. The more people who knew about it, the more dangerous it was for him. He needed to protect himself.

"Sorry, never heard of him. You were given faulty information."

Matia smiled indulgently. "Relax, Lazo. We know you and Mederos were friends. And we know what you did for him. It was an act of bravery. There's no point denying it."

Lazo looked up at the sky. This was an unexpected development, and a lot to take in. He felt disoriented.

"All right, I knew him. But how can I verify what you're saying? How do I know this isn't a trick?"

"Because Mederos told a CIA agent something that would prove you can trust us. It's a story he said only you and your friend Manny would know."

Lazo crossed his arms. "Go on. Convince me."

"You and Manny were fellow ATGM operators. One day you left a basketball game and went together to a bar in Havana. Frank mentioned a girl named Regina—"

Lazo shook his head, held up his hand, and smiled. "All right, you don't have to elaborate on that story. It's not something I care to relive. I believe you." He shook his head, remembering. "How is Frank? Do you know?"

"We've been keeping an eye on him. He's fine. Living and working in New Jersey."

"Did he ever marry Magda?"

"Yes."

"Good. Then it was worth it."

"Pardon?"

"Nothing."

Matia threw his cigarette to the pavement and crushed it with the toe of his shoe. He looked at Lazo. "Tomás thinks very highly of you. He believes you are smart and cautious—a combination the agency values. We can't afford cowboys or nitwits in this line of work."

"I'm sure."

"Would you like to continue this conversation with Tomás? Perhaps at my house?"

"Yes."

"And while we're at it, let me be perfectly clear. Would you be willing to work with us for the good of Cuba?"

Lazo looked somber. "Yes. As a matter of fact, I've been waiting for an opportunity like this for some time now."

"Good. Then we understand each other."

"We do."

"Okay. I'll set it up. We'll meet with Tomás in a couple of days and go over things."

"Fine."

"One more thing. I don't need to tell you that I'm talking to you like a brother here. Do not breathe a word of this conversation to anyone. Anyone! My life and the lives of my family are at stake."

"I understand. I look forward to our meeting."

CHAPTER THIRTY

For several weeks First Lieutenant Torres had been aware that a new group of officers would be called to the Soviet Union for further military training. This was an honor and privilege afforded to Cuba's brightest, most loyal, and competent military officers. To his delight, Torres had been selected to be among one hundred and fifty officers from throughout the communist world to be part of the contingent.

What's more, he had been given an opportunity to select an officer of lesser rank to accompany him, someone who could handle the intellectual demands of advanced training, someone fiercely loyal to the Party, someone whom he could guide and mentor.

Torres's last discussion with Pino had convinced him that the former lieutenant was the man for the job. Now he had to convince the oversight committee. He told the committee that Pino had been humbled by his stint in the fields, that he now better understood the needs of the people, and that his loyalty to the Party was unwavering, despite the hardships and rigors of his punishment. He tried to convince them that Pino was a new and reformed man, that he was completely rehabilitated.

Some members of the committee bought his argument, others did not. No matter. Torres vowed to himself that he would continue to speak on Pino's behalf until the former lieutenant was again allowed to bring his full knowledge, expertise, and talents to bear to benefit Cuba and the Party.

Meanwhile, he was eager to broach the subject with Pino, eager to impress him with the fact that he was highly regarded in the eyes of the Party, eager to share the good news with someone he liked and respected.

Pino was in the midst of hacking cane when Torres arrived at the plantation. The day was blistering hot, and perspiration dripped like rain from the tip of Pino's nose. His sweat had mixed with field dust, filming his skin like pond scum.

He was wiping his brow with the back of his hand when someone tapped him on the shoulder and told him to report to the foreman's office immediately. It had only been a week since Pino had last seen Torres, so he knew he was not being summoned for his regular interview. But being ordered to the foreman's office usually spelled trouble. His throat clutched as he wondered why.

When he opened the door to the office, Pino was surprised to see Torres sitting behind the foreman's desk with a copy of the *Granma* butterflied between his hands. Torres stood, neatly closed and folded the newspaper, and shook Pino's hand.

"What brings you here?" asked Pino. "We're not scheduled to meet until the end of next week."

Torres waved his hand dismissively. "I've got some good news to share." A smile played on his lips and he gestured toward a chair. "Please, sit down."

Pino took a seat opposite Torres, attempting to disguise his hope. *Maybe my strategy has worked. Maybe they're sending me to do something more in keeping with my intellect and abilities.*

Torres looked at Pino for a long minute, imagining their days together in Russia. He was looking forward to being Pino's sponsor, someone Pino would need to come to for answers and advice.

"As you know, I've been getting consistently good reports about you over the past several months," said Torres.

"Thank you, sir. I've been working hard at improving my behavior."

"That's obvious."

Torres enjoyed a moment of silent anticipation before he broke the news to Pino.

Pino shifted his weight in his chair and said, "Is there something I can do for you, sir?"

Torres's smile broadened. "I might as well come right out with it. The Party has requested that I travel to the Soviet Union to advance my knowledge of communism and to further my study of Soviet weaponry."

"Congratulations," said Pino. "You must be thrilled."

Torres continued without acknowledging Pino's comment. "I don't know the duration of my training yet. It will be at least four years, maybe five."

Pino's heart sank at the implications of Torres's revelation. With Torres gone, he would be assigned a new political investigator. He had worked hard to prove to Torres that he had learned his lessons and learned them well. Now he would have to prove himself to someone new. This was a body blow to his strategy. A headache coalesced across his brow.

Pino nodded at Torres without speaking. It suddenly dawned on him that he would miss this man. Over these many months, Pino had discussed things with Torres that he had never talked about. He had told him about his family, the beatings at the hands of his father, and his struggle in trying to capture Mederos. He was unaccustomed to speaking at such length to anyone, let alone about matters of such an intimate and personal nature. In fact, Torres was one of the few friends that Pino ever had. Pino thought that Torres's announcement had all the makings of a disaster for him. But he was wrong.

Torres cleared his throat and said, "Which brings me to my question."

Pino's eyes widened, wondering what more Torres had to say. "I have been granted permission for someone to accompany me to Russia, someone who would be capable of learning at a higher level. Is that something you might consider?"

Pino looked at Torres, flabbergasted. "Accompany you?"

"Yes."

Pino shook his head in disbelief, speechless. This was a totally unexpected turn of events.

"We will be stationed in Moscow," continued Torres. "We will meet with the top officials of the Communist Party and will receive military training on all of the new weapons and technology coming out of the Soviet Union. It is a long and thorough course of study that will also include economics, history, communications, and philosophy. When you return to Cuba, you will be on the cutting edge of military matters. You will have knowledge equal or superior to anyone in Cuba, which will make you an extremely valuable asset to the military."

Pino's eyebrows lifted and he let out a whistle, stunned. "I don't know what to say."

Torres smiled, savoring the moment. "We will take in the sights of Moscow, visit Red Square, Lenin's tomb, the Kremlin. It would be a privilege for anyone to go to the Motherland under these circumstances."

"Of course," stammered Pino. He looked briefly out the window and smiled. *If Torres can pull this off, this will be a dream come true. I'll have a future again. Hell, if I play my cards right, I might even get a promotion.*

"Is that a yes?" asked Torres.

Pino beamed his delight. "Definitely," he said, almost tripping over his words. "It would be a great honor. Thank you so much for thinking of me, sir."

Torres nodded. "It will take me a little more than a week to finish up my business. I still need to convince some people regarding your appointment. Let me make myself clear: I am not promising anything. But should I be successful, I will come to get you in ten days. Be ready. Understand?"

"I'll be ready, sir. That goes without saying."

When Torres left, Pino sank into a chair, lost in thought. This was an unprecedented opportunity. He hoped against hope it would materialize. Closing his eyes, he marveled at how well things had

evolved. He had avoided a jail sentence, and now a possibility ex-
isted that could greatly advance his career.

He smiled, thinking of the events of the past year: Mederos's
escape, his fruitless attempt to catch the worm, his loss of rank,
and his misadventures in the cane fields. But now he might be able
to put that all behind him. He vowed that, if approved, he would
make the most of his time in Russia.

He congratulated himself. He had played the army's little game,
and he had played it well. He smiled wryly as he drew himself up,
standing tall for the first time in what seemed like an eternity.

CHAPTER THIRTY-ONE

Torres had his work cut out. Led by First Captain Victor Flores, the committee had deep reservations regarding Pino's proposed trip to Russia, expressing grave concerns regarding the former lieutenant's judgment and temperament.

They felt that his offense was indicative of a deep personality flaw and that he could not possibly have been rehabilitated in such a short time. What's more, they maintained that he should not be rewarded by being placed in a position that could lead to a promotion.

Torres argued that Pino had been an excellent leader in the past and that it was important that he remain current with political philosophy and military issues so he could serve the country in the future. He tried to convince the committee that Pino's behavior, while egregious, did not reflect poorly on his abilities and skills.

What's more, Pino had supported the Party through his many years of service and had not betrayed the revolution in any way. He had not blown up a munitions factory, sabotaged communications, or fomented dissent.

Torres further submitted that the pool of qualified candidates for such an assignment was small. Many officers had obtained their rank by dint of their service to Fidel while fighting in the hills. Yes, they were loyal to *el líder maximo*, but they were basically rough, uneducated men who would embarrass Cuba and undermine her image with the Soviets.

On the other hand, Pino had a keen intellect, a fine education, and a highly polished manner. And despite his previous failure, he remained the best candidate to represent Cuba during these volatile and highly sensitive times.

After more than a week of discussion, the committee relented. But not before making it perfectly clear that the blame would lie at Torres's feet should anything go wrong. He would be held personally responsible for Pino's behavior. Torres, in turn, reminded the committee that he had always been successful in his undertakings and that this endeavor would prove to be no exception.

The next day Torres summoned Pino to the foreman's office to give him the news. Pino had spent the past several days thinking about what it would be like to travel to Russia. Although he exuded an air of sophistication, he had never been on an airplane or even traveled outside Cuba.

The idea of going to such an exotic place had invaded his imagination like a commando on a raid. In fact, he had been so preoccupied with the idea that he had cut himself on the hand with a machete, something he had taken great pains not to do.

Torres greeted Pino with an incandescent smile. Pino's heart skipped a beat in anticipation when he saw the officer's face. The two men looked at each other knowingly, aware that something momentous was about to transpire.

"I have two matters of interest to discuss with you," said Torres. His voice was excited, exuberant.

Pino smiled and nodded.

"First, due to your exemplary behavior, I have recommended that your rank be reinstated along with the salary, rights, and privileges that accompany it. The oversight committee has accepted my recommendation, Lieutenant."

Torres hesitated a moment, watching Pino's expression.

Pino looked at Torres, shocked. This was a development for which he was totally unprepared. Being stripped of his rank was a humiliation that had nearly eaten him alive. Pino considered it an act of satanic surgery, a blow akin to losing his arm. And, like losing a limb, he had abandoned all hope of getting it back. Now Torres had addressed him as lieutenant.

The word pleased more than one of Pino's senses. He silently turned it over in his mouth. It tasted like a chocolate truffle, velvety smooth and sweet. It sounded like the rounded vowels of a creek's burble, like the tenor of his mother's voice interrupting his father's abuse.

A glint of tears entered Pino's eyes before he blinked them away. He was not a man to show emotion.

Pino returned Torres's gaze, feeling gratified and self-satisfied. His strategy had worked. His discipline had paid off. He tried to suppress a smile, but it was almost beyond his ken.

"There's more," said Torres. Pino looked up, hopeful. "This morning your candidacy for training in the Soviet Union was approved."

"I'm going to Russia?"

"You're going to Russia, Lieutenant."

That simple sentence sent something akin to a bolt of electricity through Pino's body. He was awestruck. The excitement was enough to make him dizzy. He knew he should respond in some way, but no words gathered on his tongue. Every cell in his body vibrated in anticipation.

He imagined himself touring the Kremlin. He saw himself drinking vodka and eating borscht with top communist officials. He pictured himself warmed by a fur coat while marveling at the jewel-toned onion domes of St. Basil's Cathedral.

Torres gave Pino a moment to recover. "It's taken a lot of convincing to obtain permission for you to accompany me." His voice had assumed a somber tone. "I've taken a big risk in recommending you. I expect you to pay attention, to follow orders, and to respect the chain of command. You are to have no altercations, not even a hint of conflict arising from your high opinion of yourself. I want you to apply yourself to the best of your ability, to remain humble and on your best behavior. Do I have your word on that?"

Pino gulped down his pride. "You do."

"Good. Then it's settled."

Torres turned and handed Pino a package wrapped in brown paper and string.

"What's this?"

"It's your uniform. We're going to a hotel so you can get cleaned up and change your clothes." He gave Pino the once-over and wrinkled his nose. Pino's beard blued his cheeks, dirt yellowed his ragged nails, and circles of perspiration blackened his shirt. Torres reached into his pocket, withdrew a nail clipper, and tossed it to Pino. "Use this for starters. You certainly can't go to Russia looking like that."

"Yes, sir. Thank you, sir."

Pino's gaze drifted down to the package on his lap, looking at it as if it contained a miracle. *It's strange that my dealings with Mederos have opened a door for me that I never would've dreamed possible.* He smiled at the thought of his nemesis and said to himself, *I'm back in the game, Mederos. You'd better watch out! It may take me years, but this is my ticket to revenge.*

CHAPTER THIRTY-TWO

January was a long, dreary month in Union City. Frank walked down Bergenline Avenue with the wind tattooing his face. A light drizzle misted the sidewalk and hung like crystal beads beneath the streetlights. Crumpled Kool cigarette boxes, crushed Pabst Blue Ribbon cans, and broken beer bottles choked the gutters.

A copy of a crime magazine lay curled beside a Volkswagen Beetle painted in a rainbow of psychedelic colors. Its cover offered a lurid image of a big-busted woman in a tight black skirt. Her torn blouse revealed half-exposed breasts. Fishnet stockings clung to long, shapely legs.

The menacing figure of a criminal lurked behind her, looking like he was ready to attack. She stared at the viewer with fear in her eyes. A gust of wind flipped the magazine's pages, leaving nothing of the image behind.

A chill filled the air, and Frank was eager to get home to Magda. He drew himself up and cinched his scarf tighter around his neck. Red streaks marched across a bruised blue sky. A lone crow cawed from a telephone wire. He stepped over a pile of urine-soaked rags that cushioned a wall sprayed with black paint; jagged, irregular shapes that marked a gang's turf.

Suddenly, the pile moved and an arm emerged. A murmur arose from a mouth Frank could not see. A hand with bony fingers and jagged nails turned against the broken concrete. The man opened his hand beseechingly. Frank leaned down and dropped a quarter into his weathered palm, feeling sympathetic to the circumstances of this poor creature.

On the street corner five men held gloved hands over an oil can fire, its resinous smoke rising in arabesques around their heads. On the opposite corner several young men gathered outside a neighborhood bar, kicking empty cans and cuffing cigarettes. Red neon lights lit their eyes, haunted eyes that were far too old for their faces. Their voices were coarse, their laughter rough. One boy pushed another, a shove that could've easily erupted into a pitched brawl. Frank dug his hands into his coat pocket and slipped past them, unnoticed.

He climbed the stairs, turned the key in the lock, and entered the living room to the apartment. Magda was watching an old movie set in Paris. Her feet rested on the coffee table. Frank looked at the image on the television screen and thought that that's where Magda should live—in a home decorated with silk drapes and mahogany furniture as rich and dark as sable.

Had history taken a different turn she would never be in this city, in this small apartment with its stained porcelain sink, its rusted electric stove, its worn linoleum floor. Frank remembered the house she lived in with her parents in Havana, a place filled with flowers, fine china, and crystal. He wondered whether he would be able to provide his wife with life's necessities, let alone its luxuries.

But more than that, he worried about her safety. He shuddered to think what he would do if something ever happened to Magda. She was his rock, his touchstone, and his raison d'être. He constantly reminded her to lock the doors, and she was good about it, but sometimes it slipped her mind. It was not her habit in Cuba.

Magda looked up and smiled, sweeping her glossy hair away from her face with her hand. She stood, switched off the television set, and nodded toward the bedroom.

The couple walked into the room together, arm and arm. Frank sat down on the bed, untied his shoes, and slipped them off.

He watched as Magda grabbed the bottom of her blue mohair sweater and lifted it above her head, releasing a crackle of static electricity that created small fireworks in the dark. She stood in the shadows in her white nylon slip, the lace cups covering her firm breasts. Her waist was trim, her belly flat. She was still a little shy about revealing her body to Frank, no matter how many times he told her how beautiful she was.

Magda stripped the barrette from her hair, releasing her tresses into a jumble of curls. She kicked off her shoes and unzipped her skirt. Then she walked toward Frank and held his head to her breasts. He buried his face in them, smelling her Jean Naté cologne. He pulled her down next to him in the bed and ran his finger along the length of her nose. She giggled.

"You're tickling me," she said, pulling her face away from his reach.

He began tickling her for real, under her ribs, under her arms until she collapsed, exhausted from laughter. Then he laid her gently back on the pillow and looked at her.

"What?" she asked.

"It's just that I can't believe we're really here—together," he said.

"I know," said Magda. "And we're going to be together forever." She smiled, convinced of her words.

Frank grew quiet for a moment. "Do you mind living here?" It was a question that had nagged him for a while.

"What do you mean? In the States?"

"No, in this apartment."

Magda laughed. "Of course not. Why do you ask?"

"Well, it's nothing like the house you grew up in. I just wondered if—"

Magda wrinkled her nose as if to scold Frank. "Stop," she said. "This is our home. *Ours!* It has everything we need—a bedroom, a bathroom, a living room. My parents are nearby. We have a good landlord. It's just fine. It doesn't matter where we live as long as we're together."

"You're sure?"

"Of course. Besides, we won't live here forever. We'll make our way, get a car, buy a house. You've got to believe, Frank."

"I do. But sometimes I doubt my ability to make a nice life for us."

A look of concern crossed Magda's eyes, as if she were searching for words of encouragement that were beyond her grasp. Then her face brightened.

"What?" Frank asked.

Magda took his hand in hers and looked him in the eyes. "Remember the refrigerator?"

Frank pictured Pedro holding up traffic and laughter bubbled up his throat.

"How could I forget?"

He thought about the dogs, the cockroaches, and Pedro giving drivers the peace sign. He thought about the look on his uncle's face as they pushed the refrigerator up three flights of stairs. He knew Magda was thinking the same thing. They began to chuckle and then the laughter overtook them. They howled until their stomachs ached, and they had to wipe tears from their eyes. They lay back on the bed, exhausted. Magda turned and said, "You know, it's all about the refrigerator, Frank."

"What do you mean?"

She lifted her body on her elbow. "When you heard about the refrigerator, you grabbed the chance to get it. It didn't matter that you had to drag it up and down ten city blocks. Sure it was difficult. So was defecting. But when you set your sights on something, you do it. You don't give up. That's who you are, Frank. That's why I'm not worried about our future."

Frank returned Magda's gaze, amazed at how positive she was, always encouraging him. "That's what you think?" he said, wanting her to go on talking, but not wanting to say so.

"That's what I think. We're going to make it, Frank. We have skills and abilities. We're a team—a great team. We'll figure it out. You'll see. Besides, I'm just grateful to have you here with me and to be in America."

"Thanks, I needed to hear that." Frank gathered Magda in the crook of his arm and looked at the ceiling. "I'm grateful to be in

America too. It's so good to be able to speak your mind without fear of repercussions."

They lay in silence for a moment. Frank lowered his chin on top of Magda's head. "Do you miss Cuba?" he asked.

Magda's expression softened. "Yes. I miss the birds, the beach, the flowers—"

Frank nodded. "Me too, but I miss the people more."

Magda grew more somber. "So do I, but at least I have my family here. But you left everyone behind."

"Not everyone. I have you."

"I know, but still—"

Frank heaved a sigh. "I do miss them terribly."

"Who do you miss the most?" A look of concern marched across Magda's eyes.

Frank thought for a moment. He was feeling a dull ache of vacancy, like he was lost in the woods and couldn't find his way home. "It depends," he said. "Sometimes it's my mother and father. Sometimes Abuelo. To tell you the truth, I'm afraid they'll die before I get to see them again."

Magda nodded and lifted a hand to stroke Frank's cheek. "And your siblings, your friends?"

"Of course, I wonder how they're doing, how they're faring under Fidel." Frank hesitated a moment. "I got a letter from my mother yesterday."

"And you didn't show it to me?"

"I needed some time before I talked about it."

"Why, what happened?"

"The communists tore down Abuelo's house and sent him to an old-age home. My mother said he's devastated."

Magda shook her head in consternation. "Your grandfather is perfectly healthy and able to care for himself. Why would they do such a thing?"

"It may be in retaliation for my escape. That's the kind of thing those bastards do. I can't be sure, but I feel terrible. I haven't been able to get it out of my head all day."

Magda covered her mouth with her hand. "That's terrible. And there's nothing anyone can do about it?"

"Of course not. You know that."

The couple sat in silence for a while. Magda looked at Frank. "What else can't you get out of your head?"

"I worry about Manny and Lazo. Last night I had a nightmare about something happening to them. I can't bring it to mind, but I know it was bad. They stuck their necks out for me. I owe them, really owe them."

"I know. You always say that."

"Because it's true. I wouldn't be here without them. In fact, I wouldn't be here without a lot of people."

Magda brightened. "But you are here," she said, reaching for Frank. Frank took his wife in his arms and kissed her on the lips, lightly at first and then more eagerly. His melancholy lifted, and he suddenly felt lightheaded with anticipation.

Magda opened her mouth to accept his tongue, responding with a passion that matched his own. He ran his fingers through her hair, feeling its texture, its silkiness. He laid her on her back and covered her body with his, reveling in her curves and the sweetness of her skin.

He thought about all the times he had longed just to touch Magda's hand. She was his first love, his only love. She always seemed so beautiful, so unattainable, at least to him. He remembered walking past her parents' house on a spring evening, hoping she would be outside on her balcony and honor him with a wave. That was before Fidel interrupted their lives. Before the army. Before his escape.

For as long as Frank could remember, he had carried Magda's face in his mind's eye, heard her voice in his dreams. He still couldn't believe it when he found her in the same room with him. Her mere presence lifted his spirits. And here she was, laughing and talking with him in bed.

"Just a minute," said Magda. She sat up briefly, worked her slip over her head, and unhooked her bra. Her breasts stood out straight from her chest, her nipples the color of wine. The sight of them made Frank drunk with desire. "If only the nuns could see me now," she said, and laughed merrily.

Frank reached for Magda, took her in his arms, and laid her gently down on the sheets. He held her breasts in his hands and moved his mouth to her nipples as she wrapped her slim legs around him. He kissed her neck, her shoulders, and the hollow between her breasts. Heat suffused his body, and he felt himself stiffen. He made love to her gently, patiently, waiting for her to want him as much as he wanted her. Magda made a muffled cry as Frank entered her, slowly, carefully, watching her expression to make sure he wasn't hurting her. She moved beneath him, her breathing becoming more labored. She grabbed his back, pulling him toward her, holding his buttocks, taking him deeper inside her. Finally, she shuddered and called out Frank's name. Then they made love again. They were insatiable. It was hours before they fell off to sleep.

When the early morning sun danced on his eyelids, Frank rose on his elbows and studied Magda asleep next to him. Her hair was strewn about the pillow like cherry blossoms. He couldn't help himself. He reached over and touched her forehead, running his forefinger along the ridge of her eyebrows, stroking her cheeks with the back of his hand.

He looked down at her hands and saw the trinket ring he had given her when they first declared their love for each other. She was fourteen at the time. He told her then that it was a token of his love, but that he would buy her a real diamond someday. He hadn't been able to afford one yet. Someday, perhaps.

Magda murmured incoherently, sighed softly, and turned over. She pulled her knees to her chest and nestled her head deeper into the pillow. Frank pulled the sheet up to cover her back, draped his arm around her waist, and nuzzled her neck. *How could her skin be this soft, this smooth? Impossible!* He listened to the rhythm of Magda's breathing, and thought how lucky he was to have such a wonderful woman in his life.

Frank worried whether he'd ever speak English well enough to find a good job, to succeed. He knew the best time to learn a language is when you are a child, and he'd have to work extra hard to learn English at his age. But he was determined to do it. Between Magda and Marcos he was starting to get the hang of English vocabulary, grammar, and syntax, but he had much work to do before he was fluent.

Frank thought about his inadequacies and the skeleton of fear that had shaped his world since he arrived in America. He was always looking over his shoulder, startled at the slightest noise, afraid that someone was after him, or worse, after his beloved. His nightmares were frequent and frightening.

Magda said it would take time for his nerves to settle down after his escape, and he wanted to believe her. But the men standing outside on the street corners reminded him that tyranny takes many forms. The last thing he wanted was for Magda to be stalked by the kind of fear he had come to know.

Some women were too beautiful, too sweet, too trusting for their own good. Magda was one of them. He wanted to protect her. She had led a sheltered life, but at least she was smart. Very smart. That would help.

Frank glanced at the nightstand and saw a paper sitting near the lamp. He picked it up and squinted, adjusting his eyes so he could read the words in the dim light. It was a poem, written by Magda, scribbled in Spanish, words smudged, erased, crossed out, circled with arrows to be inserted here, there. It spoke of love, of Frank.

Suddenly, he thought of his mother, her gestures, her hands, soft and brown, as she removed a dessert from the oven, drew a needle through a button, tucked him into bed. He remembered being a child and her washing soapsuds from his hair and teaching him how to tie his shoes one loop at a time.

He tried to conjure up her face, but it was like a dream he couldn't hold onto. But he could still hear her voice telling him to be brave, to be strong. He thought of Cuba, of the waves crashing like shattered glass along the *Malecón*, of bright butterflies riding the wind like horses galloping the plains.

Suddenly a song by Up with People ran through his head. Some- one had recently sung it at the factory.

> *Freedom isn't free!*
> *Freedom isn't free!*
> *You've gotta pay a price*
> *You've gotta sacrifice*
> *For your liberty.*

He was free, and he was so grateful to be in America, in a land where he could make his way, pursue his dreams, and speak his truth without the threat of torture or death. But he had paid a price. Everything has a price.

But Frank didn't want the price to include Magda being robbed or mugged—or worse. He comforted himself with the thought that Abuelo once said that life's troubles seldom turn out to be the ones you worry about.

Frank wondered what life was like for Abuelo in the old-age home. Did he know people there? Had he made friends? Did he play dominoes? Frank couldn't imagine his grandfather without his boat and his fishing pole.

Frank missed his family. And he knew they missed him. He leaned back on his pillow, looked up at the ceiling, and allowed his tears to muffle his memories.

CHAPTER THIRTY-THREE

Pino arrived in the Soviet Union, grateful to First Lieutenant Torres for the opportunity to rebuild his career. He was in Russia to pursue the equivalent of a master's degree in one of the Motherland's finest military academies. This was a chance of a lifetime, and Pino was determined to make the most of it. But it was not easy.

Born and raised in Cuba, Pino found the Russian winters to be long, dreary, and gray as mud. Beginning in October, ferocious winds funneled down Russian streets as steady and relentless as an army on the march. The winter brought snow that swirled in blinding sheets, hugging the trunks of trees before obscuring windows and doors.

Freezing rain slicked the lieutenant's thick hair and frosted his eyebrows with tiny icicles. Ice crunched beneath his boots and his feet rebelled with toenails as brittle as bone. Pino's hands, ears, and lips became permanently chapped, and he was constantly scraping dead skin from his lips, heels, and hands.

Although brilliant, Pino found his studies to be tedious. He excelled at math and science but struggled to learn Russian. The language sounded harsh to his ears, and the Cyrillic alphabet was strange and unfamiliar. Although the academy offered classes for Spanish-speaking students in their native tongue, the professors' accents were often thick and incomprehensible. Still, Pino was determined to finish at the top of his class.

In addition to his rigorous physical training, Pino tackled a wide range of subjects, including history, philosophy, psychology, and political science. He enjoyed reading the writings of Chekhov,

Tolstoy, and Dostoevsky, but he preferred classes in military leadership, strategy, and tactics. He improved his parachute jumping and survival tactics. He excelled at the use of explosives and gained further expertise in the demolition of bridges, factories, oil refineries, and utility companies.

He was schooled in Soviet weapons, their nature, use, and deployment. He became skilled in the assembly and disassembly of firearms—rifles, pistols, and machine guns, including AK-47s. He memorized the location and purpose of strategic Soviet and American bases around the world and knew their strengths and vulnerabilities.

Having learned his lessons in the cane fields, Pino worked diligently to bond with the other soldiers. He expressed an interest in their families and friends and helped them with their studies. He did favors for his fellow officers, knowing the contacts he made in Russia would serve him well when he returned to Cuba.

But it was not all work. While in the Soviet Union, Pino broadened his horizons in a number of ways. A former scotch drinker, he developed a taste for vodka and drank it with relish and near abandon with his comrades. He dined on bowls of borscht and lobio, a thick red bean soup, which he enjoyed with hearty peasant bread. He even ate some Ukrainian delicacies, including homemade sausages and black bread with salo, a dish made from salt-cured pig fat. He attended the ballet, gained an ear for poetry, learned to play chess, and improved his backgammon game.

Due to his excellent performance, Pino was among a group of select soldiers who were treated to a trip to Leningrad. The city was constructed on what was originally more than one hundred islands formed by small bodies of water that flow into the Baltic Sea. Gazing at the map, Pino wondered how much Leningrad resembled Venice or Amsterdam, cities he hoped to visit one day.

The entourage arrived during the "White Nights," the eighty evenings when the sun barely sets on this grand city. Full of wonder and enthusiasm, Pino traveled by riverboat toward the former winter palace of the czars, the Hermitage.

Pino and his comrades gazed at the art museum that contained priceless treasures. Their minders explained how Catherine the Great had begun to acquire the collection and had chosen to spend her private time in the shadow of her beloved paintings and sculptures. Pino was dazzled by the palace's scale and splendor.

He then boarded a barge that wended its way down the Neva River to Zayachy Island where he toured the Russian Orthodox Cathedral of Saints Peter and Paul. The building was turned into a museum in 1924 and contained the remains of almost all the Russian emperors and empresses, including Peter the Great.

Looking up at the breathtaking bell tower reminded Pino of pictures he'd seen of the destruction of the gold-domed Cathedral of Christ the Savior in Moscow. The largest Orthodox cathedral in the world had been demolished to make way for the Palace of the Soviets, which was never completed. In 1958 Nikita Khrushchev turned the gaping hole into the world's largest outdoor swimming pool.

On the afternoon of January 22, 1969, Pino stood with a group of soldiers outside the Borovitsky Gate at the Kremlin. They were awaiting a special motorcade bearing the cosmonauts of the Soyuz 4 and Soyuz 5 who had recently completed their successful space mission.

The heroes were to be honored at a ceremony inside the Kremlin's Palace of Congresses. They rode in an open-air limousine, waving to the crowds. Suddenly, several shots rang out. Pino ducked and covered his head. All hell broke loose with security officers scrambling to do their jobs. The KGB soon whisked away a young man disguised in a police uniform.

The would-be assassin had assumed the limo carried General Secretary of the Soviet Union Leonid Brezhnev. It did not. The Soviet leader was traveling in a different car and escaped unharmed. The ceremony continued as planned, but it made Pino think of Mederos. It left him feeling even more convinced that worms who oppose the government should be wiped from the face of the earth.

Torres had told Pino that if he worked hard he could earn a promotion upon graduation. Pino did everything in his power to make that happen.

On a fine day in May, Pino learned that his disciplined study, his extraordinary dedication, and his keen intellect had served him well. Torres informed him that he was one of only ten graduates of the academy to be awarded the rank of captain. For a brief moment, Pino's heart felt as light as helium. He accepted the news with smug satisfaction and an internal smile.

Captain Pino stood at his graduation ceremony, thinking of the might of the Soviet Union, proud to have his diploma of this great nation in hand, and even prouder that his five years in Russia had proved so productive. He was rehabilitated. He had acquired a plethora of new skills and a host of powerful friends. More importantly, he had a gleaming medal on his chest that announced his rank. He was happy. His hand drifted upward to caress the scar on his jaw. His time in the cane fields had been worth it.

Now he had important work to do.

CHAPTER THIRTY-FOUR

Thanks to Marcos's tutoring, Frank received his GED a year after he arrived in the States. Frank and Magda started taking courses at St. Peter's College in Jersey City. Frank took some business courses while Magda pursued a degree in computer science.

Frank had left his job in Clifton and had been hired by R. G. Thomas Corporation in Palisades Park. He made aluminum shells for bombs used in the Vietnam War.

Magda had landed a job at Merrill Lynch in New York City. She commuted to the city and was making a good salary. By Cuban standards, it was a small fortune. She had been promoted and was overseeing an exciting new project. Her goal was to become one of the few women computer scientists on the East Coast.

On a Friday night in mid-September, a night when Frank and Magda usually dined out, Magda called Frank at work. She didn't sound like herself. She told her husband that she wanted to eat at home. She said she had something important to tell him. Frank wondered whether she had received a promotion. Puzzled, he hurried home.

When Frank walked in the door, the house was clean, the table was set with flowers and candles, and Magda was in the kitchen cooking Frank's favorite meal—roast pork, mashed potatoes, and salad. A bottle of red wine sat uncorked on the table.

After kissing his wife, Frank showered and changed his clothes for dinner. Magda lit the candles as he came to the table. She wore a black skirt and a white silk blouse. A strand of pearls circled her neck. Candlelight danced off her hair.

Frank settled himself in his chair and looked across the table at Magda. She had a coy look on her face.

"What's up?" asked Frank. He glanced at the table. "This looks lovely. It must mean good news."

Magda smiled. She had never looked so happy. "I just got a call from Dr. Alexander."

"And?"

"And you are going to be a father."

Frank sat back in his chair and dropped his napkin on the table. His face lit like a grassfire. He whistled his joy. "Really? You're sure?"

"I'm sure."

Frank got up from his chair, beaming. This was totally unexpected news. He was filled with a sense of pride and wonder. He and Magda were going to have a child, and their baby would be born in America—free from the treachery of Fidel. This was the icing on the cake, the fulfillment of Frank's dreams.

"We're having a baby, our baby—an American citizen," he said. "Can you believe it?"

Magda laughed. They stood and hugged. Frank's thoughts turned to his mother, father, and grandfather. This would be his parents' first grandchild and Abuelo's first great-grandchild. He imagined how thrilled they'd be when he telegrammed them the news.

Frank remembered when his mother was pregnant with his siblings. By the seventh month of her pregnancies, her belly was so big she couldn't find a comfortable position to sleep. She suffered from swollen ankles, heartburn, and back pain. Suddenly, Frank felt very protective of Magda.

"Do you feel okay?"

Magda laughed. "I feel fine."

"So what do we do now? Did you tell anybody? Does anybody else know?"

"No, you are the first."

"Wait till your parents find out!"

Magda giggled and held her hands over her stomach. "I know."

"Have you thought of names?"

"I have."

"So?"

"I was thinking of calling the baby Frank, if it's a boy."

"And if it's a little girl?"

"If it's a girl, I'd like to call her Darlene."

"Then Darlene it is."

"It's okay with you?"

"Whatever you want is okay with me. I'm just so happy we're going to have a child."

"Would you rather have a boy or a girl?"

Frank laughed. "It doesn't matter. It's our baby either way."

Magda smiled. "Are you sure you don't want a boy?"

"I want a baby—whatever we have."

"Good. That's how I feel too."

Frank and Magda were so excited they could hardly sleep. They talked into the wee hours of the morning about what it would be like to have a child of their own.

They made plans for the baby's christening and talked about the colors for the nursery. Frank told Magda he hoped the baby would look like her, and she said she hoped it would look like him.

Frank was afraid something might go wrong with the pregnancy, but he didn't want to voice his concerns to Magda. She must've been thinking the same thing. She said she wanted to wait a few weeks before telling anyone—even her parents—the news.

Frank felt like he was harboring an amazing secret, like he was the first man in the world to have a baby. His friends kept asking him what he was always smiling about, and he told them "the weather"—even when it was raining. He'd never been so excited in his life.

All of that paled when he first felt the baby kick. For several days, Magda had sensed butterflies in her stomach, but she thought it was gas. A week later she felt the baby move.

Three weeks later, Magda placed Frank's palm on her swollen belly and covered his hand with hers. "There," she said. "Do you feel it?"

Frank felt what he thought was his child's foot kicking against his wife's stomach. It was a moment he would never forget. He wiped a tear from his eye.

Frank accompanied Magda to all her doctor's appointments to make sure her pregnancy was progressing normally. By the end of April, she looked like she would burst. Her breasts had almost doubled in size. She cupped her stomach with both hands when she walked, and she held the small of her back with one hand when she stood.

At one o'clock on the afternoon of May 5, 1970, Magda called Frank to tell him her water had broken. Frank called Magda's parents and asked them to come to the Union City Hospital.

Frank was a wreck, pacing the floor like a caged animal. Drinking great quantities of coffee, he was so wound up he asked every doctor and nurse he saw about Magda's condition. None of them knew a thing. Time unraveled at the pace of a drugged turtle.

Finally, the doctor emerged from the delivery room, removing a pair of latex gloves from his hands. His surgical mask sat beneath his chin. He was smiling ear to ear. Frank looked at him, sensing good news.

"Is Magda okay?"

"She's fine. You have a healthy baby girl."

"A girl," said Frank, elated. "Darlene. Little Darlene." He closed his eyes and whispered a prayer of thanks. "Does she look like Magda?"

"She's beautiful, just like your wife."

Frank laughed and hugged Magda's parents. He went home that night feeling like he had conquered the world, like he had a hundred medals on his chest.

●　●　●

Darlene was the spitting image of her mother. From the very start, she was the apple of Frank's eye. He held her, fed her, and diapered her. He walked with her at night so Magda could get some sleep.

As Darlene grew, the couple realized that they needed more space, so they bought a house in Lincoln Park, a short drive from Union City. Darlene's room was decorated with pictures of fairies and a zoo of stuffed animals. Darlene liked to dress up in sparkly things, the more sparkles the better. A swing set occupied a small plot of land in back of the house. Magda went back to work in New York City, and her mother and aunt helped with child care.

By 1975, Frank and Magda were living the American Dream. Magda had earned a bachelor's degree in computer science and had attained her goal of becoming a computer analyst. Frank owned a Blimpie's franchise in Montclair, New Jersey, where he sold sandwiches, sweets, and beverages. He would soon open another franchise.

Frank and Magda had made a number of friends and enjoyed a full social life. The couple's calendar was crammed with an endless parade of weddings, showers, and baptisms. They entertained at home, dined out in restaurants, and had just seen the summer blockbuster movie *Jaws*.

Magda was loving and cheerful and could not have been more fun. Frank had a beautiful wife, a good job, and a five-year-old whom he adored. He was happy and content. He had no idea life could be so good.

That summer Frank and Magda rented a rustic cabin in the Pocono Mountains for a week with some friends. Overlooking Sunrise Lake, it was a quiet spot with oak, maple, and cedar trees circling a pristine body of water. Pine scented the air.

Perched high, the cabin provided a spectacular view. It had three bedrooms and a large, wraparound deck. Frank liked to get up early, make coffee, and watch the mist rise over the lake. Dew sparkled from evergreen needles. It was his quiet time, his time to think and reflect.

Motorboats were forbidden on the lake. Frank wasn't sure why. Perhaps, it was so not to disturb the tranquility of the area. Or maybe it was to protect the wildlife. Occasionally, a canoe paddle slapped the water.

The two couples spent their time hiking, fishing, and swimming. From the deck, they watched snow-white ducks skim the lake and listened to the trill of birds and the honk of Canada geese. Darlene spent her time practicing the doggy paddle and splashing around in her yellow Mickey Mouse tube. On several nights the vacationers ate the day's catch, freshly filleted trout. The men argued over who had caught the biggest fish. Although Darlene declared it "yucky" and covered her eyes, fish cleaning held a fascination for her. She was curious about the fish's organs and ran to Frank's side whenever he was about to slice open a trout.

The next-to-last night of their vacation was hot and humid. Nobody felt like cooking, so they decided to eat at a local restaurant. As they waited in line to be seated, Frank wondered about the yellow silk scarf Magda had tied around her neck. It struck him as odd—she never bothered with scarves in the summertime. He turned to her and asked, "Aren't you hot with that on?"

Magda drew a noticeable breath, raised her hand to her throat, and fingered the scarf.

"I'm fine," she said. But her voice was strained.

"I know you're fine," Frank said lightly. "I just thought you might be hot."

Magda shook her head and stiffened before releasing his hand. "I'm not hot."

She turned to her friend and said, "I'm off to the ladies' room. Want to join me?"

Magda turned and walked away. Frank shrugged his curiosity to his friend and decided not to press the point further.

Although the temperature climbed well into the nineties the next day, Magda wore her scarf again. She sat on an Adirondack chair reading a romance novel with the brim of her straw hat covering her neck. She had turned up the collar of her blouse. Frank made a mental note, but did not question her about it.

As the day progressed, Magda became more and more distracted. She would read a couple of pages of her book, place it on her lap, and stare into space. She was a voracious reader, devouring books one after another. This was not like her.

"What's the matter?" Frank asked. "Aren't you enjoying your book?"

Magda looked at him blankly, like she didn't know what he was talking about.

"What?" she said and then looked down at her book. "Oh, no, it's fine."

Late that afternoon Magda excused herself to take a shower. As Frank walked past the bathroom he thought he heard Magda crying. He listened at the door, wondering what could be wrong.

He knocked softly. "Are you okay in there, honey?"

The pipes moaned as Magda turned off the shower and hollered back, "I'm fine. Really!"

"You're sure?"

"Yes, don't worry about me. I'll be out in a minute."

Hearing the hum of Magda's hair dryer, Frank closed the bedroom door to allow her to dress for dinner. He wondered whether he had imagined her sobs.

When Magda came down the stairs, she was wreathed in smiles. She was dressed in a sleeveless shirtwaist with her collar upturned and the same scarf wound around her neck. A pair of red, beaded earrings dangled from her lobes.

Magda chatted merrily at dinner, refilling glasses with beer and iced tea and serving hamburgers, potato salad, and Jersey corn. Everyone loved the juicy beefsteak tomatoes. She served Breyers vanilla ice cream and ripe watermelon for dessert while the conversation turned to politics and sports.

After dinner the couples played a game of hearts. As usual, Magda counted all the cards. Twice she dumped the queen of spades on Frank. Twice she took the jack of diamonds. As usual, she won.

It was a wonderful week and, with the exception of the scarf, everything seemed perfectly normal.

CHAPTER THIRTY-FIVE

When they got home, Magda sat at the kitchen table in white shorts and a blue blouse that hugged her waist. She slipped off her sandals, crossed her legs, and began twirling a strand of hair around her finger. Darlene ran outside and hopped on the swing. Every time she pumped her legs, the swing squeaked in protest. Frank would oil the chains later, but right now he had more important things on his mind.

He put a kettle of water down to boil and made Magda a pot of orange pekoe tea. She liked it light and drank it plain, no milk, no sugar, no fuss. He unwrapped a sleeve of graham crackers and reached for the jar of peanut butter.

He placed the snack on the table in front of his wife. Magda nib- bled on half a cracker and then pushed the plate away. She wiped her hands on a napkin and turned her gaze toward the hallway. The suitcases sat on the floor.

"I need to unpack and do the laundry," she said.

"I know, but right now we have to talk."

Frank sat on the chair opposite Magda and took her hand.

Magda nodded, her gaze drifting out the window. They heard a basketball bouncing down the sidewalk. A boy challenged someone to play.

"Okay," said Magda. She sounded resigned. A minute crawled by while they listened to the hum of the refrigerator.

"Do you want to tell me about the scarf?"

Magda released Frank's hand and touched her scarf with her fingers. "It's nothing. It's just—"

"If it's nothing, let me see."

Magda sighed, used one hand to lift her hair and the other to unknot the scarf. Frank sucked in his breath when the silk rectangle slipped to the floor. He stood and ran his fingers over Magda's throat. Lumps lined both sides of her neck.

"How long have you had these?"

Magda hesitated. "A few days. I noticed them before we went on vacation. Do they look bad?"

Frank shook his head, wondering what in the world could've caused such a thing.

"Bad enough. Do they hurt?"

"Not really. Do you think I should see a doctor?"

"Yes, I think you should see a doctor. In fact, I think you should make an appointment right away."

A week later Frank and Magda sat awaiting test results in the pine-paneled office of Dr. Vincent D'Alessandro. A prayer plant grew next to a snake plant in a yellow glazed pot on the doctor's desk. Its mahogany-spotted leaves were open, supplicant. Frank wondered whether the doctor had chosen to combine those varieties of plants on purpose. Their juxtaposition seemed significant.

Magda and Frank stood when the doctor entered the office. He was in his mid-forties with graying hair and a small paunch. A pair of horn-rimmed glasses framed his warm brown eyes and a stethoscope circled his neck. Thick-soled shoes supported his feet. He took a seat behind his desk and looked back and forth at Frank and Magda in a paternal fashion.

He took a deep breath. "I'm afraid I have bad news for you," he said. There was a slight break in his voice.

Magda and Frank exchanged worried glances. They had no idea what the news could be.

Dr. D'Alessandro hesitated. "There's no good way to tell you this."

"Please," said Frank. "Just spit it out."

"The tests show that Magda has Hodgkin's disease."

Frank and Magda looked at each other, puzzled. Neither of them had ever heard of this disease. But the look on the doctor's face told them that it might be something serious. Frank was the first to speak.

"I'm sorry. I don't understand. What exactly is Hodgkin's disease?" The doctor's eyes clouded over. He looked somber and sad.

"It's a disease of the glands. It often strikes people in their twenties."

"Okay," Frank said, slowly digesting this information. Whatever it was, he couldn't imagine it could be that bad. He looked at Magda. Her face was strained, and she held her body the way she did when she expected bad news. But her complexion was rosy, her weight normal. With the exception of the lumps, she looked perfectly healthy.

"What can be done about it?" Frank asked. "Will she need surgery?"

The doctor's face grew grave. "Well, as you know, this is a form of cancer—"

Suddenly, Frank felt like the floor had collapsed beneath him. The room swam before his eyes and his vision blurred. The air became still. He heard Magda suck in her breath. He watched the blood drain from her face as she raised her hand to cover her mouth.

"Cancer?" Frank croaked. "I'm sorry, but my wife doesn't have cancer. Look at her. She's the picture of health. This must be a mistake. Besides, she's only twenty-four—far too young to have cancer."

The doctor entwined his fingers and placed them on the desk in front of him. It reminded Frank of how he folded his hands in grammar school. "I'm sorry. I know this comes as shock to you both. But Magda does indeed have cancer."

Frank's first instinct was to grab Magda by the hand and run out the door. He told himself this had to be a mistake. That the tests must be wrong. That she had been misdiagnosed. Instead, he took a deep breath to steady himself. He looked for Magda's reaction. Her expression was frozen, as if she were silently processing the information.

"Well, what can be done about it?" asked Frank, surprised that his voice sounded so harsh.

"Hodgkin's is a very serious disease. We need to conduct more tests to see whether the cancer has spread. In any event, Magda will have to undergo chemotherapy and radiation therapy."

Frank furrowed his brow, trying to maintain his equilibrium. He didn't want to show his alarm in front of Magda. "Can this thing be cured?"

The doctor shook his head. "Chemotherapy is very powerful at killing cancer cells. But it doesn't discriminate. It kills bone marrow as well as healthy cells, making it very tricky. Sometimes you think you have killed all the cells, but they are stealthy."

Frank tried to wrap his mind around what the doctor was saying. He sat in silence for a minute before he managed to ask, "What can we expect in terms of side effects?"

The doctor's gaze fell upon Magda. He puffed out some air. Frank could tell this was a difficult conversation for him. "Your wife will lose her hair and will be very nauseated." He pursed his lips. "She will develop mouth sores, lose her appetite, and drop some weight."

"How much weight?" Frank asked, more to hear the sound of his own voice than to learn the answer. He felt disoriented and was desperate to act like he was in control.

The doctor studied Magda for a moment. "It depends on how her digestive system responds to the treatment. But twenty to thirty pounds would not be out of the question." Magda was slim, and Frank tried to imagine what she'd look like with that kind of weight loss.

"Anything else?"

"She will experience a great deal of fatigue and will require a lot of sleep. It won't be an easy or pretty process for either of you. But it's her only chance."

Frank felt like a jackhammer was pounding in his chest. "So you're telling me that this disease could kill my wife?"

The doctor glanced out the window. Frank got the feeling he was trying to avoid the question. Finally, he said, "No one knows what the future will bring. But as it stands now, without treatment, she will be dead within three years." He hesitated. "Even with treatment there's no guarantee she will live that long."

Frank sat back in his chair and reached for Magda's hand. Neither of them had the wherewithal to speak. Moisture sprung to Frank's eyes, and Magda wiped a tear off her cheek with the back of her hand. Her jaw trembled as she tried to control her emotions.

Dr. D'Alessandro studied them for a moment before grabbing a pen. The sound of paper being ripped from a notepad sliced the air. A string of dried glue hung from the corner of the pad. The doctor rolled it into a ball between his thumb and forefinger and dropped it into the wastebasket.

"We don't have all the answers yet," he said. "We need to run more tests—biopsy the liver and lymph nodes. We can either do them here in Montclair, or I can refer you to the top man in the field at Mount Sinai Hospital in New York City. He's had some success with this disease." He scribbled something quickly on the slip of paper and handed it to Frank.

"Here's the name of the man I recommend—Dr. Hoffman." He nodded toward the reception area. "Have my secretary make an appointment for you."

"How soon do we need to move on this?" Frank asked.

Dr. D'Alessandro tapped the face of his watch with his forefinger and said, "If she were my wife, I'd have her at Mount Sinai Hospital first thing in the morning."

Frank nodded to Magda, and they stumbled out the door.

CHAPTER THIRTY-SIX

Magda was beginning her thirteen-week course of chemotherapy when Frank went to the local library to do some research. He was eager to learn all he could about Hodgkin's disease. He pulled pertinent books and magazines from the shelves, and settled himself at a long, wooden table. While the material was difficult to understand, he got the gist of what he sought, and it was devastating.

The literature confirmed that the average life expectancy for Hodgkin's disease following diagnosis was three years. But the doctor failed to mention that no one, but no one, survived the disease. It was a virtual death sentence.

The reality of what he and Magda faced hit Frank like a blow from a heavyweight boxer. For a moment, he felt like he couldn't breathe. He leaned back in his chair and tried to recall the name of the saint of lost causes. He thought he was an apostle. Saint Peter? Saint John? Saint Jude? He couldn't bring his name to mind. He said a quick prayer to him anyway.

As Frank recalled the side effects Dr. Hoffman had told them about, it felt like blue shadows blurring his mind. He looked out the window. The leaves on the trees looked like daggers, and the air smelled of a thunderstorm. He closed the periodical he was reading and folded his arms behind his head.

He was used to thinking his way out of a problem. Fighting his way out. Working it through. Was that possible in this situation? Or did he have to resign himself to losing Magda to this dreadful disease? The thought was almost too much to bear.

This can't be happening. Not now. Not to my beautiful Magda. Not after we've made such a nice life together. Not after all I've been through to get to her. And what about Darlene? She's only five. She's so close to her mother. How will I comfort her? How will she cope? How will I?

Fear invaded every cell of Frank's body. Never had he experienced such a feeling. Even when Pino stalked him in Cuba. Even when he battled the open sea.

At least then he had a chance. He could use his strength and his wits to survive. But this? With this he was helpless. He tried to analyze his fear, but it was primal, beyond rational thought. It was fear of loss, fear of facing a life without Magda, fear of raising his daughter alone.

A headache gathered above his eyebrows and he rubbed his forehead, wondering how he and Magda could turn the odds in their favor. It seemed undoable, overwhelming.

Frank's throat clogged with sorrow, but he couldn't cry in the library. Eyes moist with tears, he stumbled to the men's room and entered a stall. He had just latched the door when the sobs erupted like a warm geyser, and his whole body shook with grief.

That night Frank and Magda had a long talk. Seeking hope, they comforted each other with the idea that if conquering Hodgkin's disease were somehow doable, they were the ones to do it. They decided they could beat the cancer the same way they had beaten the communists—with extraordinary effort and determination.

They reasoned that new therapies were entering the pipeline every day. That radiation and chemotherapy would soon be a thing of the past, that medical technology would quickly advance to the point where a pill alone could cure cancer. They just needed to buy time. In the meantime, Magda would endure the treatments and fight the cancer with every fiber of her being. They would shield Darlene as well as they could from the emotional trauma of the situation. And Frank would do everything possible to help.

A couple of days later, while Frank was taking Magda to the hospital, he rolled down the car windows to get some air. They were driving about fifty miles per hour and the breeze caressed his face. Out of the corner of his eye he saw something black fly by and hit the back windshield. At first Frank thought it was a bird. But it made no noise. And how could a bird get into the car? Frank looked at Magda. A bald spot the size of a half dollar had appeared on her head.

Frank was horrified but Magda only laughed. "My hair is not only blowing," she said, "it's blowing *off*. I want you to shave my head tonight, and tomorrow I'll get a wig."

"Are you sure?"

"I'm sure."

After dinner, Magda sat on a kitchen chair. Wrapped in a white sheet, she handed Frank a pair of scissors and a razor. "Take it off," she said. "I'd rather be in charge of losing my hair than have it fall off by itself. There is no point in drawing out this process."

Frank made a small noise in his throat, took her hair in his hands and drew it to his lips. He wanted to feel its texture, to run his fingers through it, to smell its fragrance one last time. He sheared off her hair at the base of her head. It fell in strands of curls that decorated the linoleum floor.

Magda sat stiffly, resisting the urge to cry. Darlene entered the room.

When she saw her mother, she began to sob. Magda comforted her daughter in her arms, casting aside her own emotions. "It's okay," she said bravely. "Mommy just got a new haircut."

Darlene looked up at her mother and said, "I don't like your haircut—you look like a daddy instead of a mommy."

"I know," said Magda. "It's funny looking, isn't it? But tomorrow I'm going to get some brand-new hair, and you will like it very much!"

"Promise?"

Tears formed in Magda's eyes. "Promise," she said.

The real suffering began shortly thereafter. Life soon devolved into a series of physical assaults visited upon Magda's body, from projectile vomiting to fevers and night sweats. Sores sprouted in her mouth and she found it difficult to eat all but the softest and smoothest of foods. Frank made her fruit shakes in the blender using bananas, blueberries, and milk. It seemed like Jell-O and ice cream kept her alive.

Magda gave up her job at Merrill Lynch, finding it impossible to continue. She missed her coworkers and talked about going back to being a computer analyst someday. She dreamt about her work almost every night and told Frank her dreams in the morning. They were always about a new project she was working on, one where she was just on the cusp of a breakthrough.

Magda's illness took its toll on Darlene, who argued with her doll and woke up several times a night pounding her little fists against the mattress. Clinging to her "blankie," she would join Frank and Magda in bed to banish her nightmares.

Sick and exhausted, Magda mothered Darlene the best she could. But there were days when the energy level of a five-year-old became too much for her. Frank tried to distract his daughter by taking her to the park or out for an ice cream cone. Sometimes it worked. And sometimes Darlene could not be comforted.

Fighting this disease was going to be a very long battle, a battle the whole family needed to win.

CHAPTER THIRTY-SEVEN

True to her word, Magda did all she could to fight the disease. Despite considerable side effects, she suffered through her treatment with occasional crankiness but few complaints.

Magda went into remission after she completed chemotherapy and life took on a semblance of normalcy. The lumps in her neck disappeared, her hair grew back, and Dr. Hoffman declared her blood work "clean." Magda's energy level returned enough that she could care for Darlene and do a few chores around the house. Frank felt like he had his old Magda back, and he savored every moment of it.

Around Christmastime of the following year, Magda had difficulty breathing and complained of fatigue. Frank and Magda had been invited to a holiday party given by a friend. Frank urged his wife to stay home and rest, but she insisted on going.

Shortly after greeting their hosts, Magda began to feel worse. Frank took her to the hospital where she was told another round of radiation was necessary. The doctors also requested permission to remove Magda's spleen so they could study it for medical research. They told her the research might help people suffering from similar conditions some day. Bravely, Magda agreed, and surgery was scheduled. When the time came, Frank squeezed his wife's hand and kissed her good-bye.

When he got home from the hospital, Frank paid the babysitter and sent her on her way. From his window he watched the young woman's red Chevy successfully navigate the icy street. Darlene was still up, playing with a collection of Legos on the floor. Frank grabbed a cup of coffee and plopped down on the sofa. Darlene stood and smiled. She regarded her father for a moment and then climbed next to him on the couch.

She snuggled against Frank's chest, and he cradled her in his arms. "Tell me the story about the good grandpa," said Darlene. She was already in her flannel pajamas and smelled of Johnson's baby lotion. She clung to the remains of her "blankie," which was now little more than a ribbon of satin. She had given it up once, but was using it again, perhaps due to her mother's illness.

"I thought you didn't like that story anymore," said Frank. "I thought you liked *Black Beauty* now."

Darlene wrinkled her nose. "I never said that!" she said defiantly. Despite his concerns about Magda, Frank threw back his head and laughed.

"Okay," he said, "but just once, because it's way past your bedtime and your mommy will get mad if she finds out."

Darlene brought her thumb to her mouth and snuggled closer to Frank. Her hair was still damp from her bath and hung in tangles against the front of his shirt.

"Once upon a time there was a very good grandpa who lived on a beautiful island where palm trees swayed in the breeze—"

"And the birds sang a hundred different songs," added Darlene.

"Yes, and the birds sang a hundred different songs." Frank rubbed a lock of Darlene's hair between his thumb and finger and brushed it away from her face. "He lived with the lovely grandma who made chocolate cookies for her grandchildren who lived down the street. The grandpa loved the grandma very much, and every day he brought her home fish to cook."

"Because he was a good fisherman," said Darlene.

"Because he was a *great* fisherman," Frank corrected.

Darlene looked up at her father and nodded. "What was the grandpa's name again?"

"The grandchildren called him Abuelo, which is Spanish for grandpa."

"Then what happened?"

"Abuelo had a favorite grandson whose name was Frankie."

"Same as yours."

Frank nodded. "Same as mine. The grandpa took the boy fishing with him whenever he could, and taught him to read the stars so he could get to places he needed to go."

"What did the grandpa say?"

"He said, 'Pay attention, Frankie, because what I'm telling you may come in handy someday.'"

Darlene nodded. "Tell me about the mean man."

"Then one day a man with a dark beard came to rule the land. He did not let the people go where they wanted to go, or to say what they wanted to say. If they spoke against him, he sent them to prison. Many people were killed and many people went to jail. On the first day it happened, the palm trees stopped swaying and the birds stopped singing."

"But the birds didn't *really* stop singing," said Darlene.

Frank laughed. "No, the birds kept singing, but the people could no longer hear them."

"Because they were afraid," prompted Darlene.

Frank sighed. "Yes, because they were afraid."

Darlene removed her thumb from her mouth and fingered a button on her pajama top as Frank continued. "One day, the grandson decided to come to America to be with his beautiful girlfriend."

"Because she got here first," said Darlene proudly. She smiled up at Frank.

"Yes. So the grandson used the lessons Abuelo had taught him and made his way across the mighty ocean so he could be with his love."

"This is my favorite part," said Darlene. "The part where they get married."

Frank smiled at his daughter. "Yes, Frankie and the beautiful girl got married and had a very special daughter." He poked Darlene in the stomach with his forefinger. "And that little girl is *you*."

Darlene laughed, her brown eyes bright with delight. Then her face darkened with a frightening thought.

"What about the boy's father?"

"His father died of a heart attack," said Frank. His eyes misted over as he said the words. Darlene looked at him, eyes wide, thinking.

"What happened to Abuelo?" she asked. "Did he ever see his grandson again?"

Frank pressed his lips together. "No, he didn't," he said. He tried to keep his voice even.

"Why not?"

"Because Abuelo died before it could happen," he said softly.

"The father and the grandfather both died?" asked Darlene.

"Yes," said Frank. "They both died."

Darlene lowered her chin and her bottom lip quivered. "What did the grandpop die of?"

"I don't know for sure. But the grandma says he died of a broken heart."

Darlene's eyes assumed a faraway look. She thought for a moment and said in a soft, sweet voice, "Will you die of a broken heart when Mommy goes away?"

Frank did not answer. Instead, he lifted his daughter in his arms and carried her up to bed. He tucked her in and kissed her on the forehead. She gave him an enigmatic smile before he turned out the light.

When Frank returned to the couch, he thought about Darlene's question. She knew more about the severity of Magda's condition than he and Magda thought. *That's often the way with kids. They are far more aware of the reality of situations than adults give them credit for. And they usually know their parents better than we know ourselves.*

Frank didn't know whether it would be best to talk to Darlene openly about her mother's cancer, or to let things ride until the situation worsened.

He decided it would be best to discuss the matter with Magda.

CHAPTER THIRTY-EIGHT

When Frank told Magda about Darlene's question, she began to cry. She had been stoic up to that point, but the thought of Darlene spending the rest of her life without her mother was almost more than she could bear. Frank could hardly keep a stiff upper lip himself. Magda thought it best to prepare Darlene for the worst, and he agreed.

That night Frank and Magda sat Darlene between them on the couch. Magda started. "You know your Mommy is very sick, don't you?"

Darlene nodded.

"Well, sometimes when people are sick, they don't get better."

"But you are going to get better," said Darlene. A look of desperation filled her eyes.

"I hope so," said Magda. "But sometimes God wants people to come and be with Him."

Darlene's lower lip quivered, but she didn't respond. A moment elapsed, pregnant with emotion.

"Darlene, listen—" Frank said.

Darlene stood and flung her arms in the air in wild gestures of defiance. "I don't want to listen, and I don't want to talk about it." She started to walk away.

Magda pursed her lips and turned to Frank. "Maybe another time. She's not ready." Frank leaned down and rubbed the back of his neck, unsure of how to handle the situation. At least they had introduced the subject. They'd have another conversation, probably more than one, when Darlene was more open to discussing the issue.

• • •

A month later Frank stopped by the supermarket for some groceries, feeling desperate to find something—anything—to help
Magda. He was almost without hope. Not a good place to be.

He filled his cart with fruits, vegetables, yogurt, and Jell-O and
searched for Rice Crispies, Darlene's favorite cereal. She was still
enamored with Snap, Crackle, and Pop.

As he waited in the checkout line, a tabloid newspaper caught
his eye. Amid the stories about alien abductions and people with
four hands was an article about an American doctor who claimed
to have a cure for cancer. Curiosity piqued, Frank read the first few
lines of the story. He paid for his order and placed the newspaper
atop the bag of groceries.

He opened his umbrella, shielding the newspaper against a sudden torrential downpour and headed for his car. Once he unloaded
the groceries, he spread the paper against the steering wheel and
switched on the overhead light.

His breath steamed the windows while rain pounded the roof
like a herd of wildebeest. He knew most of the stories in these
kinds of newspapers were pure poppycock, but, occasionally, they
held a kernel of truth.

He scanned the article with deep concentration, flipping the
page-one story to its jump on page six. The article described a
treatment that was very different from what was practiced in the
United States.

A doctor in Freeport, Bahamas, advanced the idea that chemotherapy and radiation weakens patients' immune systems to the
point where they can't fight the disease. As far as he could tell,
the doctor removed the patients' plasma, treated it, and returned
it to them minus the cancer cells.

Frank ruminated for a few minutes, rereading the article a
couple of times. When he finished, he felt more sanguine than he
had in months. *Maybe this is a fraud. Or maybe it's the answer to our prayers.*

He went home and showed Magda the article. She was skeptical at first, but Frank convinced her that it was worth a try. They had nothing to lose.

"But what about Darlene?" asked Magda.

"I think it would be best if she stayed with your parents. That way we won't have to take her out of school. But the decision is up to you."

Magda shook her head and pursed her lips. A pained look crossed her face. "I really want to have her with us."

"So do I. But we don't know what's ahead of us. You may have a bad reaction to the treatment, and I'm not sure Darlene can handle it. As much as I'd like her to join us, it may be better if she stayed behind."

"I guess you're right," said Magda, struggling with the idea of leaving Darlene.

"I'll pack us all up and will make the airline arrangements," said Frank. "We may be able to get a flight to Freeport tomorrow."

"But what if I never get to see Darlene again?" asked Magda.

"Don't worry, if it comes to that, I will make sure she is there. But right now we need to focus on getting you well."

Magda leaned forward, covered her face with her hands, and wept. Frank had never seen her so distraught. Her whole body shook with grief. Frank sat next to her and took her in his arms. They rocked back and forth on the sofa, thinking of Darlene, fearing the unspeakable, holding on to dear life, while tears fell on each other's shoulders.

CHAPTER THIRTY-NINE

Magda and Frank dropped Darlene at her grandparents' house before they boarded the plane for Freeport. Mother and daughter sobbed as they said good-bye, and Frank tried his best to comfort them. He hated to leave Darlene behind, but he was at a loss about what to do. This was a nightmare from which he couldn't awake.

The plane ride seemed to take forever. When they arrived, Frank and Magda were exhausted, physically and emotionally. Neither had slept well the night before, worrying about Darlene and the outcome of Magda's treatment.

The next morning, after a Danish and a cup of coffee, Frank and Magda strolled to a Florida-style house—pale-green cement flanked by bird-of-paradise flowers. An office occupied the front of the house and a lab occupied the back. They entered through a louvered door and approached the secretary. A sign on her desk informed them that her name was Corinne.

"I read about your clinic in the newspaper," Frank explained. He turned toward Magda. "My wife has Hodgkin's disease, and we were hoping your treatment could help."

The secretary looked at Magda and smiled wanly. "Please, sit," she said, waving toward a couple of wicker chairs. Corinne opened her appointment book and ran her forefinger over the calendar while making small clicking sounds with her tongue. She looked at them with a troubled face.

"I'm sorry, the doctor is totally booked. I'm afraid we can't fit you in."

"But we've come all the way from New Jersey. My wife is very sick. She needs to see someone immediately."

"I'm terribly sorry. I know this is difficult, but Dr. Hunter's schedule is simply impossible."

Frank glanced at Magda. It hadn't occurred to him that she would be refused treatment. He had assumed it was a given. Magda's face was white as cotton. Her chest heaved with weariness. This was their last chance, their last hope for a cure. Surely, there was a way to make it happen.

"I understand," said Frank, trying to control his quaking voice. "Would it be possible for us to see Dr. Hunter for a few minutes—just to talk?"

The secretary glanced at her book. "His day begins at seven a.m. If you could get here around six-thirty, he might spend a few minutes with you."

Frank looked at Magda, and she nodded. "We'll be here," he said.

There was no time for breakfast before Frank and Magda met with Dr. Hunter the next morning. The building was open and they took seats in the waiting room. Magda glanced through some magazines on the coffee table while Frank rested his eyes.

Ten minutes later, Dr. Hunter stepped through the door. He was a handsome man, about six feet tall. He sported a beard of very short nap and wore a white lab coat with his name embroidered in green thread over his right pocket. Owlish glasses framed his crystal-blue eyes, and a signet ring with a blue carved stone circled his finger.

The doctor shook Frank and Magda's hands as they introduced themselves. "I'm sorry," he said. "Corinne tells me Magda has Hodgkin's disease and would like to avail herself of our services."

"Yes," said Frank.

"And she has informed you that we have no openings?"

"She has."

Dr. Hunter leaned back in his chair. "Then what can I do for you?"

"Could you explain in layman's terms what you do?" asked Frank.

Dr. Hunter leaned forward. "Our work here is totally experimental. But I believe it is the treatment of the future." He hesitated a moment. "We are clear and open about the nature of our treatments. We ask all our patients to sign a form that releases us from any liability. We make no claims of a cure, but we do offer hope."

Frank looked at Magda, and said, "We're all for hope."

The doctor nodded. "That being said, our philosophy is to build up the body, not tear it down with radiation and chemotherapy. As far as I'm concerned, chemotherapy is nothing more than poison—it does little in the long run to extend life, and it erodes the patient's quality of life."

Frank nodded, thinking about what Magda had been through. "What's involved in the treatment?"

"I won't get into the technicalities. Let's just say we purify the patient's blood by removing the cancer cells. We work with the blood and the bone marrow. We run a lot of tests to determine whether the treatment is working and how best to alter it if it is not. We also provide nutritional support with large doses of vitamins and minerals."

"Do you succeed?"

"We have more success with some patients than with others."

"I see." Frank thought for a moment. "How much do you charge?"

"Five thousand dollars if you only have to have your blood treated once. More if you need further treatment."

Dr. Hunter turned to Magda. "Do you have any questions, dear?"

Frank thought Magda would bristle at being called "dear," but her face showed no annoyance.

Magda glanced at the office's rudimentary computer. "What do you use this for?"

"To record patients' names and addresses."

"Do you use it to track treatment results?"

The doctor shook his head. "No one here is equipped to do that."

"Would it help if I wrote you a program so you could analyze the results of your patients' blood work?"

A look of astonishment crossed Dr. Hunter's eyes. "You could do that?"

Magda nodded. "I was a computer analyst for Merrill Lynch. I'm fully capable of doing that and anything else you might need. I could simplify and streamline your practice. And you could use the time you save to treat me."

Dr. Hoffman looked as if he'd been struck by lightning. It took him a minute to process what Magda had said. Sensing an opportunity, Frank interrupted the doctor's train of thought.

"If we were to pay you ten thousand dollars, and Magda could help computerize your practice, would you accept her as a patient then?"

Dr. Hunter leaned back in his chair and exhaled. "This is a very tempting proposition."

"It is meant to be," said Frank.

"Very well. Let's give it a shot."

CHAPTER FORTY

Magda started treatment immediately and began to feel better. The more time that went by, the better she felt. According to the doctor, her blood work was improving and she was responding well to therapy.

As soon as she felt up to it, Magda made good on her promise to work on the clinic's computer system. She tackled her new responsibilities with determination and enthusiasm, and quickly became the darling of the office. The staff simply loved her.

Frank rented a condo and a car for their use in the Bahamas. He traveled back and forth to New Jersey, dividing his time between his job and Darlene. Frank had several talks with Darlene about her mother's condition, and she seemed to understand the severity of the situation as well as could be expected.

Darlene visited her mother on many occasions, often accompanied by Magda's aunt and uncle or her parents. Magda's family had been devastated at the news of Magda's disease and had done everything possible to make the situation easier for Frank and Darlene.

Frank worried about how Magda's disease was affecting his daughter. Sometimes she acted as if nothing were the matter, laughing and singing like she did before Magda's diagnosis. At other times, she was lethargic and irritable. She was sucking her thumb more often than usual, and her teacher said she was moody and distracted.

Darlene talked to her mother on the phone several times a week. Sometimes it cheered her up. And sometimes it made her cry uncontrollably. At those times, Frank would hold her in his arms like he did when she was a baby. She clung to him for solace, but he never felt more inadequate in his life. Whenever Darlene had a holiday from school, Frank flew with her to see her mother. Their reunions were joyful, their departures filled with despair.

For a while, Magda's cancer went into remission. She continued treatment in the Bahamas for almost a year, and Frank and Magda treasured their time together, aware that her condition could worsen at any time. Magda sat in the sun and gazed at the crystal-blue waters of the Caribbean. She talked to Darlene and the rest of her family on the phone. She read and she prayed.

Frank and Magda often talked well into the night about family, religion, and the nature of love. They discussed what would be best for Darlene if Magda should pass, a difficult topic for them both.

In the spring of 1979, the lumps in Magda's throat returned. She experienced extreme fatigue and slept most of the day. Frank flew her to Miami, and took her to the hospital to see if anything could be done to extend her life. The prognosis was bleak. Magda had only a short time to live. The oncologist mentioned further surgery. Distraught, Frank heard only half of what was said.

Frank entered Magda's hospital room, sat on a vinyl-covered chair, and took her hand. "The doctor said something about surgery."

Magda tensed and set her jaw. "I'm finished with doctors and hospitals, Frank." She gazed out the window. "Just take me back to the Bahamas so I can live out the rest of my life in peace."

Frank left the hospital and made the flight arrangements. Despite the medications, Magda's pain was so severe she couldn't get comfortable on the plane. When they arrived, Dr. Hunter and his staff were devastated that their treatment hadn't worked. But to a certain extent it had. Magda had lived a year longer than the medical community had predicted.

Two weeks elapsed. Magda's pain worsened, her appetite disappeared, and she shed more weight. Her face and limbs looked skeletal. Every day, every hour, was precious.

On Mother's Day Frank brought Darlene to say good-bye to her mother. It was a bright, sunny day. Darlene tiptoed into her mother's room. Magda smiled and nodded for her to approach. Darlene laid her head on Magda's chest, while Magda stroked her daughter's hair. Darlene sobbed and tears ran down Magda's face.

Frank stood, not wanting to interrupt them. This was their moment, theirs alone. He watched for a minute. When it became too much for him to bear, he left the room, silently closing the door behind him. Darlene emerged from her mother's room with red, puffy eyes.

Frank held his nine-year-old daughter close to his heart.

CHAPTER FORTY-ONE

Twilight. The time when the sun offers its final long kiss to the sky and the sky kisses it back. Frank watched as clouds shifted shapes and colors, embracing yellows, purples, and splashes of orange. Halfway up the horizon the silvery moon played peek-a-boo with a rhubarb-colored playmate, a cumulous cloud that was finely etched and clearly defined. The cloud slowly morphed, its outer edges fringed in gold. It was a spectacular interlude, the closing curtain before the sun marched to its bloody demise.

The coral-washed firmament faded to gray as Frank entered Magda's room, knowing this might be the last time he'd ever be with her. He looked at her with hungry eyes. Her hair was thin and brittle yet it decorated the white pillowcase like calligraphy on parchment, gracefully curling and turning. Her face was pale—almost translucent—her forehead smooth. Her molasses-colored eyes rested beneath her lids.

He approached her bed and sat quietly in the chair at her bedside. Her eyes fluttered open, and she smiled slightly when she saw him. He took her hand in his, wanting to say so many things but not knowing where to begin. He sighed and looked at her. How could such a remarkable creature be granted only twenty-eight years on this earth? How could this be the end?

"I'm so sorry, Magda." he managed. "I'm sorry nothing worked. I never thought it would come to this."

Magda looked at Frank with such tenderness he thought his heart would buckle under her gaze. "Don't, Frank," she said softly.

Frank stopped talking and regarded her closely. She appeared peaceful, resigned, almost ethereal.

"You mustn't speak that way," she said. "We did everything we could. There's nothing to regret."

She sighed and glanced at the crucifix on the far side of the room. She moved her lips slightly, like she was reciting a prayer beneath her breath. A long moment elapsed, pregnant with memories.

Magda started to speak and then stopped.

"What is it?" Frank asked.

"I will miss everyone." Tears swam in her eyes and she looked at Frank with all the love they had bestowed on each other over the years. "I will miss you more than you know," she said in a voice choked with emotion. She hesitated while Frank folded her hands in his. "I will miss my parents, my brother. But most of all, I will miss—" Her lips quivered. Quiet filled the room like a vulture.

"I know, I know," Frank soothed.

"I can't even bear to think about Darlene," she said, and started to cry.

"She'll be okay," Frank said, with as much conviction as he could muster. There was nothing he could say that would mitigate Magda's pain. "She loves you, and she knows how much you love her. You've been a good mother. She'll always carry you in her heart."

"It will be so hard on her."

She stopped speaking, and Frank nodded his understanding. He didn't know what else to say. Magda pulled her right hand from his and pointed a frail finger at the dresser. Frank followed her gesture with his eyes and saw her gold locket sitting in a pottery dish. "Put a picture of me in my locket and give it to Darlene," she said, her moist eyes signaling grave concern. "It's important for my child to remember her mother's face."

"Of course," Frank said, sucking in his breath at her words. As he did, he glimpsed the trinket ring he had given Magda years ago nestled next to the locket. An explosion of pain ripped at his stomach, demanding release. He struggled to control it.

He ran the back of his hand along Magda's cheek and said, "And we will miss you. Darlene will miss you. *I* will miss you—" He stopped, aware of the words' pathetic inadequacy.

Magda nodded then hesitated a moment, contemplating.

"We have always been honest with each other. And I need to be honest with you now. We've touched on this subject, but I want to be very clear about how I feel."

Frank looked at Magda, conscious of her chest rising and falling with each breath.

"There's not much time," she said.

"Shhh, Magda."

"No, let me speak." She pulled herself up in the bed. Her eyes assumed a somber cast, but her feisty spirit was still evident in the muscles around her mouth. The delicate chain that held her gold cross was wrinkled at her collarbone and stuck to her skin, displaying the cross at an oblique angle. She leaned back on her pillow and offered Frank a small smile.

He nodded. "Whatever you want."

Magda's shoulders relaxed, and she said, "You are the kind of man who needs a woman, to love, to care for, to cherish."

Frank made a sound that indicated he didn't want to pursue this conversation, but Magda held up her hand to silence him. "You are too young not to remarry. Promise me you'll find someone else and make another life for yourself."

"I can't," Frank said. "I'm sorry, I can't even think about that now."

Magda set her lips in a stern line. "But in time you will, Frank, and I want you to know that you have my blessing. Just make sure to choose someone who will be good for you and kind to Darlene."

Grief constricted Frank's throat. He couldn't respond. He sat immobile, thinking about his soon-to-be motherless daughter. How would he care for her? How would he manage his grief while assuaging hers? How could he ever begin to teach her the things that only a woman can impart to a daughter? She would need the help of Magda's mother and aunt. Frank wanted Darlene to have the comfort of his own mother, but she was far away, in a land of no return.

Banishing the thought, he studied Magda's hands sitting lightly on the sheets. They looked fragile, like ice crystals ready to dissolve under the sun's steady gaze. The couple sat in silence for a moment. Magda was the first to speak. "Frank," she whispered, "will you do something for me?"

Frank looked at her with tears in his eyes. He brushed her hair away from her face. "Of course, darling," he said. "Anything."

"Will you make love to me one last time?"

Frank sucked in his breath and studied her. "Oh, Magda, is that what you really want? Or would you rather I just hold you? You are so frail, so fragile. Are you sure?"

"I've never been surer of anything in my life."

Frank looked at her thin, bruised body, wondering how to do this. "I don't want to hurt you," he said. "You've been through so much—"

"You won't hurt me, Frank. You have never hurt me. Besides, it doesn't matter anymore. I won't be in this body much longer."

Frank shook his head. "Dear God, Magda, I don't think I can."

"Why?" she asked in a voice that was thin and papery. A tear escaped from the corner of her eye and landed on her upper lip. Her tongue darted out and quickly retrieved it. At that moment, Frank realized he had hurt her, the last thing he wanted to do.

"Because if I make love to you now, I will remember every detail for the rest of my life," he said. "I will never be able to get it out of my mind. It will be too painful—"

Magda sighed and turned her head to face the window. Her eyes assumed a faraway look. She knew he had spoken the truth.

"It's 'Now or Never,' Frank."

"I'm sorry?"

"I keep hearing it in my head."

Frank's eyes opened wide, expelling a line of warm, salty tears. It was their song, the one Magda sang to Frank when he was thinking about leaving Cuba.

She turned her face toward him and said, "Sing it with me, Frank."

Frank opened his mouth, but no sound sprang forth. Magda started to hum, then to sing in a tremulous voice. Her words were soft at first, almost imperceptible. "*It's now or never, come hold me tight. Kiss me my darling, be mine tonight—*"

Her tongue tripped over consonants, dropped an octave, and then grew stronger, as if the notes were bells, iron bells, injecting the tensile strength of metal into her bloodstream, providing her with one final surge of energy.

Frank stared at the white cotton bedspread that floated lightly over her body, hoping his voice would find its wings. He thought of things long since forgotten—the color of the ribbon in her hair the first time he met her. The way she smiled at him, shyly. The way her body looked stretched out on a beach blanket. The small geysers she created when she skipped into the waves, kicking the sparkling spray waist high.

His breath caught in his throat as he listened to her. It was clear what she wanted. For months she had been too mired in the work of survival to allow the vibration of song to sweeten the air. Now it refused to be silenced. Her voice was raspy, weak, but it grew clearer, brighter, stronger, as she picked up the tempo.

He turned his face to the window. Tears streamed down his cheeks like condensation on a water glass. They sequined his hands, sparkling in the light. He did not bother to brush them away. They were as right as sun on a summer's day, essential to their parting, a testament to their love.

"Please," she said. Frank cleared his throat, afraid no sound would exit his larynx. Then his love for her eased the kink in his throat. He took Magda's hand and finished the lyrics to the song with her: "*Tomorrow will be too late. It's now or never, my love can't wait.*"

The words drifted from her lips like wisps of smoke drawn through an airshaft. Then silence. Magda lifted her chin slightly, offering Frank her lips. She took his hand in hers and drew it to her breast. He looked at her, trying to memorize her eyes, her lips, her cheeks, her profile. "Please," she said.

He held her face in his hands, bracketing her cheeks with his palms, leaned down and kissed her. Her face was warm. Too warm. Feverish. Her lips were dry. Chapped. She made a small forlorn sound, almost a whimper and parted her lips. His tongue darted for hers, hungrily, instinctively. His chest was heavy with grief, yet he managed to run his hands over her legs, her arms, her belly. "Yes," she whispered.

"I love you so much. I always have," he said.

He nibbled Magda's lower lip, softly at first and then with a sudden urgency that surprised him. She responded, kissing him back. He pulled away and looked at her. "Oh, Magda, Magda—"

"Yes, Frank."

"How will I live without you? I don't know if I can go on." He swallowed hard. "I can't even conceive of it."

Magda expelled a breath and a tear found its way to her pillowcase, leaving a small circle the color of clouds. "You will, you will go on—"

"Dear God—" Frank shook his head and gripped his thighs to steady himself.

Magda took his hands in hers. "I love you, Frank," she said in a voice filled with enough conviction to fill an ocean. He knew it would be the last time she would utter these words, and his ears scrambled to save them, to retrieve them like a lioness rescuing a cub from beneath a falling tree.

He knew what he had to do. He stood and disrobed, leaving his clothes in a heap on the floor. He looked at Magda, his heart aching with the loss of all that could have been, with all he believed was meant to be.

He slipped into bed and drew his body along the length of hers, feeling her silky skin against his own. Even now, after all she had been through, she was still lovely. He wrapped her in his arms, brushed her hair from her face, and buried his nose in her tresses.

When he looked at her again, Magda said, "Please remember me."

"How could I ever forget you?" he responded.

A moment elapsed. "It's time," she said. "I can't fight it any longer."

"Don't," Frank pleaded.

"No, Frank. Hear me out. You've been very brave. You've done everything that could've been done. It's God's will that I go now. I don't want you feeling guilty over this."

"God's will," Frank repeated numbly, not knowing how that could possibly be. Did God need her more than him? Could anyone? Any being? Was there not enough pain and suffering in the world to spare Magda?

"I'm sorry," he said. "It makes no sense. Why would He take you now?"

"Perhaps it was meant to be," said Magda. "Perhaps I was meant to be the catalyst that brought you to America so our daughter could be born in freedom."

Frank shook his head, not knowing how to respond. "Perhaps," he said. "It's the only explanation that begins to make sense."

"Then believe it. Hold on to it."

"I can't."

"Try."

"All right," Frank said, attempting to please her but finding little solace in the idea.

"Good. Now let's make love."

Magda leaned back against the pillow and made a movement with her eyes for Frank to begin. Slowly, button-by-button, he opened her nightgown to reveal her body. Pink rosebuds dotted the cotton fabric. He shivered, thinking he could almost feel their thorns prick his fingers. Not even the thought of roses offered him comfort now.

Magda's skin was as soft as dandelion fluff. He ran his hand down the full length of her body, tracing her clavicle, her breasts, her nipples, her belly. His palms sought the silkiness of her inner thighs, and she heaved a sigh.

Suddenly, the aroma of orange blossoms scented the air. Or perhaps he had imagined it. His thoughts turned to their wedding night, the first time he made love to Magda. She had worn such a fragrance then. His heavy heart began to flutter.

Magda sighed and opened her legs, signaling she was ready to receive him one last time. "I'm sorry," he said. "I can't. Not with you like this. Let me just hold you and look at you."

Magda nodded. He held her close and smoothed her forehead, not knowing whether she wanted to make love for her sake or his. It didn't matter. They would make love with their eyes, their lips, and their hands. That was enough, more than enough. He gazed at his wife, wanting to look deep into her soul, to savor every precious moment left to them.

He kissed her. At first her breathing was ragged. Then it slowly became rhythmic, pushing and pulling, in and out, their heartbeats beating in unison, their breaths tumbling over each other like the ebb and flow of the endlessly churning sea.

Frank wanted to bequeath his breath to Magda so she could own it, use it, and extract every bit of love and energy from it. He wanted his breath to serve as a currency, a balm that would heal her, sustain her and nurture her for years and decades to come. But he could not. He was powerless to bestow this gift.

He took her in his arms and treated her body like fragile porcelain, fine and easily broken, never to be whole again. He was afraid of hurting her, yet she showed no sign that he was doing so. He wanted this moment to last forever, to carry them to a different time, a different place, a place of gentle breezes and blue-green water filigreed with lacy foam.

He wanted time to reverse, to expand, to stand still, to do anything but to advance in its inexorable progression into the dark, empty inevitable. Lines from a Carl Sandberg poem sprung to mind:

I never knew any more beautiful than you:
I have hunted you under my thoughts,
I have broken down under the wind
And into the roses looking for you.
I shall never find any
greater than you.

Magda's body was as familiar to Frank as a glass of milk. He wanted to transport her to a place where she could forget what Fate had in store for her. At least for a while. But he couldn't.

It was his last chance to please her, and he was determined to give it his all. She cried, and he comforted her as best he could. They repeated each other's names as if the repetition would fix their place on this earth and stave off their parting. He remained with Magda until he could stand it no longer and then collapsed in a torment of grief.

He screamed his pain into the ether in a keening that arose from the depth of his being. He wanted to extinguish it, but it rolled over him, a swell of anguish that rivaled the thrashing waves of a storm, a tsunami of sorrow that could no more be contained than a comber reclaimed by the tide.

Magda gathered his head to her bosom and began rocking back and forth, making a cooing sound she used when Darlene was a baby. "There, there. It's okay, don't you worry," she murmured, running her fingers through his hair and blotting the tears from his eyes. He looked at her and she smiled, a strained smile that informed him it wouldn't be long before she was gone.

He wanted to return her smile, to fondle her again with his eyes, but he could not. It was impossible. He was helpless in the face of her impending death. How many breaths did she have left? Enough to count? Fifty? A hundred? A thousand? An hour's worth? A night's worth?

Grief welled in him as loud and mighty as a hurricane, shattering time, place, self, obliterating everything but this moment, this precious moment that refused to last, that refused to stand still, that could not be savored but could only be devoured like the menacing cells that were eating her body, endlessly dividing, multiplying, while at the same time plundering, destroying, diminishing, extinguishing.

Finally, he could stand it no longer. He rose from her bed and stumbled to the door, hoping to find refuge in another room, another place, wanting to lean against the steady trunk of a tree, to gain comfort from the murmur of the nocturnal sounds of nature. He longed to hear the chirping cicadas, the croaking frogs, the birds calling their mates back to the nest. But he could not leave her.

With his hand on the doorknob, he dropped to his knees like a fallen icon, feeling the warmness of her body still on him and the coldness of the floor piercing his skin. He gulped great breaths of air, filling his lungs with sweet, precious life while knowing her eyes were upon him, watching him in sympathy, loving him faithfully to the end.

He put his head between his legs and pounded his fists on the floor until his hands were swollen and bleeding and his throat was so dry and parched from sobbing that he had to stand and stumble to her bed stand for a drink of water. He slurped it greedily, the water dribbling down his chin, wetting his chest, his fingers, his toes. It was the essence of life, and he would have all of it, every drop.

Magda looked at him with alarm in her eyes and reached out her hand to comfort him.

"I'm so sorry," he said.

"It's all right. Come lie with me."

Magda moved to one side of the bed, and Frank lay down next to her. They clutched each other like children in a typhoon, until his tears finally ceased, his hiccups of grief subsided, and the great heaving sobs no longer racked his chest and polluted the air. Frank took her hand in his, as delicate as a paper crane, and held it the way a child holds a kitten, gently, softly, petting her skin, her fingers, her nails. Frank struggled to stay awake, but soon found himself dreaming of a lone tree standing on a rocky hill. It was barren, stripped of its leaves, its bark, its flowers. The rock dissolved into dense sand, ebony grains that ran like hot oil through his fingers, leaving them black, charred, and numb.

He was watering the tree, trying desperately to provide it with nourishment, but its slender roots were turning inward, curling in upon themselves, seeking something Frank could not provide.

From the edge of consciousness, he heard his name being repeated ever so softly—Frank, Frank, Frank. He awoke with a start and looked at Magda. Her eyes were closed, and she was turning her head from side to side. Her forehead was dotted with perspiration. He wet a washcloth in a glass of water on her bed stand and placed it on her lips. She raised her chin and sucked briefly. Her eyelids fluttered, but her mind was no longer focused.

The sun was lighting the sky to a bruised purple as he looked at her. Magda winced as a lance of pain gripped her and her body convulsed. She whispered Frank's name in torment, beseeching him for relief, for rescue, for redemption.

But he could not save her.

It was a coarse, inconsolable sound that soured the air and singed his soul like flames consuming a martyr's stake.

But he could not save her.

His throat clogged with a thousand tears. But he could not save her.

It was the last sound she ever made.

CHAPTER FORTY-TWO

For several months after Magda's death, Frank experienced an odd combination of grief and relief, grief that he had lost his wife and relief that her suffering had finally ceased. He couldn't sleep, couldn't read, and couldn't think properly. He felt like he was walking through a thick mist, unmoored and unfocused. For a while he lost all faith in life, in God, and in love. He simply could not accept the fact that this awful thing had happened to Magda. Or that she was gone.

The emptiness rolled over him like white sheets of fog. There was no one to confide in, no one to shop with, and no one with whom he could discuss the day's events over a glass of red wine.

He would turn to ask Magda a question, forgetting she was no longer alive. He would pick up the phone to check with her regarding an upcoming event, only to drop the receiver back in its cradle. He would reach for her in bed in the middle of the night, only to find an empty space. Those moments snuck up on him. He was continuously ambushed by surprise.

He'd see Magda wheeling a cart down a supermarket aisle, carefully checking her list. He'd glimpse her standing on street corners, her hair draped around her shoulders. He'd observe her waiting at stoplights, sunglasses perched on the bridge of her nose. Then he'd realize his mind was tricking him. It was not Magda he saw. It was someone else. She was everywhere and nowhere, and he feared his longing for her would never end.

Frank's biggest concern was Darlene. Her world had been turned upside down, and he had no idea how to make her feel better. His answer was to surround her with as many loving people as possible. Frank took his daughter back and forth to school, and her grandparents and Aunt Sophia babysat her whenever they could, sometimes at their houses in Union City and sometimes at Frank's house in Lincoln Park. On Saturdays, Darlene would go to work with Frank, content to do her homework in his small office while he made sandwiches and waited on customers.

At night they'd have long conversations. He'd describe the house her mother lived in when she grew up in Cuba, and what she looked like when he first met her. He told her how smart her mother was and how everyone loved her at school. He told her about the childhood pranks he played with his cousins and friends. Those stories cheered Darlene up—at least for a while. But Magda's death had left a giant hole in her life, one Frank felt unable to fill.

He approached work with little enthusiasm. Days went by when he was barely aware of what he was doing. He was short, irritable, and grumpy with his staff, complaining about their slightest transgressions.

The thought of remarriage never crossed his mind. Frank was of Spanish descent, and in some circles tradition demanded that a man not remarry after his wife died, at least for what was considered a respectable time—fifteen to twenty years. Frank was resigned to the idea and accepted it without examination.

One day an old customer came into Frank's store. He had made small talk with the woman on several occasions when Magda was alive. Her name was Chris Ann, and she had moved from Montclair to Bellevue, a short distance away. She came back and forth to visit friends.

She was curious and inquisitive. Smart. Kind. Fun. She exhibited a keen interest in Cuba, questioning Frank about its history, geography, climate, and foliage. She wanted to know about the country's politics, about Castro and Batista. After a while, she started to visit the store more regularly. When business was slow, she and Frank would have a cup of coffee together. And talk, talk, talk.

As they got to know each other, Frank told her about Magda and

Darlene. She was sympathetic about Magda's death and concerned about Frank's daughter. To Frank's surprise, she asked whether he'd like to go bowling with her and her friends some time. He was pleased at her suggestion.

One thing led to another, and Frank and Chris began going out together. For the first time in his life Frank learned how to date the American way, which was far different from what he had experienced in Cuba. No one oversaw his dates with Chris, no chaperone came between them. The experience was strange but liberating, and it made Frank feel more integrated into American society.

Chris and Frank walked, talked, drank coffee, and laughed. She listened to his stories about Lieutenant Pino, his escape from Cuba, and the family and friends he had left behind. Frank listened to her stories of being adopted and growing up in a single-parent home. She told Frank how hard her mother worked, and how much she loved and admired her.

One day Frank told Chris about getting his first refrigerator. When they finished laughing, she sat back in her chair and asked, "Now that you have a house, two cars, and a business, would you do it over again?"

"Do what again?"

"Go to all that trouble for a discarded refrigerator."

Frank considered for a moment and said, "No, I don't think I would."

Chris made a face.

"What?" he asked.

"You need to rethink your answer."

Frank was surprised at her challenge. "Why?"

"Because it's important to remember who you are and where you came from. The persistence it took to get that refrigerator is part of you, and you need to honor it."

Frank sat back in his chair, stunned. Chris had spoken the truth. And he liked it. For the first time, he noticed the beauty of her shiny red hair, her big green eyes, and her lovely smile. And for the first time, he began to look at her not as a friend but as a woman.

CHAPTER FORTY-THREE

In the early seventies, Frank's father and grandfather had died, both of heart attacks. He was devastated at the news. One of his biggest fears when he left Cuba was that family members might die before he got to see them again.

At the time, Frank had been so busy building a life that he had given short shrift to the grieving process. He had tried to push down the pain, and it had worked—for a while. Magda's demise had brought these previous losses to the front of his mind and had triggered a primal need in him to see his family in Cuba again, especially his mother.

More than a decade had passed since Frank had seen his mother's face. During that time, they had corresponded, careful to avoid any reference to Frank's escape or any discussion of politics in their letters. But Frank desperately wanted to talk to her in person. He wanted to tell his mother about his life in America and about the death of Magda. He wanted her to meet Darlene, his daughter, her granddaughter. He missed his siblings, cousins, nieces, and nephews, and he yearned to meet his many relatives who had been born since his escape.

For years Frank had wracked his brain for ways to get his relatives out of Cuba and had come up with nothing. It seemed well-nigh impossible. But in the spring of 1980, a glimmer of hope surfaced.

In early April, almost a thousand Cubans stormed the Peruvian Embassy, located in an upscale suburb of Havana. They were protesting the living conditions in Cuba and the policies of the Cuban government. Soon ten thousand Cubans petitioned the Peruvian government for political asylum. The media dubbed them the "Havana 10,000."

In response, Fidel announced that anyone wanting to leave Cuba could do so as long as they obtained an exit permit. It was his way of ridding the country of "troublemakers and undesirables."

President Jimmy Carter agreed to welcome up to thirty-five hundred refugees from the embassy. No one could foresee that one hundred and twenty-five thousand Cubans would eventually leave the country as a result of these events.

Frank soon realized that this was an unprecedented opportunity. He spent two sleepless nights thinking about it. Timing was such that he couldn't get word to his family in Cuba that he was coming, so he decided to wing it. The next night after dinner he told Chris he was leaving for Florida to bring his relatives back to the States—come hell or high water!

Chris hung up the dish towel, looked at Frank, and said, "I think you're crazy. What if the authorities figure out who you are and arrest you? They could throw you in jail and torture you. You are risking your life. You might not get out alive."

"I'll be careful," said Frank, hoping his words would reassure her.

Chris shook her head. "It could be very dangerous. What if Pino finds out you are there?"

"It's been a long time," said Frank. "I'm sure Pino's forgotten all about me. Besides, the authorities probably executed him for treason or sentenced him to life in prison."

"Still—" said Chris.

Frank cut her off. "Don't worry, honey, I won't get off the boat."

Chris thought for a moment. "Make sure to bring your American passport. You can't be too careful."

"Of course. That goes without saying."

Chris placed some dishes in the cabinet and asked, "How will you get to Cuba?"

"I don't know yet. But if there's a way, I'll find it. The important thing is to take the first step. I'll figure out the rest when I get to Florida."

The next day Frank hopped aboard an Eastern Airlines flight for the Sunshine State. The plane was populated with Cubans hoping to rescue their relatives. When Frank arrived in Miami, he called his Uncle Luis. He was living in Miami with his new wife. It had been a long time since the two men had spoken. To Frank's delight, Luis sounded like he had mellowed over the years.

After a few minutes of small talk, Luis told Frank that he was planning to go to Cuba on a shrimp trawler to rescue his former wife, Rosa, and their two daughters. He apologized that there was no room on his boat, but he suggested Frank contact his Cuban friend, Rolando, a man who had captained several boats and had excellent navigational skills.

Frank spent the night of April 25 at a Holiday Inn in Key West and called on Rolando the next day. As it turned out, Rolando wanted to go to Cuba to bring back his brother. While he was an experienced captain, he did not own a boat. He was willing to serve as the captain if Frank purchased the boat. Considering the risk of traveling to Cuba alone, it seemed like a reasonable offer.

After making several inquiries, Frank bought a twenty-five-foot boat from an old, sunburned fisherman. Boats were in high demand and price gouging was rampant. He paid eight thousand dollars. The boat was in fair shape and the price was outrageous, but it was the best deal Frank could make.

Approximately thirty years old, Rolando was amiable, smart and handy—a winning combination. The two men worked well together and spent the next day fixing and preparing the boat for the journey. They tuned up the motor, bought life jackets and floatation devices, and obtained three fifty-five-gallon barrels that they filled with gas.

They collected kitchen items—cutlery, bowls, aluminum glasses, and a can opener. They filled a cooler with ice and secured an ample supply of water. Rolando donated two flashlights and a ragtag collection of towels from his house. Once they put these supplies in order, they went to a general store for sunscreen, blankets, and hats. The lines were horrific. It took them almost two hours to check out.

They had no idea how long they might have to wait for their relatives' paperwork to be processed, and Frank knew it could be a death sentence for him to step foot on Cuban soil. So they needed to bring enough food to sustain them.

They purchased canned goods at a local supermarket—tuna fish, ham, salmon, beans—as well as peanut butter, crackers, nuts, and other nonperishable items. They put some fruit in the cooler, including apples, which Frank thought would be a nice welcoming gift.

Frank and Rolando named the boat *My Way* in a gesture of defiance to Fidel. Rolando attached an American flag to the back of the boat to signal American citizens were on board. Frank imagined how happy his family would be when they saw the flag. His chest swelled with pride as he watched the flag flap in the wind.

The morning of April 27, Rolando placed his compass on board and studied a map of the ocean. By lunchtime boats were lined up on trailers a hundred deep, waiting to be launched. Everyone was headed southbound. The circuslike atmosphere led Frank to believe it would be hours before their boat touched water.

Shortly before one o'clock, the sky darkened and a ferocious wind kicked up. Rain followed in blinding sheets, pelting windshields, flooding boats, and drenching people to the skin.

Boats already in the water became swamped, and people hastened to get off them. Several boats had slammed into each other and littered the beach like dead fish. People swore, shielded their heads with newspapers and umbrellas, and scrambled for safe haven. Fortunately, the mini hurricane was short lived and was over in a couple of hours. Frank and Rolando bailed out their boat and waited to depart.

On Chris's advice, Frank had taken a couple of Dramamine pills to ward off seasickness. Although they made him feel a little loopy, it had been a good idea. Once Frank and Rolando launched their boat, they found themselves battling the waves. The water was choppy, and they struggled to stay afloat. Their small boat bobbed in the ocean like a rubber duck. They motored past many boats that had capsized and been abandoned.

The American Coast Guard was out in full force, rescuing people in trouble and towing disabled vessels back to Florida. The skies were filled with planes and helicopters conducting aerial reconnaissance and radioing the Coast Guard for assistance.

The water was dark and treacherous, and their boat rocked incessantly from the wakes of other boats. The combination of sun, waves, and the churn of the sea soon lay waste to Frank's stomach. The Dramamine helped, but, to his chagrin, he became well acquainted with the side of the boat. It was a long fourteen hours.

Frank felt a welter of emotions as they approached the coast of Cuba. As soon as he saw the lights on the Havana harbor, a thousand memories washed over him. He remembered kissing Magda on the *Malecón*, her lips soft and warm and her hands caressing his back. He remembered fishing with his grandfather on warm spring days and eating lunch with him out of a lunchbox decorated with Lone Ranger stickers. He remembered playing baseball with his cousins and friends, not ending the game until the last ray of sunshine departed and the ball was impossible to see.

But, most of all, he remembered his time running from the force, the waiting, the hiding, the fear. Lieutenant Pino's face floated before his eyes. He had a hard time pushing it from his mind. For a moment his stomach constricted—he knew he would dream about his escape that night.

Weaving among many boats, Frank and Rolando made their way to the Mariel Harbor, twenty-seven miles west of Havana. They arrived around eight p.m., tired, eager, and excited. Frank was thrilled at the possibility of seeing his family again.

Despite the size of the harbor, they had difficulty finding a place to anchor their boat. Once they did, they sighed in relief, leaned back in their seats, and surveyed their surroundings.

The sight was astounding. Hundreds of boats—pleasure boats, motorboats, shrimp boats, catamarans, fishing boats—had arrived, almost all flying Cuban or American flags. Some had suffered mechanical failure and needed assistance. Frank estimated that more than a thousand boats were waiting to retrieve loved ones from Cuba.

The moon slipped from beneath a bank of clouds as gentle waves lapped the *My Way*. Arcs of searchlights cast a silvery glow upon the water, and flashlights winked on and off like fireflies. The atmosphere was festive. Cuban and American music filled the air. People hollered back and forth to each other, some in Spanish, some in English, offering information and assistance. Frank almost expected fireworks to explode.

Frank and Rolando looked at each other and smiled. Frank grabbed two bottles of beer and offered one to Rolando. Melting ice floated at the bottom of the cooler.

They opened a couple of cans of tuna fish and drained the oil into the sea. Frank unscrewed a jar of peanut butter, slapped some on a hunk of bread, and shared it with his boat mate. They wanted to eat the bread before it got stale. Oranges and bananas completed the meal.

Frank looked at the patchwork of stars overhead and his heart ached for Magda, his father, and Abuelo—three people he loved so dearly, now gone. He thought about Chris and Darlene and smiled.

After Frank and Rolando satisfied their hunger and quenched their thirst, they settled down to sleep, hoping tomorrow would be a good day.

CHAPTER FORTY-FOUR

The next morning the port was abuzz with activity. Small government-sponsored boats cruised from vessel to vessel, selling cigarettes, cigars, water, and fruit.

Water taxis took people into the port to buy foodstuffs, gas, and other essentials in government-run stores. Everyone who went ashore complained of unconscionable price gouging.

People were conversing freely from boat to boat—the rumor mill was at full throttle. Frank heard they might have a long wait since Cubans wanting to leave the country were required to have their possessions inventoried before departure, ensuring their property reverted to its true owner, the State. He recalled Magda's family enduring the same tedious process before they left Cuba for America.

A patrol boat came by at mid-morning on their third day in port. An official with a brown clipboard recorded the name of Frank and Rolando's boat and the names and addresses of those they hoped to claim.

The young man held a thick pad of loose-leaf paper containing a long list of names. Rolando gave him the name of his brother, and Frank gave him the names of eight family members whom he thought would want to leave Cuba, including his mother, siblings, nieces, and nephew.

The official, who looked about eighteen, appeared overwhelmed and disorganized, wrongly repeating the names he was given. He appeared to have no idea what he was doing, and Frank wondered whether he could actually spell. His papers flapped in the wind, and he held them down with his thumb. Frank feared the list would blow into the water.

"We'll get back to you in a day or two," said the official. Frank and Rolando looked at each other, hoping their paperwork would be processed properly.

On May 1, a series of thunderstorms battered the seas from Key West to Cuba, kicking up high winds and twelve-foot waves. The storms lasted for several hours, starting and stopping intermittently. Frank and Rolando watched with apprehension as vessels banged into each other. Several boats were smashed beyond repair. Fortunately, theirs sustained little damage.

About a week later, Frank and Rolando heard that Fidel had opened the prisons and mental institutions, releasing the inmates to go to America. The authorities warned those waiting in the harbor to prepare to transport hardened criminals and lunatics back to the States. The two men looked at each other in alarm. Not in their wildest dreams had they thought Fidel would do such a thing.

A young man in the next boat told them that refugees were required to report to a fountain in Havana before being sent to a "holding camp" called *El Mosquito* where their paperwork was processed. On the way to the camp, pro-Castro Cubans pelted their fellow countrymen with eggs and tomatoes, deriding them as worms, and harassing them for abandoning their country. *They're up to their old tricks*, thought Frank. *They did the same thing when I lived in Cuba.*

Once the refugees arrived at *El Mosquito*, they were required to sleep on dirt floors and to consume a diet of rotten eggs, raw potatoes, and uncooked rice. The water was filthy, rats were ubiquitous, and guard dogs attacked people trying to use the toilet. Frank shuddered to think how his mother was faring.

A couple of days later, the patrol boats announced that due to the volume of requests for exit permits, it could take a month or more to process the paperwork required for people to leave the country. No one could predict the time frame involved. The authorities urged people to go home and return in a month or two to claim their relatives.

Frank's mind immediately turned to Darlene. Her grandparents were babysitting her, so she was safe. That was a given. But Frank had not anticipated such a long wait, and he had not prepared his daughter for the possibility of his extended absence.

He hoped the delay in taking people out of Cuba was being reported on the news back in the States, and that Magda's parents had reassured Darlene that her father would be home as soon as possible. Unfortunately, he couldn't count on media coverage of the event, especially when dealing with Fidel.

Frank faced a terrible dilemma. If he remained in port, Darlene might fear something happened to him and would feel abandoned. She was still struggling with the loss of her mother, and Frank did not want to add to her suffering.

But if Frank departed, he would leave his mother to an uncertain future. People who tried unsuccessfully to leave Cuba were shunned and scorned by their neighbors and friends as being disloyal to the cause. By not waiting, Frank was creating an untenable situation for his mother and his other relatives for whom he had placed a claim.

Making matters worse, Frank knew Fidel was so unpredictable he could seal the exit channels at any time. Policy decisions were determined by the dictator's slightest whim.

Frank decided to sleep on it. The following morning, he discussed the matter with Rolando. Both men faced similar issues. Rolando didn't want anything to happen to his brother any more than Frank wanted anything to happen to his relatives.

They each had concerns about work, but nothing that couldn't wait.

Frank had arranged for an employee to run his sandwich shop in his absence, and he assumed that person would continue to do so until he returned. Frank decided that the possible consequences of leaving were far more serious than those for staying, and Rolando agreed. They would see their plan through.

Frank and Rolando had the will and the wherewithal to stay in port. But many people appeared to have neither the time nor the resources to wait. The two men watched with sympathy as men in boat after boat lifted their anchors, started their motors, and turned their empty vessels in the direction of Florida.

Days passed and Frank and Rolando received no word about their family members. Twice, different officials requested their relatives' names and addresses, acting as if this were the first time the information was obtained and recorded. Frank and Rolando became increasingly afraid that their paperwork had been bungled or lost. Other boats had received their passengers, but they had not.

After twenty-three days of waiting, the authorities announced over a loudspeaker the names of the boats that would form the next flotilla. Due to the noise in the harbor, Frank found the news difficult to understand. Although he and Rolando paid close attention, they failed to hear the name of their boat.

Finally, the official announced *Me Why*. The name didn't register with Frank, but Rolando stood up and beamed. "That's us!" he said. Frank looked at him and realized that the Cubans were pronouncing *My Way* as *Me Why*.

Rolando pulled up anchor and motored to the dock to see about their passengers. The guard handed him a list of eighteen people, twice their carrying capacity. Frank figured that overloading the boats was Fidel's way of making life miserable for anyone wishing to leave Cuba. There was no use protesting. Frank closed his eyes and ran his hands through his hair, dreading the trip ahead.

Frank and Rolando eyed their passengers. Rolando's brother was nowhere to be found; neither were Frank's relatives. Frank shook his head. Several burly Haitians climbed aboard, swearing and sweating profusely. Their stares were hard. Their arms were well muscled.

The men had shaved heads, indicating that they might have been released prisoners. Frank and Rolando had no idea who these people were or what they had done. Their passengers could be rapists or murderers for all they knew. Frank tensed and watched Rolando's throat work, fear entering his eyes.

The rest of the group comprised middle-aged men, several housewives, three teenagers, and two children. A little boy clutched a teddy bear, the only passenger carrying anything more than the clothes on his back. Frank wondered who had granted this gesture of kindness.

The last one to climb aboard was a pretty young girl wearing a yellow sundress and red plastic sandals. She looked about eight. She was unaccompanied by an adult, and carried herself with poise and determination. She asked for Frank by name. Rolando ushered her to Frank's side and her eyes grew wide.

"Are you Frankie Mederos?"

Frank nodded, surprised that she knew his name. "Yes, and you are—?"

The girl swallowed hard and pushed her bangs from her forehead. "You don't know me because I was born after you left. But I've heard a lot about you—everybody has."

Frank looked closely at the girl. She was the spitting image of his deceased sister Teresa. Her father was in prison for political reasons, and Frank wondered whether he was one of the inmates who had been released. She interrupted his thoughts.

"I'm your niece, Mari—Maribel."

Delighted at this turn of events, Frank threw back his head and laughed. Then he gathered his niece in his arms and kissed her. She seemed a little uncomfortable at his gesture.

"Where's your grandmother?" he asked. "She was supposed to be here. So was your father, your Uncle José—"

Mari interrupted him. "I don't know what happened." She looked around nervously. "They told Grandma that you put in a claim for her. She was so excited about seeing you. That's all she's been talking about. She gave away all her stuff, but she was never issued a visa."

Frank blanched and his throat tightened. "What do you mean she wasn't issued a visa?"

"Just that—I don't know why." Mari hesitated. "But Uncle Carlos and Uncle José made it." She looked around. "They were with me for a while. Uncle Carlos was holding my hand, but we got separated. I think he's on another boat."

"And the rest of the family? Cousin Sonia?"

"I don't know. She was here but—" Mari began to tremble. "There was so much confusion. I don't know what happened to everyone." Tears welled in her eyes. "Will you take care of me?" Her voice was small and plaintive.

"Of course!" said Frank, taking her hand. "Here, sit between Rolando and me, and don't talk to anyone but us. This could be a long trip, and I don't want anything to happen to you."

Mari settled herself on the cushion next to Frank. He tried to appear positive, but he was bereft that he couldn't get his mother out of Cuba. He wondered whether he'd ever see her again. He shook his head, thinking this is what happens when you get involved with Fidel.

Once Frank fastened his niece's life jacket, Rolando started the engine and pointed the boat toward the officials standing at the departure dock.

CHAPTER FORTY-FIVE

As they waited in the forty-boat queue for the Cuban authorities to finalize their paperwork, Frank announced the rules for the journey. The area where Frank, Rolando, and Mari sat was off limits, not to be breached by anyone, for anything.

No fighting or swearing was allowed. No one was permitted to speak to Mari. Women and children had first dibs on water and blankets, and the women were to be respected at all times. Coast Guard boats were everywhere, and Frank threatened to turn troublemakers over to the authorities for the slightest infraction of the rules.

"Try any funny business and you're going back to Cuba," Frank warned. A man smirked, and Frank stared him down. A stony silence blanketed the group.

With the wind against them, the trip back to Florida was longer and more difficult than the one going to Cuba. The sun beat down relentlessly and the sea rolled beneath the boat. Frank rubbed sunscreen on his niece and distributed his remaining Dramamine to the passengers. Still, some people became sick enough to vomit.

The passengers watched with apprehension as shark fins broke the surface of the water. Everyone realized the danger. Mari held on to Frank for dear life, occasionally shooting him a bewildered glance. To keep her calm, Frank talked to her about school and questioned her about her family and her life in Cuba. He reassured her that everything would be all right, and that she'd love living in the United States. But fear never left her eyes.

The Haitians were surprisingly well behaved, and Frank had to reprimand them only twice. The weather held for the entire trip—no rain, no storms—and the passengers thanked their lucky stars. The boat rose and fell with the swell of waves, occasionally struggling to stay afloat. Many disabled boats punctuated the way. Frank was grateful that his boat was not among them.

With a strong headwind against them, the trip took close to twenty hours. The last two hours were the most difficult. People were tired, sunburned, and eager to stand on solid ground. Frank and Rolando yearned for a home-cooked meal.

With so many people on edge, Frank feared a fight would break out. He watched everyone carefully, ready to act should things get out of hand. When everyone's patience was on the verge of exhaustion, Frank spotted the harbor in Key West. A *V* of geese heralded the boat's arrival, and the passengers let out a rousing cheer.

Rolando motored ahead. Hundreds of boats choked the harbor with thousands of people in need of food, water, and medical assistance. The number of people who had participated in Operation Boatlift greatly exceeded the American government's expectations. The system for processing immigrants into the country was overwhelmed. President Carter was under heavy pressure to deal with a situation that was spinning out of control.

As *My Way* inched into port, the Coast Guard approached. Two officers stepped aboard to examine the boat. They had a checklist and were looking for safety violations.

"Who owns this vessel?" asked the officer.

"I do."

"Name?"

"Frank Mederos."

The man raised his CB radio to his ear and talked to someone for several minutes while the other officer inspected the boat. After ten minutes, he handed Frank a list of citations, stating his boat lacked a horn, a sufficient number of flotation devices, and proper lights.

The officer directed Frank to report to the court in Key West. He handed him a ticket with a list of citations before placing a red "impounded" sticker on the windshield of his boat.

The passengers disembarked, trying to regain their land legs after their voyage at sea. They were beaming. The Haitians faced Cuba and flipped their middle fingers in a gesture of contempt, saying *"No mas Fidel!"*

With Mari and Rolando at his side, Frank made his way to a crowded courtroom, a short distance from the dock. Petrified, Mari clung to her uncle's side like a barnacle to a pylon.

They sat in court for three hours before the judge got to their case. He was a balding, middle-aged man with age spots dotting his head. He rifled through some papers and adjusted his robes. The judge pounded his gavel and looked at Frank over a pair of black reading glasses.

"Mr. Mederos, correct?"

"Yes, Your Honor."

"I see that the boat you took to Cuba was cited for several safety violations."

"Yes, Your Honor."

"What have you to say regarding this matter?"

"I'm sorry, sir. I bought the boat in Miami and was unaware of the violations. I was in a hurry to get to Cuba to rescue my relatives."

"My notes indicate that you returned today—May eighteenth. Correct?"

"Correct."

"So you were in the port of Mariel on May fourteenth?"

"Yes, Your Honor."

"And when you were in the port were you aware that on May fourteenth the President of the United States, Jimmy Carter, temporarily suspended acceptance of Cuban refugees into America?"

Frank looked at him, confused. "No, sir. I had no knowledge of that."

"Did you not see empty boats leaving the harbor?"

Frank considered for a moment. "I did, but I thought they left because the Cuban government asked them to."

"Why would they do that?"

"Hundreds of boats were in the harbor, causing delays in processing paperwork."

"Were you aware that the president's order had been broadcast on the radio?"

"I heard nothing to that effect, Your Honor. By the time in question, I had already given the names and addresses of my relatives to the Cuban authorities."

"I understand. But you still must abide by the laws of the United States. As a result of your actions, the passengers you brought to the States are illegal. According to the law, you should have returned to Florida without them."

Stunned, Frank looked at the judge. He was unsure of what to say. It occurred to him that he might be required to take his passengers back to Cuba, a sobering prospect.

Frank thought for a moment and said, "I hadn't seen my family in thirteen years. If you were in my position, Your Honor, would you turn back?"

The question took the judge by surprise. He thought for a moment and said, "No, under the circumstances, I don't think I would." He hesitated. "How many people did you take out of Cuba?"

"Eighteen."

"How many of your relatives were in your boat?"

"One," said Frank, turning to Mari. "My niece."

The judge looked at Mari and surrendered a small smile. "All right, then. You can go, but I want you to respect the laws of the United States from here on out."

"Yes, Your Honor."

The judge pounded his gavel, and said, "Case dismissed."

Frank and Mari waited for several hours to get her papers processed before looking for the rest of the family. They finally located Frank's cousin, Sonia, her husband, and children. Frank's brother Carlos and his Uncle José were nowhere to be found. Mari was inconsolable.

Frank and Rolando got the family settled in a local motel, and Frank called Chris for assistance. She volunteered to fly to Florida and help Frank get everyone back to New Jersey.

Once Chris and Frank got Mari and Sonia's family to Frank's home in Lincoln Park, they had a small family celebration. Magda's parents brought Darlene back to Frank's house, and he introduced her to long-lost relatives. Darlene showed Mari her room, and the two girls began to bond.

Frank's relatives spent the first few days sleeping on his living room sofa and floor, and catching up on family news. They were curious about the American lifestyle. Frank and Chris took them shopping to buy clothes, shoes, and toiletries, and they were amazed at the quality and quantity of consumer goods in the stores.

Around noon on May thirtieth, the phone rang. Frank had just gotten home from grocery shopping and was unpacking fruit and vegetables at the kitchen table. Chris picked up the receiver and quickly handed it to Frank. He beamed when he heard the person on the other end of the line say, "Frank?"

Although it had been thirteen years, Frank recognized the tone and timbre of his brother's voice. For a moment Frank's mind flashed back to games of hide-and-seek, to times when Carlos would holler, "One, two, three. Ready or not, here I come."

Tears sprung to Frank's eyes as he said, "Jesus, Carlos. Where the hell are you? We've been worried sick about you."

"You won't believe it," replied Carlos. Thinking his brother had arrived in the States, Frank expected him to sound happy, but he didn't.

"Try me."

"I'm in a place called Fort Chaffee."

"Fort Chaffee? Where in God's name is that?"

"Wait a minute. I have the information here somewhere." Frank heard Carlos struggle to retrieve what sounded like a piece of paper. "It's a place called Arkansas. Is that a state?"

Frank laughed. "Yeah, it's a state, but it's hundreds of miles from New Jersey. How in God's name did you get there?"

"There were too many refugees for the authorities to process in Florida, so they sent us here. We came by plane."

"Is Uncle José with you?"

"Yeah, as well as about twenty thousand other people."

"That many?"

"I wouldn't kid you."

"What's happening there?"

"It's bedlam. The place is a hellhole. It's hot as Hades and people are going crazy. A bunch of people are high on marijuana and God knows what else. They're stealing raisins and sugar from the barracks' kitchens to make rum alcohol. Fights are breaking out all over the place. The authorities have confiscated all kinds of weapons—knives, clubs—the works. At the rate it's going, somebody's going to get killed."

"What are they doing about it?"

"The governor is trying to deal with the situation."

"Who's the governor?"

"Some guy named Clinton. Bill Clinton. Ever hear of him?"

"Can't say I have."

"Well, things are really bad. You've got to get us outta here, Frank."

Frank looked at Chris and signaled that something was wrong.

She raised her eyebrows in curiosity. "All right. We've got a houseful of people here, but Chris and I will get there as soon as possible."

Frank explained the situation to Chris and asked Darlene whether she wanted to stay with her grandparents. She said yes. Once they made necessary provisions for the other relatives, Frank and Chris jumped into Frank's car and drove to Arkansas, wondering what in the world they'd face when they arrived. The experience was more than they anticipated.

The fort was enormous, having served as a relocation center for Vietnamese refugees in the 1970s. Shabby wooden barracks were located on approximately seventy-six thousand acres of earth so barren and parched it looked like the moon. Federal troops had been called in to maintain order. Dust and fear hung in the air.

Frank and Chris arrived just in time for a riot. Tired of being fenced in and waiting to be processed, the refugees began attacking authorities with pieces of broken sidewalk and live snakes.

Having heard that Fidel had released inmates of the prisons and mental institutions, the residents of the bordering town of Barling feared for their lives. They had armed themselves to the teeth and wanted the refugees gone.

Hooded Ku Klux Klan members demonstrated outside the front gate, proclaiming white supremacy and demanding action. Locals wielding rifles and clubs egged them on. Two guards escorted Frank and Chris into the fort. Chris's face had turned white with fear. They hurried toward shelter. Never in his life had Frank been more aware of his light-brown skin.

Frank and Chris made their way through the angry crowd and gave the authorities the names of Carlos and José. Shortly thereafter, they were escorted to a crowded waiting area. It contained several couches and a dozen battered chairs. The room was filled to capacity.

Frank wrinkled his nose and looked at Chris. "I smell something burning," he said. He looked out the window to see a gray plume of smoke rise to the sky. Screams suddenly filled the air. The refugees had set several buildings on fire, and hundreds of people were running from the conflagration. Flames devoured doors and window frames.

The National Guard had its work cut out, attempting to extinguish the fire and to keep the refugees from leaving the fort. Soldiers worked to protect Cubans from being shot by angry locals wishing them dead. State troopers used billy clubs and tear gas to quell the riot.

When Frank finally saw Carlos, he had several days worth of beard on his face and dark bags under his eyes. Frank hugged him for a long time and then pulled back to take a good look at him. While he had changed a lot, he was still the brother Frank remembered. Frank hugged him again before introducing him to Chris.

"Where's Uncle José?" asked Frank.

Carlos shook his head. "He's around here somewhere. I saw him this morning."

"What's the next step?" asked Frank.

"The authorities won't release us unless we have a sponsor willing to provide for us. You have to sign forms to that effect. Once that's settled, we have to undergo a medical examination and an interview. Things go much faster if your sponsor is an American citizen." He exhaled. "I hope you're a citizen, Frank."

"I am. I became one in 1974."

"Good."

Frank patted Carlos on the back. "Don't worry, we'll get it all straightened out."

"I was hoping that would be the case," said Carlos.

Chris chimed in. "We have some good news. Frank has rented the house next door to him. You can use it until you get on your feet. You are more than welcome to stay there."

Tears sprung to Carlos's eyes. "I couldn't be more grateful," he said.

"Don't worry. Everything will be fine," said Frank.

Carlos smiled. "I sure am glad to see you, brother."

"I'm glad to see you too," said Frank. "And by the way, Carlos, welcome to America!"

CHAPTER FORTY-SIX

With his stint in Russia completed, Pino desired to be stationed at the large Santa Maria base on the outskirts of Havana, the base where he had served before. But his hopes were dashed. Since the powers that be wanted to keep close tabs on him—at least for a while—they stationed him at military headquarters in Managua.

Having acquired the virtue of patience in the cane fields, Pino bided his time, devoting his energies to impressing his superiors. Although he was now a captain, it was still necessary for him to rebuild the military's confidence in his ability to comply with official practices and procedures.

The knowledge he had acquired in Russia came in handy. His job was to train Cuban captains and commanders on Soviet weaponry—the capabilities and optimum placement of land-to-sea and air-to-air missiles, as well as technical aspects of other weapons. Slowly but surely he was regaining the trust he had squandered with his inglorious past.

Since he returned to Cuba, Pino had suffered one grave disappointment. When he heard about the Mariel boatlift, it occurred to him that Mederos might come to Cuba to claim his relatives. This would provide Pino with a convenient opportunity to exact revenge.

Having developed close connections with members of the Cuban intelligence over the years, Pino approached the officers several times to see whether they had any information regarding Frank's arrival. But with the number of people needing to be processed in the tens of thousands, the operation was slow, cumbersome, and chaotic. Pino was relentless in his inquiries. But days passed with no word regarding Mederos.

Finally, Pino learned of his nemesis's presence in the harbor. Records showed the names and addresses of the relatives Frank had requested to claim and the name of his boat. Pino hoped to apprehend Frank if he ever came on land for supplies. But Pino learned of Frank's presence in the harbor several hours too late. By the time he had been given the paperwork, Frank was in the middle of the Florida Straits.

Pino was furious. He railed against the incompetent system and the lazy intelligence officials, cursing them and threatening them with retribution. But all was for naught. Once again, Frank had gotten away. Once again, he had evaded Pino's clutches.

While Pino had not managed to have Mederos arrested, he had gained an important piece of information: his address in America. Hoping it would come in handy someday, he carefully recorded it in a small leather-bound book. Mederos may have eluded him twice, but Pino vowed it wouldn't happen again.

Pino's other frustration was how long it was taking him to gain re-admittance into the Communist Party. It seemed like an eternity. Pino viewed this not only as an emblem of power, but as a testament to his ability to overcome adversity.

It took some time, but thanks to his friend, Torres, Pino was finally granted his wish. On that day, Pino gazed with pride upon the red document that contained his name, picture, and credentials. The captain smiled and brought his treasure to his heart in a gesture of affection, knowing it was the key to his future military success.

Finally, after painstaking work to prove himself to the authorities, Pino was named commander of the base at Santa Maria. This was the base where all his troubles began, the base he had left in disgrace, and the base from which Mederos had escaped. It gave Pino great satisfaction to finally be in charge here, and he planned to take full advantage of the opportunity.

Pino now had considerable power. As base commander, he had seven hundred men under him, including three cannon batteries, three hundred members of the infantry, and three hundred and fifty members of the Special Forces. He had handpicked his lieutenants, and he knew that at least one was totally loyal to him.

To the casual observer, Pino seemed rehabilitated. Unlike other commanders, he took a keen interest in the members of the Special Forces, congratulating those who performed well in exercises, those who excelled in academics, and those who exhibited political purity and revolutionary ardor.

This was not the way he behaved when he was a lieutenant, in the days before his trial, in the days when Lazo worked under his command. Although Pino's behavior was reassuringly different, remnants of his old affect remained.

Periodically, Commander Pino invited thirty to forty soldiers to feast with him in the officers' dining room, an invitation that was highly prized and eagerly sought. Waiters served elegantly prepared food and fine wine to the select soldiers in the beautifully appointed dining chamber. It was not only a coveted honor to eat with the commander, but an opportunity for members of the Special Forces to gain prestige in the eyes of their fellow soldiers.

Pino was exceedingly gracious, inquiring after the men's well-being, their families, and health. He was known to say, "How about another glass of wine? Here, help yourself to one of these juicy steaks—a young man needs protein!" This was music to the ears of those soldiers lucky enough to sup with their commander.

Pino knew what he was doing. He took his time. He was in no hurry. He had formulated a plan, and now he was in the position to recruit the right man to execute it.

He had spent months—no, years—reviewing various scenarios in his mind, weighing their pros and cons, planning for contingencies, assessing the skills of the person needed for the job. He had to pin his hopes on one of these men, but which one?

Pino watched them all with a sharp eye, asking them leading questions that would shed light on their character, their risk tolerance—and most importantly—their total loyalty to him.

Eventually, Pino narrowed his list to five or six, eliminating men lacking the requisite intelligence, determination, and ambition. He needed a soldier with a rare combination of qualities to serve his needs.

And he dare not make a bad selection.

CHAPTER FORTY-SEVEN

After months of meetings, Pino identified two privates who filled the bill: Alberto Alanis and Damian Baez. Alberto was smart, loyal, and eager to please. He exuded a confidence born of his good looks and fine physique. He had a superior intellect and the added distinction of being top in his class, a real plus in Pino's eyes. Several members of his family were active in the Communist Party, and there was no reason to suspect he would be anything but loyal to the cause.

Damian also came from a family of loyal communists, and it was no surprise that Pino found him even more engaging than Alberto. The young man was ruggedly handsome with a shock of black hair, sparkling brown eyes, and an aristocratic nose.

When Pino spoke, Damian hung on his every word, adding to the conversation in ways Pino found satisfying and insightful. Damian exhibited extraordinary patience, excellent judgment, and keen powers of concentration and observation, useful qualities under a variety of circumstances. Damian also had "the killer instinct," a hard edge necessary to carry out his mission.

Pino was close to a decision. But he needed to be circumspect. He would approach both men carefully, feel them out, and watch for a telltale sign that would indicate the better choice.

One evening after dinner, Pino asked Alberto to join him in his office. Both men were in good spirits, having imbibed a bottle of wine between them. The commander extended his hand toward the chair. "Sit, please," Pino said pleasantly. Alberto took a seat opposite Pino's desk, careful not to let his spine touch the back of the chair. His feet were planted firmly on the polished-wood floor. Even under these circumstances Alberto knew it was prudent to obey protocol.

Pino smiled amiably, as if he had not a care in the world. He studied Alberto for a moment before saying, "I'm very impressed with you, young man. You have an excellent grasp of military matters, and your dedication to your work is exemplary."

"Thank you, sir," said Alberto.

Pino was not a man to bestow compliments lightly. Pino cleared his throat. "As your commander, there's something I must talk to you about."

Alberto looked into Pino's wolverine eyes, and a shudder surged through his body. "Yes, sir."

Pino hesitated before speaking. "Occasionally I get a call from Managua regarding highly sensitive missions. This information comes right from the top." Pino narrowed his eyes, studying Alberto. "If a mission like this were to arise, would you be interested?"

"As an assignment, sir?"

"Exactly."

"Yes, sir. Of course."

"Good. Because it has come to my attention that the army has a mission on the drawing boards that would require the skills of someone highly intelligent, someone knowledgeable and earnest like yourself."

Alberto looked confused. It was highly unusual for a base commander to discuss such matters with a private.

"What kind of mission?"

"Top secret—a special assignment directed at the highest levels of government."

"Top secret?"

"A grave matter regarding national security. Do you understand?"

Alberto gulped and nodded. "I'm trying to understand, sir." Pino watched Alberto closely. "Any questions?"

Alberto squirmed in his seat. "Could you tell me more about the mission, sir?"

"I'm sorry. I'm not at liberty to disclose any details. Again, this is a highly confidential matter."

"I understand, sir."

"The authorities have not made a final determination on the execution of this mission. But if it is to take place, I must have a man in mind, someone I feel comfortable recommending. Due to your excellent scholastic performance and your exceptional leadership skills, you are being considered."

"I see, sir." Alberto shifted his body in his chair, a slight smile distending his lips.

"I understand your family are members of the Party."

"My father and brother are both Party members."

"Then I don't need to tell you about the importance of loyalty."

"No, sir. My father has lectured me on that subject my entire life. And, of course, the force has reinforced his teachings."

"Of course." Pino thought for a moment and drew his lips together while Alberto looked on curiously. "In this business, you must be scrupulous in following orders. You must remain above reproach. You must not question authority—ever!"

"I understand."

"You also must be willing to risk your life for your country. And you must be willing to kill if necessary. Am I making myself clear?"

"Yes, sir, that goes without saying."

"So, you concur."

"Of course."

"Say it!" snapped Pino, suddenly annoyed.

"I concur," said Alberto in a tremulous voice. Pino leaned forward, placed his elbow on his desk, and rested his chin on his fisted hand. The two men regarded each other like boxers in a ring.

Alberto broke the silence. "Is there anything else you could tell me about the mission, sir?"

"There's little I can tell you now other than the assignment is highly dangerous, and it is of utmost importance to me and to our nation." Pino's voice dropped its edge. "And, if you are offered and accept this assignment, you will be rewarded handsomely."

Alberto's face brightened. Pino watched the soldier's expression with concern. He believed that monetary reward should not be the prime driver for the man who took this assignment. It would be a consideration, of course. But he wanted someone with fire in his belly—someone who would complete the mission for three reasons: loyalty to him, dedication to the cause, and love of country. In that order.

"I assume the assignment would be in Cuba," said Alberto.

Pino's nostrils flared as he inhaled sharply. "This mission will not be carried out in Cuba. I cannot divulge its location, but it would take place outside the country."

For a brief moment Alberto's face soured.

Pino watched Alberto carefully, unhappy with his expression.

"You seem concerned. Are you still interested?" Pino asked sharply.

Alberto paused before he spoke. Pino interpreted his hesitation as reluctance.

"Of course I'm interested. It sounds like an opportunity of a lifetime," said Alberto. "Who wouldn't be interested?"

"Good. But give it due consideration. There's no need to decide now. I need someone smart and sensible, and you may be the man for the job."

Pino stood and extended his hand. Alberto did likewise. "We will speak again. Meanwhile, this conversation is to remain between the two of us. Do I have your word on that?"

"Yes, sir. I understand. I will think it over carefully."

Once Alberto left his office, Pino sat on his chair and expelled his breath. He didn't expect Alberto to hesitate the way he did, and he didn't like it. Didn't like it at all.

Pino leaned back in his chair and propped his feet on his desk.

What's wrong with him? That kid should've been chomping at the bit for an opportunity such as this. Then it struck him. *He probably has a girlfriend. Of course! A girlfriend. Why was it that the damn women always got in the way? That was the problem with Mederos. Couldn't wait to be with his honey. Well, I learned my lesson on that score. I'm not falling into the trap of dealing with another man whose judgment is compromised because he's love crazy. If Alberto gets antsy to see his girlfriend, he could jeopardize the whole mission. He could get hasty. Careless. Sloppy. Then where would I be?*

Pino lit a cigarette and dropped his gold lighter onto his desk. It landed with a thud. Memories of the sugarcane fields flashed through his mind. *The stakes surrounding this mission are too high. This guy is bright, but I can't chance it.* He shook his head. *No, I can't take a chance, not when I could face a court martial for what I plan to do.*

CHAPTER FORTY-EIGHT

A couple of days elapsed before Pino decided to discuss the mission with Damian. He was still disappointed with Alberto's reaction and was hoping this interview would prove more fruitful.

The two men met in the officers' dining room, where they dined on steak and lobster, and finished their meal with snifters of brandy. Pino lead the way back to his office and switched on the light. A dog barked in the distance. The hum of insects grated the evening air.

Pino was eager to begin the conversation. It was time—past time—for his mission to get under way. After both men settled in their chairs, Pino turned to Damian, and said, "I have a serious matter to discuss with you." The commander's demeanor was somber.

"Please," said Damian, nodding to Pino.

"I'm obliged to inform you that there exists a grave threat to Cuba's national security."

Damian's back stiffened. "I'm sorry to hear that, sir. Can I help in some way?"

Pino thought for a moment. "Perhaps." Damian waited for Pino to continue. "I've received word from the highest authority that a former Cuban—a worm—may need to be eliminated."

"I see, sir."

"Question: if you had the opportunity to kill a traitor, someone who was a threat to this nation's very existence, would you take it?"

A feral look flashed in Damian's eyes. Pino liked it.

"Without hesitation," said Damian.

"Why?"

"A traitor is a threat to everything Cuba stands for—our traditions, our values, our way of life. I'd have no trouble stomping out a worm. Anyone who has betrayed the Motherland deserves to be killed."

"True."

"What do you have in mind?"

"I'm awaiting orders—nothing is certain, mind you. But I've been asked to recommend a man who would be willing to carry out an important mission if necessary. And I thought of you."

"I appreciate the thought, sir."

Pino glanced out the window before he returned his gaze to Damian. The moon lit the sky with a stainless steel glow.

"Due to the classified nature of this mission, the man selected will have the full backing of the Cuban government. No matter where you go, no matter what you do, you will have a safety net. All resources will be brought to bear to make the mission successful."

"That's good to know," said Damian.

The young soldier glanced at the ceiling as if in deep thought. Pino interrupted his reverie. "In case you were wondering, considerable compensation awaits the man who accepts this assignment."

Damian looked unimpressed. Since he did not respond, Pino continued, "If you are given this opportunity, you will be granted the rank of full lieutenant as soon as your feet touch foreign soil. Upon successful completion of the mission, you will return to Cuba where you will take command of a Special Forces unit. With your new rank, you will receive a generous salary. You will be set up in your own apartment and will be given your own jeep."

Pino expected Damian to smile, but he did not. He waited a moment for this information to sink in. Finally, Pino said, "You don't seem very excited about the benefits."

"Those things are of little consequence to me," said Damian. "What's important is that I be able to eliminate a worm that may threaten our country. It sounds like this guy could do a lot of harm."

"He has in the past and he can in the future."

"That's all I need to know."

Pino smiled inwardly, knowing he had found his man. Silence

deadened the air for a moment before Pino asked, "Do you have any questions?"

"May I inquire where the assignment would be?"

Feeling certain of his selection, Pino volunteered, "Should I receive the go-ahead order, the mission will take place in the States."

"Good. There are a lot of traitors there. And we know full well that they've infiltrated our military. The world will be better off with one less worm."

"My sentiments exactly," said Pino.

"May I ask how I would get there?"

"Just as the Americans have their people here, we have people in the States who would tend to you. The Cuban government will guarantee safe passage in and out of the country."

"When will the mission occur?"

"I'm awaiting word from higher authority. I'll let you know when and if it's a go. Meanwhile, I don't need to remind you that this conversation never happened."

Damian stood and saluted. "Never happened," he said, and turned for the door.

CHAPTER FORTY-NINE

Other than Torres, Pino had only one real friend in the army, one man in whom he could confide, one man who would tell him exactly what he thought without the usual obsequiousness: First Lieutenant Franco. A sandy-haired man with a double chin, Franco was as smart as anyone Pino had ever known.

But what Pino really appreciated was the man's loyalty and wise advice. He had steered Pino in the right direction on more than one occasion. The two men saw eye to eye on most matters, and their friendship had withstood the test of time.

Late the next afternoon Pino strode into the lieutenant's office. "We need to talk," he said, closing the door behind him.

"Pull up a chair," said Franco. "What's on your mind?"

"I want you to know that I've identified my man for the mission."

Franco shook his head in disapproval. "You know what I think of this 'mission' of yours."

Pino waved his comment away. "I'm here to discuss the man who will do it."

"So, you've chosen someone against my advice?"

"I have."

"Who?"

"Damian Baez."

Franco slapped his forehead. "Christ! And he's agreed?"

"He considers it an honor—he can't wait to kill a traitor."

The lieutenant pressed his lips together and rubbed his temples with his forefingers. "What did you promise him?"

Pino shrugged. "He didn't seem that interested in the reward."

"But you promised him something, nonetheless."

"I told him he'd be made a full lieutenant as soon as he landed in America."

"And—"

"And he'd get his own apartment, a jeep, a good salary, glory—the works."

"Anything else?"

"He'd command a Special Forces unit when he returns."

Franco tilted his chin toward the ceiling before lowering it. "Do you want my opinion, or do you just want me to shut up and listen?"

"I'm willing to hear you out."

Franco closed his eyes for a moment. "I understand your reasons for this mission. I know you paid a high price for what happened with Mederos. But you're making a big mistake."

Pino raised his chin at the lieutenant's words, but refrained from silencing him. "Go on."

"This whole thing is lunacy. You're still harboring a grudge about something that happened, how many years ago?"

"What happened was big. Real big. Time doesn't matter with that kind of thing."

"Yeah, it matters. Mederos is probably married and has a couple of kids by now. I'm sure he's forgotten about the whole episode. I doubt he poses any threat to Cuba."

"Well, I haven't forgotten about the 'whole episode' as you put it. Justice is justice. And I'm going to make that little worm pay."

"Well, you asked, and I'm telling you. I think you should leave Mederos alone. What you're planning will just cause trouble—it's not worth it."

"It is to me!"

Pino's remark hung in the air while he stared out the window, stewing.

Franco blew out his cheeks. "You are a smart man, Commander. But this thing is eating you alive—it has been for years. When are you going to let it go?"

Pino stared at Franco with a vulturine look. "Mederos is a traitor and a worm, and it is my duty to bring him down. I can't let that go."

"All right. I hear you. But is this the best way to do it?"

"What do you mean?"

"For starters, we both know you can't make good on your promises to Baez. That's the kind of trouble that will blow up in your face someday. Sooner, I'd say, rather than later."

"Not the way I've got it planned—"

Franco eyed Pino warily. "I have no idea what you have planned. But if you are determined to get Mederos, there are cleaner and easier ways to do it. We've got people in the States who handle these kinds of assignments. We've been over this before. It's way too risky for you to get personally involved. Why don't you just put the word out and let somebody else take care of it?"

Pino scowled. "You don't understand. I don't want to *hear* that Mederos went down, I want to *know* he went down. I want to be as close to this thing as possible. I want you, and only you, to tell me what happened. I want you to describe to me exactly how Mederos died so there are no doubts in my mind. I want Mederos to know that I was the one behind taking him out. I need to know he's dead not only in my head, but in my heart, in my soul, in my *bones*."

"Have it your way, Commander. But remember, I'm dead set against this whole operation."

"Frankly, Lieutenant, I don't give a damn whether you're for or against it. I'm not asking your permission. I'm going to carry out this mission regardless of your opinion. I need you to help me refine and execute my plan. Are you up for that?"

Franco looked disgruntled. "Fine," he said, grabbing a pencil. "Then we need to nail down the details. First, how are you going to explain Baez's absence from base?"

"I'll say he had a family medical emergency."

"And after that?"

"After that I'll claim he defected. He'll never be seen or heard from again."

The implication of what Pino was saying hit Franco in the face like a flyswatter. "So you're—and you want me to—?" He dropped his pencil. "I'm sorry, Commander, but that's plain crazy!"

Pino's fingers formed a fist on his lap. "There's no other way. I know I can't keep my promise to Baez. And I know what he'd do if he learned I lied to him. He'd run at the mouth to anyone who'd listen to him—his mother, his father, his siblings, his fellow soldiers—until it got back to the brass in Managua."

"That's what I'm telling you."

Pino raised his hand threateningly, and his voice shot up an octave. "Listen to me and listen to me well. Damian Baez will never make it back to Cuba. Do you understand? You, my dear and trusted first lieutenant, are going to make sure of that. Appoint someone to do the dirty work. You don't have to do it yourself. You will oversee the operation. But I want to be clear: once Baez leaves this base, I never want to see his face again."

Franco started to speak, and Pino held up a hand to stop him. "I trust you—and you alone—to complete this mission. If you do this for me, I will take care of you. You have always wanted to be a base commander. I'm in a position to make that happen. There's an opening coming up. Complete your mission and the sky's the limit. Are we clear?"

Franco inhaled noisily. "We're clear."

"We have an understanding?"

"We do."

Pino smiled. To Franco's dismay, he also licked his lips. "Then good hunting, my friend."

CHAPTER FIFTY

Lazo was dismayed when he heard Pino had returned to serve as commander of the Santa Maria base. Given Pino's behavior in the past, Lazo could not imagine how Pino had managed this feat. He was well acquainted with Pino's demeanor when he served under him, and he doubted the man had changed. He had recently heard about Pino's stint in the cane fields and his military training in the Soviet Union, and he was at a loss to explain how one had led to the other.

He wondered whether the former lieutenant still harbored resentment toward him regarding his friendship with Frank and, more importantly, whether he would do anything about it. Lazo knew he would have to be especially careful to keep a low profile and not antagonize the captain.

At first Lazo gave short shrift to the fact that Pino was entertaining solders in the officers' dining room. He had more important matters on his mind. But as the number of men Pino wined and dined dwindled, Lazo became increasingly concerned. Recently, he had seen Damian and Alberto with the commander, and in both cases the soldiers had dined alone with Pino.

Lazo decided to discuss the situation with Tomás. He closed the office door and pulled up a chair. "Pino's got something up his sleeve," he said.

"What do you mean?"

"He's been meeting with a couple of privates one-on-one, and that just doesn't happen at his level."

Tomás nodded. "You think he's up to something?"

"I think he's recruiting these men for some kind of mission. I don't know what, but I'd sure like to get to the bottom of it."

"Well, keep an eye on him and get back to me with anything pertinent."

The following weekend, Lazo saw Alberto sitting on a bench outside the barracks. Lazo lit a cigarette as he approached him. "How's it going, Alberto?"

Alberto looked startled. He had been lost in thought. "Okay," he said, but his voice held no enthusiasm.

Lazo sat down on the bench. He had had long talks with Alberto before, and he was very fond of him. "C'mon, Alberto, why so glum? Aren't those steaks you're having with the commander agreeing with you?"

Alberto made a face and shook his head. "I just want to do my job and be left alone."

Lazo chuckled. "Are you telling me that the commander won't let you do your job? That doesn't sound like him."

"No, quite the opposite."

The hairs on the back of Lazo's head suddenly stood on end. "What do you mean, Alberto?" he said softly.

Alberto pushed some dirt around with the toe of his boot as the palm trees rustled in the breeze. "It's classified. I can't talk about it."

"Okay," said Lazo.

The two men sat in silence for a few minutes, but Lazo could tell Alberto was dying to continue the conversation. A monarch butterfly alighted on a nearby rock, flapped its wings, and flew away.

"I'm afraid I'll have to do that too," sighed Alberto.

Lazo was momentarily confused. "Do what? Fly away?"

"Yeah, fly away."

"What do you mean?"

"Commander Pino spoke to me about a job where I'd have to go somewhere, and I don't know what to do."

"What are your concerns?"

"I don't know if I can do it."

"Well, I don't know what the job is, but I have full confidence in you and your abilities. I'm sure you could handle any assignment Commander Pino gives you."

Alberto shook his head and considered for a moment. He took a deep breath. "Even if it's a secret mission—straight from the top?"

Lazo gulped, weighing his response. He didn't want to appear like he was pressing for more information, especially if Pino had sworn Alberto to secrecy. "I'm sure you could handle whatever it is. Why do you doubt yourself?"

"It's not that I think I can't do it. I don't want to leave my girl-friend. I don't want to be away from Cuba. It's bad enough that I only get to see her when I'm on leave once a month. She's not very patient, and a lot of other men find her attractive. I'm afraid she'll break up with me if I'm away too long. That's what I'm worried about."

"So the mission isn't in Cuba?"

"Pino didn't say exactly where it would be. But he did say it would be out of the country. I figure it could be anywhere—Vietnam, South America, Mexico. Even Russia or America."

"I see."

"I thought Pino would come down really hard on me if I refused the assignment, so I said I'd accept it."

"That was a wise move."

"The good news is that Pino says the mission isn't certain yet. He's awaiting orders from Managua. Maybe I won't have to do it."

"That's always a possibility."

Alberto smiled slightly. "There's also a chance he'll pick some-one else."

"Like who?"

"Damian Baez. He has dinner with him as often as he does with me."

"There you go," said Lazo, trying to sound lighthearted. "Maybe it won't be a problem after all."

"I hope so."

"Me too." Lazo patted Alberto on the shoulder and stood up, shaking his head as he walked away.

CHAPTER FIFTY-ONE

Pino was so excited he could hardly contain himself. After years of planning, scheming, and brooding, the time for final preparation was at hand. He trusted that Franco and Baez would not let him down, and he could imagine the satisfaction he'd feel when he heard the news of Mederos's demise. His phone rang, and he leaned over his desk to answer it.

"What do you have for me?" asked Franco.

"I've made the necessary arrangements. Your associates' names are Sebastian and Elias. They will pick up you and Damian when you arrive in Key West. You will spend the night with them in a safe house in Miami."

"What's the plan after that?"

"Damian, Sebastian, and Elias will leave for Union City the next morning. You will remain in Miami and direct operations from there. A man named Adán will assist you."

"What do you know about these guys?"

"Not much. One of my Russian contacts recommended them. He assured me they are up to the job. He said they were the best he could do on late notice."

"Right. What's happening in Union City?"

"My contacts there are scouting Mederos. They know where he lives, where he works, and what his habits are. He'll be an easy target."

"Who's in charge there?"

"A guy named José."

"Anyone else involved?"

"Someone named Chico. He'll help José, should the need arise."

"When do we leave?"

"Everything's set for next week. You'll leave on Monday."

"Is there anything I should do before that? Any preparations I need to make?"

"No. I'll give you Mederos's file and picture. When the time comes, give them to Baez so he can identify the target."

"Should I tell him anything now?"

"No, I'll brief him after dinner. Don't give him any information. We don't want it to leak out that I'm after Mederos. Everything's on a need-to-know basis."

"How should I explain my absence from base?"

"You have a vacation coming. Claim it."

"Easy enough."

That evening Pino met with Damian to finalize plans regarding the mission. Pino looked at Damian with confidence. He liked what he saw—a man in great physical condition, well-trained in guerrilla tactics, and willing to sacrifice his life for the cause. He was perfect!

"You'll be happy to learn that I've chosen you for the special mission we spoke about," said Pino.

Damian's eyes shone. "I'm delighted to hear that, sir."

"Sit down, and I'll give you some background on our mission." Damian took a seat opposite Pino's large desk. "First, I want you to know that we did not seek this mission. It came to us."

"Came to us? How so?"

"As you know, Cuba has enemies all over the world—people who want to bring our country to its knees."

"I understand."

"We have an enemy in the United States—someone who was a member of the Special Forces—just like you. This worm works for the CIA and is in constant contact with an entire network of subversives hoping to overthrow our government. That includes

Alpha Sixty-six. He meets with them, trains them, and conspires with them at the highest levels. He hates Cuba, Fidel, and everything we stand for. Believe me when I tell you he has the knowledge and the will to bring us down."

"That's very worrisome, sir."

"It is."

"I assume he's an excellent fighter."

"He knows everything you know about fighting and more. As you know, members of Alpha Sixty-six played a key role in the Bay of Pigs invasion. They are experienced fighters. Mederos has their respect. His deep knowledge of our military secrets puts our great nation at risk."

Damian shook his head. "After all Cuba has done for him." He hesitated. "Mederos is the worst kind of traitor."

"The worst kind," echoed Pino. "He is using the training and skills he acquired in our military against us. And he's done so for years. Now he's amassed enough power and contacts to do our nation irreparable harm."

Damian looked puzzled. "In what way, sir?"

Pino was warming to the subject, wanting to drive home his point. "I'm not at liberty to go into details. But based on an in-depth analysis of the situation, it has been determined that an invasion of Cuba is imminent. Mederos has been engaged in counterrevolutionary activity for years. He gives speeches and stirs up thousands of other worms to overthrow our government. Their plans are now coming to fruition. Time is critical. We must act before it's too late."

"I understand the importance of this mission, sir."

Pino cleared his throat. "I have not received final word yet on the desired outcome of the mission. Orders could be to eliminate him. You once said you wouldn't hesitate to pull the trigger against a traitor. Does that hold true, even if he is a former member of the Special Forces?"

Damian spoke with heat in his voice. "A traitor is a traitor. So it does."

Pino straightened his back. "I hope you realize what an honor this is. I knew this man some time ago. He is a worm of the first order. I would be more than happy to pull the trigger myself." He waved his hand to indicate the scope of the base. "But I have other duties to attend."

"Of course," said Damian. "These things must be left to men like myself."

"So I can trust that you will not hesitate to complete the mission when the time comes?"

"You can."

"Good."

Pino sat back in his chair, looking satisfied. "Now, let's talk logistics. We have many friends in the United States just as we have enemies. And the Americans have friends in Cuba, so we must be careful."

"Of course."

"You will have safe passage to and from the United States. We will provide you with a safe house where you will stay when you arrive in Miami. Our people will greet you in Key West and will supply you with everything you need—a weapon, food, and gear. A safe house will also be established in New Jersey. You will learn of its location when you arrive in Miami."

"Excellent. Will I be going alone?"

"No, First Lieutenant Franco will accompany you. He will oversee the mission from our base in Miami."

Damian nodded. "When do we leave?"

"Monday. I will inform you of the time and method of departure. Until then, keep your head low."

"I will."

The two men stood and saluted. When Damian left, a satisfied smile danced on Pino's lips.

CHAPTER FIFTY-TWO

Early Tuesday morning Lazo walked into Tomás's office, and said, "Remember what I told you about Captain Pino?"

"Yes."

"My suspicions have been confirmed."

Tomás put his paperwork aside. "Tell me more."

"Pino's going after Frank. He's using Franco to oversee the operation, and he's using a member of the Special Forces to carry it out."

"Jesus! How do you know that?"

"I talked with another soldier that Pino was trying to recruit for a top-secret mission outside Cuba. On orders from Managua."

"And?"

"That's not how things are handled, you know that. There are too many steps between Pino and the brass in Managua—too many ways word could leak out. Pino would never be asked to execute a secret mission. This is his own private vendetta to get Frank."

"You're sure?"

"Positive. A member of the Special Forces named Damian Baez left yesterday on emergency family leave. Meanwhile, Franco has taken an unscheduled vacation."

"Adds up, doesn't it?"

"Damn right it does."

Tomás thought for a moment. "Who else is Pino using for the operation?"

"Pino made a lot of friends while he was in Russia. He's got people all over the world who owe him favors, including men in the States. I have no idea who he's using, but there's no government involvement."

"You're sure?"

"Positive."

"That guy never gives up, does he?"

Lazo chuckled. "You have no idea."

Tomás thought for a moment. "This guy, Baez. Is he smart?"

"He's smart, and he's got ties to the Party."

"Okay. You've convinced me. I'll get my people on it right away. We'll have somebody find and warn your friend Frank."

Lazo shook his head. "That's not what I want."

Tomás looked at him askance. "What do you mean?"

"I understand protocol. God knows how many times I've done this kind of thing for the agency. But I don't want to do this one by the book. This time it's different."

Tomás eyed Lazo warily. "How do you figure?"

"This operation hits home—it means a lot to me. I want to go myself to warn Frank. If I tell him he's in danger, he'll believe me. If somebody else delivers the message, he may dismiss it as nonsense, especially after all the time that's elapsed. Frank's my friend, and I want to personally see this thing through."

Tomás looked nonplussed. "I don't like the sound of this. You are far too important to our operation to take a chance like that. If you get caught, it will totally blow your cover. Our people can handle this situation. You can add nothing to the operation that can't be done by someone else."

The lines of Lazo's mouth turned downward. "You are forgetting one important element."

"What's that?"

"I'm the only one who can identify the trigger man. Besides, I trained Baez. I know his strengths and weaknesses, and how he's likely to react in a given situation. Frank has never even seen him— he's a sitting duck."

"I'll grant you that. But this is a very dangerous mission, and I don't want to compromise it for one man's agenda."

Lazo's face revealed his frustration, but his voice remained calm, rational. "Look, Tomás, in all the years I've worked for you, I've never asked a personal favor. But I'm asking for one now, not as a CIA agent, but as a person."

"Have you and Frank corresponded over the years?"

"No, Frank knows better than that. He would never put me in danger by contacting me."

"Of course." Tomás thought for a minute. "You really care about this guy?"

"Frank and I bonded in the force. He is a good man, and I could never live with myself if I thought I could've saved his life and didn't."

Tomás pursed his lips. "Don't take offense. But what guarantee do I have that you won't stay in the States once you get there?"

Lazo smirked. "If I wanted to live in the States, then I wouldn't be here. My entire family lives in Cuba. I have no desire to live anywhere else."

"I understand. But getting you involved in this mission is not as easy as you may think. I have to talk to my supervisors about it. We'll have to contact members of Alpha Sixty-six. They're the ones who would take care of something like this. They are very independent-minded. I doubt they'll want one of us tagging along."

"Well, do what you have to do. But do it fast. Because my friend is in danger, and I'm going to help him—with or without your permission."

Tomás rubbed his forehead. "Do you know when the hit will take place?"

"No. But Baez and Franco have already left base, so the operation is well underway."

"You're bound and determined to do this, aren't you, Lazo?"

"Yes, sir, I am. In my eyes and in the eyes of many others, Frank is a beacon of freedom. He gave us hope. I'll be damned if I will allow something to happen to him. And I'm willing to risk my life to make sure it doesn't. Pino failed once to kill Frank, and I want to make sure he fails again."

"I hear you," sighed Tomás. "We'll talk again later."

CHAPTER FIFTY-THREE

The next day Tomás asked Lazo for a full description of Frank Mederos: name, last known address, skills, and distinguishing physical characteristics.

Lazo tossed and turned for the next two nights, worried about the outcome of the mission. Deep down, he knew Tomás was right—his proposal was riddled with risk. He would be operating in a foreign country with people whose methods and procedures were unfamiliar and unpredictable.

He was jeopardizing years of dangerous espionage work for a mission of uncertain outcome. His deep understanding of Cuba's military operations, its strengths and vulnerabilities, would be worthless on this mission. If the mission did not succeed, the consequences would be grave. He would fail Frank, Tomás, and the CIA. Not to mention himself.

But his gut told him to go to Frank's aid. He knew emotions drive decisions more often than not, even his. This was an emotionally driven choice. But one he was willing to make. Now he was sitting outside his superior's office awaiting orders.

When the door opened, Tomás gestured to Lazo to enter. "Sit down," he said.

Lazo glanced out the window and took a seat. Several men were dragging pipe off a refinery truck. The sound of metal upon metal grated the air. Tomás stood and closed the window. It rattled shut.

"I won't beat around the bush," said Tomás. "I'm not in favor of your proposal. I think it's foolish for a number of reasons, not the least of which is the danger posed to you and to the agency."

He took a breath. "But I understand the personal nature of this mission, and I respect that."

"Thank you, sir."

"Against my better judgment, I've prevailed upon my superiors to grant you your request. Given your distinguished service to this agency, they've agreed. And I am willing to go along with it—just this once."

Lazo smiled slightly. "I appreciate that, sir."

"Now, let me fill you in on what we know so far."

Lazo pulled his chair up to the desk while Tomás opened a folder. "I've put out some feelers to find out what's happening."

"What have you learned?"

"Pino has set up an apartment in Miami for his people."

"Describe it."

"It's your basic high-rise. Small. Spartan. Two bedrooms, living room, eat-in kitchen. Nothing fancy. Nothing that would draw attention."

"That's their headquarters?"

"As far as we can tell, it's where decisions are made. Lieutenant Franco and a man named Adán will work from there. Damian has either arrived or is on his way. We're not sure. Cuban operatives named Elias and Sebastian will pick up Baez and Franco at the dock. They will take Franco and Baez to the safe house and then accompany Baez to Union City."

"What do they know about Frank?"

"They know his address, his place of work, and his personal habits."

"Which are?"

"Nothing out of the ordinary for an American. He owns a couple of restaurants in New Jersey. He works long hours. Dines out on Friday nights. We know which restaurants he prefers."

"Anything else?"

"He's a sportsman. Likes to fish and hunt."

"For what?"

"Fishes for trout. Hunts for deer."

"What kind of gun does he use?"

"We don't know yet."

"Well, find out. It's important. He's an excellent shot."

"It's on the list."

"What about Magda?"

"Magda?"

"His wife."

"We haven't heard about anyone named Magda. He brings a young girl to work with him sometimes. She often stays with an older couple and another woman. We figure they're her aunt and grandparents."

Lazo thought for a minute. "It must be his daughter."

"That's what it looks like."

"How do you know all this?"

"One of our guys posed as a washer repair man for their safe house in Miami. He dropped a bug. We overhear all their intelligence. It's simple."

Lazo shook his head. "Nothing's ever simple in this business. We both know that." He looked at the ceiling before his gaze returned to Tomás. "I want to be very clear about something. Franco and Baez are hard-core communists, loyal to a fault. They know Pino hates Frank with a passion, and the commander will not look kindly on them if they fail to kill him. They will eliminate anyone in their path to complete this mission. Your people need to be careful."

"Don't worry. Our guys from Alpha Sixty-six have faced worse. Hell, two of them fought with Fidel in the hills until they figured out what a nutcase he is. The other two worked the Bay of Pigs invasion—spent time in a Cuban jail as a reward for their efforts."

"What do they do now?"

"They patrol Cuban waters, try to blow up military installations. Cause trouble. Sometimes they're successful. Sometimes not."

"Sounds like the mission's in good hands."

"The mission *is* in good hands." Tomás thought for a moment,

"Listen, I hate to reiterate something you already know, but if you are apprehended by the Americans, do not mention your connection with the agency. If you do, we'll deny knowing you. Just go to jail. We'll take care of everything after that."

"Understood. Do you have a weapon for me?"

"You'll be issued a gun in case of emergency. But remember, your role is to warn Frank and to identify Damian. Nothing else. I don't want you involved in any gunfight. I don't want you killing anyone. Those are my orders. Do you understand?"

Lazo ignored the statement. "What kind of danger does Frank face now?"

"He's fine. Our people are keeping close tabs on him. If anyone moves on Frank, we'll take care of it."

"Why haven't they made a move yet?"

"They're doing the same thing we are: reconnaissance. They know as much about Frank as we do. They are waiting for the proper moment. They're being very careful."

Lazo nodded. "When do I leave?"

"Tomorrow."

"It can't be soon enough for me."

"I understand. Go pack your bag."

Lazo stood with a smile and started out the door while Tomás said, "And, by the way, this shouldn't take long. Pack lightly."

CHAPTER FIFTY-FOUR

It was late afternoon when Sebastian and Elias picked up Damian Baez and First Lieutenant Franco from a boat in Key West. Sebastian was pushing fifty and Elias had just celebrated his fortieth birthday.

When the four men arrived at the safe house in Miami, Sebastian grabbed a beer from the refrigerator, while Elias unpacked. The older man popped the tab and upended the can. He gulped the beer, wiped his mouth on his shirtsleeve, and reached for another. Elias shook his head. He disapproved of drinking—he thought it fogged a person's thinking. His weakness was Coke and pie à la mode.

Finicky since birth, Elias insisted on using the top two drawers of the bureau. He arranged his toiletries in alphabetical order, labels turned out. He hung his shirts in the closet according to color, plaid to the left, striped to the right. He went to the bathroom and brushed his teeth, something he did four times a day. He sheeted the mattress and folded the spread at the foot of his bed.

Sebastian watched him with disdain. Grunting, he threw his suitcase on the floor without bothering to open it. He figured he'd unpack as he went along. Tomorrow they would head north, so he saw no need to bother with sheets. The bare mattress would do just fine.

While Sebastian and Elias both lived in Dade County, they had never met. But they had something in common: they were of Cuban descent and had relatives living in Havana. They hated America for its invasion of that island country, and they were willing to pass information to the Cuban authorities to prevent a similar occurrence. A mutual friend, who had trained in Russia, had assigned them this case.

Sebastian and Elias spent their days working, vacationing with their families, and leading normal American lives. Sebastian's hobby was fishing, and Elias fixed cars in his spare time. He always wore gloves when he worked. Their families had no idea of their clandestine activities.

The two men were now engaged in a mission they believed originated at the highest levels of the Cuban government. Being selected for such a job was a new experience for them, an opportunity to feel important. They were thrilled.

Damian and Franco changed their clothes for dinner. The four men drove to a small Italian place, quiet and out of the way. Sebastian ordered a large plate of baked ziti accompanied by a full loaf of bread slathered with butter. He downed several beers and chased six meat- balls around his plate with his spoon before eating them whole.

And it showed. Rolls of fat layered Sebastian's abdomen and a double chin hung from his jaw. Puffy red bags almost obscured his eyes. The fabric of his shirt strained at the buttons. His stomach rumbled like a thunderstorm. He patted it, adjusted his belt, and expelled a loud burp.

Elias was in no better shape. Although he carried most of his weight in his shoulders and back, it was all fat. His upper arms were soft and his stomach was spongy. *These guys might be great at making bombs and doing espionage,* thought Damian. *But I hope I don't have to depend on their strength or stamina, or I could be a dead man.*

Franco leaned back in his seat and wiped his face with his napkin. "Bring us up to speed with what's happening, Sebastian."

"Our people in Union City have Mederos under surveillance. We know all about him."

"Fill us in," urged Damian.

"He works in a sandwich shop—we think he owns it due to his hours. He works from seven in the morning until ten or eleven at night."

"He'd better own the place at the rate he's working," quipped Franco. He smiled at his own remark. "What else?"

"He's a hunter—goes to the same place every Saturday during hunting season. We're hoping he gets together with other subversives so we can kill two birds with one stone. José and Chico haven't seen suspicious activity yet, but they're keeping a close eye on the situation."

A look of concern entered Franco's eyes. "Tell them not to wait for Mederos to meet with other subversives. Our mission is to kill him and him alone. Nothing else matters."

"But—"

Franco held up a hand. "Do I need to repeat myself?" he said in an authoritative tone. "Nothing else matters."

Sebastian grumbled and turned to Damian. "We'll stay at a safe house in Union City with José and Chico. José will direct the operation from there. You are to take orders from him, Private."

Damian's eyes turned cold. "Do not address me as Private, Sebastian. I have been promoted. From now on call me Lieutenant Baez. And for your information, I don't take orders from anyone."

Confused, Sebastian glanced at Franco for confirmation. Franco nodded.

"I'm terribly sorry, Lieutenant. I didn't realize. I thought you were a private—my mistake."

Damian cut him short. "It's of no consequence. You know now."

Sebastian's face reddened, and he turned to Franco. "I understand you will direct operations from the command center in Miami to the command center in Union City."

"Correct."

Sebastian glanced at Damian. "As I just said, José is in charge up north. He will follow Franco's orders and keep him abreast of what's happening in Union City. A man named Adán will arrive in Miami tomorrow to assist Franco." Sebastian turned to Franco and said, "Under no circumstances are you to leave the safe house in Miami."

"Pardon me?" said Franco. He pushed back his chair and folded his arms. "Who do you think you are? I don't take orders from you."

Sebastian ignored Franco's remark. "Phones have been installed for your use, and food will be brought in to you. You will provide advice and direction regarding the mission where needed."

"I'm quite aware of what's expected of me," said Franco. "I'd like to know what your role is in all of this." He almost added the words "fat man" to the end of his sentence, but he thought better of it.

Sebastian chuckled, revealing a mouthful of disordered teeth. "My mission is to make sure your mission is completed. Do you understand?"

"Don't ask me if I understand. I'm not an idiot."

Franco finished his drink and wiped his face with his napkin. He leaned down, opened a paper bag, and handed Damian a thick manila envelope.

"Here's all the information you'll need on Mederos—where he lives, what he did as a member of the force, how he escaped, and the role he's playing in bringing down the Cuban government. The picture was taken several years ago, so his looks may have changed."

Damian opened the envelope, extracted the photograph, and held it up to the light. "Study the eyes," urged Franco. "It's all about the eyes and the height. Mederos could've gained or lost weight, changed his hair color, started to wear glasses. Who knows? But the eyes don't change."

"How tall is he?" asked Damian.

"Five ten," said Franco.

Damian scrutinized a photograph of Frank standing in front of the Santa Maria base. "He's not bad looking. Nice teeth, regular features."

"Don't get hung up on that either," interrupted Sebastian. "If he gets wind that we're following him, he could blacken his teeth and change the contours of his face. A skilled makeup artist could give him a big nose, puffy cheeks—whatever. They can do a lot. But as Franco said, the eyes don't change."

"I'm aware of that," snapped Damian. He returned the photograph to the envelope and then folded and tabbed the flap.

"Elias and I will accompany you to Union City. We leave first thing in the morning. The sooner we get this mission completed, the better. Once you settle in up north, José will call Lieutenant Franco every night to update him on the day's events. Do you understand?"

"I understand the situation," said Damian. "I wasn't born yesterday."

CHAPTER FIFTY-FIVE

Lazo arrived in Key West the next day, exhausted. Despite Tomás's reassurances, he had tossed and turned the night before, failing to get more than three hours' sleep. He was worried that Franco's team had a couple days lead on him. *They could've completed their mission by now. What if I'm too late? What if they've already gotten to Frank?*

Tomás had been very specific in his directions. Two members of Alpha Sixty-six—Augustin and Curro—would meet Lazo at the dock in Key West and take him to a safe house in Miami for the night. They would begin their drive to Union City the following day. Augustin and Curro would stay with Lazo until the mission was completed. A man named Javier would help them in Union City. Reinforcements would be brought in if necessary.

Lazo's orders were clear: to identify Damian and return to Cuba as soon as possible. He was not to get involved in any dirty work. It sounded simple.

The men stopped for sandwiches on their way to the safe house in Miami. It was the first time Lazo had been in America, and he was amazed at the similarities between Havana and Miami. The weather, the flowers, the colors, all reminded him of Cuba.

When they arrived at the safe house, Augustin unfolded a map of New Jersey and flattened it on the kitchen table. He was a tall, amiable man who exuded confidence. His intelligent eyes and quick wit reminded Lazo of a friend from high school.

Less outgoing, Curro was a handsome man who resembled Cary Grant. His hair was combed to the side, his features were aristocratic, and his teeth were perfect. Although both men were middle aged, they were strong and limber with muscles bulging beneath their shirts. From the way they carried themselves, they had obviously handled similar missions. They inspired confidence in Lazo.

Curro glanced at the clock, and then pointed his finger to a dot on the map. Still single at forty-five, he filled his spare time thinking of ways to rid Cuba of Castro. "This is Montclair where Frank works," he said. He moved his finger slightly and pointed to Lincoln Park. "And this is where he lives, about twenty miles away. He drives to work in a blue Grand Prix. He has a daughter around nine or ten and a red-haired girlfriend."

Lazo's face creased in puzzlement. "He's not already married?"

"Our surveillance indicates that he dates a woman named Chris," said Curro. "But they aren't married."

Lazo's eyes narrowed, trying to make sense of this information. As far as he knew, Frank was married to Magda. He wondered what had happened to her. He couldn't imagine Frank and Magda getting divorced. He furrowed his brow but decided not to pursue the subject. "What's happening with the communists?"

"Four guys are holed up in a headquarters in Miami. One has a military haircut—he's not from around here."

"That would be Lieutenant Franco," said Lazo.

"There's another military guy. We didn't get a good look at him, but he sounded young on the bug we planted."

"That's the hit man," said Lazo. "He's been given orders to shoot Frank. He is smart and well trained. Don't underestimate him."

"Name?" asked Augustin.

"Damian Baez," said Lazo. He stumbled over the name, knowing he was signing the young man's death warrant.

CHAPTER FIFTY-SIX

Damian left Miami the next day for Union City, accompanied by Sebastian and Elias. It was a long drive, much longer than he anticipated. He and his companions took turns at the wheel, spotting each other when they got tired.

Damian found the company of his fellow travelers to be less than enthralling. While he considered himself to be a loyal communist on a vital mission, his companions showed no desire to talk about anything serious. They couldn't care less about world events, and Damian's attempts to discuss the merits of communism or Marxist doctrine fell on deaf ears.

Instead, Sebastian and Elias argued about cowboy movies, TV sitcoms, and Cuban beer. They agreed on nothing. Once they exhausted these topics, they blasted the radio to the point where Damian thought his eardrums would burst. *How can these guys be polar opposites and still be a couple of nitwits? Neither one has a convolution to his brain or a thought in his head.*

They drove on two-lane highways through Georgia and South Carolina. Damian was amazed at the miles upon miles of squalid shacks that lined the roads. Barefoot children dressed in rags clung to the skirts of toothless, downtrodden mothers. Broken tractors and cars rusted amid piles of debris. The sights confirmed what Damian had been taught: Cuba was superior to the States in every way.

When he wasn't driving, Damian pulled out his envelope to examine Frank's information, memorizing his profile details, and his daily routine. He was a full lieutenant now, and he viewed this mission as good preparation for the role he'd play when he returned to base. His mission was honorable. He was defending his country. He would be thorough. He would do a good job.

He thought about the despicable actions taken by the United States against the Cuban people, the exploitation by the sugar, fruit, and tobacco companies. He thought about the heroes who had lost their lives in the Bay of Pigs invasion. That atrocity was bad enough. At least the Cubans had defeated the Yanks. But what would happen to his loved ones if the United States attacked again? What if it were a nuclear strike?

Damian had seen pictures of Nagasaki and Hiroshima during his training. He had studied the images of the devastation, great swaths of land where nothing remained but bones, dust, and ash. Would Cuba fare any better? Could it?

Soviet-supplied ballistic missiles had been removed from Cuba during the Missile Crisis in 1962, rendering his country powerless in the face of a nuclear attack. According to Pino, Mederos was involved in subversive activities that could turn Cuba into a vast wasteland. Who knew what kind of threat he and his cronies posed? The freshly minted lieutenant smiled with pride at the thought of protecting his homeland from such a menace.

Around ten p.m. the three men stopped at a cheap motel. A neon sign blinked the word "Vacancy." Sebastian checked in, while Damian and Elias unloaded the luggage from the car. When Damian opened the door to the room, a foul odor assaulted him.

The room reeked of mold, smoke, and urine. Crumpled, lipstick-smudged cigarettes sat in an ashtray on the nightstand. A couple was arguing in the room next door. Elias banged on the panel-covered walls and hollered for them to stop. The noise ceased momentarily but continued on and off throughout the night.

The room held two single beds and a foldout cot, which Damian volunteered to take. The thought of climbing into bed with Sebastian or Elias gave him the willies.

Before heading for Union City the next morning, the three men stopped at a local diner for ham and eggs. They had a long drive ahead of them, and everyone was grumpy. No one had gotten much sleep.

They made good time and were lucky not to be stopped for speeding. When they arrived in the city a little past midnight, José and Chico were there to welcome them. They said a few words of greeting, and took a cursory look at the safe house before going to bed.

The next day Damian, Sebastian, and Elias scouted the area by car, driving past Frank's house and his place of work. Damian made a mental note of the location of the police station, the layout of streets, and the local landmarks, wanting to be prepared for any eventuality.

In the days thereafter, Sebastian and Elias took turns accompanying Damian while he tailed Frank. They followed him from morning until night, observing his home routine, and watching him go back and forth to his sandwich shop.

As time went on, Damian began to see a different side of America than the one he witnessed in the Deep South. He also saw a different side to Americans than the picture presented to him by the Cuban military.

Americans got up early for work, drank coffee, dealt with traffic, and pushed their babies in strollers. He didn't see them beat Negroes or use Whites Only restrooms. They didn't seem arrogant, belligerent, or nasty. In fact, they didn't seem very different from his friends and relatives in Cuba.

What's more, Frank didn't seem any different from anyone else. As Damian watched Frank wipe his counters, order his produce, mow his lawn, and fix his car, questions arose in his mind. Something was wrong. Something didn't compute.

The days dragged on with Damian watching, waiting. Meanwhile, Lieutenant Franco was growing impatient. Nervous about being away from base too long, he called José from Miami every day, wanting to know when the mission would be completed. The clock was winding down, and he couldn't fathom the delay. But Damian was not to be rushed, nor was he to be intimidated—not by Franco, not by Sebastian, and not by José.

Damian watched and ruminated for a few more days before José approached him. "Why the hell are you futzing around? Don't you have the guts for this mission? Just kill the damn worm and be done with it. I've got better things to do than watch you pussyfoot around!"

"I have to make sure of a few things before I go and shoot this guy," Damian replied.

A week elapsed with still no action. Finally, José read Damian the riot act: "This is your assignment, but if you can't come up with a decent plan and execute it, I'll kill the worm myself. Then you can go back to base and explain yourself to your superiors."

"Don't give me that crap!" snapped Damian.

José shook his head in frustration. "What crap? I've never seen anything like this in my life! What the hell is your problem? Are you afraid of killing someone?"

"Are you forgetting I'm a member of the Special Forces? I've been trained to kill. I know how to do it. Fear is not part of this equation."

"Then what?"

"I'm questioning—"

"You're questioning what, Lieutenant? The mission?"

Damian turned to José with fire in his eyes. "No, I'm not questioning the mission, goddamnit. I'm questioning the target."

José looked incredulous. "What are you talking about? You have his picture. You can tell for yourself that we have the right target."

Damian drew his lips into a straight line. "I have a picture but it's old, wrinkled, and faded. I can't tell for certain whether it's a photo of the target or not. What I do know is that the man we've been following is behaving just like a normal guy. He could be anyone for Chrissakes. I've seen no evidence of anticommunist behavior. He's not meeting with Alpha Sixty-six or other subversives. He's not leading rallies. He doesn't even carry a gun."

"What difference does it make?"

"You're not a professional, so you wouldn't know. But I am, damn it. I'm a full lieutenant, and I don't go around shooting people unless I'm certain about what I'm doing."

"Are you saying you're not going to kill him?"

"No, I'm saying I'm unsure about the target, and I'm sure as hell not going back to Captain Pino and tell him I killed the wrong guy. Then there would be hell to pay."

José's face grew red with frustration. "I don't give a damn about your rank or your so-called professionalism. Just do your job. Shoot the guy! That's your mission! You weren't brought here to waste time and to question orders."

Damian glared at José, and José glared back.

The next day Damian sent Elias into Frank's shop under the guise of buying a cup of coffee, while he and Sebastian waited in the car. He hoped Elias could obtain some actionable information. Elias drank his coffee, placed some coins on the counter, and left with a smile.

When he got back to the car, Elias told Damian that he overhead Frank on the phone making plans to meet someone that night. Excited, Damian went to a phone booth and called José.

"Mederos is leaving work early to see someone at six o'clock," he said.

"This could be our big break," said José. "Maybe Mederos is going to meet with counterrevolutionaries. The three of you follow him and report back."

Good, thought Damian. *Maybe Mederos will finally give me a reason to shoot him. Then I can return to base with some peace of mind.*

CHAPTER FIFTY-SEVEN

Damian, Elias, and Sebastian tailed Frank until he turned into the Willowbrook Mall. They pulled in to a nearby parking space, got out of the car, and followed him at a distance as he entered the mall. It had been a lovely day, bright and sunny. Frank was thirsty so he stopped for a drink from a water fountain. His shoelace came undone, and he leaned over to tie it.

Frank did a little window-shopping before he entered an Italian restaurant that he and Chris frequented. It was Friday night and the place was mobbed. He stood in line and ordered a large pizza with mushrooms and extra oregano. He paid the tab and brought the pizza to a table dressed in a red-checkered cloth.

Chris appeared at the door, a bright smile lighting her face. She wore a fall sweater embroidered with acorns and carried several packages, which she placed on an empty chair. Breathless, she released her hair from a ponytail and took a seat.

"Sorry I'm late," she said and held up her fingernails for Frank to see. "I tried a new nail salon, and they took longer than I expected."

"No problem. Your manicure looks great. I ordered us some pizza."

Frank separated the slices with a knife so they'd be easier to lift and placed one on Chris's plate. He wound the dripping cheese around his finger and sucked it off. Suddenly, he got a chill. He turned his head to the left and looked over his shoulder.

Chris tilted her head in Frank's direction. "What's the matter, honey?"

Frank attempted a feeble smile. "Nothing. How was work?"

"The usual," said Chris with a shrug. "I'm just glad the week is over."

Frank nodded as the muscles in his neck grew tense and the hairs on his arms stood on end. Turning, he thought he saw a figure duck behind a wall, but he wasn't sure.

Chris looked concerned. "You seem jumpy. Are you sure nothing's wrong?"

Frank faced her. "I'm fine. Sometimes I just get these feelings—"

He bit off the end of his pizza and swallowed. The mushrooms were fresh, and the cheese was warm and gooey. It tasted great. He sipped his Coke while looking over the top of his glass. His eyes darted from side to side.

"What?" asked Chris, alarmed.

Frank threw his napkin on the table. "Something's wrong," he said. He stood and walked to the front of the restaurant. He looked out, scanning the interior of the mall. Seeing nothing, he went back to the table and sipped more Coke.

Damian watched Frank from the mall's second-story balcony. He turned to Sebastian and nodded. "The target knows we're here. He knows we're watching him."

"You're crazy," said Sebastian. "He doesn't know. How could he?"

"You're wrong," said Damian.

Sebastian looked at Frank again. "How can you tell?"

"He's a member of the Special Forces. He was part of *my* army. He's one of the best. He's been trained to sense stuff like this. But you wouldn't know that, would you?"

"What are you saying?"

"What do you think I'm saying? I'm saying Mederos can sense us, damn it. He knows he's under surveillance."

"What do you want to do?"

"You and Elias get outta here," said Damian. "Wait for me in the parking lot. I need to make a quick stop. I'll meet you back at the car."

● ● ●

Frank looked at Chris. She was finishing the last of her pizza, chomping on the hard crust. "I'm sorry, but I need a little space," he said. "I'll be right back."

Frank got up and walked to the bathroom. He used the toilet and went to the sink to wash up. He leaned over, inhaled, and stared at himself in the mirror. *What the hell is wrong with you? It's been a while since you've felt this way. You thought you'd put your fears behind you. But something's got you rattled.*

Frank rinsed his hands, shook them, and reached for a paper towel. He crumpled it and tossed it into the trashcan. As he turned to leave, a young man stepped through the doorway. The two men jostled for position, determining who should go first.

Then Frank looked up. Neither man smiled. Frank stared at a handsome man with intelligent eyes and dark hair. He looked to be about nineteen. Frank recognized something of himself in him. He noted the posture, the affect. The young man wore civilian clothes, but he had a military haircut, one a little different from the American cut. Frank knew he wasn't from New Jersey.

Frank locked the man's image in his brain.

CHAPTER FIFTY-EIGHT

The following Wednesday night Frank was closing up shop, putting things away, cleaning the windows, and sweeping the floor. It was unusually warm for late September.

His friend, Gary—a local cop—stopped by for a cup of coffee before he went off duty for the night. Talkative, middle-aged, and overweight, he was not the picture-perfect cop. His bulbous nose, ruddy complexion and bushy eyebrows lent him a comic look. He sported age spots on his forehead, and he would soon have little use for a comb.

A regular customer, Gary constantly groused about his life as a police officer. He complained that the department was riddled with corruption, and the work was so stressful it was ruining his marriage.

After months of conversations, he and Frank came to an unspoken agreement: Frank would give Gary free coffee, and Gary would drive around Frank's restaurant a couple of extra times a day to make sure everything was okay. Frank thought he was getting the better part of the bargain.

Gary hopped on a stool and ordered a cup of coffee. He took it with cream, no sugar. Frank set the coffee on the counter along with a glazed donut he was about to discard. Elton John's song, "Mama Can't Buy You Love," played on the radio. The police officer stirred some cream into his coffee while Frank tidied up the refrigerator.

Gary set down his cup, looked up at Frank, and asked, "How'd you get to own this restaurant?"

Frank laughed. "I worked my ass off."

"Do you make much money?"

"It pays the bills."

"I was thinking it might be a good way for me to make a living, but I guess I'd need a hefty down payment."

Frank nodded. "You'd have to get some cash together."

"I don't have much in the way of savings."

"Is there anyone who could loan you some money?"

"Just my father-in-law—he's loaded."

"Talk to him. Tell him you'll pay him back with interest once you get your place going. That's how it's usually done."

"I'll think it over. Maybe I'll give him a call."

The next night's business was especially brisk, and it took Frank longer than usual to close up. Having been on his feet all day, he was tired and eager to get home to Chris and Darlene.

Chris had moved in with him a few weeks before. Although she was only nineteen, she was wonderful with his daughter, taking her clothes shopping and to the movies. The two of them baked cookies together while discussing television shows, hairstyles, and friends. Frank loved to watch them interact.

One night when the couple was out to dinner, Frank told Chris he had fallen in love with her. His feelings had developed slowly and, even now, they surprised him. Every time he talked with Chris he felt more at ease, more comfortable, more connected. He found himself thinking about her during the day, longing to touch her, and to be with her. As he did, the pain over Magda's death began to subside. He knew it would never disappear entirely, but he hoped it would become less pronounced someday. When Frank was with Chris, his heartache became manageable, and his loneliness disappeared.

Frank shifted a couple of packages to his left arm as he locked up the store and pocketed the key. The streets were deserted save for a couple of cars and a black cat that lurked behind a telephone pole. It meowed softly. Its eyes glowed eerily in the dark.

Frank walked toward his car, which was parked in a small public lot. His was the last car left. Clouds kissed a sliver of moon. Across the street a television blared a talk show. A dog barked from a second-floor window.

As Frank opened the car's back door to deposit his belongings, a vehicle approached. Black and nondescript, it was traveling well below the speed limit. The situation gave Frank pause. He strained his eyes to identify the occupants, but their faces were hidden in shadow.

Inside the car Sebastian turned to Damian. "It's time," he said. "It's dark, the street's deserted, and Mederos has his arms full. Let's take him out *now* while we have the chance."

"Shouldn't we clear it with José?" asked Damian.

"The hell with José," said Sebastian. "He doesn't know any more about how to do things that we do. You're a lieutenant. He's no smarter than you."

"Give me a minute to think about it," said Damian.

"C'mon. These opportunities don't come along often. I say strike now and explain later."

Damian heaved a sigh and shifted in his seat. *Sebastian might have a point*, he thought. *I'm tired of being harassed for my lack of action. I'm tired of dealing with this joker sitting next to me. And I'm tired of José bossing me around. At least this way, we can get the operation over.*

Damian considered the upside of taking the target out then and there. An image of Pino congratulating him on his success flashed through his mind, making him smile. *I'll get my own apartment and jeep. That will make it all worthwhile. This might not be the perfect place to finalize the mission, but it's probably as good an opportunity as any.*

"I guess you're right," said Damian wearily.

"Good," said Sebastian. "I'm pulling over."

Frank saw a dark car park adjacent to the sidewalk, and watched two men get out. They pulled something from their pockets and kept their arms tight at their sides. Frank feared they were armed. They nodded to each other and took opposite sides of the street.

Frank couldn't see the men's faces, but he watched their movements, his muscles on high alert. He noted that one man carried himself as if he had military training, while the other did not. His fingers ached for the trigger of a gun. But he didn't have one with him.

As Frank watched Sebastian and Damian, the doors of a second car opened. It was parked not far from Frank's vehicle. Frank hadn't noticed it was occupied. Curro and Javier emerged, looking tense and determined. They stood tall and scoured the area with hard eyes. They glanced at Frank, but did not make a move. Experienced in guerrilla warfare, they knew when to strike.

Frank closed his back car door and opened the one to the driver's side. As he did, Gary's police car swung out from a side street. When he saw Frank, he applied his brakes and pulled his vehicle alongside Frank's. He turned on his flashers. Red and blue lights bubbled away the darkness. Frank looked over his shoulder. The four men had returned to their respective vehicles. Both cars drove off. Frank shook his head.

Gary rolled down his window and hollered. "Hey, Frank, I want to tell you something."

"Something's fishy," interrupted Frank.

"Whaddaya mean?"

"I'm not sure. Just now. Did you see those guys?

Gary looked around. "What guys?"

"They're gone now."

"Sorry, I didn't see a thing."

"Well, keep an eye out, would you?"

"Sure."

"By the way, what did you want?"

"I talked to my father-in-law."

"What did he say?"

"He seems interested. Said he'll think about lending me some cash. We're going to talk again next week."

"Good."

"I'm pretty excited about it. It'll give me a chance to get out of this racket—too many ways to get killed in this line of work."

"You're right about that. Keep me posted."

"I will." Gary held Frank's eyes for a moment longer than necessary. "Are you okay?"

Frank glanced around. Everything seemed normal. He closed his eyes briefly, wondering why goose bumps dotted his arms.

"Yeah, I'm okay."

"See you tomorrow, then."

Frank raised his chin in a farewell gesture. Gary nodded and turned off his flashers while Frank switched on the ignition.

Frank drove home feeling his skin was too tight for his scalp. His stomach was knotted like a skein of yarn. He knew Darlene's aunt, uncle, and grandparents would care for her if anything should happen to him. But that was out of the question. The child had been through too much already, and Frank was determined for her not to undergo another loss.

Frank's thoughts turned to Chris. He wondered how his in-laws would react if he married her. Based on Spanish tradition, he expected them to object. It was much too soon for him to remarry. Tradition was tradition, difficult to fight. He had been brought up with Spanish traditions himself. He knew how easily they could rule your life.

But his heart told him it was right to marry Chris.

Frank pulled into his driveway, turned off the motor, and rested his head against the back of the seat. He stared at the car's roof liner. He needed time to think. The past year had been difficult on Darlene. Frank and Magda's family had done their best to help the child through her grief while dealing with their own. It was a big job.

Frank was busy with work and tried to spend as much time as he could with his daughter, letting her hang out with him at Blimpie's after he picked her up at school. She did her homework there and helped him make sandwiches on occasion. But the routine grew old for both of them.

Sometimes, Darlene stayed with her grandparents. She loved

being with them, but the transitions were difficult. Even though she had recently turned ten, she would cry when she packed to go to her grandparents' house, and cry again when she packed to come home. She also sobbed when it was time for bed.

Magda used to read her bedtime stories, and Chris tried to do the same, but Darlene wanted no part of it, saying she was too old for stories. Frank would try to comfort her and would lie next to her in bed until she drifted off to sleep. Then he would tiptoe out of the room like he did when she was a baby, careful not to awaken her.

While her relatives had been wonderful about helping with Darlene since Magda's death, his daughter needed a mother. She needed stability. She needed to know where she belonged.

The situation was difficult. Frank pushed his fingers through his hair and closed his eyes. He thought for a minute. Then he asked himself three questions: Did I give my all to get to Magda? Did I love her with every fiber of my being? Did I do everything I could to save her?

The answer to every question was a resounding yes. He had loved Magda unconditionally, and he had done his best to help her deal with her illness.

He thought about what advice Abuelo would give him in this situation. His grandfather was a practical man. Frank knew he would tell him to follow the dictates of his heart, to do his best for Chris, and to do his best for Darlene.

Frank remembered how Magda's eyes sparkled on their wedding day, and how happy they were to get married. He recalled placing the wedding ring on his bride's finger and walking her up the aisle while their family and friends smiled and clapped. Frank's vow "to love and to cherish her until death do us part" was still fresh in his mind. It was a beautiful sentiment, one to be honored and obeyed. And he had done just that.

But our marriage is over, he thought. *Death has parted Magda and me. It was a terrible thing, but there's nothing I can do to change it. I can only control what happens now. Life must go on, regardless of what anyone thinks. Regardless of how much time has elapsed. Regardless of tradition, life must go on.*

Frank knew what to do. He opened the car door feeling like a terrible weight had been lifted from his shoulders.

CHAPTER FIFTY-NINE

When Damian and Sebastian returned to headquarters in Union City, Elias and José were in a snit. The two men had just finished arguing about drying the dishes. Elias had accused José of leaving lint on the glasses with the dish towel, and José had smashed a dish in response. José ordered Elias to clean it up, but Elias refused. Tension filled the air, and pottery shards littered the kitchen floor.

José removed a newspaper from the couch to make room for his associates to sit. Sebastian plopped on the sofa with a thump. His legs barely supported his weight as his buttocks met the cushions. The couch creaked beneath him.

"How did surveillance go today?" asked José. "Did the target do anything unusual?"

Sebastian took no time to answer. "No, he just followed his normal routine." He inched himself forward on the couch and held onto the coffee table to help him stand. He grabbed a bag of Wise potato chips off the counter, brought it to his mouth, and ripped the cellophane with his teeth. The packaging squeaked open. Sebastian shoveled handfuls of chips into his mouth, leaving a trail of crumbs behind. He filled his mouth to the point where it was impossible for him to talk.

"Nothing out of the ordinary?" confirmed José. He watched Sebastian with contempt.

"Not exactly," said Damian. Sebastian shot him a steely look, and it dawned on Damian that Sebastian would rather he not discuss the evening's events. But Damian didn't care. After all, it was Sebastian's idea to make an attempt on Mederos's life.

"What then *exactly*?" said José in an annoyed voice.

"Mederos left work a little late. It was dark. There was no one in sight, so we—"

José's eyes narrowed. "So you *what*?"

Sebastian's breathing thickened, and he ran his tongue over his teeth before he interrupted the conversation. "The situation was perfect. Mederos was distracted. He was parked in a deserted lot and was putting some packages in the back of his car. It was a great opportunity."

"So?"

"So we decided to take him out."

"You *what*?" José made a movement so sudden he almost knocked over a lamp. His voice was harsh, hoarse. He raised a threatening fist. "What made you think you could do such a thing without consulting me? I'm in charge. You had no authority to take an action like that!"

Damian had had enough. "I'm tired of you busting my chops for making my own decisions, José. For your information, I am not without authority. I am a full lieutenant, and I expect to be treated as such."

"You may have rank, but you have no expertise in matters like this," returned José. He put his head in his hands before he looked up again. "All right, get to the point. What happened?"

"We aborted the mission," said Damian.

"Why?"

"A police car appeared out of nowhere. The cop was obviously a friend of the target. They chatted for a while. There was nothing we could do, so we drove away."

"Did Mederos see you?"

"Hard to say, since he was talking to his friend."

José looked first at Damian and then at Sebastian. "What the hell's wrong with you two? You tried to take Mederos out in a parking lot? In Montclair? Are you crazy? You can't just kill someone off the cuff. You need to plan something like that. What if the cop showed up when you were in the middle of this thing? Our whole damn operation could've been jeopardized. It could've been a disaster for everyone, including me."

Damian stiffened. He was fed up with everything. The chain of command was muddled. José was overbearing. Sebastian was a buffoon. And Elias acted like a spoiled brat. He had a lot of issues to sort out in his mind, including why Commander Pino had sent him on this mission.

He turned to Sebastian. "Let me ask you something. What do you do for a living?"

Sebastian's eyes widened at the question. "I'm a plumber."

"And you, Elias?"

"It's none of your business, but for the record I'm an electrician. I work with my father. We wire factories and apartment complexes. And we're damn good at it."

"Did you know each other before this assignment?"

The men looked at each other and shook their heads no.

"Sebastian, how did you get activated for this job?"

"I got a phone call that we needed to take out a worm. I was told to report to Miami. Nothing else."

"Were you ever activated before?"

"I've passed along information. But I've never worked on something this big. I've never been on a mission to kill."

"Never?"

"Never."

"How long have you been working in this line of business, Sebastian?"

"Five years."

"And you, Elias?"

"I've been at it for seven years. But this is my first time doing this kind of thing."

"Don't you find that strange?" asked Damian.

Elias shrugged while Sebastian dropped the last of the potato chips into his mouth. He didn't seem concerned. He swallowed and said, "That's the way it's done."

"Well, I want to tell you something," said Damian. "I've come all the way from Cuba for this mission. And so far the target hasn't shown me one iota of evidence that he's involved in subversive or counterrevolutionary activity."

"What are you saying?" snapped José.

Damian pursed his lips and turned toward José. "I don't have a good feeling about this. So far, I have no confirmation of what is written in my report about this guy. He's not hanging out with members of Alpha Sixty-six. He's not attending anti-Castro meetings. He's not training people to overthrow the Cuban government. As far as I can see, he doesn't even have Cuban friends. I've never seen anyone act less suspicious in my life."

"I have to agree with Damian on that," said Elias.

"Shut up, Elias," said José. "No one asked your opinion." He turned to Damian and smirked. "So what's your point?"

"I was told the mission is to defend Cuba against somebody who is putting our country in danger. That he is playing a role in an imminent invasion. That he is a threat of the highest order. Well, I'm not buying it. Either we have the wrong guy or something bogus is going on." Damian hesitated. "I've given this some thought. I made a mistake by trying to take this guy out tonight, but not because I wasn't following your orders, José. I shouldn't have gone after him because I'm still not sure he's the right man. I'm an honorable man. I'm a patriot, not a murderer."

José's face bloomed crimson. His throat constricted, and he covered his mouth with his hand. He licked his lips. Damian had his orders and he had his—to make sure Damian completed this mission. And then shoot him. He didn't know what Damian had done to deserve this fate. But it was his job to make sure the young man never returned to Cuba.

José had been a little squeamish about carrying out his own

order, but now he was feeling better about killing Damian. *If this smart aleck keeps challenging my authority and questioning the mission, killing him will be a lot easier than I anticipated.*

"You're here because of the nature of the target," said José. "Mederos is a member of Alpha Sixty-six, that's a given. He's a dangerous subversive, and he's working to undermine the regime. And you, big shot Lieutenant, are not to challenge facts or to disobey orders. If you continue to carry on this way, you could be arrested for insubordination. Or treason."

A moment elapsed while the two men glared at each other. Menace filled their eyes. Damian broke the silence. "Well, one thing's for sure. If Mederos was a member of the Special Forces, we're not chasing just anybody. He was trained the way I was—to withstand hunger, torture, and deprivation. He will fight for his life, and he will kill if necessary. He can smell danger a mile away. If we miss him the first time, we'll have a hell of a time getting him the second time. Given this, do any of you feel qualified to take him on?"

Elias and Sebastian looked down, chastened and embarrassed. José coughed and set his jaw. Damian's question hung in the air, unanswered.

José crossed his arms and looked at Sebastian and Elias for support. "Well, I can see you think you are better than us. Being in the force, you may be in better shape. But regardless of your qualifications, I don't like what went down tonight."

"Why? I thought it was my mission to put three bullets in this guy's brain," said Damian.

"It is," said José. "But where and when I say."

"So when are you going to say?" challenged Damian. "You don't like my ideas, but you haven't come up with any of your own."

"We'll do it Saturday," said José.

"Where?"

"If the target runs true to form, he'll hunt with a friend in Sussex

County. It's bow season, so he won't be carrying a gun. His only defense will be his bow and arrows. He should get to the woods first thing in the morning. He'll be easy prey. Just put three bullets in his head and this whole thing will be over. Then you can stop fretting about your damn conscience. You can go home and enjoy your life as a lieutenant."

"Fine with me," said Damian. "I just hope Mederos shows up, and that he gives me good reason to shoot him."

"Don't worry," said José. "He'll be there."

CHAPTER SIXTY

When Alpha Sixty-six members Curro and Javier returned from their surveillance that night, they stopped at a diner for coffee and pie. Lazo joined them, along with the local Alpha Sixty-six leader, Augustin.

Augustin was a well-muscled man of thirty-seven, a father of four who served as a supervisor in a shoe factory. He had escaped Cuba in a wooden boat six years before. Sharks had been his companions for much of the trip, and he arrived unnerved, exhausted, and determined to find an avenue to bring about change in Cuba.

Augustin's brother had been sentenced to five years in jail for counterrevolutionary activity, namely for visiting his mother in the next town without permission from the CDRs. He made the mistake of speaking against the regime while imprisoned, and his sentence was doubled. Ten years in jail just for trying to see his mother. The whole episode struck Augustin as criminal.

Augustin had been a member of Alpha Sixty-six for four years and had worked with Curro and Javier on other missions. He joined the organization as a way to avenge his brother's sentence and to bring down Fidel. He liked working with the group. It kept him in shape and in touch with like-minded people.

Being involved with Alpha Sixty-six was a way for the men to bond. They had all escaped Cuba and had a common enemy, Fidel. They loved Cuban food and shared a love of fishing. Javier had a small boat. On Saturday mornings, the three men fished together. Fishing served as a vehicle for them to laugh, drink beer, and talk about the day when Cuba would be free.

Once they settled themselves in a booth, Curro turned to Lazo and said, "It's a good thing we were there for your friend tonight."

Lazo sucked in his breath. "What do you mean?"

"The Cuban operatives were ready to put a hit on Frank when he left work."

"Damn! What did you do?"

"Not much—we didn't have to. A policeman—looked like a friend of Frank's—showed up in the nick of time and scared the bastards off."

"Jesus!" said Lazo. "Sounds like a close call. I should've been there."

"You deserved a few hours off."

"Yeah, but I still should've been there. That's what I'm here for."

Augustin nodded. A black curl fell on his forehead. "I don't know what they were thinking, trying to make a hit in a public place. That's unusual behavior. People in this line of work are generally more disciplined."

"It figures," said Lazo. "These guys were recruited by someone close to Pino, probably by a contact he made in Russia. Who knows what their backgrounds are. They could be Russian trained, but I doubt it. Their behavior doesn't support that supposition."

"Well, I assure you they were about to take Frank out tonight," said Curro. He turned his fork on its side and scraped a puddle of pie filling off his plate. The waitress arrived and removed his dish.

Lazo lifted his cup to sip his coffee and pulled back from it. It was still too hot. He liked his coffee warm and black. He placed his cup on its saucer and stirred the dark liquid with his spoon to cool it. He gulped it down in one go and leaned back in his chair.

"Pino and Franco must be getting desperate," said Lazo. "Franco needs to get back to base before his absence raises suspicions. Pino is probably pressuring him to return. They're running out of time."

Augustin looked concerned. "It may account for what happened tonight. We were damn lucky they didn't kill Frank."

"We were," added Javier.

Augustin turned to Curro, and asked, "What's Frank doing tomorrow?"

"It's Saturday, the day he hunts."

"What does he hunt again?"

"Deer, with a bow and arrow."

"No gun?"

"Not at this time of year."

Augustin leaned forward, his eyes sharp as knives at a sudden realization. "That's where it's going to happen!"

Lazo raised his eyebrows. "Of course, it makes perfect sense."

"Lazo," said Augustin, "I want you to get up early and follow Frank. Let me know if the Cuban operatives are in the woods. If so, I'll join you with reinforcements. There's a phone booth in the parking lot. Use it. But don't take any chances."

"Don't worry," said Lazo. "I'll take care of it."

Curro and Javier stood, signaling their return to headquarters. "Are you coming, Lazo?" asked Curro.

"Not yet. I need another cup of coffee."

"Me too," said Augustin. He reached behind him and pulled a pack of cigarettes from his jacket. "Wanna smoke?"

Lazo shook his head and signaled for the waitress. The two men watched as she refilled their cups. A toilet flushed behind a closed door and a hand dryer switched on.

"I was wondering," said Lazo. "How do you identify Cuban agents?"

The Alpha Sixty-six leader looked out the window at a bunch of girls getting out of a car. They were dressed in jeans, giggling, and applying lipstick.

"We don't."

"What do you mean?"

"It's almost impossible. They could be anybody from the local grocer to the guy next door. They look just like you and me. They live among us, and even talk against Cuba, Fidel, and the revolution. Some of them work for the Cuban intelligence, and some work on their own. I think this group works on its own. They are too sloppy to be in the Cuban intelligence. Either way, we have to get very lucky to find them."

"How do they get activated?"

"We don't know. Sometimes they remain dormant for years before they are called to perform a mission. They don't know each other. They are activated on a case-by-case basis. They perform a mission and disappear, making it almost impossible to know who they are."

"So, it's unusual that you've identified this many Cuban operatives?"

"Highly. The fact that we've identified five in Union City, including a member of the Special Forces, and two more in Miami, including a first lieutenant, is a real bonanza for us." Augustin thought for a moment while he lit another cigarette. "By the way, your friend knows he's being watched."

"What do you mean?"

"He was on high alert in the parking lot tonight. He sensed something was wrong."

"I wouldn't expect any less of him." Lazo frowned. "How do I know the operatives won't come after Frank when I leave, regardless of what happens tomorrow?"

Augustin exhaled a line of smoke. "There's nothing to worry about. We've photographed all the Cuban operatives in Union City and in Florida. Their pictures are in the hands of the CIA in Miami. When the time comes, somehow, someway, the CIA will get the pictures into the hands of the appropriate person in the military command in Managua as proof of Pino's insubordination. So you can relax."

Augustin finished his coffee and stood. "Your friend may be in danger now, Lazo, but after tomorrow no communist will attempt to hurt Frank again. You have my word on that. From what you've told me of Pino, the world would be better off without him. Now let's get home. We have a big day tomorrow."

CHAPTER SIXTY-ONE

For several years Frank had hunted with his friend Raúl, the man who supplied him with sandwich makings for his shop. Raúl was an avid hunter, a good marksman, and Frank's best friend.

Raúl was Frank's only Cuban friend. When Frank first arrived in the States, he had exercised great caution not to socialize with groups of Cubans, afraid he might come into contact with spies. Cuban spies were common in north Jersey at the time. Given the events surrounding his escape, Frank couldn't be too careful. Besides, he wanted to blend into American life, to get to know Americans, and to become one of them.

Over the course of time, Frank had come to trust Raúl. He was smart, funny, and so enthusiastic about hunting that he'd often arrive at Frank's house long before the appointed hour, ready for black coffee and as much conversation as Frank could muster in the wee hours of the morning.

Frank hadn't slept well the night before, having been twice awakened by nightmares. The incident in the parking lot had left him anxious and unsettled. He had a foreboding that something terrible was about to happen. He couldn't shake his feelings of dread.

True to form, Raúl arrived at three-thirty a.m. Frank was still in bed. He banged on the door, hollering, "You have any coffee in there, Frank?"

Annoyed, Frank stumbled down the stairs to open the door. "Jesus, Raúl, Darlene and Chris are fast asleep. You'll wake the whole damn house if you don't keep your voice down."

"Sorry," laughed Raúl, "You know me. I can't help myself. I'll make some coffee while you change out of your pajamas. Then you can get me outta here before I rouse the sleeping beauties."

Frank took a quick shower and dressed in his camouflage shirt and pants. He downed a cup of coffee and loaded his aluminum folding chair, his bow and arrow, and a small pair of binoculars into his Jeep Cherokee. He went back to the house and reached for his deer-dressing knife that he kept in his gun cabinet. He hesitated, eying a pistol.

Should I bring it with me just in case? What if someone's after me? What if they follow me back to the house and harm Darlene? Or Chris? Frank shook off the thought. *Get a grip. Darlene will be fine. Chris is taking her shopping. And nobody's going to bother you in the woods. Besides, you're a law-abiding citizen, and it's illegal to carry a gun during bow season.*

Frank's attention turned to a larger, serrated knife. He usually didn't bring it hunting with him. But something in the back of his mind prompted him to add it to his backpack.

Frank and Raúl set off for deer country, the rugged hills of Sussex County, about a mile from Routes 15 and 206 in northern New Jersey. Autumn leaves scented the air. On the way, they stopped at an all-night diner for coffee and bagels for the road. When they returned to Frank's vehicle, the steam from the coffee fogged the windows. Frank wiped the windshield with his hand before he switched on the ignition.

Raúl was in high spirits, and the friends chatted amiably for the hour or so it took to get to their destination. When they arrived, Frank parked his vehicle on grass that was still soft and spongy from a recent rain. They unloaded their equipment around five fifteen a.m., and Frank locked the car door behind him. Wisps of clouds crossed a crescent moon.

The area where they hunted consisted of two forested hills that formed a V. At the bottom of the V bubbled a shallow, rock-strewn creek. At the top of the far hill was an expansive meadow surrounded by forests. An old logging road skirted the trail. Raúl and Frank had hunted in the area for years and were familiar with the terrain.

The two men trudged a mile up the side of the nearest hill, walking slowly so they wouldn't break a sweat. They didn't want their body odor to signal their presence to the deer. Frank was happy to be outdoors and was anticipating the day ahead.

When they reached a fork in the trail, Frank and Raúl shook hands and wished each other luck. As was their custom, they promised to remain in their respective blinds until noon. That way they wouldn't scare off the deer for each other. They went their separate ways carrying flashlights.

Dropping his bow and arrow, Frank set about building his blind. He had done it so many times, it was almost second nature to him. He gathered branches, hammered them into the soft earth, and crossed them with a thick stick for support. He added some beech limbs to help confuse the eyes of the deer. Their pear-shaped leaves created a perfect camouflage. He finished his work using small twigs, leaves, and greenery.

Frank built his blind facing north so he'd remain in the shadows when the sun rose. A fallen tree was at his back. He eased himself into the blind, settled himself in his chair, and switched off his flashlight, assuming Raúl was doing likewise in his blind. He had time to relax. He sat in thought, occasionally drifting off to sleep, as he awaited the pale glint of dawn.

At five forty-five a.m. Damian, Sebastian, José, and Elias pulled up and parked next to Frank's Jeep. Damian was dressed for guerilla combat in camouflage shirt and pants. His face was covered in greasepaint. Sebastian, Elias, and José wore camouflage shirts and jeans, but had forgone the greasepaint. They all carried flashlights.

Damian got out of the car and began to jog up the hill. He felt invigorated, easily making the run. This was the first time in his life he had experienced crisp autumn air, and he was surprised at how refreshing it felt. He was making good time, and he assumed his companions were not far behind.

Red in the face and sweating, José, Elias, and Sebastian slowed their pace. It had been a long time since any of them had exercised.

Panting like a golden retriever, Sebastian stopped and leaned against a tree. He needed water.

Sensing no movement behind him, Damian stopped and turned around. His patience had long since been exhausted. He retraced his steps, threw Sebastian a canteen, and swore profusely.

"Damn you, what a bunch of amateurs! We've just begun this operation, and you can't keep up. You're already complaining. Next, you'll be squabbling among yourselves. At this rate, we'll never accomplish our mission."

Sebastian grunted and slid his body down the trunk of the tree. He sat in a mound of leaves. "Gimme a minute, will ya?"

"One minute, that's it," spat Damian.

A short while later, the men were on the move. Guessing Frank's location, Damian told the operatives to stop at a clearing. It was still dark. He put his finger to his lips, signaling quiet.

"Turn off your flashlights and don't smoke," he said in a voice that was barely a whisper. "We don't want to disclose our location."

The men sat and waited, not knowing they were only a hundred yards from Frank's blind.

At six a.m. Lazo, Javier, and Curro pulled into the parking lot and extinguished their engine. Seeing Frank's and the Cuban operatives' vehicles, they scanned the area until they saw a flash of light in the distance. The light flickered and bounced off the leaves before it winked out.

Lazo turned to Curro, excited.

"It must be the Cuban operatives. I'll trail them while you call Augustin for reinforcements. We still have time. Nothing will happen until daybreak. Tell them to get here as soon as possible."

"On it," said Curro.

Lazo and Javier started up the mountain while Curro phoned Augustin from the parking lot. Curro informed Augustin that the mission was on, and that all the parties had arrived.

"Glad to hear it," said Augustin. "Reinforcements are on their way."

Forty-five minutes later Augustin and three members of Alpha Sixty-six arrived to join Lazo, Curro, and Javier. Lazo was happy to have such able men on his side. They climbed the hill to the vicinity of the Cuban operatives and prepared themselves for a fight.

Everyone was ready. Everyone was in place. Everyone knew something momentous was about to transpire.

Except Frank.

CHAPTER SIXTY-TWO

Frank was sitting in his blind and thinking about Chris when a sharp cramp gripped his leg. He hopped out of his blind and leaned over to massage his calf. Wincing, he walked back and forth until the pain subsided. When it did, he beheld a spectacular sunrise.

Ribbons of coral and indigo unfurled against a sky populated with red, popcorn-shaped clouds that numbered in the thousands. Tendrils of mist rose from the earth to lace the trees like a giant spider web. A flock of Canada geese honked plaintively as they winged their way across the color-drenched sky.

The budding sun turned the landscape peach. It yellowed Frank's hands as he held them against the light. They looked like they were dressed in fairy dust. He had seen few sunrises to rival this one. It was so magical he wondered whether it presaged a special day. He returned to his blind and waited.

Soon Frank spotted his quarry—a full-grown buck with a large rack. He had almond-shaped eyes and a white-tipped tail. The morning sun dappled his back. He was almost too beautiful to kill.

Suddenly, the deer lifted his head, straightened his body and fixed his brown eyes directly on Frank. His ears stood straight up. Frank tensed as adrenaline coursed through his veins. A vulture circled overhead. It was so quiet Frank could hear his wings flap.

Frank slowly lifted his bow and arrow, drawing it up inch by inch. The buck stood stock-still, staring, its antlers pointing skyward. It was an eight-point-buck. Frank felt like they were the only two creatures in the world.

Adjusting his spine, Frank pulled back his arrow and released it.

It whistled past his ear, straight as a ruler, and hit the deer square in the neck. Frank had accomplished his goal with only one arrow. Five arrows remained in his quiver. Startled, the deer wobbled, emitted a small sound, and fell to the ground, making a soft thud as it landed on a bed of leaves.

Frank crouched down in the blind, bow still in hand. The deer panted, working its legs as if he were riding a bike. The vulture circled low, soon joined by another. The movement ceased. Frank sat in his blind for thirty minutes, making sure the deer was dead.

When the time seemed right, Frank retrieved his dressing glove, his knife, and his binoculars from his backpack and cautiously approached the deer, bow and arrow in hand. He traversed the fallen tree. The deer lay motionless on its side. Its eyes stared blankly into space. Frank poked it with his bow. It was lifeless. Frank smiled, feeling elated. It was a great day. He was happy.

But that feeling was to be short lived.

CHAPTER SIXTY-THREE

When the sun rose, Damian scoured the surroundings with his eyes. He hoped Frank was somewhere in the vicinity, so his companions would not have to walk too far. He knew they weren't up to the challenge.

Damian turned and looked through the trees. To his surprise, he had a clear view of Frank. He was leaning over something, examining it. Damian didn't know whether it was a deer, an elk, or a moose. He nudged his companions and nodded in Frank's direction. Keeping his eyes on Frank, Damian drew his .45-caliber pistol. He hesitated, knowing he didn't have a good shot. Frank was beyond the range of his gun. He waited, hoping for a better opportunity.

Damian's trigger-happy companions scrambled to their feet. Failing to await an order, Sebastian and Elias preempted Damian, firing their shotguns in Frank's direction. Sebastian shot first. Elias followed suit. José held his fire.

Frank crouched down and listened, adrenaline boiling his blood. He tried to think, to calm himself, while a spray of pellets penetrated nearby trees. Frank took cover and shielded his eyes from the sun, trying to see who was shooting. Three more shots rang out in rapid succession. Bang! Bang! Bang!

What the hell is this about? Who's trying to kill me? And why? Well, whoever they are, they're using shotguns, not rifles. And they're terrible shots.

Then Frank heard it—the familiar sound of someone banging on a pail. It was the same sound he heard when the Special Forces were about to apprehend him in Cuba. Although Frank didn't see him, he knew the sound came from the blue-eyed boy, the one he considered his guardian angel.

The sound grew louder, more insistent. The hairs on Frank's arms spiked like porcupine quills. The drum was calling him to safety, telling him which way to go. A voice in Frank's head said: *Pay attention, this is real. This is what you've feared all these years. This is your nightmare.*

Frank fell to the ground, covered his head, and wedged his body beside the fallen tree. When the shooting stopped, he leaned on his elbows and looked between the branches. To his surprise, he glimpsed the young man he had encountered at the mall. Frank's heart skipped a beat. He knew this was trouble.

The man's arms were muscled, his shoulders squared. His thick head of hair bore no hat. He looked furious, speaking in Spanish and gesturing to his companions. Frank inched forward, straining to hear what was being said. He was amazed at the conversation.

"Damn it, you assholes. What the hell do you think you're doing?" asked Damian. "You couldn't hit a brick building ten feet away."

"What are you talking about? I got him!" said Sebastian.

"Put your guns down."

"Really, I think I hit him. If not, I'll give it another try."

"Damn you, Sebastian. You didn't hit anything but a bunch of trees. Your shotgun doesn't have the range to hit him from here. All you've done is disclose our position. You've made this an even fight. Prepare for the worst."

"What? You think Mederos is going to get us with his lousy bow and arrows?"

"You know what, Sebastian, you just don't get it. You disgust me."

Sebastian started to speak, and Damian held up his hand to stop him. He thought for a minute, and said, "I figure Mederos will do one of two things: either run up the hill, or run down the hill and follow the stream. I bet he'll take the stream. If we split up, we can surround him.

"Sebastian and Elias, you go down the logging road and up the other mountain. Stay low." He nodded and gestured to José. "We'll try to catch up with him at the stream. Let's go."

Sebastian looked at Damian, and asked, "Can I shoot the bastard if I see him?"

"Shut the hell up, Sebastian."

"Can I?" pleaded Elias.

"No, damn it. Neither of you have earned the right to shoot Mederos. I know how he operates. I'll do the shooting."

Lazo was dismayed to hear the shots. They echoed through the hills, reverberating in all directions. He turned to Augustin, and said, "That's them—the Cuban operatives. Let's go."

"Not yet," said Augustin.

"But Frank could be wounded."

"I doubt it. There were too many shots. Chances are they didn't hit him. He's probably alive and running for cover. We need to wait for the Cubans to shoot again to determine their exact position."

Lazo shook his head, unsure of the strategy. "I hope to hell you're right."

Sitting in his blind, Raúl unscrewed his thermos bottle, poured some coffee and brought the red plastic cup to his lips. Just as he was about to drink, he heard gunshots. Startled, Raúl spilled the coffee down the front of his shirt. He swore and grabbed a rag to wipe himself off.

Hearing a rustle, he capped the thermos and set it aside. He hoped a deer had made the sound. He waited twenty-five minutes for the animal to appear, while cursing what he thought were fools shooting birds.

Frank grabbed his bow and arrow, retrieved his large knife from his backpack, and slipped it under his belt. His didn't have time to secure it properly.

Knowing his pursuers expected him to run along the stream, he took a shortcut. He knew where he was headed, and the shortcut would give him a head start. He hoped to beat his pursuers to the stream. He inched his way to a nearby ridge and scrambled down the rough terrain on his butt.

He descended as quietly as he could, cringing at the sound of rocks that tumbled in his wake. He forded the stream at its narrowest point and ran up the opposite hill toward the meadow, thinking of the generous forests surrounding it. They were thick and almost impenetrable, a perfect hiding place. He moved over the wet earth, carefully, silently, glad he had outmaneuvered his stalkers.

While Damian and José headed toward the stream, Sebastian and Elias set off toward the logging road and began ascending the opposite hill. They were out of shape. They couldn't walk fast enough. They had made a strategic error.

CHAPTER SIXTY-FOUR

Having reached the far hill, Frank hurried up the mountain toward the meadow. The last part of the climb was so steep he had to crawl on his hands and knees. He adjusted his knife several times so it wouldn't slice his stomach or leg.

As he inched his way upward, a thousand thoughts clogged his mind. He felt like he had spent the best part of his life on the run, first from Fidel's forces and then from the fear and horror surrounding his escape. The more he thought about it, the angrier he became. He needed to tame his emotions.

He crested the hill and gazed at the meadow, his way out. The expanse looked like a beacon of hope. Sun warmed the earth, and wind danced on the yellowed grasses. The forests loomed in the distance, a beckoning sanctuary. The forest on the left was closer and denser. Once Frank entered it, he would disappear. His pursuers would never find him. If he ran fast enough, he could make it to safety before they spotted him.

Frank began to sprint, feeling his adrenaline flowing. His muscles responded, his arms and legs worked in unison to propel him forward. The wind lifted his hair and the breeze kissed his face. He felt like a kite skimming the sky, exhilarated. His speed surprised him. No burn singed his lungs. He could do this. He managed a quick smile.

A hawk circled overhead. The forest came closer. He would make it. He would escape. Then a feeling struck him like a boulder rolling downhill. It felt like a blow to his gut. He had no idea where it originated, but it was so powerful it made him suck in his breath.

He stopped and bent over, hands on his knees. He gathered his wits and stood, rubbing his forehead and eyes.

He thought about *el lider maximo* and all he had done to his people: more than a million Cubans having fled his tyranny and millions more living in abject fear. He thought about the men, women, and children lost at sea, about those who were jailed for requesting more food, about those imprisoned for speaking against a system that robbed them of their freedom and dignity.

He thought about his family, still suffering under Fidel. He thought about the government razing his grandfather's house, about young Joey Lopez being shot in the back at the age of thirteen, just for trying to escape. He thought about living under a bed for five long months, deprived of sunlight and the ability to move. He thought about hiding in the wretched outhouse.

Now he was in New Jersey, in America, in the land of the free. And yet he was being stalked. He was on the run. Again! Why, he did not know. But he knew he had a choice.

I can run and hide. Or I can do what I can to eradicate evil. Would it be evil to eradicate evil? I don't know. That's a question for theologians and philosophers, one beyond my ken. But one thing I know for sure. Whoever these bastards are, they are out to kill me. I'm not running any more. Not here. Not in America. Enough is enough!

Frank's killing instinct surfaced with surprising vengeance. He extracted his serrated knife from his pants, looped the case through his belt, and tied it securely to his thigh. If worst came to worst, he could defend himself with it.

He gripped his bow and arrows so hard his knuckles gleamed white. His mouth turned cottony. He had never felt more furious. *This is the end of it right now. If you guys want a fight, you'll get one. Now let's see what's going to happen.*

Frank pivoted and marched down the hill, jaw set, spine steeled. He grabbed a couple of branches for cover and headed toward his pursuers. He walked two-thirds down the hill and stopped. About twenty-five yards away he spotted two men collapsed on the ground, shotguns in hand. He stooped and studied them. They were the men he had seen in the clearing: the ones called Sebastian and Elias. The ones who had tried to shoot him. They looked exhausted.

Sebastian leaned against a tree, red in the face and panting. Despite his physical condition, he was barking orders. His shirt hung open, revealing a massive mound of flesh. His face glistened with perspiration, and his hair clung to his cheeks. He wiped the sweat from his forehead with his shirttail. He licked his lips. He looked thirsty.

Frank had no second thoughts. He plucked an arrow from his quiver, cocked his compound bow, and let it do its work. His arrow sailed toward Sebastian at lightning speed—right on target. Sebastian moved, ever so slightly, but not enough to avoid Frank's arrow. The arrow missed his heart by a couple of inches, slicing his shoulder. Blood spurted like water from a fire hose. Frank had nailed Sebastian to a tree.

For a moment, Sebastian looked stunned. He tried to get up before he realized he was pinned in place. He grabbed his shoulder, his screams sawing the air. He writhed in pain, blood wetting his hands.

As soon as the arrow hit, Elias scrambled to his feet, shooting wildly in all directions. Frank covered his head with his hands and hid behind a tree as pellets filled the air. He needed to hurry down the hill, get Raúl, and make their way home. He had created a nice diversion, which he hoped might buy him some time.

Raúl hoped Frank was having more luck hunting than he was. He was not happy that someone had scared away the deer. But it happened sometimes. He shrugged, ready to finally have some coffee. He brought the cup to his lips and had just taken a mouthful when more shots exploded. He jumped in surprise. To his dismay, he spat his coffee all over his hands. "Jesus Christ. What a mess I've made. Something's wrong when a man can't drink a cup of coffee in the woods."

Upon hearing Sebastian's screams, Damian and José hurried toward him and Elias. Frank saw them advance through the forest, periodically taking cover. Damian entered the small clearing before José did, his eyes darting back and forth, his body coiled for action.

Frank watched Damian closely, wondering about his mission. *Why are these men trying to kill me? I've never done them harm. I'm just living my life, minding my own business.*

When Damian turned around, Frank saw something chilling. The young man was wearing an enamel belt buckle stamped with the communist hammer and sickle. Frank shook his head before he took off in the direction of the stream.

Fearing Sebastian was giving away their position, Damian approached him with fire in his eyes. He covered Sebastian's mouth with his hand, and said, "Shut up, you worthless slime. I don't want to hear another peep out of you. It's your job to withstand pain."

Damian took a knife and sawed off the aluminum arrow, which stuck out on both sides of Sebastian's shoulder. His action released the Cuban operative from the tree. Had he tried to extract the arrow from his shoulder, Sebastian would have bled to death.

Damian turned to Elias, and said, "Stay with Sebastian. José and I will go after Mederos. I know where he's headed. He's got to get out of here, and he's not going to leave his friend behind. His buddy might try to help him. Don't mess with him. Take him out only if he gives you trouble." He glanced at Sebastian. "Just make sure this jerk doesn't start screaming again."

Damian and José descended the hill, careful to make as little noise as possible.

As soon as Frank reached the bottom of the hill, he looked around. To get to where he needed to go, he had to ford the creek and climb the opposite hill. He hesitated, thinking. The water was only ankle deep. While it wouldn't take long to cross the stream, doing so would make him easy prey.

Frank waded into the creek and stepped over some rocks, glancing from side to side. He walked as fast as he could while trying not to fall. About six feet in, his foot met a moss-covered rock. For a moment he lost his balance. He bent over and then straightened up. He winced, knowing he was in a vulnerable position. He extended his arms to steady himself. When he looked up, he saw two figures standing amid the greenery, about thirty yards away.

Frank recognized them as two men who had come to Sebastian's aid. The younger one had a strange look on his face. No one said a word.

To Frank's surprise Damian stepped forward, enabling him to view the full length of his body. This was highly dangerous and unusual behavior. His manner was military, resolute. But something else was going on with him, something Frank couldn't fathom. Frank watched in amazement as the man waded into the creek. Frank had no idea what he was doing. He focused his mind.

You are not going to die. You are not going to die. You are not going to die. Not here. Not now. You have too much to live for. You have Darlene. You have Chris. Steady, steady, steady.

Rattled, José stood on the sidelines, shotgun aimed at Damian's body. His mission was to shoot Damian, not Frank. He watched Damian's strange behavior, confused, fascinated. José inched toward Damian and hollered, impatience shredding his voice. "Why the hell are you waiting, damn it?"

Damian kept his eyes on Frank. The two men sized each other up. Without breaking his gaze, Damian screamed to José, "Put your goddamn gun down, and shut the hell up." His tone of voice demanded compliance.

José hesitated, befuddled. He inched forward, taking small sidesteps, his weapon aimed at Damian's chest, his eyes darting back and forth between him and Frank.

"*Now!*" commanded Damian.

Swearing, José dropped his gun. An airplane flew overhead, leaving a white contrail against a blue vault of sky. Damian waited a moment. Then he stood tall, dragged his feet through the water and squared his toes. Frank was astonished to see Damian take the military position. Water gurgled as it tripped over rocks.

Damian nodded to Frank before raising his hand in a crisp salute. He held Frank's gaze, looking at him with an intensity Frank had never seen. Damian's eyes telegraphed conflicting emotions.

Frank drew his body to full length and saluted Damian back. The two men stared at each other, taking stock, paying each other respect. A moment elapsed that seemed like an eternity. Frank was not about to wait for Damian to kill him.

Frank raised his bow. His finger and thumb joined to pull back the string. A muscle pulled at his jaw.

Frank and Damian looked at each other straight in the eye. To Frank's surprise, he heard Damian say one word: sorry.

Then Damian slid his hand to the holstered pistol at his thigh, swiftly withdrew it, and aimed it straight at Frank's chest.

CHAPTER SIXTY-FIVE

Once before, Frank had faced the barrel of a gun. On the run in Cuba, Pino had cornered him and had ordered members of the Special Forces to shoot him.

Lieutenant Brown, the officer in charge of Frank's unit, countermanded Pino's order while Frank made a beeline for cover. Pino took several shots at Frank, but missed. Now, Frank faced a similar situation. He was standing face-to-face with someone as skilled at guerrilla warfare as he.

The idea of an afterlife flashed through Frank's mind. *Will I soon join Magda in heaven? Will I see my father, my grandfather? Will they be waiting for me, as the Church would have me believe? Or is this all there is to life? You do your best. You love. You live. You die.*

Darlene's face danced before his eyes. Frank pictured her long eyelashes, her mischievous smile. She was a girl in every sense of the word, intelligent and high-spirited. She wore frilly clothes and played with dolls. Frank wanted to watch her grow into a beautiful woman like her mother. He knew she would. He couldn't bear the thought of her being orphaned.

He wondered whether he'd live to marry Chris. She was a remarkable woman and had made such a difference in his life. When Frank was with her, he felt alive again. She and Darlene gave him a reason to hope, a reason to live. He had to live. He had to.

He refocused on Damian. He identified with the man standing before him. He was young and determined. But also misguided. Somewhere along the line, someone had sold him a bill of goods. And Frank had his suspicions as to who could have done it.

Damian hesitated a second too long. A shot rang out. Frank looked up, startled. Damian dropped his pistol and brought his hands to his chest. Blood soaked his clothes. Frank heard Damian's screams through a fog of fear. Covering his head with his hands, Frank fell to the ground as another shot sliced the air. Boom! Then another.

Gunfire echoed and skipped through the hills. The trees trembled. The sound was so near and so loud Frank thought he'd been shot. But he felt no pain. Panicked and confused, he scrambled about, patting his body parts, searching for wounds.

A second bullet pierced Damian's chest. He sank to his knees, writhing in agony. He screamed his pain into the sky. Blood spewed forth like gushing oil. Another shot rang out, and Damian fell on his back. Within a few seconds his body went limp.

Damian floated in the stream, face up, his shirt blooming crimson, his eyes staring blankly at the steel-blue sky. The creek reddened with blood. The smell of death fouled the air. Crimson water traversed the rocks.

Frank looked at the young man, aghast. *Such a waste! And for what?*

Frank drew his fist to his mouth. His face felt hot. He was afraid he would vomit.

Three more shots rang out. Frank heard a moan. Then silence. He glanced toward the woods. José fell to the ground with a bullet in his head. Blood streamed down his face. Frank looked at the two dead men in horror.

A rustling of leaves and the crackle of twigs caught Frank's attention. Someone was closing in on him. Fear grabbed him like a gorilla.

He whispered a silent prayer, rose on his haunches, and readied his bow and arrows to shoot. He was out in the open—a sitting duck. No match against a man with a gun. A moment passed. Time stood still.

Then someone hollered in Spanish, "Don't even think about it, Frank!"

Frank felt disoriented. Visions of Cuba flashed before his eyes.

The voice was familiar, making Frank feel at once comforted and terrified. He stood. Tense. For a second, he wondered what to do.

Then Lazo appeared, walking in Frank's direction. Frank couldn't believe his eyes. He felt as if he were in a dream. His old friend came up beside him, a knowing smile lifting the corners of his lips.

"What the hell—?"

Lazo's eyes brightened. "It's over," he said reassuringly. "Relax. It's over. It's clear."

Frank nodded, trying to comprehend what Lazo was saying. Lazo looked his friend up and down.

"You okay, Frank?"

Frank looked at Lazo as if he were a mirage, an apparition. A million questions sprang to his mind, but he couldn't ask them now. He had to focus on the situation at hand.

"I'm not okay yet," he said. He pointed toward the hill. "Two more guys are up on that ridge—both armed. One is wounded. And I've got a friend in the area. He's a hunter."

"My men will take care of it," said Lazo. "I'm sure your friend's okay. These guys have no interest in him."

"You're sure?"

"I'm sure."

Frank nodded, suddenly feeling dizzy. He sat on a rock on the side of the creek to steady himself. He shook his head and looked at the two dead bodies. "What—?" Frank closed his eyes, trying to piece the scene together.

"Surprised to see me, Frank?"

Frank looked at Lazo, wondering how to respond. He gathered his wits and croaked, "Who the hell are these people, and what in God's name are *you* doing here?"

"It's a long story," said Lazo.

"I bet it is. Try me."

Lazo motioned to the stream bank, and the two men sat side by side. Lazo draped his arm around Frank.

"It was Pino's idea."

"Pino? I figured that bastard had something to do with this. So, he's still around?"

"Yeah! He's as hateful and vengeful as ever. And he still has it in for you."

Frank shook his head. "After all this time? I don't understand."

"He's commander of the Santa Maria base now."

"How did that happen?"

"It's a long story. Do you have time?"

"For you? After this? Yeah, I have all the time in the world." Frank looked at Damian's remains. "Who's the kid?"

"Damian Baez. Special Forces just like you and me."

Frank covered his mouth with his hand. It took him a moment to recover. "That explains it."

Augustin emerged from the woods and approached the bodies. He kicked José with the toe of his boot to make sure he was dead. Then he removed his gun. He did the same to Damian.

Frank looked at Lazo, trying to formulate a question that would explain these bizarre events. Instead, he said, "Do you live in the States?"

"No, I still live in Cuba."

Frank wondered how Lazo got to New Jersey. His mind was a blur. He wasn't thinking clearly.

"You saved my life—again. Why?"

"For friendship, Frank." Lazo smiled. "Funny, isn't it? Seems like I'm always saving the same old friend."

Frank looked at Lazo in amazement, unable to wrap his mind around the fact that his buddy was sitting beside him. A squirrel scampered through the brush, carrying an acorn. He sat on his hind legs, holding his food with his paws, nibbling. He looked like a picture.

Shots rang in the distance. Frank glanced at Lazo who nodded. It dawned on Frank that his pursuers had met their fate. Elias was dead, and Sebastian had been put out of his misery.

Frank took a minute to settle his nerves. "Are you still in the army?"

"Permanent reserves."

Frank sat in silence for a moment, groping for some way to make sense of the day. "What can I do for you? Do you want to stay with me? Defect? I'll take care of you."

"No, Frank, you did your job more than a decade ago. You were the first member of the force who had the guts to defy Fidel. You inspired thousands of Cubans. My job is to do what I can to overthrow the regime from within, and to tell as many people as I can about your escape."

Frank was dumbfounded. He shook his head, amazed at Lazo's words. Tears sprang to his eyes, remembering a time long past. Seeing Lazo made it all come back again. The two old friends sat for a minute in silence. Then they began to reminisce. They talked, laughed, hugged, and talked some more. Frank felt at home in Lazo's company.

Frank was hungry for the latest news about his family, and Lazo filled him in about what he had heard. Lazo expressed his sympathy for the death of Frank's father and grandfather and told Frank that his mother was healthy and well. Then he talked about Cuba. Lazo spoke in broad strokes. Details would come later.

Lazo related what had transpired in the army during and after Frank's escape, and Frank told him what had happened on his end. While Frank was surprised to learn about Lazo's position with the permanent reserves, he was more surprised to hear about Pino's rehabilitation and plans to kill him. He had thought Pino would spend the rest of his life in jail.

"Whatever happened to Manny?" asked Frank. "I think about him often."

Lazo turned his head. "Manny joined the Cuban intelligence."

"Jesus, that's a surprise."

"His heart wasn't in it," said Lazo. "He couldn't find a job. He needed to do whatever he could to survive."

Frank considered this for a moment. "What about Lieutenant Brown?"

"Brown? The army sent him for more military training. He's now back at the Santa Maria base. I see him all the time."

"Did he ever become a member of the Party?"

"No. He still hates the communists for confiscating his family's land. Besides, the Party would never consider his candidacy after what happened."

"I figured as much."

Lazo's face turned somber. "I hesitate to ask, but I'm dying to know: Whatever happened to Magda?"

Frank pushed his lips into a neat, tight seam. Seeing Lazo brought back memories of Magda, some pleasant, some painful. "She died," he said simply. "Cancer."

Lazo shook his head, sickened at the news. "I was afraid it was something like that."

Lazo placed his hand on Frank's forearm.

"I'm so sorry, Frank."

Frank puffed out his cheeks and said, "Me too."

They sat in silence for a couple of minutes, paying homage to Magda.

"Did you have children?"

"A daughter. Darlene. She just turned ten."

"It must be tough on her."

"It is. When we have time, I'll tell you more about her. I'd love you to meet her."

"That won't be possible. I've got to get back to Cuba."

"I understand."

"But I'd like to hear more about your escape. I've thought about it often."

"Not as often as I have, especially in the middle of the night."

Lazo exhaled. "Sometimes it gets to us all in the middle of the night."

Frank looked at Lazo, thinking about their friendship. "I've never had a chance to thank you."

Lazo waved the comment away.

Frank shook his head. "My thinking is a little fuzzy. Tell me again why you're going back to Cuba."

"To do my job to infiltrate the army and to support the Cuban underground."

"That sounds like gobbledygook. What does it mean?"

"It means I work for the CIA."

"So, you and Manny work on opposite sides?"

"It's more complicated than that. But I can't discuss it."

Frank looked at Lazo with heightened respect. "Jesus."

"Why are you surprised, Frank? You gave the agency my name, remember?"

Frank thought for a minute and nodded. "I almost forgot about that. It seems so long ago. What about Pino? What will happen to him?"

"Pino's in for a big surprise. He won't be happy."

Frank tried to grasp the full implication of Lazo's words. But he was too tired to think.

"I feel so helpless. There must be something I can do."

"There is," said Lazo.

"What?"

Lazo looked across the stream, past Damian's and José's bodies, and said, "Be a good American."

Frank was speechless. He knew what Lazo meant. He'd been trying to be a good American for years. Lazo hesitated a moment, and added, "One more thing—"

"Anything!"

"Tell your American friends that the embargo isn't working. It's hurting the Cuban people and giving Fidel an excuse for his failed policies. Cubans need to see more of America—your goods, your values, your way of life—not less."

"I understand."

Members of Alpha Sixty-six appeared and prepared to remove Damian's and Jose's bodies. They had spent the past hour burying

Sebastian and Elias in the woods. As they unrolled a body bag, Frank stood to help.

"No need," said Lazo. "We'll take it from here."

"Just let me do this," Frank said. He leaned over and closed Damian's eyes with his fingers.

As they carried Damian away, Lazo and Frank stood and raised their hands in a salute. After all, he was a member of the Special Forces. He was one of them.

Lazo moved to Frank's side and draped his arm over his shoulder. They turned and hugged for a long moment, their hearts beating in joint rhythm. In a low voice, Lazo said, "Forget about all this, Frank. You've had enough to deal with in one lifetime. Go home, take care of your daughter, and marry your girlfriend."

Frank pursed his lips. "I will," he said. "I've struggled with the idea that it's too soon after Magda's death to get married—tradition and all. But I've come to terms with it."

"How long has it been?"

"A little over a year."

"It's not very long."

"I know. But Chris has found a place in my heart."

Frank stood and shook Lazo's hand, noting the web of lines that netted his eyes. He looked a lot older than he remembered. He guessed they both did.

Lazo withdrew his hand from Frank's, stepped back, and saluted. Frank returned the favor.

Before turning to leave, Lazo reached into his pocket and pulled out a card with a phone number penciled in. "Call me early tomorrow," he said. "I don't have time to meet with you, but we can speak on the phone. We have much to discuss."

Frank smiled. "Don't worry, I'll call. I have a few more stories to tell you."

Lazo laughed. "It would take a lifetime to tell each other our stories."

CHAPTER SIXTY-SIX

Frank made his way back to his blind in hopes of finding Raúl. He sat on the ground, still in shock, put his head in his hands, and sifted through his thoughts. He couldn't believe that Lazo had come all the way from Cuba to save his life.

He stood and fingered the pellets that riddled the trees near his blind. He imagined them entering his body, and he thought about how close he had come to dying. He was a lucky man.

An hour later, Raúl showed up, his shirt stained with coffee. Astounded to see the deer, he slapped his forehead and whistled.

"Jesus, Mary, and Joseph!" he said. "How the hell did that happen? I wasted my whole damn morning hunting, and I didn't get a goddamn thing. Not even a squirrel. And you go and bag this big old buck!"

Raúl leaned down, examined the deer, and shook his head. "How in God's name did you do this, Frank? There weren't any deer anywhere. *Nada!* I never even spotted one. Those shots scared them away. Did you hear them? Must've been a bunch of jerks."

Frank nodded. "Yeah, I heard them."

"You're such a lucky bastard. Why don't I ever get lucky like you?"

"Lucky," Frank repeated wearily.

Raúl examined Frank's face. "Hey man, what's wrong with you? This is a big damn deal. You should be ecstatic."

"I am ecstatic," said Frank. "Ecstatic."

"Well, you don't look it. Anyone who bags a deer like this and isn't jumping for joy is nuts." Raúl looked at Frank and laughed. "I think you need a shrink. I'm taking you to a psychiatrist as soon as we get home."

"That might not be a bad idea," said Frank.

Raúl handed Frank a line of rope to tie up the deer. They secured his front and hind legs. When they finished, Frank looped his arm around Raúl's shoulder.

"It was quite a day," said Frank.

"For you, yes. For me, it was pretty boring. The day is still young. Maybe we could do something interesting once we get this buck in the jeep."

"No, I think I just need to go home," said Frank.

Raúl made a face. "To do what?"

Frank smiled, and said, "To be a good American."

CHAPTER SIXTY-SEVEN

Chico sat on the couch watching television in the Cuban operatives' headquarters in Union City when a knock came at the door. He had just grabbed a can of beer from the refrigerator. It was a little early for a drink, but he thought *what the hell!*

He popped the tab and mumbled to himself. He sure as hell didn't want to be disturbed. He placed his beer on the kitchen counter next to a bottle of Cuban rum and wiped his hands on his pants. He walked down the hall and opened the door to see a man dressed in a brown United Parcel Service uniform.

The impostor glanced down at the paperwork, and said, "I have a package for a Damian Baez from Miami. Someone needs to sign for it."

Chico glanced at the television. He had been absorbed in a John Wayne movie.

"All right," he said, eager to get back to the show.

The impostor reached into his breast pocket for a pen. "Sorry, I must've left my pen in the truck. Do you happen to have one?"

Chico nodded. "Yeah, come in." The man stepped inside the apartment and closed the door behind him. The lock snapped shut. A look of terror crossed Chico's face as the UPS man drew a gun. His silencer muffled the shots.

When the deliveryman man left, Chico was dead on the floor. The imposter gathered the paperwork he found in the apartment and stuffed it under his jacket before he walked out the door.

Franco had been calling Damian in Union City all morning, but he was getting no answer. He was anxious to learn what had hap-

pened on the hunting expedition. He couldn't wait to notify Pino
that the mission had been completed. And he couldn't wait to return to Cuba and become a base commander—as Pino had promised. He smiled at the thought.

He had just finished a breakfast of bacon and scrambled eggs
when the doorbell buzzed. He swallowed the last of his coffee and
signaled to his associate to answer it. When he did, a man with a
UPS uniform stood before him, smiling congenially.

"I have a package for a Lieutenant Franco from Union City," he
said. "Sorry, but I need a signature."

Adán turned to Franco with questioning eyes. The lieutenant stood and began walking toward the door, but not before the
deliveryman stepped inside. When the imposter left, the files on
the mission were under his arm, Franco and Adán were dead, and
the deliveryman still held the package in his hands.

CHAPTER SIXTY-EIGHT

The file of Damian Baez sat open on the desk of First Captain Victor Flores. Flores was a seasoned soldier and had been in the Revolutionary Armed Forces for more years than he cared to admit. He had risen through the ranks, and he prided himself on his ability to piece things together.

Flores had seen a lot of shenanigans in his day, including those of the now infamous Captain Pino. He never could cotton up to the man. There was something about him that made his skin crawl. Years ago he had railed against Pino going to Russia for further military training. He couldn't see what good it would do. Pino was too hotheaded and stubborn for him. And, as far as he was concerned, zebras don't change their stripes. But the authorities had ignored his advice, and the views of First Lieutenant Torres had prevailed.

Absorbed in thought, Flores rifled through some papers. Although defections were uncommon, he had seen them before. Several worms had taken it upon themselves to abandon their country after the escape of Frank Mederos in the late sixties. But standard protocol was followed. Hence, they were usually apprehended and suffered the consequences.

This case was different. Damian Baez was one of the most talented and dedicated members of the force. His family had a history of loyalty to the Party, and demonstrated unwavering dedication to the cause. He couldn't imagine that Damian would defect.

The fact that he had was out of character for this ardent young man, and the fact that he did so without leaving a trace was even more troubling. Something about this case didn't add up. Damian had been labeled a worm, but Flores had his doubts.

The captain placed his pencil behind his ear and reclined in his chair. He had been thinking about this issue for a while, and he still had no answers.

He stood, yawned, and looked out the window. No rain had fallen in weeks. For a few minutes, he watched the birds peck at the hard, dry earth. *The poor things can't even find a worm.* The captain smiled at the irony. *And neither can I.* He sighed, heavyhearted. *Maybe I'm getting too old for this work. Maybe I'm losing my edge.*

Flores sat down, reached to the credenza, and switched on the radio. He liked to listen to The Voice of America. The station was funded by the United States government and provided news on a wide range of topics.

The captain had listened to the programming for several years and enjoyed the music, especially the Beatles' songs. Periodically, Fidel tried to jam the signal, but Flores disagreed with that policy. He felt the military was better off knowing what the enemy was up to than not.

The captain settled himself in his chair and listened to the news—the weather, the state of the economy, the upcoming elections. Routine stuff—nothing out of the ordinary.

As he was about to turn the dial, his face froze. He extended his hand to increase the volume. The report was clear and succinct. A man with an authoritative voice stated that reliable sources from Alpha Sixty-six had reported that a member of Cuba's Special Forces, Damian Baez, had been shot and killed in the hills of northern New Jersey in a failed assassination attempt on the life of a former member of Cuba's Special Forces who had defected to the United States in 1967.

As a result, four Cuban operatives had been assassinated in Union City, and two more had been killed at the group's operational headquarters in Miami. The victims in Miami included First Lieutenant Franco of Unit 2572 of the Santa Maria base in Havana.

Flores closed his eyes. As he was trying to piece the puzzle together, his door opened. A messenger dropped a manila envelope stamped top secret on his desk. Flores opened it and rifled through a stack of photographs. First Lieutenant Franco was pictured in a restaurant with a sign in the background that read Miami. Private Damian Baez sat at his side. The two were engrossed in conversation. Another photograph placed Baez in Union City. It all made sense.

Flores pursed his lips, fuming. Then he picked up the phone and barked one sentence to his secretary: "Get the Commander General on the phone, and do it pronto. I need to talk to him about Captain Pino."

"Right away, sir."

Flores slammed down the receiver, stared out the window, and smiled smugly. *Well, the chickens have finally come home to roost. This time there's no way out for Pino. This time it's treason.*

And this time we're going to execute the bastard.

EPILOGUE

In 1981, Mrs. Mederos came to the United States to visit Frank and his brother Carlos, who had escaped Cuba during the Mariel Boatlift. After her arrival, she applied for and was granted political asylum. She now lives in Florida, and Frank visits her several times a year.

In addition to Carlos, Frank's brothers Robert and Raúl also escaped Cuba. His widowed sister and her three sons live in Cuba, and her daughter lives in Mexico. Frank's brother George and his wife still live in Cuba along with their son, daughter, and grandchildren.

Shortly after the incident in the woods, Frank married his girlfriend Chris. They have two sons and live and work in New Jersey. Frank credits Chris with giving him the will to go on with his life. Darlene lives not far from her father.

In the spring of 2011, Frank took advantage of relaxed government regulations regarding Cuban visitation and returned to his homeland for the first time in forty-four years. He was astounded to receive a warm and enthusiastic welcome from family and friends in his hometown of Guanabacoa. He visited again in 2012.

Frank found the living conditions in his former country to be deplorable. After fifty years of communist rule, many people had given up their fight for freedom. He was saddened to see them resigned to their fate.

Frank donated all the money and possessions he had with him at the time to his Cuban friends and relatives, including his hat, his watch, and his belt.

Following the incident in the woods, Frank had several talks with

Lazo. The information he obtained served, in part, as the basis for this book. After his time in the States, Lazo returned to his position at the oil refinery and continued to work for the CIA.

However, when Frank went to visit Lazo's home in 2012, he found it to be nothing more than a pile of rubble. No one knew of Lazo's whereabouts, nor had they heard from him or his family in years.

Frank will continue to visit Cuba, and he hopes to be reunited with his friend Lazo someday.

Frank still suffers from nightmares, but they occur far less frequently.

The drum of the blue-eyed boy has been silent since 1980.